A LEGACY WITCH

Spellcasters Spy Academy, Culling Year

A MAGIC OF ARCANA UNIVERSE SERIES

ASHLEY MCLEO

Meraki Press

Cover by Ravenborn Designs

Editing by Jen McDonnel

ISBN e-book: 978-1-947245-22-8

ISBN paperback: 978-1-947245-23-5

ISBN audiobook: 978-1-947245-52-5

ISBN hardback: 978-1-947245-42-6

CONTENTS

SPELLCASTERS SPY ACADEMY READING ORDER

The best reading order for Spellcasters Spy Academy Series:

A Legacy Witch: Year One - also available in audiobook format

A Marked Witch: Internship - also available in audiobook format

A Rebel Witch: Year Two - also available in audiobook format

A Crucible Witch: Year Three - also available in audiobook format

Or get this:

The Spellcasters Spy Academy Boxset

CHAPTER ONE

"We're not in L.A. anymore, Toto," I said as Maine's summer greenery whipped by the window.

"No, honey, we're not." Mom's tone was quieter than normal. "Are you having second thoughts?"

"No." Irritation that I normally didn't feel toward my parents flared at the question. We'd been over this at least thirty times. "I don't understand why you're so against me going to Spellcasters. You always said I could be whatever I wanted. Do you think I can't hack it?"

Dad grasped Mom's hand as his gaze caught mine in the rearview mirror, his hazel eyes understanding. "We're just worried, little pea. And believe me, we *know* you can do anything you put your mind to. Would we have flown across the country, driven from New York to Maine, *and* stayed overnight in Portland to drop you off on orientation day if we thought otherwise?" Hesitation flickered across his face, which was just beginning to show lines that came with age. "It's just that becoming a spy isn't easy. Even if you can use magic."

"And working in Hollywood is a cakewalk?"

"By comparison, yes," Mom replied. "And *much* safer. Besides, you love theater. You know we can help get you started. As a dancer you'd be a double threat."

"Honey . . ." Dad squeezed Mom's hand, and she shook her head, resigned.

I rolled my eyes, and we fell into silence.

I didn't have the desire to argue that following in their footsteps was a good thing. Sure, working in Hollywood would have been glamorous and fun, but espionage had always interested me more. The choices made by Spellcasters graduates rippled out into the rest of the world on a large scale. Even if I was never known publicly for it, making a positive difference meant a lot to me.

I'd always thought it mattered to my parents, too. They'd attended Spellcasters, spied for the U.S. government, and even patronized the academy after they quit espionage. It was because of their history that I'd expected them to laud my choice.

Their resistance to my enrollment was baffling and frustrating in equal measure.

Unfortunately for my parents, I was eighteen and an academy legacy. I didn't need their permission. Spellcasters had accepted me the moment I'd written the headmistress and expressed interest. There had been no stopping me after that. Dad recognized my drive, but Mom was still holding out.

The terrain beneath the wheels changed dramatically, and my suitcases rattled in the trunk. I glanced out the window. Smooth pavement was still flashing by even though it felt like we were traveling down a dirt road. My eyebrows furrowed.

"That's the signal. We're almost there." Mom twisted her long, brown hair and laid it over her shoulder—an anxious tic.

"They haven't changed the first marker after all these years," Dad noted with a shake of his head.

Mom snorted. "They *will* change it. And soon."

I was about to ask what she meant, when a sign came into view that sent chills up my spine. I could just make out the words.

'Saint Albert's Academy for High-Risk Boys and Girls.'

My heart rate sped up, and I pressed my nose against the glass in anticipation.

Barbed wire flashed by in the spaces between trees. It looked menacing, and from what I'd read about Spellcasters before I applied, the precautions were even more dangerous than they appeared. The fences would not only keep out curious humans, but fae and demons trying to sneak in from Faerie or Hell.

Spellcasters was one of the most secure places I'd ever seen. That was saying something, considering my parents had warded every nook and cranny of our Beverly Hills home.

Dad slowed the car to a crawl as we neared the sign. He whispered a word under his breath, and the silver prophetess seal of Spellcasters split and the academy gates opened. A shimmering blue cloud engulfed the car, seeped in through the closed windows, and caressed my skin. A laugh tipped my tongue. It tickled.

Then, just as suddenly as it materialized, the cloud disappeared.

I was about to ask my parents what the magic had been detecting, but something else caught my attention first. The letters on the sign had begun to rearrange themselves, morphing into new words. My heart thumped hard when the letters stopped.

'Spellcasters Spy Academy.'

I held my breath as we drove through the gates, barely able to contain my excitement.

Woodlands dominated the grounds, although I was sure I'd spotted a lake and a golf course peeking through the dense trees. As the drive narrowed, long branches started to bow inward, creating the effect of a stunning green tunnel.

My legs shook as if I'd just chugged three espressos. When the trees broke, and the school emerged, I squealed out loud.

"It's like a mix of Neuschwanstein and Westminster Abbey," I whispered.

The white facade and green-topped towers mimicked the German fairytale castle, while the stained-glass windows above massive front doors, and gargoyles resting at various intervals on ledges and windowsills reminded me of the famed abbey.

Dad laughed for the first time since we'd left Portland, Maine. "I suppose it is. In my day, we coined it 'Gothic-cheery,' but your description is more precise." He shot Mom a smile she didn't return.

Dad parked in front of the double doors, which looked like they belonged on an old Spanish cathedral. I shot out of the car and straightened my dress and the long leather jacket that gave me the perfect spy-in-training air. Spell-casters would eventually provide me with a job after graduation and I wanted to look the part. Plus, what if I met my spouse here, like Mom and Dad had found each other? First impressions were important, I didn't want to mess this one up.

I took a big breath of piney air, soaking in the fresh scents of summer.

"Where do we go?" I asked once I felt grounded.

"Someone will be here in just a second." Mom waved her hand.

"How do you know? Did you call ahead?"

"They always send someone, pea," Dad said, his tone more gentle than Mom's.

As if on cue, the doors burst open, and a tall, thin woman about my mom's age strode outside. Her chocolate brown hair was pulled back in a heavy bun that coiled at her nape. She was smiling, a tight, thin affair that didn't reach her appraising eyes.

"Pris Wake!" I blinked as the corners of Mom's mouth

quirked upward for the first time in hours. "This is a surprise. Usually, they send a junior spymaster, not the headmistress."

Wake. I knew that name. I had studied her lineage after receiving an acceptance letter bearing her signature. She was a descendant of a famed spy from World War II—Nancy Wake, also known as the White Mouse, one of the Gestapo's top five most-wanted Allied spies.

A thrill ran through me. This woman could teach me a thing or two about changing the world for the better.

"It's not every day our most esteemed donors drop off their only daughter." Headmistress Wake's eyes drifted from Mom to me and looked me up and down. "Odette Dane, I presume?"

My hand shot out. "Yes. It's nice to meet you, Headmistress Wake. I've heard a lot about you and your escapades."

She cocked a pencil-thin eyebrow.

"The ones that are public," I amended, not wanting her to assume my parents had shared secrets about her spy days. That would have broken protocol, and my parents *so* did not do that. They never even talked about *their* spy days, or why they had quit. Probably because they didn't believe I could live up to their reputations.

I planned on proving them wrong.

"I suppose there are a few of those," the headmistress said and turned back to my parents. "Will you be staying a while? As benefactors, I'd love to lunch with you in my chambers."

"We're not leaving Odette until we have to, right after the orientation dinner."

Mom had been so dour on the ride upstate, but now her tone was light as she gazed wistfully at the academy grounds. It seemed that, although she hadn't wanted me to come here, returning to her alma mater was lifting her spirits.

"Wonderful." Headmistress Wake glanced at her watch. "My daughter should arrive at any minute."

Once again, the front doors to the school flung open. A statuesque, attractive girl appeared and made her way over to us. Her pin-straight, blonde hair was so thick and heavy that it barely moved against her shoulders as she walked.

It's like they time these things.

The girl stopped to stand next to the headmistress.

"Odette Dane, this is my daughter Diana Wake. You're both first years—or as we call your class at Spellcasters, initiates. If you're amenable to parting with your parents, she'll show you to your rooms."

"Hi! And totally!" I beamed at the girl who returned my exuberance with a tight smile similar to her mother's. "Should I grab my bags?"

The headmistress shook her head. "Just what you'll want right away. The rest will arrive shortly."

I snapped up my backpack and waved at my parents. Mom's face fell, the bit of joy that had made an appearance since arriving on the school grounds, gone in a second.

"See you at the orientation dinner." I turned around quickly so I didn't have to dwell on Mom's anxiety.

She'll be fine. She's just nervous about her baby girl leaving home and playing with the big boys. Once I start killing it in classes, she won't worry so much.

With those reassurances in mind, I followed Diana into the hallowed halls of Spellcasters Spy Academy.

CHAPTER TWO

The moment I walked through the double doors of Spellcasters, I knew I'd made the right choice.

Growing up in Hollywood with parents who were well-respected film producers meant that I'd spent a lot of time on set. I'd seen many amazing productions created and walked through scenes pulled straight out of the storybooks.

None of that compared to Spellcasters.

The entry hall was cavernous, its ceiling soaring at least fifty feet high to dome at the top in an intricate display of latticed wood. Light filtered through stained-glass windows depicting serene scenes from nature. Across the entry hall, two staircases split and spiraled up three stories. Between the staircases hung an enormous green and silver banner of a prophetess, the Spellcasters mascot. Moving back down, my gaze trailed a ways along each landing, trying to make out the paintings that hung at regular intervals on the walls.

"Whenever you're ready, Dane."

I jumped, the voice slicing through my dreamy wonder. Diana waited at the bottom of the staircase that veered left, her foot tapping and blue eyes gleaming.

"Oh my God!" Heat flushed my cheeks. I'd stopped in the middle of the foyer to stare with my mouth hanging open. "I'm so sorry. I'm just taking it all in. Who wouldn't be impressed with *this*?"

Diana shrugged. "My mother's been the headmistress here for the last fifteen years. I don't remember the first time I saw Spellcasters. To me, this has always been home."

Well, duh. Priscilla Wake had become the headmistress of Spellcasters Spy Academy when I was around three or four years old. Although the histories said nothing about a daughter, here she stood, in my year.

"Of course." I joined Diana and noticed that she smelled like Ivory soap. "I'm sorry. I'm being such an idiot. It's just that I've wanted this for years and now I can't believe I'm actually here."

Diana nodded, turned, and walked up the stairs. "Come with me."

We climbed to the third floor and made our way down a long, wide hallway. Many of the paintings on this level depicted notable witches and wizards who had been spymasters during their time.

It was strange to see witching history on display. In the real world, magicals hid their existence from humans. Only in the last couple generations did global governments discover that we existed.

"So, growing up here must have been interesting, huh? I bet you've seen a lot of cool stuff. People always ask me about living in Hollywood. They think it's unique and glamorous, but this is so much more impressive. Are there any academy secrets I should know about?" I grinned at her, trying to break through her shell. "And how's the cafeteria? I try to eat healthy, but I hope it's varied because sometimes I just *need* a slice of Hawaiian, you know?"

Diana's beak-like nose wrinkled for a millisecond before her face smoothed out into an unreadable expression.

Noted—Diana is a pineapple on pizza hater. Just as well. More for me!

"It was an intriguing place to grow up," she answered, her tone flat. "I learned a lot and finagled some early training. Did you do much of that in Hollywood?"

Early training? In what? I hoped she didn't mean running or some other horrible type of cardio. I'd never stepped foot on a track, but I'd seen others running around them. It looked like hell.

"I'm not sure what you mean," I confessed.

"Oh, that's right. My mother mentioned that you opted for the legacy route. Probably no training for you, then."

I cocked my head. "Did you take the entrance exam? But you're a legacy too."

Diana snorted, and for the first time since we climbed the stairs, her bright blue eyes locked with mine. "Why would I want to be here if I didn't possess the skills necessary to succeed?"

"Because there have been spots for both of us since we

were born?" My eyebrows furrowed. Why would someone take a test—one that I'd heard was beyond difficult—if their spot in the academy was a sure thing?

"Yes, well, some of us aren't used to the 'I'll pat your back if you pat mine' mentality. I thought it best to test myself and make sure I *earned* my spot."

Whoa, judgy much?

"You know, I really don't believe—"

Diana halted before a doorway and spoke over me. "Here's the initiates' tower. Bedrooms are on the upper levels. You'll find your level on a paper pinned to the stairwell."

"Err . . . okay. Thanks," I said, thrown off-kilter by her vibe.

"Don't mention it, *Legacy*." Diana turned and strutted down the hallway.

I frowned. What a bummer of a welcome. I couldn't enter my dorm with a storm cloud like this hanging over my head.

I took a deep inhale and began reciting mantras in my head:

You will love it here.

You will be amazing at this.

Everything will work out as it should.

People sneered at mantras, but I would defend them to the death. Growing up, I had been painfully shy and had only come into my own at thirteen—after Mom taught me about mantras. After a year of recitation, I'd gained enough confidence to audition for a role in my local theater. In the end, I not only performed in a play, but I scored the starring role. Shortly after that I dabbled in contemporary dance. While I'd quit dancing my senior year, I still loved it, and never would have even started without help from my mantras.

After only a few repetitions, my trusty mantras worked like a charm, and my mood lifted. I inhaled a huge breath and pushed the door open.

Immediately, the pleasant aromas of sage and coffee relaxed me. Walking into the room, my eyes trailed from the floor to the ceiling. Various levels—six of them—climbed skyward and ended in a dome with a lunette so large that it flooded the entire space with sunlight. Every level boasted eight doors. Somewhere up there, *my* dorm waited for me.

I hitched my backpack higher and spun around, taking in the common area. The walls were dark wood in here too, but the furnishings gave off a cozier, younger vibe. Gray armchairs and side tables that looked like they belonged in a mid-century home littered the space. A massive fireplace dominated the wall across from the stairwell. A few maps were tacked here and there, and what looked like a list of rules was posted at the bottom of the stairs.

To my dismay, no one was relaxing or socializing out here, but I could hear noises from above. People were probably getting settled into their rooms.

I made my way to the staircase and began climbing. Just as Diana had said, there was a bulletin of student names on each floor. My name was on the list tacked to the third-floor banister. I scanned the sheet, taking in the names of my closest neighbors:

Wilhelmina Köhler
Evanora Proctor
Alexander Wardwell
Hunter Wardwell

Some rooms were empty, which I was cool with. While I loved going to parties and socializing, at home I preferred the quiet.

As each floor was circular, I turned right, figuring that either way, I'd run into my room. A gold plaque hung against the gleaming wood of the first door. It read, 'Hunter Wardwell,' and I kept moving.

The next door didn't have a plaque, I supposed because it was empty. After that, I found Wilhelmina Köhler's room and then another empty room. Alex's dorm was next, followed by yet another unclaimed room.

Then, *finally*, I ran into mine.

I took in my name on the shining plaque with awe. My fingers brushed the metal, and a thrill ran through me. This was it. Where I'd spend the next year learning and growing. I bit back a squeal and, unable to savor the moment any longer, placed my hands on the handle and turned.

The metal stopped with a resolute click, and I frowned. It was locked.

Diana hadn't given me a key—or even mentioned one. Maybe they'd been at the bottom of the staircase by the list of rules, and I'd missed them? I ran back downstairs. After a fruitless search, I returned and searched around my bedroom door. Still nothing. Feeling stupid, I knocked on my door. Unsurprisingly, no one answered.

I frowned and clenched my fists. "How the hell do I get in, then?" I said, my voice louder than normal as I kicked the door.

Pain shot up my leg as my toes hit just right, and I squeezed my eyes shut. "Ouch! Shitballs! Ouch!"

A door down the hall, the one labeled with Alex Wardwell's name, creaked open, and a boy stepped out. I stilled and sucked in a breath. Alex—if that was in fact who he was—was freaking gorgeous. He was tall and lean with just the right amount of muscle bulging out of his tight t-shirt, and cheekbones that could cut glass. He had gleaming, black hair and wore thick, square-framed glasses which I normally would've found nerdy, but they looked hot as hell on him.

And, to my utter embarrassment, he had just caught me ogling him.

I shook myself and put on my most charming smile. "Sorry if I startled you. I didn't know that anyone was around. I'm having trouble getting into my room. Did you get a key? I think they forgot mine."

Alex's beautiful face remained impassive as he came my way. Now that he was closer, I noticed his eyes were bluer than the Caribbean Sea. *How am I going to study with a hunk like that hanging around all the time?*

He stopped beside me and read the plaque on my door.

"Odette Dane? As in the daughter of Lauren and Joseph Dane?"

"That's me!" I chirped and did my best not to twirl my hair. Spies in training did not twirl their hair.

"You're a legacy and you don't know how to get into your own room?" Alex frowned. "Didn't you read the orientation paperwork?"

"Ahh, not yet. I figured I would when I got here."

"So *typical* of a legacy." Alex rolled his eyes.

My lips parted in surprise, and I was about to retort when he spoke again.

"The professors enchant our rooms to open for us and us alone. Put your hand on the door handle and say your name. That's all you have to do. It's voice activation, not rocket science."

"Oh . . . thanks. I—"

But before I could finish, Alex Wardwell, one of the most beautiful guys I'd ever seen, walked back to his room and slammed the door shut behind him.

CHAPTER THREE

Alex was right. Getting into my dorm room had been easy once I knew the trick.

I felt like an idiot for not knowing, when it had been so simple. Why hadn't I read through the orientation paperwork? Of course I'd been busy before I left California. Saying goodbye to my friends and packing up my life had taken priority. Still, I probably *could* have made time on the plane from L.A to the east coast. But even if all that was true, there was another part of me that felt super annoyed by Alex's attitude. Was everyone at the school a big jerk?

I hoped not, but at the very least, my room didn't suck. Actually, it was *awesome*. My window looked out over the lake. A desk sat against the wall opposite my bed, with a pamphlet of rules and information on top. A shoulder-height dresser graced the other wall. There was a door to an en-suite bathroom, complete with a claw-foot tub and shower combo, toilet room, and ample storage for linens.

Judging by the size of my closet, it was a good thing Mom had limited me to five suitcases. Not even a quarter of my clothes back home would fit in the dinky space.

Most surprising of all was the fact that my bed was way larger than I'd imagined it. Just laying eyes on the queen-size mattress made me grateful that I'd chosen Spellcasters and not some normal college where they stuck adults into twin beds. How did people even smoosh themselves into those?

Alex wouldn't fit, he's too tall and . . . I caught myself nearly swooning, and shook the image of Mr. Grouchy from my mind.

I opened the window, and cleansing, pine-scented air flooded my room. My lips pulled up in a smile as I tossed my bag on the bed and began dumping out my belongings. I hummed softly as I lined up my favorite books on top of my dresser. I'd just perfected color coding them when the sound of a door closing nearby was quickly followed by a loud crash.

My spine straightened. Had that come from my bathroom? I strode to the door, flung it open, and let out a yip of astonishment.

A girl stood before me, covered in white powder—baby powder, judging by the smell. Other products littered the floor, also covered in baby powder.

"I'm so sorry!" the girl wailed, her cheeks coloring to match her scorching red hair. "I dropped the damn bottle and kept trying to catch it like a total klutz, but the lid was loose and it bounced *everywhere*! I didn't mean to make such a racket and freak you out."

My fingers pressed against my lips as I tried to hold back the laughter bubbling up my throat. "It wasn't so much noise, but I didn't expect to find anyone in here. I'm guessing that door goes to your room?" I pointed to the door I'd thought had been a linen closet.

"Yup. It's a Jack and Jill bathroom. Thankfully, the toilet has its own room. That way one of us can brush our teeth while the other pees in peace."

I'd never shared a bathroom, but I knew at regular colleges, an entire floor often shared too few toilets and showers. This was much better.

"Works for me. I'm Odette." I stuck out my hand.

"Evanora, but I prefer Eva. Less pretentious." The girl brushed the baby powder off her hand before shaking mine. "Did you get here recently?"

I nodded. "You?"

"I arrived last night with most of the new students. My parents couldn't wait another minute to drop me off. Well, I guess they didn't really drop me off. They'll leave after the orientation dinner."

"Yeah, mine are still here too. It's gonna be weird seeing them leave. I'll miss them."

I bit my lip, realizing how much I meant the words, despite my parents trying to dissuade me from attending Spellcasters every other minute. It was the first time I'd be away from them for longer than two weeks. No matter how excited I was about the academy, that prospect was still intimidating.

Eva waved her hand, and a cloud of powder filled the air. "Mine can't leave fast enough. Then I can have some flipping peace!"

A giggle escaped me. "Have they been helicoptering since you got here? Mine would, if Headmistress Wake hadn't invited them to lunch."

Eva raised a ginger eyebrow. "My parents would kill for that privilege!" A thoughtful look crossed her face. "Now that you mention it, I haven't seen them all morning. They must have found someone to hang out with. They were dying to return to Spellcasters and see if any of their old classmates were around. My parents love this place."

"I wish mine were like that."

Then it wouldn't have been such a struggle to get them here.

My suitemate washed the baby powder off her arms, and her blue eyes caught my brown ones in the mirror. "Eh, it's not that great, because while *they're* obsessed, I'm less than enthused. They told me I had to enroll, though. Said it would be good training, no matter what I did with my life after the academy—which I can kinda understand. Also, they promised they'd pay for a college and a grad school of my choice . . . if I still wanted to go after Spellcasters." Her pert nose wrinkled. "Like I would change my mind! Once I get out of here, *no one* is changing my mind about applying for my dream archeology program."

I blinked, taking in all the information Eva had shared.

Apparently, my suitemate wasn't at all shy. After realizing I was staring, I grabbed a washcloth off the counter and helped her clean up.

"Wait, a minute—" Eva's head snapped up. "You're Odette! The sign on the banister said your last name was Dane, right?" She turned off the faucet and began drying her arms.

"Yeah."

"As in Deliverance Dane? From Salem?" Her voice rose excitedly as she spoke.

"A witch on my dad's side," I affirmed.

"This is so cool!" She clapped her hands together with academic enthusiasm. "I'm a descendant of John Proctor! Do you think our ancestors knew each other in Salem? I wonder if they were in the same coven? What do you know about Deliverance?"

I shrugged, and my long, brown ponytail fell over my shoulders. "Not much. To be honest, I don't know the history of Salem well. Or much about my ancestry."

Eva's face fell, but lit up again almost right away. "I wonder if they did this on purpose . . ."

"What's that?"

She gestured in the hallway's direction. "The other two are Wardwells. That's a name from Salem, too. Köhler isn't, but maybe Wilhelmina's mom's side was involved. The fact that four Salem descendants live on the same floor is odd. Being able to claim ancestry isn't *that* common among witches. It had to be on purpose."

"So the other two are related?" I'd assumed so, but Eva seemed like she actually knew.

"Yup," Eva popped the "p," and it vibrated in the echoey bathroom. "Cousins. Both arrived with their parents the same time I did. It was a *frosty* encounter."

Alex Wardwell's irritated demeanor played in my mind, and I snorted. "I believe that."

Eva cocked an eyebrow. "Meaning?"

"I ran into Alex in the hall. I didn't know how to get into my room, and he was a *total* ass about it."

My suitemate waved her hand as if to say not to worry about it. "He was in a sour mood last night, too. They have family issues, for sure. His parents were screaming at Hunter's. Alex and Hunter just sat there, staring at each other, all pissed off and brooding and hot." Her cheeks flushed as she realized what she said. "I mean—if you're into that."

Alex's muscular, trim form and crystalline blue eyes were too unforgettable to deny his hotness.

"Yeah, I get you. Why do all the good-looking ones have to be such a-holes?"

"Oh, if you think Alex is hot, wait until you meet Hunter. I talked to him earlier today while our parents were schmoozing, and he is so *not* a jerk." Eva fanned herself. "He's *dreamy*."

I threw the towel I'd been using in the hamper. "I can't wait until orientation to see for myself." I wagged my eyebrows, and Eva released a peal of laughter.

A loud knock came from outside my room, and we both jumped.

"Who is it?" I asked.

"Luggage," a voice grunted.

I turned to Eva. "I'm going to unpack a little. Wanna explore later? Maybe we'll run into Hunter."

A sly grin spread across her face. "I like where your head's at, Dane."

I beamed at her. I liked where hers was at, too.

CHAPTER FOUR

My gut hurt from laughing so hard.

Eva was the funniest and most badass person I'd ever met.

"And then," she continued her story, "I dressed in all black, went into my parents' room, and rearranged everything in their sleep! I even moved their underwear into the shower! After freezing them, of course." She chuckled and shook her head. "They were so pissed, but honestly, they had it coming. I'd been talking about that trip non-stop for a week!"

I howled, imagining a sixteen-year-old Eva plotting revenge on the parents who'd sprung training exercises on her the day that she'd planned a trip to a theme park with her friends.

Eva grinned, delighted to have entertained me so well. "So, what about you? Did your parents make you do anything crazy to prepare for Spellcasters?"

"I wish! No, they pretended that this place didn't exist. I had to pull the 'I'm an adult now and will do it whether or not you want me to' card." I looked out over the lake we'd chosen to chill next to after meandering the academy grounds for hours. So far, it was perfect—if a little quiet. "Where do you think everyone is, anyway?"

Eva ripped a hunk of grass out of the ground and tossed it into the air. The green threads danced on a current of yellow magic, until she released her hold and they fell into the lake. "They're probably spending time with their families while they still can. There's a little supernatural town around here—Wandstown. I bet some went there to hang out and get last-minute supplies."

"What about the second and third-years?"

"Oh, I saw some of them when I was exploring this morning. They're already training. I guess they don't call our second year 'the Grind' for nothing. Apparently, a whole month off can make people rusty." She rolled her eyes.

Training already? Wow. Everyone seemed über-serious here.

I couldn't remember the last time I'd used my magic. My parents preferred that I completed tasks using my fortitude. And to be honest, I didn't feel the need to use magic all the time. Especially during senior year, when I'd been preoccupied with graduating high school, theater, hanging with my friends, and . . .

I sat straight up. "I know what this place needs!"

"Go on . . ." Eva leaned forward.

"A party! We should set up a first year mixer. It would be the *perfect* ice-breaker!"

Eva bit her lip as if she was mulling over what I said. "I guess so. But I think our classmates may surprise you, Odette. I've met a few of them over the years, and they're not very social. And many of them are crazy competitive."

My interactions with Diana and Alex were prime examples, but I refused to believe that everyone else was *that* standoffish. "Well, we're all in a new place, which makes things weird. Plus, when parents are around, sometimes people act differently. I think we should ask Headmistress Wake if we can set up an optional party after the orientation dinner!" I leapt up and held a hand out to Eva.

The trepidation that had lined my new friend's face vanished. "Maybe you're right."

Eva knew where Headmistress Wake's offices were, so she led the way through wide hallways, all lined with artwork, or outfits worn by spies from previous eras. Unlike the corridors that led to our dormitories, it seemed that the rest of Spellcasters was more of an experience rather than an education.

We turned down a dark hall, and I stopped short in front of a mannequin. "Oh my God, Eva, do you see this?"

The gown before me was one of the most gorgeous items of clothing I'd ever seen. Red as a crushed raspberry, with dark crimson threading decorating the cinched-in bodice, the dress was soft as goose-down to touch. The skirt bloomed out so large that both Eva and I could crouch beneath it together. The bottom of the skirt was trimmed with an intricate, red lace pattern I'd never seen before.

"Whose is it?" Eva asked.

I read the plaque, barely visible behind the large skirt.

"Ursula Shipton." My eyes trailed down the lettering, taking in every word. "Holy crap! She was a spy for her coven."

Witches and wizards had acted as spies for centuries to benefit their own kind. Only after WWI did certain governments discover our existence and seek our services.

"That's amazing. I can't wait until we start classes and get access to the library." Eva's face lit up.

I loved that she was such a mismatch. Part of her was a clear bookworm and wanted to know everything about archaeology and history. The other part was sassy and rebellious.

"If it has stuff like this in there, I'm with you," I agreed.

A squeal of hinges echoed somewhere down the hall, and we jumped back, away from the gown. Footsteps followed, multiple sets, and I heard familiar voices.

"I'm just not sure our money is being put to the best use, considering . . . everything," Mom said.

There was a cough, and Headmistress Wake piped up. "Rest assured, Mrs. Dane, we have used the funding you provided to beef up security around the academy. We've even—"

"Lauren has a point though, Priscilla. We didn't read the instructions you sent Odette, and entered Spellcasters without issue. There's been no update on the charms on the road, and the password is even the same as it was years ago. Taking into account the first years' predicament, don't you think some safeguards should be changed?"

I cocked my head. *Predicament?*

"Possibly, Mr. and Mrs. Dane," Headmistress Wake said grudgingly. It struck me as odd that she insisted on using my parents' last name while they called her Priscilla. Hadn't they all been in the same Spellcasters class? "If it concerns you so—oh dear!"

Headmistress Wake turned the corner and nearly ran right into me.

Mom's hand flew to her heart as she jumped. "Odie! You startled me!"

"Sorry, Mom," I said, although I thought she was being a touch dramatic. We were in a school. Did she think there wouldn't be other people around? "We didn't mean to sneak up on you. We were coming to talk to Headmistress Wake."

The headmistress glanced at her watch. Growing up with parents on the go, I understood that signal. I'd better get to the point.

"Eva," I gestured to my friend for my parents' benefit, "my suitemate, and I noticed that everyone seems solitary. I wondered if it would be possible to set up a mixer after orientation? You know, like a welcome party for the first years, so everyone can get to know each other before classes?"

Mom smiled. She'd always been the party-planner at

our house and threw some of the best movie industry shindigs.

"Hmm." Headmistress Wake's thin lips flattened. "I'm not sure. Classes start early tomorrow, and most students find them rather more rigorous than they expected."

My mom turned to her. "But don't you think this could be a chance to solidify bonds, Pricilla? When people know each other better, they look out for one another more."

My eyebrows knitted together, sensing a subtext that I didn't understand.

"I suppose you're right. Yes, Odette, you may put together a mixer. We will hold orientation in the Agnes Sampson Hall, so you can't use that space. Why don't you set up a few tables in the Marie Laveau Room? It should be sizable enough for your class. You may also speak to the kitchens and have them supply *appropriate* refreshments. Please make sure it's over by ten."

"Perfect!" I squealed. "We'll get right on it! Thank you, Headmistress Wake. See you guys at dinner!"

I tugged on Eva's arm, and we scampered off to plan the party.

CHAPTER FIVE

Eva and I sprinted through the corridors. We'd spent the last three hours party-planning, and were cutting it close to make orientation on time.

"This way!" Eva panted, taking a corner I'd darted right past.

I bunched up the hem of my dress—a long, red maxi that seemed appropriate for orientation and the party—and followed her. While I always liked to make an impression, I *hated* being late. Tardiness implied sloppiness, and I was so not about that. The door up ahead began to close.

"Wait!" Eva yelled. "We're coming!"

We were there seconds later, chests heaving and perspiration dotting our faces. *Who knew Maine was so darn humid in July?*

"Thanks." I acknowledged the male witch manning the door before turning to Eva. I pulled a tissue from my clutch and dabbed at my face."How do I look?"

"Perfect, you've got that dewy look. Me?"

"Hot as hell."

Eva beamed, and we high-fived.

"Girls?" The wizard gestured for us to enter.

"Sorry!" I chirped and gave him a sheepish grin. "But you know, first impressions and all that!"

Agnes Sampson Hall was enormous, although it appeared only a third of the way filled. The overall vibe of the hall was dark, with its chocolate-colored wood walls, thick, red curtains at the sides of a stage, and decorative paintings done in brooding tones. Tables of varying sizes dotted the dining hall, and families chatted amongst themselves. In the corner, just by the stage, I could see servers holding trays, waiting for the signal to serve the families of Spellcasters' students.

I spotted my parents. They were at the front, their table for three positioned beneath an iron chandelier that made Mom's gold Moroccan print dress shimmer and shine.

"I found my parents. See you after?"

"You know it," Eva said and headed the opposite direction.

I sashayed through the crowds, giving anyone who looked my way a welcoming smile. Most didn't catch my attempt to connect, but one did. He was Hollywood hot, with shaggy, honey-blond hair, high cheekbones, emerald-green eyes, and a golden tan. As soon as we locked eyes, he winked. A shiver ran up my spine, and I diverted my attention to where Mom and Dad sat, a couple tables over.

My parents would have stuck out even if their table

hadn't been in such a prominent position in the room. Whereas every other family seemed jubilant, including Mr. Winky's, Mom and Dad did not. The allure of arriving at their alma matter seemed to have worn off, and just like when we departed LAX, a palpable tension rolled off them in waves.

"Hey." I joined them. "How was your day? Did you have a good time going down memory lane?" I hoped that by reminding my parents they'd had fun here, it would reduce their anxiety concerning me.

"It was . . . better than it could have been, pea," Dad spoke up, his tone diplomatic and hazel eyes careful.

What kind of answer is that? I opened my mouth to ask what he meant, but at that exact moment, a server appeared.

"Good evening, Dane clan. Might I offer you still or sparkling water?"

We requested still water, and the waiter filled our glasses before launching into the menu for the evening. The server disappeared once we'd ordered, and right away, someone else swooped in.

Mr. Winky.

"I heard the famed Mrs. Lauren Dane and Mr. Joseph Dane were at this table?"

He held out his hand to Mom, who took it to shake. But the young man pulled a fast one and brought her hand to his lips instead. Mom blushed, and I worked not to gape. This guy was a charmer.

"That's right," Dad said, looking amused. "And what's your name?"

"Hunter Wardwell, sir. It's a pleasure to meet such legends of espionage. I've studied your public cases." Mr. Winky—Hunter—shook Dad's hand. "And this stunning woman must be your daughter?"

Dad's chest puffed up, signifying a pride that he reserved only for me and particularly well-done films that he'd produced. I pressed my lips together tightly, trying not to laugh. Not only was Hunter too handsome for his own good, he knew *exactly* how to work my parents.

I extended my hand, which he had the good sense to shake and not kiss. "Odette Dane. Nice to meet you, Hunter. I think you met my suitemate, Evanora Proctor?"

"She's a charmer. I believe we're on the same floor."

"All three of us." I considered it pretty rich that Hunter was calling Eva a charmer.

Mom jumped into the conversation. "Wardwell. I've heard that name, but I don't believe I know your parents. However, I am familiar with John and Alice Wardwell. Their son is Alexander, I think." She pointed to the table at the back of the room. "Is there any relation?"

The grin slipped off Hunter's face, and I remembered Eva's mention of a family feud. "They're relations of mine. An aunt and uncle—although we're not close."

"That's a shame, but we can relate. We have little family. Odette is the last of our line." Mom's eyes shifted to me. "It's part of the reason I'm so reluctant to let her move all the way across the country."

Hunter's face lit up again. "My parents had their doubts too. Perhaps after orientation, I can finagle an introduction, and you four can commiserate?"

Mom gave him a watery smile. "Being in contact with other Spellcasters parents is a good idea. I'd like that."

The tinkling of a bell rang through the chatter of families, and a slow hush descended in the room. Hunter excused himself, and I turned my attention to the stage, where Headmistress Wake stood, backed by an entourage of men and women.

"Thank you all for being here tonight," the headmistress began. "The professors and I are pleased to welcome our newest class of future spies." Headmistress Wake pulled her lips up in what I guessed was her approximation of a genuine smile, but looked more like grimacing. "This is a friendly reminder that after orientation, parents are no longer permitted on the grounds of Spellcasters. Once the term commences, visitations are limited to the Yule holiday and a one-month break after internships end next summer. Cell phones will be confiscated. It sounds draconian, but as our parents know, spies must often sever all ties. We consider this isolation yet another aspect of your training. Therefore, I urge you to soak up your family time now."

The headmistress shot a glance at the corner of the room, where servers held trays laden with sumptuous smelling food. "The rest shall wait for after dinner." She clapped her hands, and the servers rushed forth.

A plate of chicken, roasted to perfection, with honeyed carrots and rosemary mashed potatoes, Mom's favorite comfort foods, landed before her. Dad had opted for steak tacos, whereas I'd chosen seared ahi tuna on a bed of jicama and greens. Since I'd skipped lunch, I quickly became engrossed in my meal, which was spectacular.

"So, Hunter is handsome," Mom said, after I'd inhaled over half my meal.

My face heated, and I stuffed a few more bites into my mouth. I'd had a few boyfriends before, but I rarely divulged relationship information to anyone. My circle of high school girlfriends had only heard the most superficial tidbits, and my parents knew the guy's name and phone number, but that was it. While I was open with them about everything else in life, talking about guys made me super uncomfortable.

"Yeah," I choked out, my eyes fixed on my plate.

"And he's not the only one," Mom released a heavy sigh. "I knew once you saw this place, you'd fall in love, but I suppose with men like Hunter around there's no hope that we can change your mind about going home?"

I sucked in a breath and prepared to start the same old fight, but when I looked up, I found that I couldn't. Mom just looked too sad.

At least my parents want me around.

After tonight, we'd be out of touch for months. No matter how much I wanted to be here, I had to admit that sucked. Plus, a spy academy was bound to be dangerous. Mom and Dad just didn't want me hurt. I was their only kid.

"There's no way I'm leaving." I kept my tone measured.

"I'm sorry, but you guys have always said I need to follow my own path. I haven't been here long, but I'm sure this is where I'm meant to be."

Mom nodded. "No witch or wizard could lay eyes on Spellcasters and not want to stay. It's a special place. I'll just miss you—and worry."

I reached across the table and took her hand. "I'll miss you too, Mom." Our eyes, the same shade of brown, connected, and for the first time since I announced my intent to enroll at Spellcasters, I felt like Mom understood.

Everyone had finished their meals, and servers swept the plates away, when a bell tinkled through the cavernous hall. A moment later, Headmistress Wake stepped on stage.

"Now that it appears everyone has finished their meals, I shall begin the commencement speech for the incoming Spellcasters class." She straightened the jacket of her pantsuit and pulled the microphone off its stand.

"I'd like to welcome our class of initiates into the elite halls of Spellcasters." Headmistress Wake smiled, but once again, it didn't reach her eyes. I wondered if she even knew how to smile warmly. "A calling such as espionage is not an easy road, and I commend you for your choice. However, just because you arrived today, does not mean you'll make it to the end of the year."

Mom squirmed in her chair. Murmurs filled the hall, and I leaned back, wondering what she was talking about.

The headmistress began to pace, and her steps echoed in the vast room. "Your first year at Spellcasters is known as the Culling. It will be filled with two trials, one challenge, and many more tribulations, designed to ensure that you actually belong among the top students that Spellcasters accepts." Wake's dark eyes moved across the crowd with hawk-like intensity.

"These trials will take place on Samhain and Beltane. The challenge is on Imbolc. You must succeed in two of the three Spellcasters tests to graduate from initiate status and be admitted into year two. There is no guarantee that this will be your reality. Spellcasters is *not* some normal human college, and yes, there have been fatalities over the years. We have made no secret about that. You are adults, and it is not our responsibility to baby you. It *is* our mission to train you so that you might progress from initiates to members of the Supernatural Society of Spies. Make sure you are entering these halls with full knowledge of what we expect. To move forward in this world, you must be willing to risk everything you know. You cannot coast by on the hard work of others." The headmistress caught my eye, and I looked away as whispers rose from the crowd.

Headmistress Wake cleared her throat. "As you know, the U.S. government contracts Spellcasters alumni as agents. Because of this, we at Spellcasters work diligently to assure that our graduates are the best trained in supernatural espionage." She sniffed. "That being said, if you're not up to being the *absolute* best in the world, please leave now."

Unsurprisingly, no one stood up. I caught Eva's gaze from across the room, and she mouthed, *"What the hell?"*

Yeah, what *was* up with Headmistress Wake's speech? I

thought Spellcasters was supposed to welcome us tonight, not scare us off.

"Excellent," the headmistress said, once it was clear no one was taking her up on her offer. "At the very least, you have a fighting spirit. Now let's see if you have sufficient skill and strength to back it up. Classes will begin at eight tomorrow morning, and you all have a full roster of seven classes. A staff member has placed your schedules on your desks. Until then," Wake performed a shallow bow, "I welcome you to Spellcasters and bid you goodnight. Parents, we shall see you during the Yule break." She returned her microphone to the stand and marched out of the room.

You could hear a pin drop in Sampson Hall. Mom leaned closer to me, as if she wanted to say something, but a wavering voice interrupted her.

"Excuse me, ladies, gentlemen, and students." A man on the stage with round glasses and elbow patches on his sleeves spoke. "I'm Professor Tittelbaum, the Magical Languages instructor for the Grind and Crucible-years. If you're all finished with your refreshments, please show yourself to the front lawn. Goodbyes will be said there."

People began to stand. I was missing my opportunity to announce the mixer. I stood up, threw my shoulders back, and turned to my mom.

"How do I look?"

Her appraising gaze ran over me. "Beautiful as always, Odie."

I gave her a grateful smile and then, harkening back to

my theater days, projected my voice. "Excuse me! Before everyone leaves, I have an announcement."

Everyone turned, and I beamed. "My friend Eva Proctor and I, Odette Dane, would like to invite the first year class to a mixer. Whenever you're ready, we'll be in the Marie Laveau Room."

"Sweet," someone said, but I barely registered their excitement, because Alex Wardwell was in my direct line of sight, and he actually had the audacity to *scowl* and cross his arms over his chest.

"There's no obligation," I added, trying to ignore the ridiculous, yet insistent pang of hurt that shot through me at his reaction.

He's no one to me. Just a pretty face. Why should I care what Alex thinks?

"We thought getting together before classes to bond would be nice. I hope to see you all there." I sat and hoped that no one noticed the slight waver in my voice that Alex's reaction had sparked.

CHAPTER SIX

Tears brimmed in Mom's eyes and reflected the pale moonlight. My heart clenched, knowing these would be our last moments together as a family until Yule break.

"You realize I'll miss you so much, right honey?" Mom took a stuttering breath. "And worry. I know you're all grown up, but like Headmistress Wake said, Spellcasters isn't exactly safe."

"I'll miss you guys too."

Mom bit her lip and glanced at Dad. Their eyes connected, and Dad shook his head. I hoped that he was using their marriage bond, or whatever married people had, to psychically tell her not to push it.

"We understand it's time for you to spread your wings, little pea," Dad said, his tone soothing, a balm to Mom's anxiety. "We won't try to stop you any longer. Just know, if you ever want to leave—like this is too much, or you don't fit in—you can *always* come home. There's no shame in that. Also, we have something for you."

Dad pulled something thin and cylindrical out of the pocket of his sports jacket.

I blinked. *Is that a can of mace?*

He handed me the object. "This is a blend of metals and potions. It's to keep you safe, and should be effective against hostile fae, shifters, vampires, and demons. Keep it with you at all times."

"Err, alright, thanks." I glanced down at the can, perplexed. "Is this because of the trials the headmistress mentioned? Will they allow a weapon like this?"

I wasn't sure what else to think. Only witches attended Spellcasters. And the academy was so heavily warded that other magicals couldn't just waltz onto school grounds.

"Please, keep it handy. For us," Mom replied, her tone shaky.

I nodded and stuck the item into my clutch. It was a small ask, and if it made them feel better, I'd do it.

Trying to lighten the mood, I smiled. "Are you sure this isn't to keep away the guys? Hunter was pretty smooth with that hand kiss, huh?"

Mom sniffed and let out a tiny laugh. "That boy *is* a touch too winsome for his own good." Then without another word, she wrapped her arms around me.

My shoulders released as I took in the scent of my mother, vanilla and myrrh. I buried my face into Mom's long, brown hair, and Dad's large hand landed on my shoulder. My heart felt like it was ready to burst.

We stayed like that until Dad whispered something unintelligible on the other side of Mom. She clenched me tightly, and for a moment, my blood flow seemed to speed up before returning to normal. I furrowed my eyebrows, but my confusion vanished as Mom choked out a sob and Dad let go of me to steady her.

"It's time for us to go," he said.

I pulled away. The sudden movement made me feel strangely lightheaded and over-energized all at once.

I shook my head, trying to rid myself of the odd sensation so my parents wouldn't worry more. "Right, me too. Can't have a party without a host, can we? Just think, tonight, I may meet the best friends of my life."

"I hope you do, honey." Tears fell fast and free down Mom's face. "I really hope you do."

I wiped the moisture from my eyes as I meandered down the academy hallways. I'd held myself together until my parents' taillights disappeared down the tree-lined drive. Then the floodgates had opened.

By the time I reached the Marie Laveau Room, I'd pulled myself back together. After one quick outfit check, I pulled my shoulders back, tilted my chin up, and entered.

The room resembled a den, with books lining the dark mahogany walls, and antlers mounted above a massive hearth. The staff had removed most of the furniture for the mixer, but two larger tables and chairs remained in case people wanted to sit and chat. Thick, red velvet curtains were pulled to the sides of the floor-to-ceiling windows to allow in the right amount of moonlight. Candles littered the room, providing a warm ambiance and adding to the illumination from a crystal chandelier.

I shivered. Although I'd helped set up for the party, that had been in the light of day. Hours ago, it had reminded me of a stuffy library, but now it resembled something out of a James Bond film.

Eva was already there, as was the wink-happy Hunter Wardwell.

And he was spiking the punch.

A giggle burst from me as I took in the scene that was unfolding. Eva was clearly distracting the adults, who were doing last-minute prep, so that Hunter could pour a flask of who-knew-what into the punch.

The moment he'd emptied the flask, Hunter capped it and whipped around. He spotted me watching, grinned like the devil, and strolled to meet me.

I shook my head as he approached. "And to think I thought spy school would be *so* different from high school."

Hunter winked. "A little . . . social lubricant never hurts in situations like this. Not all of us grew up rubbing shoulders with celebrities or giving speeches to rooms full of important people." His tone was teasing and light, eliciting a smile from me.

"Telling people we're having a party is *hardly* giving a speech. And please inform people that's spiked before they drink, in case they're not into alcohol. They can always request something else from the kitchens."

"Absolutely," Hunter agreed.

Eva jogged up, her blue eyes twinkling. "Did you get the job done?"

"He did." I smirked. These two were going to be trouble.

Over the next half hour, our classmates trickled in. I tried to greet each person and warn them about the spiked beverage. Eva had branched off and was talking to a girl—Amethyst Rhines—who she'd met once with her parents.

When my latest peer excused herself to visit the punch bowl, I sighed. A few groups had formed, and some close-lipped peers who I'd been talking to were chatting animatedly with others. Maybe Eva was right. Was I too much for our classmates?

"What's up, buttercup?" Hunter asked. He, at least, hadn't left my side.

I shook my head. "I keep trying to engage people, but they all scurry away so fast. It's like they don't want to talk to me."

Hunter leaned closer. "Because they're intimidated by you."

I narrowed my eyes. "Excuse me?"

He quirked an eyebrow. "Your parents are legendary. They took down entire crime rings of demons, and tribes of dangerous faeries."

I blinked. My parents had done those things? How had Hunter found this out? And why didn't they tell me?

A spurt of jealousy that Hunter was so well informed about my parents' past shot through me.

"And then there's the dragon wrangling—my favorite tale," Hunter said. "That's definitely scaring a few people off."

My grip tightened on my drink. "Dragon wrangling! What are you—"

"*Or* they feel obligated."

A sharp tone cut through my disbelief, and I whipped around to find Diana standing before us.

"I'd say people are ignoring you because they're aware that you shouldn't be here."

My mouth opened and closed like a fish's. "E—e—excuse me?" I sputtered.

"Did I stutter?" Diana arched an eyebrow. Seriously, what had I done to deserve her ire? "You may have dodged the entry testing, but perhaps Culling will weed you out sooner than I thought, if you can't grasp such a basic concept."

"Are you telling me they're *all* being standoffish because they're upset that I didn't test in?" I challenged.

Diana shrugged. "I can't speak to their motivations, but since our performances in the testing were made public in our orientation packets, I'd have to say it's a distinct possibility. I bet that some didn't want to come, but their parents insisted. Our parents' generation is far too concerned with appearances."

The music, which had been soft before, picked up, and Diana wrinkled her nose. "Thankfully, our peers seem to be of a different mind. Less inclined to put up a front for a freeloader, living off her connections."

"I'm not—!"

"Anyway," Diana waved her hand in front of her face as she spoke over me, "I've made my appearance, and that's all I'm willing to give. Class starts early tomorrow, and you can bet that I'll be ready."

She turned on her heel and strutted out of the room as if she owned the place. I was about to follow and set her straight when I noticed five other classmates scurrying after her.

My heart plummeted. I recognized that scurry. It was the mass exit, the one that followed after the first person brave enough to leave a party made their move.

People wanted out.

My stomach hardened as an unavoidable question popped into my mind.

Did they even want to be here in the first place?

CHAPTER SEVEN

The next morning, snippets from the mixer replayed in my mind like a bad dream as I walked to my first class. My inability to hold anyone's interest, Diana's hoity-toity attitude, and the mass exodus that had followed her out of the room, being the most memorable and hurtful.

At least there had been a couple wins. Like meeting Wilhelmina "Mina" Köhler, the other girl who lived on our floor, and Amethyst Rhines, whose family was friends with the Proctors. Those girls hadn't seemed to dislike me. And as Mina was another L.A. native, we'd been able to bond over our love of good tacos.

Still, that left the vast majority of my class that potentially thought I was riding on my parents' coattails.

I heaved a massive sigh.

"Hey, just forget about it, all right?" Eva said. "I told you, people who attend this school are just a little . . . different. Most are from East Coast power families, and they're competitive. I mean, to be a spy you *have* to be. But I'm sure they'll warm up. No one wants to spend three years with no friends."

I nodded but said nothing. The thing was, people hadn't seemed standoffish the entire time. Many of them talked to each other. Only I had seemed like a social pariah, which supported Diana's theory. It was a fact that I didn't want to bring up to Eva, for fear that she'd ditch me too.

"Here we are." Eva brushed my arm so that I stopped walking, and gestured to a dark, wood door.

Unlike normal colleges, where the room number would be on the door, at Spellcasters, gold plaques declared which subject was taught in each room. This one proclaimed that we were about to enter *"Basics of Demonology"*.

"How do I look?" Eva and I asked at the same time, before bursting into giggles.

"You look great. Like a hot scholar," I assured her.

Dressed in a short blue skirt, a gray tank, and a jacket with elbow patches, Eva looked smart and smoking hot at the same time.

"You too. Very cute dress. The color is fabulous on you." Eva's eyes traveled over the green maxi dress that hugged my torso, plunged at the neckline, and then flared out.

"Thanks. Mom always says emerald is my color. It goes well with tanned skin."

"She was so right." Eva gestured to the door. "Shall we?"

We pushed the door open and stopped in our tracks.

The room was already full, and our classmates quiet, waiting. A tall, dark, surprisingly young, and attractive professor stood at the front, staring at his watch. I glanced at the clock on the wall, and my eyebrows knitted together. We weren't late. There were still two minutes until class started.

This must be part of what Eva meant by our peers are competitive. What a bunch of suck-ups.

"You two must be Odette Dane and Evanora Proctor," the professor stated. "Welcome to the Basics of Demonology, or D1 as we at Spellcasters like to call it. We have much to cover this year, so take a seat, and we'll get started." He spoke in a clipped tone which tolerated no dilly-dallying, just like his perfectly styled black hair and gunmetal gray eyes.

Eva and I rushed to the back of the room, where two desks sat side-by-side with books bound in burgundy velvet atop their scratched wooden surfaces.

"I'm Professor de Spina. In D1, you'll learn what you need to know to defeat various races of demons." Professor de Spina flung his arms behind him, exposing a well-muscled chest as a spray of shimmering gray magic burst from his hands to mold into a life-sized hideous beast with wrinkled skin, an oversized mouth, webbed fingers, and worst of all, glowing red eyes.

I wrinkled my nose. *Sick.*

"This," the professor gestured to the creature he'd just conjured, "is a representation of a lesser demon called a wraith. Is anyone familiar with wraiths?"

At the front, Amethyst raised her hand. I noticed that her purple hair seemed even more vibrant than just the night before. I wondered if she'd used magic or regular dye to color it, and made a mental note to ask her.

Professor de Spina nodded, his eyes boring through her. "Please introduce yourself."

"Amethyst Rhines, Professor. I believe wraiths are a class of demons skilled in possession?"

In response, de Spina twirled his hand so that the wraith's mouth cracked open wide. Someone in the group let out a lone "ewww", and even from my spot in the back, I could see why. The inside of the demon's mouth was filled with rows upon rows of teeth, like a shark's, and most of them were rotting.

"Very good, Amethyst. As you can all see, wraiths have many teeth." De Spina approached the wraith, and ran his finger over the first three rows of teeth.

I shuddered at the motion—the wraith looked too real and disgusting. There was no way in hell I'd stick my hand into that thing's mouth.

"Wraiths constantly lose their decayed teeth and regrow new ones," de Spina continued. "This makes it easy for them to possess people. In fact, I'd dare say they're the species of lesser demon that higher demons send on possession missions most often."

Wait, a hot minute! Demons possess people by using their teeth? My hand shot up.

De Spina lifted an eyebrow. "Yes, Miss Dane?"

I cleared my throat. "I'm wondering how having so

many teeth would make it easy for a wraith to possess people?"

The professor's full lips flattened, and a few people at the front, Diana among them, turned to stare at me with amusement.

"Are we sure she's not human?" a girl—Tabitha Goode, I recalled from the mixer—said. While her tone was light, the narrowing of her eyes let me know that she meant the jab.

Professor de Spina cleared his throat, and the few people who had chuckled fell quiet. "Most demons that are capable of possession use their teeth and claws to dig their way into humans. Hence, having more teeth would make it easier."

My lips formed the shape of an "O," and the professor stopped.

His eyebrows furrowed. "I'm sorry . . . have I confused you?"

A few people sniggered, and I blushed. Did they already know all this?

"No! I just . . . please continue. This is fascinating."

Professor de Spina nodded and moved on. Slowly, those in front turned back around to give the professor their full attention, but the burn in my cheeks lingered for much longer.

My head spun. I'd learned more in a single hour of Demonology than I'd learned in four years of high school. And that wasn't even including the *six* other classes I had that day, one of which I was dreading more than the others —Physical Conditioning.

We had Physical Conditioning every day of the week and for *three consecutive hours* every other Saturday. Thinking about it made me cringe. I mean, I understood that spies needed to be fit, but wasn't that a little much? If my brain didn't explode, my body was probably just going to give out.

"It looks like Battle Magic is next," Eva said, reading the schedule that all the first years had received. "On the lower level."

I snapped to attention. The lower levels? Like a dungeon? I gulped and allowed Eva to lead the way. She seemed to be a natural with directions, unlike me. Even in L.A., where I'd lived all my life, I'd needed GPS.

We rushed back toward the entry hall. Having only fifteen minutes between classes meant that students had to scramble from class to class. Even though it was annoying, I understood why Spellcasters ran such a tight ship. We had a lot to learn in three years; they had to pack it all in somehow.

Speaking of packing it all in, where's the rest of our class? Shouldn't we be traveling in a herd? I glanced around and saw that a few first years trailed behind us, but not everyone. Or at least, I couldn't see them all. Now that the second and third-years weren't actively training and were attending classes too, the halls were actually kind of crowded.

"What are you looking for?" Eva asked, striding between the two staircases that spiraled up the three levels.

"Our classmates. I thought we had every subject together."

"Usually," Eva replied. "There's a note that until after Samhain, the Physical Conditioning professor and Battle Magic professor split us up. I guess dividing newbies into smaller groups makes us more teachable." She shrugged. "It makes sense. These classes are more hands-on, and they have to keep us safe."

"Oh!" My hand plunged into my bag, searching for my schedule.

"You're on the same rotation as me," Eva assured me. "I checked when we swapped at breakfast."

Thank goodness my new friend was on top of things because clearly, I wasn't. The thought was driven home a second later when Eva gripped a light fixture on the wall between the two massive staircases and pulled it down. Right in front of me, a hidden door opened with a groan.

"Whoa," I breathed, my eyes widening at the passage that wound down into the darkness.

Eva grinned. "My parents pointed out the entrance before they left. There's a more mundane route too, but I wanted to show you this one."

I beamed. My new friend was the coolest.

"Wonderful, I see we're on the same schedule," a stern voice snapped behind us. "Now, if you wouldn't mind moving out of the way while you gawk, Professor Thrax does *not* suffer tardy fools." Diana Wake pushed past me and bolted down the staircase. Phoebe Pudeator and Tabitha Goode trailed behind her, both wearing amused smiles.

I huffed. *Great, a girl gang has already formed.*

"Don't let her get to you." Eva rolled her eyes. "Diana's just upset that you're an unknown. My family's table was near hers last night, and I overheard her complaining to her father that life wasn't fair."

I quirked an eyebrow. "What do you mean?"

"You didn't test in, right?"

My cheeks colored, and I shook my head. I hadn't even been here a full day, and I was already regretting my decision to claim the legacy route.

"I don't think it's a bad thing," Eva reassured me. "It's just that most families, even legacy families, make their kids take the test. Mine did. That way they know where their child stands before entering and can work on weaknesses."

"But I still don't understand why Diana would care."

"They share the test results of those students who are admitted into Spellcasters. Diana tested as one of the top students for our year. But because you opted out, you're a mystery. She can't claim she's better than you, and I bet you she hates that." Eva arched an eyebrow.

My spirits lifted slightly.

The hoot of an owl sounded, and Eva stiffened. "We're late." She yanked my arm and pulled me down the stairs.

"Initiates, line up!" a man with braided red hair, bulging

muscles, a barrel chest, and a booming Scottish accent bellowed just as we rushed into the classroom.

We fell in line, and I took a second to look around. Cement walls surrounded us, absorbing most of the light from the plain bulbs hanging from the ceiling. Two massive racks of weapons adorned walls opposite each other. Nothing in this space whispered of the dark opulence that thrived just a floor above.

Instead, it screamed of war.

My gaze trailed down the column of students in this period, taking in Amethyst Rhines, Diana and her minions, and Hunter and Alex Wardwell, among eight others. I sighed. Of course both Diana and Alex, the two people who'd made it clear they disapproved of me, would be in this period.

Suddenly, a body appeared in front of me. I blinked and jerked backward.

The professor shook his head, displeased with my jumpy reactions. "If you two will insist on dressing so inappropriately, I suggest you arrive to my class *early* to change." His jaw clenched, and I wished I'd worn pants and a top like everyone else. "As this is yer first day, I'll let it slide. But only this once. No second chances."

I nodded. "Yes, sir!"

The professor jerked his thick neck toward the door. "There are some old sparring uniforms that we used to require students to wear through there. Go find yer size and change. The rest of you, we'll begin testing. Let's see what you got."

CHAPTER EIGHT

I readjusted my 'sparring uniform,' which was code for ugly-as-hell and smelly black jumpsuit. Either I had a long torso, or Spellcasters just thought all their female spy trainees would be short, because I only found one that fit. Sort of. And it definitely smelled of *cheese*. I wondered when the last time someone had worn one of the jumpsuits was. I suspected they'd been in their wrinkled pile for years. Whatever the case, it would have to work, because there was no way I was going to traipse out of the locker room in my dress and ask if Professor Thrax had a few more sizes lying around.

"Bout time," the professor said when Eva and I entered the classroom again. "I've split yer class into pairs. Your partners are over there, waiting."

Amethyst Rhines and a guy I'd met at the mixer named Efraim Eastey were waiting for us. "Why can't we pair together?" I asked, realizing how odd it was that Professor

Thrax had made two students wait off to the side while others had already begun practicing.

"Because, Miss Dane," I jerked back at his use of my name, which I hadn't given. Then I remembered I had introduced myself during my speech at orientation, and relaxed. "I want to see what you can do, not how friends can go easy on each other. You think this is the first class I've taught? Now pair up."

Eva and I scurried over and split. Amethyst was my partner, and we made our way to a large, empty circle drawn on the floor.

"A sparring circle," Amethyst said, catching me looking at the circle. "We'll practice inside it, often under shields so we don't hurt others."

"Gotcha," I grinned at her and was pleased when she smiled back. Making friends had been rough so far, and I'd take all the good vibes I could get. "So, any idea what we're supposed to be doing?"

Amethyst shook her head and began pulling her long, purple hair into a ponytail. "He just told us to pair off and warm up."

Warm up? I looked around, and saw people were playing with magic. Diana's power was bright purple, and she was practicing levitating a bunch of knives. Mina, my fellow taco-loving Californian, was using her power to open and close the door to the class from fifty feet away. One team was shooting weak spurts of magic at each other, none of which hit the other person, while another group was stretching.

Obviously, no one else knew what was going on either. I settled for shadowboxing, which I'd learned in a self-defense class that Dad had forced me to take. My choice earned me a few strange looks, and I was glad when Professor Thrax blew his whistle and called us to attention.

"All right, now that you've had a mo' to work out the kinks that being at a desk can bring on, we'll begin testing. I've paired you up so that I might assess your range and brute power. Yer goal is simple." He extended his arm toward the far end of the room, and targets shot up from the ground about thirty yards away. "Hit a bullseye with your magic."

I pressed my lips to the side, confused. "So why do we have to be in teams?"

An amused smile split Professor Thrax's face. "Because yer partner will try their damndest to stop you. Which team wants to go first?"

My hand shot up. If given the choice, I always preferred to go first. That way, I didn't have to watch everyone else perform while my nerves grew. Thrax nodded, and Amethyst and I stepped up to the line he indicated.

"Amethyst Rhines, correct?" Thrax asked, his Scottish accent thick.

My partner nodded.

"Very good. Stop Miss Dane."

Amethyst took up position.

I turned to face the target, which was so far away that I was almost sure I wouldn't hit it, but still, I had to try. I called my magic. A familiar sensation of squeezing something out of a tube flowed through me as my power moved from my center, through my arms and toward my fingers. A slight pressure built up, and I held it back, knowing that I wouldn't have many shots to impress the professor. When the sensation grew to be almost too much, I extended my hands and let it go.

Pastel pink magic soared out of me, flying up and away. A second later Amethyst's violet power shot from the sidelines, stopping my magic dead in its tracks before it was even halfway to the target.

Well, damn.

"Again," Professor Thrax said.

I gritted my teeth and set to it, repeating the steps. My magic released, it was slightly darker and faster than the first time. *This is it,* I thought, my hopes rising, only to be dashed once again as Amethyst's magic dissolved my own.

"Again," Professor Thrax repeated.

And so I went, again and again and again until only wisps of power emerged from my fingers. At that point, the professor took a long look at me and sighed.

"Miss Dane, you won't be stopping anyone if yer already that depleted. Join the rest of the class. Diana, partner with Miss Rhines for her test."

I trudged back to the crowd, my stomach sinking and heat warming my cheeks. Diana met me halfway, a grin the size of Texas on her face. "Maybe you should have thought about self-examination before applying," she whispered.

I was about to retort where she could stick her ideas about self-examination, when another voice caught my ear.

"I mean, what did she expect with pathetic pastel magic like that? As my mom says, what looks weak is weak. And that jumpsuit is *not* helping matters."

I turned just in time to see Phoebe and Tabitha laughing while a few others nodded in agreement.

"Well done, Diana!" Professor Thrax bellowed after Diana sent glittery purple magic across the room, picked up a couple daggers from the stockpile, and hurled them straight into a bullseye. "Who's next?" His piercing green eyes scanned our group.

I slunk back. We were on our second round of testing, which Thrax was personalizing in accordance to what he thought our strengths and weaknesses were. After my earlier display, I was well aware I had more of the latter, and didn't want to go after Diana.

"I'll go, Professor." Hunter stepped forward, his sandy blond hair disheveled from the first round of testing.

Last night, it had been perfectly styled, but I had to admit that I preferred this look. And I wasn't the only one. The girl on the other side of me sighed out loud, earning her a glare from Alex at the opposite end of the line.

Yeesh. If looks could kill, she'd be a goner.

"Hunter Wardwell, is it then?" Professor Thrax asked.

Hunter nodded, and his hair flopped into his eyes, triggering a few more sighs from the ladies.

"Have you practiced any offensive or defensive magics?"

"Sort of. We don't have a space like this to train, but my parents made me run drills."

My heart began to beat irregularly at the mention of drills. Every other student had outperformed me in the first test. Half of them, Hunter included, had even hit the bulls-eye. Had everyone here seriously been training for years?

"I thought so, based on your earlier performance. Can you create a shield?"

Hunter took a huge breath and stuck out his hands. His eyes narrowed in concentration, and I wondered if he was trying to call a sword or something to him, when suddenly, wavy, dark green lines burst from his hand. He wove them-selves together piece by piece until they resembled a dome that settled over him.

"Cool," Eva whispered, and I tilted my head, wondering what the hell I was looking at.

"Impressive work, Wardwell," Professor Thrax commented. "Shield work is tricky. That you can already accomplish one is a mighty boon . . . even if it was slow to weave together." He paused and tapped his bottom lip with his pointer finger. "Why don't we test its strength?"

His eyes swung to Hunter's partner. "Thor, can you break a shield?"

The brawny boy shook his head.

Thrax looked unsurprised, and turned to the rest of the class. "Would anyone like to break Hunter's shield?"

Once again, I wished to disappear into the crowd. I

didn't have the faintest idea how to break a shield, or make one.

My parents had always preferred that I didn't use magic for every little thing. They said it gave me fortitude. And in my family, magic was forbidden around those who did not possess it—which was all of my family's social circle. They reasoned that just because the government knew about magicals and welcomed us, it didn't mean that the greater population would react the same way. They were cautious, which I understood, but now I wished that my parents had befriended more witches. Or even joined a coven. Because damn, I was feeling behind.

"No one's up for the challenge, I see?" Professor Thrax pressed. "It seems I may have discovered my top two students, and we're only on day one."

"I'll break the damn thing," someone growled, and a second later, Alex stepped forward. He clenched his jaw, making it almost as square as the frames of his glasses. His blue eyes glinted with determination beneath dark lashes.

My heartbeat picked up at the sight of his coiled muscles. *Even pissed off, Alex is H.O.T.*

Professor Thrax stepped aside. "One Wardwell against another. This should be good."

Alex moved forward like a cat stalking its prey, slow and fluid. From his protective bubble, Hunter was staring at his cousin, arms crossed over his broad chest.

Eva nudged me, and I shot her an excited glance. The tension in the air was palpable.

Were we about to see a family feud played out before us?

As if in answer, Alex thrust his hands in front of him. A vivid crimson light that was even brighter than the magic he'd used to hit the bullseye shot from his palms and crashed into Hunter's shield.

The collision of green and red was blinding, and my gaze shot to the floor. I heard Hunter cry out, and looked up. The shimmering green dome around Hunter remained intact, but the wizard himself was on the ground, his chest heaving.

Realizing that everyones' attention was on him, he leapt up and ambled to the edge of the protective bubble. His hand brushed the green magic, testing it, and a charming grin spread across his face. "Is that all you got, Cousin?" he taunted.

Alex snorted. "Can you handle more? I'd hate to bring it and break that pretty little nose."

"Yes, that would be a shame." Hunter's gaze rolled down the line of students. "A few of these lovely ladies would probably agree."

A few girls batted their eyelashes. Eva let out a high-pitched giggle. I just smirked and gave a tiny shake of my head.

Hunter caught my reaction and winked. I couldn't help myself. I started cracking up. *This guy is too much.*

My mirth attracted the attention of Alex, who whipped around, his eyes latching with mine and lips pursing in annoyance before he dismissed me by turning back around.

My laughter ceased. Alex's scowl made me feel as though milk had curdled in my stomach. Before I could even begin to fathom why he seemed to dislike me so much, Alex swung into action, slamming Hunter's shield with red-hot magic.

The shield pulsed and shimmered, holding strong. Hunter touched it, infusing it with more energy, and the color deepened.

Although I couldn't see Alex's face, I noticed the tension building in his shoulders. He let his power fly once more, this time as a constant stream.

I watched enthralled, as the vibrant river of red flowing from Alex's fingers engulfed the green dome and pressed inward. Second by second, the red magic forced the dome to contract, and Hunter's space to become smaller.

Underneath his protective bubble, Hunter's jaw worked, and green power streamed from his palms to press out against Alex's magic. The dome was contracting at a rapid pace, and in less than a minute, it was nearly touching Hunter on all sides—threatening to shrink-wrap him.

Clenching his jaw, Hunter flung his arms up. His shield pulsed and *jumped* a few inches off the ground. Red magic flew off, and Alex was thrown backward onto the ground. Whatever Hunter had done had thrust Alex's assault off from the inside.

He shot his cousin a cocky smile, but then something caught his attention, and he looked down.

I followed his gaze and gaped. Red magic was *inside*

Hunter's dome, snaking its way up the walls. Alex had snuck a few tendrils in when Hunter had tried to toss it off.

Hunter swore and took a step back, obviously trying to assess how to reclaim his safe space.

Alex barked out a laugh at his cousin's anxiety. It was the sound of victory.

My breath tightened, and I watched with a mixture of awe and fear as Alex, not even bothering to pick himself up off the ground, raised his closed fist and splayed his fingers open. Red magic shot toward a spot on the dome where the rest of his power had congregated. When the two halves of his power met, a sound like crackling lightning filled the room, and the dome shattered into a million little pieces.

"Holy shit," I whispered.

I'd never seen magic used like that. Judging by the stunned looks on most of my peers' faces, I wasn't the only one.

A slow clap made me jump, and Professor Thrax stepped forward. "Good work today." He nodded at Alex, Hunter, and Diana in particular. "Unfortunately, we're out of time. Although I didn't get around to testing everyone to the extent that I would like, I've got enough to be getting on with. We have a lot of work to do before the Samhain Trial." His eyes turned to me. "Dress appropriately from here on out so we don't waste a second."

The sound of a hooting owl filled the room, and my classmates rushed out of the training hall to get to their next class. Eva and I still had to change, so we darted into the locker rooms.

"What exactly is the Samhain Trial, anyway?" I asked Eva once I was sure no one else was around.

Eva shrugged as she unzipped the jumpsuit, threw it on the ground, and pulled on her skirt. "According to my parents, it's different every year. They don't tell anyone in advance. Mind witches spell ex-participants from giving particular details of their experience and apparently the incantation is super strong. All my parents could say was that it's like a mini-mission. Like the ones the government will assign us after graduation."

I thought back to Demonology as I shed my jumpsuit. It had only been that morning, but it felt like much longer—years even. "So we'll probably battle a demon or rabid fae or vampire."

"I guess we'll just have to see." Eva shrugged. "All I know is we're gonna be late for Herbalism, Potions, and Poisons if we don't get moving."

I glanced at the clock. "Crap!"

I grabbed my bag, and we ran out the door to our next class.

CHAPTER NINE

My muscles groaned as I lifted myself up off my mattress to close the curtains and keep sunlight from interrupting my sleep. Once I'd taken care of business, I collapsed back into the bed, desperate for a few more hours of rest.

It was Saturday, which meant we had one afternoon class that day—Physical Conditioning, for three freaking hours. It was enough to make me cry, because after only a week at Spellcasters, I was exhausted with a capital "E". My body hurt in places I'd never thought possible. As for my magic . . . well, I felt depleted, as if I'd run a marathon—or at least what I thought running a marathon would feel like. Since I hated running, the comparison was a theoretical one.

Amethyst had assured me it was normal for someone to feel drained if they were unaccustomed to using magic and then went all out. She said that after a couple of weeks, I should be fine. All I could do was wait, practice, and hope that in the meantime, I would grow stronger and more skilled.

Because it sucked being the worst in my year. And no matter how many mantras or positive affirmations I repeated, there was no denying the fact that I was totally the bottom of the barrel.

The way Diana and her minions looked at me like I didn't belong there didn't help to motivate me, either. I simply hadn't expected to come to a new place and have only a few friends and be so terrible in comparison to my peers.

I placed my hand over my eyes, hoping that my brain would stop obsessing, and just let me go back to sleep. Worrying helped no one, but sleep did.

I snuggled deeper into my blankets and buried my face in the pillow. No sounds came from the hallway or the common area below. I wasn't surprised. After hours of training and studying every day, my classmates should all be exhausted. If they weren't, I needed to know their secret.

Minutes passed, and birds chirped outside. I let the sounds of nature lull me, and I'd almost drifted back to sleep, when a bullhorn shattered my calm.

I shot up and let out a yelp of fear. A few pounding heartbeats later, Eva barreled through my door, her eyes wide, and her sleep mask half over her mouth.

"What the heck was that?" she asked.

"No clue. It came from the common area."

After I made sure I was presentable, we tiptoed out my door. Other students already leaned over the banisters on each level to stare into the common room. Incredibly, a few people were actually down there, studying. Diana, of course, was among them.

However, the person who caught my eye was Headmistress Wake. She stood like a pillar in the dead center of the common room. Blue magic wafted from her lips as she spoke in a booming voice.

"Attention, students! Attention! Is everyone awake?"

Diana's finger wafted through the air, counting. "Everyone's awake, Mother," she said.

I stifled an eye roll. What a suck-up.

"Excellent," Headmistress Wake said. "I have a surprise for you. Consider it our first workshop of the year."

Murmurs flew all around. Even Hunter, who rarely looked surprised, tensed. From what I gathered through the rumor mill, Spellcasters' workshops were eclectic. Apparently, there was always a bartending workshop and a how-to-care-for-your-familiars workshop, but the rest varied depending on the guest lecturers who Headmistress Wake invited that year.

"This will differ from other workshops, but is nonetheless vital. Do your best to make a good impression, and be in the Shipton Solarium in thirty minutes."

With that, the headmistress gave us a quick nod and strode from the room.

I turned to Eva. "Any idea what we're walking into?"

Eva shrugged. "Just don't wear a dress. I wouldn't put it

past them for our first workshop to be something like parkour."

I groaned. Parkour in addition to the three hour training session later? I hoped Eva was wrong. If not, I probably wouldn't survive the day.

My stomach growled as I trooped down the hall. I was among the last to leave the first years' tower, and wishing that I'd been faster so stopping by the kitchens could have been an option. With all the magical training and exercise, my metabolism was burning through *everything* I ate at an astounding rate. But even though I was starving, I hadn't been willing to arrive half made up or late. If there was something I was never willing to rush, it was a first impression.

"Here we are," Eva said, turning a corner and passing through a door labeled *'Ursula Shipton Solarium'*.

The solarium was, as expected, made of glass. Sunlight streamed in to dance upon many exotic leafy plants and Moroccan-style lounge areas at both ends of the rectangular solarium. The space was brighter than any other room I'd seen at the academy. In fact, the only part of the solarium that seemed to mesh with the rest of Spellcasters was the long, dark wood table that ran down the center of the room.

And while the room was beautiful, it was the twelve men in tailored suits sitting at the table chatting that told me spending a few extra minutes getting ready had been the right choice. A man conversing with Alex and a giggling Diana noticed our arrival, excused himself, and stood. He was older, perhaps forty, fit, and still handsome in a rugged yet distinguished way.

"Welcome, ladies. I take it this is the rest of the first years? Headmistress Wake informed us that this year had only thirty-one students."

Diana nodded from her spot next to Alex, who I noticed she was sitting particularly close to. "This is everyone."

"Splendid. I'm David Chena, a non-magical spymaster for the Paranormal Intelligence Agency."

A thrill ran through me, and out of the corner of my eye, I noticed Alex's mouth drop open. Apparently, he hadn't known the high rank of his conversation partner. An ignorance my mother would argue was a folly worse than death.

Mr. Chena plowed on. "We were just chatting before everyone arrived. Why don't we settle into groups of three or four so we can all chat?"

Chat? About what? Where is this going? I stepped forward. During my week at Spellcasters, I'd learned enough to grasp what I didn't know—which was practically everything. But I did know one thing. When meeting high-powered, well-connected people for the first time, I liked to have an idea of what to expect.

"If I might ask, Mr. Chena, no one told us what we'd find down here." I smiled so I didn't seem pushy. "What is this workshop about?"

Mr. Chena grinned. "Extracting information already.

Your classmates have been here ten minutes, and none of them had the guts to ask, well, anything of note. In each conversation I've had, I've been the one doing all the prying."

The other men in suits nodded in agreement.

Mr. Chena turned to me. "That's a good sign, Miss—?"

"Dane," I replied. "Odette Dane."

The spymaster's eyes lit up. "Daughter of the famed Joseph and beguiling Lauren. Please, Miss Dane, join me." He gestured to the empty chair on the other side of him.

Unable to help myself, I arched an eyebrow. Mr. Chena burst out laughing. Just behind him, I noticed Diana scowl, while Alex's lips pressed together in annoyance.

"I can see I won't slip one by you," the spymaster said. "To answer your earlier question, my colleagues and I would like to see how your class might fit into the PIA after graduation."

I nodded and made my way over to the table. Diana and Alex could be mad at me all they wanted, but I was taking Spymaster Chena up on his offer. If there was one thing I learned from my parents, it was that it's all about who you know. And even if I didn't want to talk to either Diana or Alex, David Chena was definitely someone worth knowing.

Mr. Chena, or David as he later insisted upon, poured me another refill of coffee.

I leaned back in my chair, sated and happy. We'd been in the solarium for over an hour when I suggested that conversation always flowed more naturally around a bountiful table. David had agreed, saying that food was an excellent tactic to making people feel welcome, and breakfast was served. Now I was happy to stay here all day, networking and socializing.

Finally, something I do better than the rest of my classmates.

I didn't think it was cocky to think that, it just seemed like a fact. David had actually commented on it, leading Diana to excuse herself from our group and find a new one. But as soon as he mentioned it, I saw that he was right. The vast majority of my peers appeared uncomfortable around the spy mentor they'd been grouped with. Tabitha Goode looked more uneasy than I'd ever seen her, red-faced and tight-lipped.

I couldn't understand why others were having such a hard time. Extracting information, as David liked to call it, was just questioning your conversation partner about themselves. It wasn't as difficult as magic.

"Now that you've learned all I can tell you about my position at the PIA, I'm wondering how you're finding Spellcasters, Odette?"

I refrained from sighing. "To be honest, I'm finding my transition a bit of a struggle," I replied.

"Really?" David leaned forward, blocking Alex from our conversation for the fifth time.

My classmate huffed, leaned back in his chair, and crossed his arms over his chest. I almost felt sorry for the guy. Until I remembered how much of a jerk he'd been all week.

Karma sucks, buddy.

"And why are you finding the transition a struggle?" David prodded. "Your parents are both witches and were stellar spies. I'd just started with the service when they left, but it devastated the PIA to lose them."

I nodded. That fit what I'd heard others say about my parents, and I didn't doubt it. Everyone in Hollywood loved them too. "Well, part of it is that my parents didn't want me to come here."

David's eyebrows shot up, and I rushed to explain.

"I'm their only kid, and Spellcasters isolates us so much. Plus . . . " My cheeks warmed, and although I wasn't sure if it was smart to reveal this next bit of information to my future employer, David had been honest with me about his life at the agency, so I'd be honest with him. "They think it's too dangerous. Or that I can't hack it. And to be honest, after this week, I'm not sure they're wrong. I'm behind in all the classes where we work magic."

From the other side of David, I could hear Alex snort, and my face became even hotter. But David didn't seem to register Alex's annoyance as he leaned forward and took my hand.

I felt eyes watching all around the long table, but David's gaze bore into me with such insistence, I couldn't look away.

"Odette." He spoke in a low tone so that only I could hear. "I can understand your parents' fears. Being a spy *is* dangerous. And we don't get to live a normal life, or see the people we love often. They would know firsthand." His grip squeezed mine tighter.

I pressed my lips together as a spurt of emotion shot through me. Even though we'd only been at school a week, I missed them and had been trying to avoid thinking about them.

"But, there's also great satisfaction and reward in what we do. We make a difference in the lives of many. You, as a witch, can do far more than me."

After a week of failures, I couldn't help that his compliment brought tears to my eyes.

David's hands released mine, and his lips formed a soft smile. "I can't speak to magic, as I'm not a wizard, but from what I've learned of you today, I bet you just need more time to adjust. Knowing your pedigree, I'd be surprised if you weren't in the running for spymaster before you hit thirty."

My lips parted, but my surprise lasted only until Alex shot out of his seat and stormed out of the room.

My heartbeat kicked up as I watched him go. Alex's jaw was clenched almost as tight as his fists. Clearly he was livid and didn't believe that I belonged at Spellcasters.

But I'd finally received the tiniest shred of the validation I'd been seeking. And now that I'd had a taste of success, I wanted nothing more than to prove Alex wrong.

CHAPTER TEN

Later that afternoon, I was walking on air.

After a week of being the worst student in every class, I'd *finally* found something I excelled at—getting people to tell their stories. Spymaster Chena had actually suggested that if the rest of my class needed pointers on how to make small talk and get information out of others, they should ask me.

Me! Suck it haters!

I twirled and leapt to one side of the wide hallway, landing beside a painting of Merlin. His blue-green eyes twinkled, and I grinned. "You seem pretty crafty, but I bet I could teach you a thing or two."

I bopped Merlin on the nose and strutted a few more paces down the hall. My gaze caught on two other paintings. One was of a beautiful witch who I didn't recognize. I moved closer and read the plaque beneath her likeness.

"Morgan Le Fay."

A shiver ran up my spine as I took in the artwork. Morgan's fire red hair, full lips pulled up in a mischievous smile, and bright eyes called to me in a way a painting never had before. And her dress of cornflower blue, exquisite taste in jewelry, and confident pose made me feel connected to her.

"Girl, you've got it going *on*. No lessons for you!"

I moved on to the third painting, one of a very dour-looking Nicolas Flamel, and shook my head. "But you need all the help you can get. Start by smiling more, and try to wash your clothes. I'll check back next week to see how you've progressed. Maybe Morgan can help too!" I winked and chuckled at my wit as I continued on to the Physical Training Facility.

Most of my classmates were already there, along with many of the second and third-years, who were sweating so much, I'd have thought they'd been there for hours. After five days of working out more than I did in a typical year, my muscles were beyond sore, so I made my way past the treadmills and weight machines to the separate room in the back reserved for magical training.

When I opened the door to the warded space, Hunter Wardwell smiled at me from behind a shimmering green force field. I balked and shook my head in disbelief. My classmate was hovering a couple of inches above the ground, a difficult skill to master.

Hunter floated to the ground, released his shield, and sauntered my way. "What? You've never seen someone levitate before?"

"Actually, no."

He kicked his swagger up a notch as he joined me. "Mr. Chena seemed very impressed with you this morning. Do you accept students?"

"Like you need help. You held your own at breakfast, and no surprise there, you're charming . . . maybe *too* charming for your own good." I quirked an eyebrow and injected some sass into my tone. I didn't need Hunter thinking I would fawn over him like every other girl in our year.

Hunter chuckled. "I've heard that once or—"

"At least you found *something* you're capable of." The voice that cut through the air was ice-cold and all-too-familiar. "I was beginning to wonder when my mother would send you home for being such a disgrace of a witch. But apparently you have some skills. You're a pro at sucking up to those at the top."

Bitter much?

"I would say that I never took you for a sore loser." I tried to appear flippant as I turned to face Diana, "but that would be lying."

Behind her, Tabitha and Phoebe gasped.

"I'm a sore loser because you know how to schmooze people in power?" Diana's eyes narrowed. "Like that matters in the real world. If I was on a mission, and it was my *job* to get information from someone, I would've excelled. But I don't need to suck up now to get a leg up later. I *work* for what I get."

I rolled my eyes. "Of course you do."

"Now, now, ladies, don't you think this is getting a little heated?" Hunter tried to intervene.

Diana gave him a pleasant, not at all tight-lipped smile. "Honestly, Hunter, I don't understand why a wizard of your talents bothers trying to make everyone feel so at home. Especially when it's so obvious that they don't belong."

"Yeah, she can't even shield herself," Tabitha added, her voice like a little girl's, too high-pitched.

"And she didn't know that you can change the color of your magic to be more covert," Phoebe added with a snicker. "Imagine trying to complete a mission with watery *pink* magic giving you away."

My fists tightened. "We're here to learn, aren't we?"

Tabitha must have been really feeling herself, because she stepped in front of Diana and flipped her long, black hair over her shoulder. "Trying isn't good enough when you come face-to-face with a demon or malevolent fae. I bet you don't make it past the Samhain Trial. Hopefully, your partner will bring your body back. Then again, if they have to save your ass so many times during the trial, they probably won't have the energy."

"I won't be a burden to my partner," I stated through clenched teeth.

"Oh *please,* let's be honest, Legacy." She spread her arms wide. "Whoever gets paired with you is getting the short end of the stick. You'd be doing us all a favor if you left now. At the very least, we wouldn't have to pray not to get stuck with a magical dud. Malicious magicals aren't swayed by a pretty face and charming demeanor—which is the best you got."

My anger reached a boiling point. A beam of shimmering, pastel pink magic burst from my hands, shot toward Tabitha, and hit her straight in the heart. Diana gasped, and the smile fell from Phoebe's face as she backed away.

Unfortunately, Tabitha didn't topple. My magic wasn't strong enough for that, but it did knock the wind out of her.

Still, I barely had a second to revel in my small win before a stream of Tabitha's orange magic came barreling my way. I dropped to the ground, and smelled a nasty scent as the edge of her power caught my long hair. Quickly, I rolled to put the fire out, and leapt back up.

Tabitha had come closer, and there was a fire in her dark eyes.

"What's wrong, Legacy? Did I ruin your hairdo?" Tabitha jeered and shot another beam of magic at me.

I darted out of the way.

"Ladies! I think—"

"Stay out of this, Hunter!" Tabitha screamed. "This little witch needs to know she can't get everything she wants because of who her parents are. Not everyone will treat her like a princess!"

Yikes. So she wasn't just pissed that I'd attacked first. My *privilege* incensed her.

Before I could even consider how to calm Tabitha down, she attacked again. This time, I saw the moment her orange magic transformed midair from sheer energy into fire.

I shrieked, but didn't move fast enough. It hit my arm,

and I tried to bat it out, but it didn't disappear. At least not until Hunter conjured water and shot it at me.

The fire sizzled to nothing.

Tabitha laughed. "See, little *Legacy,* you really don't belong here. I learned how to put out enchanted flames at the age of five. It's probably best to pack up your bags now."

I gnashed my teeth, gathered up as much power as I could muster, and roared as I let it fly. A bright pink beam, much more vibrant than my normal pastel hue, soared from my palms.

My mouth dropped open at the sight of it. When Tabitha's eyes widened, a sense of victory bloomed within me.

It disappeared nearly as fast when she threw up an orange shield.

"Nice try, Legacy!" she screamed, as my power met hers, ran the length of her shield, and was deflected—right back at me.

I tried to run, but found my legs didn't work. *Damn Tabitha! She's holding me in place.*

So I did the only thing I could. I curled in on myself, and protected my head with my arms just before my own magic hit me, and I dropped to the floor unconscious.

CHAPTER ELEVEN

My eyes blinked open, and two pools of bright blue made my insides melt.

"She's awake." Alex's deep baritone hit my ear.

A thrill shot through me. *Stupid hormones, quit screwing with me. Liking him is out of the question.*

"And she's fine, I think. Someone should take her to the infirmary, though, to be sure." He averted his gaze from whoever he'd been talking to, and looked back to me. "Do you feel off?"

I felt like I had run straight into a brick wall, but other than that, nothing seemed amiss. I shook my head.

"That's a miracle." He stood and held his hand out to me. "You may be a legacy, but you'd do well not to challenge strong witches. You lucked out, not getting injured."

Someone behind Alex tittered, and he shot them an annoyed glare. "And witches who are stronger than *obvious* beginners should know better than to fight them. This is Spellcasters, not a gladiatorial ring. Have some class."

The laughing stopped, and footsteps leaving the training room sounded.

"If you're quite done, Cuz, I'll take Odette." Hunter moved forward and extended his hand out to me. As soon as I stood without a wobble, Eva, who'd been hanging back and wringing her hands like a grandma, threw herself at me.

"That B! I can't believe Tabitha did that to you."

"What . . . did she do to me?"

I recalled snippets of fighting, and that Tabitha had been far stronger than me. But whatever energy manipulation she used to knock me out had knocked a couple memories loose too.

"She shielded herself from your magic, which is within the rules of fair play. But in doing so, she redirected your own power back at you and blended it with an offensive spell of her own. You know, in case yours wasn't enough. Which it clearly was. The color looked stronger, more bright pink than pastel. What did you do differently?"

I shook my head, not having a clue, but vaguely remembered also being shocked by the hue.

"Hmm." Eva's blue gaze traveled the length of my body. "Well, you seem fine now. Alex did good work."

"Alex?"

"My cousin is skilled in the art of healing." Hunter joined us. Only then did I notice it was just us three in the room again.

My shoulders relaxed a bit. Alex put me on edge—in more ways than I liked to admit.

"Healing? Isn't that something we learn later?"

Hunter nodded. "We learn a few remedies in Herbalism, Potions, and Poisons, but not true body work. Healing starts in our Grind-year. And only advanced students go on to study the discipline in more depth in the Crucible-year." He shrugged. "But Alex's parents are physicians. They've probably been teaching him for ages. Smart, considering all the crap the school's gonna throw at us. Obviously, he'll be making it into the advanced class."

I nodded, and my neck twinged. It would be smart to have knowledge of healing. If I survived my Culling-year at Spellcasters, I'd have to pay close attention.

"You still look off." Eva's ginger brows pulled together. "You should listen to Alex and go to the infirmary. You can make up training time later. They can't make you work out if you're all shell-shocked. We'll go with you in case you fall over or something."

"Yeah, good idea," I said.

As I hobbled out of the magical training chamber and through the larger gym, our classmates and the years above us turned to stare. Some chuckled while others just shook their heads. Apparently, my fight with Tabitha had already been reported to the wider student body.

And judging from the way everyone stared at me, I hadn't come out well in the gossip.

~

That night, I couldn't sleep.

Although my body ached and my eyelids felt weighted, my brain would not let me rest. I'd been tossing and turning for hours. The voices in the common area had faded as people went to bed, leaving a lovely quiet behind. And yet, I was wide awake, thinking. My first week at Spell-casters had been unexpected to say the least. An absolute disaster, if I wanted to be dramatic about it.

Which I sort of did.

I hadn't expected to find myself so unpopular and ridiculously behind. So I hadn't trained all my life for this. My parents wanted to give me a normal childhood. Did that really mean I deserved others' ire?

Giving up the pretense that sleep was coming soon, I threw my covers off and decided to go for a nighttime stroll. Sometimes, in the past, like when I'd been nervous about taking my SATs, upon my parents' insistence, walks had helped me calm down.

Throwing on my bright yellow robe and sheepskin-lined moccasins, I left my room.

Hunter, Eva, Diana, and Thor were the only ones still in the common area. They were studying, although judging by the droop of Eva's eyes, she'd give up soon.

"Where are you going?" she asked.

"For a stroll. I can't sleep. Walking helps me relax."

"It's not your head, is it? Do you want any company?"

"No, my head's fine. I just need some alone time."

Eva nodded, though she didn't seem convinced, and I slipped out the door before she insisted on joining.

In the dead of night, the hallway was bleaker than usual, which was saying something. As I walked, I paused in front of various portraits of spymasters, reading their names and years of service. A particular portrait of a man who shared my last name caught my attention.

Is he a distant relation? Or do we simply share a last name? Had he tested in? David Chena had mentioned that he thought I would make an excellent spymaster. I'd always thought so too.

But after today, I wasn't so sure.

I sighed and kept moving. While my classmates had spent years practicing magic, I'd wasted my time. After I turned sixteen, I'd stopped mentioning Spellcasters to keep the peace in our home. Instead, I'd pretended like I was going to be a good little girl and go to a human college. I'd studied calculus, performed contemporary dance, could burn the keys off the piano, and even throw a damn good punch, courtesy of the self-defense classes Dad had made me take. But did I know the first thing about performing battle magic?

Nope.

Could I actually survive three years at Spellcasters? Although this was what I'd wanted since I was young, and had even fought my parents for my place, I was starting to have my doubts.

Were my parents right?

I was making my way down the set of stairs that led to the entry hall, when a loud clanging made me jump.

"Is someone there?" I asked. My voice echoed

throughout the large chamber, sending shivers up my spine. Although Spellcasters was always dark and a little creepy, at nighttime, the creepiness factor increased tenfold.

No one answered, so I kept descending the stairs. I wanted to walk in the full moon's light along the lake's edge.

I'd reached the front steps, and another noise, the howling of a dog outside, hit my ears.

I tilted my head. A dog? The only student who had a dog as a familiar was Olivia García. And it was a little yappy thing, definitely not capable of producing a deep howl like that. Perhaps it was a pet from Wandstown on the loose? Eva mentioned that it was a few miles away. It seemed likely that a dog could escape and run this far. But the fencing around Spellcasters was prodigious—topped with barbed wire, and enchanted to hold out magicals. Surely, it would keep out a normal dog.

"It's probably out near the main road," I whispered to myself and pushed the front door open.

As soon as I took my first full breath of fresh air, my heart rate slowed. Slippered feet whisked across the grass, as I walked toward the lake, pulling my robe closer. The full moon shone down on me, illuminating my walk and calming my frazzled nerves. I'd made the right choice in going for a stroll. Hopefully, after I returned to bed, I'd be able to fall right asleep, and be fresh to study the next day.

I reached the lake's edge and nestled into a spot where the grass seemed shorter, intent on sitting until my eyelids started to droop. The minutes ticked by, and peace settled over me.

Suddenly, another howl pierced the calm of the night.

My spine straightened. That had been closer.

I looked around, taking in the darkness, but was unable to spot any disturbances.

The air seemed to shift, and one by one, goosebumps rose on my arm. I wished that I'd brought a weapon. I wondered if Dad's can of magical mace would work against aggressive animals? Was it really closer, or was that my imagination?

As if in answer, another howl sounded, louder this time.

I shot to my feet. Nothing was moving in the nearby grass, but still—something was off. Dangerous. I spun to return to the school, and made it three steps when another sound stopped me dead in my tracks.

Was that . . . a scream? The hairs on the back of my neck stood up. I was sure it had been, and even worse, it was very close.

Not a second later, the scream sounded again and ended in a sob.

Someone's hurt. I can't just leave them with . . . whatever is out here.

I sprinted in the sound's direction, my eyes scanning the long grasses on the banks of the lake that brushed my legs. Dark woods hung ominously on one side. I'd gone about halfway around the lake, spotting no one, before I heard moaning. The sound was coming from my direct right—in the forest.

I sucked in a breath and moved toward the trees. I'd nearly broken out of the long grass and into the tree line when I saw a flash of red at eye level. The light vanished as quickly as it had appeared, but that didn't subdue my fear.

Had that been a wraith? Was the strange shift I'd sensed earlier demonic energy? All my instincts screamed to sprint back to the school, but then a hand shot out in front of me and flailed like a fish pulled from the river.

A shriek ripped from my throat as I leapt back.

Someone gurgled.

No. No. No. I knew that noise from film sound effects, and it never ended well in the movies. And even though every cell in my body begged me not to look, to go get help, I couldn't.

Heart pounding, I took a few steps toward the arm, now still.

Tabitha Goode lay just inside the tree line, blood covering her throat and her body all the way down to her hips. Her neck was twisted, and her black hair splayed out behind her.

My hand flew to my mouth. "Tabitha!" I fell upon her, trying to find a pulse in the mess of blood and torn flesh.

There was nothing.

CHAPTER TWELVE

I burst through the doors of Spellcasters and ran right into Diana. A flashlight flew from her hand, making me jump. Headmistress Wake was right behind her daughter. Professor de Spina too, his black hair slicked back and gray eyes blazing. Their mouths dropped open at the sight of me.

"Odette Dane!" Headmistress Wake scolded. "What is the meaning of this?!"

My lips trembled.

"T—T—Tabitha," I stuttered finally. "I found her body. By the lake. I tried to revive her, but . . . I couldn't." I pointed in the general direction where Tabitha's body lay growing cold.

Diana's eyes widened. "Her body? Do you mean—?"

I nodded. "Dead . . . I'm pretty sure."

Diana whipped around. "Mother!"

Headmistress Wake nodded. "Odette remain here. Diana, you stay with her."

"But, Mother!"

"No buts. Professor de Spina and I will return."

It was only once the headmistress and Demonology professor were gone that I realized shivers wracked my body. I took a step into the warmth of the academy, and Diana's attention snapped to me.

"Where are you going?"

"Just away from the door. I'm cold," I answered, rubbing my hands against the thick fabric of my robe. Wetness covered them, and I looked down to find my sunshine yellow robe covered in blood. "Oh—oh my God."

Diana's eyes narrowed. "What were you doing out there?"

"Walking. I couldn't sleep, so I wanted to walk."

"Isn't it too frigid for someone from L.A.? Why wouldn't you just walk around the school?"

"I wanted fresh air."

Diana's lips flattened for a second before she pressed on. "So it wasn't that you heard Tabitha leave just minutes before you to get water from the lake? You weren't following her?"

"What? Why would she get . . . and why would I—" I stopped as what Diana was getting at became clear. "You can't think I'd actually kill her!"

"Oh please, Dane, stop acting all innocent. We're in spy school. If you can't fathom killing someone, you shouldn't be here. And yes, I find it suspicious that you left your rooms mere minutes after Tabitha left the common space. Especially considering how hard she creamed you earlier. Did you want a little revenge on someone who earned her spot here because she tarnished your family rep?"

My fight with Tabitha came rushing back in a new light. Diana was right. That we'd fought just hours ago didn't look good for me.

"Diana, I swear . . . I didn't—"

The academy's door burst open, and Headmistress Wake and Professor de Spina shuffled inside, their magic supporting Tabitha's body.

Diana's hand flew to her mouth. "What's wrong with Tabitha, Mother?" Her icy blue eyes shot through me, full of loathing.

"Not now, Diana. Thank you for alerting us to the scream, but it's time for you to get back to your dorm. Tell everyone else to stay there too." Headmistress Wake gestured to Tabitha floating on a bed of mixed blue and gray magic. "De Spina, take Tabitha to the infirmary. Try every revival method known to witching kind. Odette, you come with me."

The moment we arrived in Headmistress Wake's enormous office, she went to a small sink in the corner with a bar above it and washed the blood from her hands. I wished that I could do the same, but I'd need something a lot bigger than that tiny sink. Tabitha's blood covered me.

To distract myself, I took in the room.

In line with the rest of Spellcasters, it was dark. The headmistress' desk was the most prominent piece of furniture, but there was also an impressive globe, many filled bookshelves on the side walls, and a luxurious chaise lounge by the window. A fire burned in the hearth right behind her desk, giving the room light and warming my chilled bones.

"Sit," Headmistress Wake commanded.

I lowered into one of two red velvet chairs before her massive mahogany desk. She grabbed a fresh towel, ran it under the faucet, and handed it to me. "Wipe your face and hands. Then we'll talk."

Again, I did as she said, and the white rag soaked through with blood within seconds. Once I finished, the headmistress held out a trash can, and I deposited the rag.

She took her seat and tented her hands. "Tell me everything."

I did so, babbling about flashing red eyes, Tabitha's non-existent pulse, and my attempts at CPR that resulted in me deciding I needed to get more help.

Headmistress Wake raised her hand, and I shut up. Silence hung in the room as she mulled over my recounting.

Unable to help myself, I broke the silence. I needed answers. "Headmistress Wake?"

"Yes, Miss Dane?"

"How many types of demons have red eyes?"

The headmistress stiffened, but did not get the chance to answer, for at that very moment, there was a knock on the door.

"It's open," the headmistress called out.

Professor de Spina entered, his suit crooked over his

broad chest and black hair slightly disheveled. My eyebrows pulled together. Why was he in a suit and Headmistress Wake in a dress? It was nearing midnight.

Feeling out of place in my blood-covered robe, I pulled the fabric tighter around me. Did these people never sleep?

"Professor de Spina. Excellent timing. Perhaps you can answer a question Miss Dane has just posed."

"Which would be?" De Spina countered, his voice still a little breathy as he took up position behind the chair next to mine, his hands laying on the top.

"What sorts of demons have red eyes?" the headmistress asked.

De Spina lifted an eyebrow as his gaze found mine. "Are you saying that you believe a demon did this to Tabitha?"

"I—I'm not sure. All I saw was flashing red. It looked like eyes," I answered. After a moment, I added, "But I also heard whimpering, like a dog."

Headmistress Wake didn't answer, and de Spina sighed. "Many demons have red eyes. But wraiths are the most common lesser demons sent to the human world who fit that description." He paused for a moment. "Although, I disagree that what happened to Tabitha resulted from a demon attack."

"Why?" I asked.

"I see no way it could have gotten onto the grounds. Not only that, but there's the fact that Tabitha was only a first year, with a week of classes under her belt. It's not like she could properly fight a wraith. The creature should have been able to possess her without issue or causing injury. If it was a wraith that had gotten onto the grounds, why wouldn't it do so?"

Was. He'd said Tabitha *was* a first year, which meant she was definitely gone. Although I'd suspected that was the case, a lump rose in my throat, and my eyes dropped to my hands. I hadn't liked Tabitha, but I wouldn't have wished this on her.

"So, Professor, what do you—or the healer on staff tonight—surmise did this to the girl?"

That got my attention. I lifted my gaze to find that de Spina was staring at me.

My heart stopped. "You two don't think I did this, do you?" My voice croaked out of me, a little shaky.

It was one thing for Diana to jump to conclusions. She hated me, and Tabitha had been her friend. The professor and headmistress, however, were people who had power over my life. People who could kick me out of Spellcasters.

Anger smothered my fear at the thought of losing my dream. *I can't let them do that.*

I shot up from my chair. "I swear I didn't! I think something got in through the fence. I also . . ." I shot a hesitant glance between my superiors, wondering just how crazy what I was about to say would sound.

The headmistress' lips pressed together, and I decided it didn't matter. I had to go for it.

"I heard howling right before I found her. If it wasn't a demon, could it have been a werewolf? Don't some have red eyes in wolf form? Like juveniles? Or could a demon have possessed a dog?"

De Spina's eyes widened, and Headmistress Wake inhaled sharply.

"I swear, I didn't do anything to Tabitha. Why would I have any reason to hurt anyone here?"

Headmistress Wake's intense, dark glare focused on me. "Do you deny you two had an altercation earlier today?"

My stomach dropped. "No, but I—"

"Perhaps you did not enjoy your shortcomings being demonstrated in front of others?"

I blinked, stunned that she'd gone there. Clearly, Diana had told her about today, which was annoying, but not unexpected.

"I've already let it slide that there was an attack outside the confines of a regulated classroom. Really Miss Dane, your parents would be appalled by that sort of behavior, but now this?"

Hold up . . . my parents. Hadn't I heard them talking to the headmistress about how the school was not secure enough? My eyes found the headmistress'. I doubted that she really believed that I did this, but still, I didn't need my reputation ruined, or to be pushed out of Spellcasters before I even found my footing.

"Headmistress Wake, didn't my parents bring up the idea of inadequate protection around the school when they were here? Particularly, how their many donations were not being used to make the school more safe?"

Her lips flattened, and Professor de Spina shuffled uneasily, but I pressed on, not willing to give them a moment to dismiss me before I'd said my piece.

"Should they hear about this attack . . . and that I believe the attackers came from the outside, I wonder what they'd do? A council oversees the academy, right? Maybe we should invite them to Spellcasters to make sure everything is fine here?"

The headmistress' mouth tightened at the corners. "There will be no need for that, Dane. We have a staff of competent witches and wizards who know the academy better than anyone. We'll see to the investigating. You are—"

The door to the headmistress' office burst open, and Eva and Hunter rushed in.

"She's innocent!" Eva yelled. "We saw Odette not even ten minutes before the attack! There's no way she'd have had time to do it!"

"Not to mention it seems totally out of character," Hunter added, his chest puffed out with surety.

My heart swelled at the vote of confidence—friendship—coming from him. I would have expected it from Eva, we were already tight. But Hunter and I were still finding our way. Or so I'd thought.

As if he could read my mind, Hunter's green gaze sought mine. "Odette doesn't have a mean bone in her body. She would never harm someone without a *very* good reason."

"Yeah." Eva stepped forward, fists clenched at her side. "Odette would never—"

Headmistress Wake shot out of her seat. "*Enough*! Miss

Proctor! Mr. Wardwell! How dare you burst into my office?"

We froze in place. Once she was sure my champions wouldn't start up again, Headmistress Wake shook her head in disapproval. "I understand coming to support your friend, but this is absurd. Never, and I mean *never*, enter my office without permission again. Is that clear?"

Eva and Hunter nodded.

"Good. And at any rate, your concern was unwarranted. Miss Dane has sufficiently just defended *herself*." Her eyes shifted to me, and I swore that through her clear annoyance, I caught a glimmer of respect. "However, the staff has a killer to catch, so I'd appreciate if the three of you moved on—together. Go to the initiates' tower and remain there until morning. Say nothing to the other students, I'll make an announcement tomorrow. Is that clear?"

We nodded simultaneously.

"Good. You are dismissed."

My defenders and I rushed out of the headmistress' chambers as fast as our feet could carry us.

CHAPTER THIRTEEN

"Tell us everything!" Eva said once we were out of earshot from Headmistress Wake's office.

I shook my head, still disbelieving everything that had happened. "I—I couldn't sleep after today . . . after Tabitha."

Hunter and Eva nodded sympathetically.

"Whenever I worried too much at home, I always went for a walk and felt better." I gulped. That mechanism of self-soothing would never be the same. I wasn't sure if I could ever go for a night stroll again and *not* remember tonight. "I sat by the lake and kept hearing a noise nearby . . . howling."

"Like a dog?" Hunter asked.

"Sure . . ." I trailed off and bit the inside of my bottom lip before continuing. "To be honest, I'm not sure what it was. But I heard that and screaming. I followed the sounds, saw a weird flash of red in the woods, and found Tabitha on the ground." My voice cracked, the anxiety threatening to overwhelm me, but I needed to get this out—wanted someone to be on my side. "I tried to help, even did CPR, but when I searched for her pulse, there was nothing . . ."

"And then you ran back in here, all covered in blood, and the headmistress tried to blame you, even though there's another obvious explanation." Eva spat the words out, as if taking great offense to each syllable.

Another *obvious* explanation? I hadn't even mentioned that I thought the red could have something to do with a demon or shifter. And the headmistress didn't seem to have a clue what was going on, so how did Eva? My eyebrows knit together. Hunter too looked more resigned than confused—which made zero sense.

"Hold up." I stopped in the middle of the hall. "What's the explanation? I haven't even told you everything yet, so what are you talking about?"

"Oh, you know. Only the freaking curse that's been killing off kids born in our year. It all adds up with what you said. Fulfilled curses give off a flash of light, usually red or a poisonous-looking green." Eva waved her hands as if her words were nothing.

My mouth fell open. "C—c—curse?" I bleated.

Hunter and Eva stared at me, their eyes—bright shades of blue and green—cutting through me like brilliant gems.

Hunter gaped. "You didn't know?"

Eva gasped. "What! No way!"

"Will someone please tell me what the hell you're talking about?"

"But—but, I just . . . " Eva looked around, as if the empty hall would supply her with an answer, before returning her attention to me. "I assumed when you said your parents didn't want you here, it was because of the curse. It seemed so obvious. Honestly, it was one argument I used to get out of *coming* here."

"What curse?!" I hissed.

Eva was too flabbergasted to speak, so Hunter stepped up to the plate. "Haven't you noticed how the first-year class is much smaller than the other years? Usually it's the opposite at Spellcasters because, well, it's not unheard of for students to die on missions, but those don't start until our Grind-year. Most classes begin with about a hundred students. For our year, fewer applied. Their families claimed it would be a poor choice to congregate us all in one place. Really, only the serious legacies tested in, and . . . a few others." His tone dipped at the end.

One hundred students? Our class had thirty-one—thirty, now that Tabitha was gone.

"So people didn't apply because the curse scared them?"

"Yes, but to be honest, kids our age have been dying every year since we were born." Eva shook her head. "I can't believe your parents kept this from you. People don't talk about it much because it scares them, but it really shook the witching community when the curse was cast."

"What happened?"

"A witch who practiced black magic stumbled into the agency and spewed off a super powerful curse. The magic was so strong that it killed her. She literally exploded all over the human receptionist at the front desk." Eva stuck out her tongue and shuddered.

My nose wrinkled. That had probably been one hell of a job for the memory witches to reverse.

"What did the black witch say?"

"The human was hysterical afterward," Hunter said, "but she remembered bits and pieces once the agents got her to calm down. The witch talked about children born in the first year of the new millennia, children whose ancestors had defied the natural order of the world and shared revelatory secrets with humans. And how the darkness would come for them."

I sucked in a breath. Although the words seemed kind of vague, they weren't. Witches weren't a large portion of the population, and unlike normal humans, we had a difficult time reproducing, so narrowing it down to the year of birth shrank the pool considerably. The 'natural order' was easy. There were factions of dark magicals all over the world—black witches included—who hated that their kind worked with humans instead of against them. Since we'd been born with gifts, they thought magicals should rule, not humans. As for 'secrets', few magicals had more secrets than spies.

Slowly, I released my inhale. "So children of spies would be the primary targets."

"Bingo," Eva breathed. "There's a theory that because the witch was at the agency when she cast the curse, it even made it easier for her magic to find those who she wanted to prey upon. There's no way to know whether that's true or not, but since the year we were born, kids our age from spy families have died under mysterious circumstances. No one has been able to figure it out, and some—like Headmistress Wake—flat out deny that the curse is real.

"We all know Spellcasters is super secure, and yet Tabitha just died. Vamps, demons, fae, shifters, humans, and even other witches and wizards can't simply waltz onto these grounds, but one thing can, no matter what."

"Magic—particularly the black kind that's been lying in wait for its chance," Hunter finished.

"Headmistress Wake doesn't believe in it? But if so many people have died, the curse has to be real, right?" My words came out slowly as I worked out the details.

Hunter and Eva nodded simultaneously.

My confusion over my parents' reluctance to bring me to Spellcasters disappeared. They hadn't thought I couldn't handle it, or probably even that a spy academy was too dangerous. Or if they had, it had been secondary to another concern.

They thought coming here made it even easier for the curse to find me.

CHAPTER FOURTEEN

Summer had slipped away in a haze of classes, exercise, long nights studying, and many, many tears of frustration. Now a fall chill permeated the air, as September gave way to October.

Despite knowing about it for almost three months, I still wasn't sure what to think about the curse.

Not wanting to risk embarrassment, the only people who I broached the subject with were Eva and Hunter. And as the Samhain challenge neared, they became far less interested in rehashing it.

For my friends, the curse was a fact of life—one they'd known about for years.

For me, it explained a whole hell of a lot. Like my parents manically warding our Beverly Hills home. Or their extreme anxiety over me attending Spellcasters. And why I'd overheard them talking to Headmistress Wake about the academy's protection being lax.

But as much as the curse helped to explain, it also prompted more questions, which suited me fine. They were a welcome distraction during a difficult time in my life.

Not only had a certain subset of peers not gotten over the fact that I was the only witch in years to decline the admissions test, but being the one to find Tabitha's body hadn't helped my reputation. Despite Headmistress Wake's assurances that I'd had nothing to do with my classmate's death, a fair number of people still regarded me with unease.

My status was not what I'd desired when I came to Spellcasters, but considering the academy was more competitive and cliquey than I could have imagined, I'd stopped fighting it.

Or at least, I was trying to.

Sometimes, it felt like all my efforts were futile. Like in our Conjuring class, when certain students produced representations of animals that walked, while I struggled to create a complete teacup. Frustratingly, mine always seemed to be missing half a handle.

As if she could sense my annoyance, Amethyst's lifelike fox loped up to me and opened its mouth. "That's a beautiful pattern you've made there, Odette," it said in Amethyst's sing-song voice.

I grunted at the unexpected quirk. Even if I could see the fox's blurred edges, telling that it was still an illusion and not a solid object, no one else had gotten their creations to talk yet. As my attention strayed, the hazy form of my teacup evaporated into a shimmer of pastel pink magic that dissipated into the air. I let out a frustrated sigh. "Thanks. Unfortunately, I don't have your focus. The damn cup has yet to materialize how I envision it—even in non-solid form."

The fox shrugged. "It'll come. Let me know if you want help."

I nodded at the fox. "Thanks, Amethyst."

The fox did a cute little head bob and ran back to its creator, whose purple hair flew everywhere as she jumped up and down. Even though I was envious of Amethyst's progress in Conjuring, I had to grin at her glee.

She was one of the few students who seemed to believe me after Tabitha's death, and she had always been kind. The number of students who shared those traits were so few that I could count them on two hands, and I clung to those people.

"All right! Everyone, release your conjurings. Class is almost over, and I want to give homework," stout and graying Professor Umbra yelled over the din of students.

Her blue eyes twinkled as she gave out the assignment —an impossible team project that made me groan—right before the hooting of an owl rang through the academy. The first-years spilled from her classroom, making our way to Faeology.

"Can you believe that homework?" Eva's blue eyes were wide with disbelief. "Three new two-piece conjurings by tomorrow! No freaking wonder they call this year the Culling. We're gonna be up all night, with all the homework we have."

"Especially if you have to wait for mine to materialize," I said. Mastering my own magic was hard enough, but with this project, I had to meld it with Eva's. "I'll understand if you don't want to partner with me on this."

"What? No way am I leaving my bestie high and dry. Plus, you've gotten better. I'm sure it will be fine." Eva's tone brooked no rebuttals.

Even though my progress felt excruciatingly slow, she was right. Over the past month and a half, I had gotten a lot better at magic—but then again, so had everyone else. And as our collective skill level increased, the professors assigned our homework and projects accordingly. My worst fear was that my halting progress would trickle to nothing, while everyone else advanced.

"Thanks, girl." I gave Eva a grateful smile. If it wasn't for her and Hunter, I'd be alone in all this.

As if my thoughts had conjured him, Hunter appeared at Eva's side. "Hey, babes." He grinned at us, and I heard a girl sigh somewhere behind us. "I need to run up to the tower before Faeology. Save me a seat?"

"Sure," I replied, and he peeled off.

I was about to comment on how silly it was that others were still so smitten with him, when I noticed Eva watching Hunter dash away *very* intently.

In the short time I'd known him, it had become obvious that Hunter was a major flirt. Eva and I had both commented on the fact many times. But maybe Eva wasn't as immune to his charms as she let on.

I opened my mouth to ask, but she spoke over me.

"I gotta stop in the bathroom. Save me a seat too?"

I didn't even respond before she took off in the direction that Hunter had just gone.

A grin split my face, and I shook my head as I watched my bestie chase after Hunter.

Go get him, girl.

When I arrived at Faeology, only three seats remained, all in the back row, where one other person sat.

Alex Wardwell.

Mr. Hot Grouch caught me staring at the empty seats, and his blue eyes pierced through me, studying me for a heartbeat longer than normal. My stomach fluttered, and I dared to hope that he wouldn't snub me. My hope was quickly dashed when a second later, Alex pointedly looked away.

Inwardly groaning, I made my way toward the back of the class.

Would it be too weird if I took the chair farthest from him? Quickly, I concluded that not only would it be weird, it would be poor form. If there was one person Alex rebuffed more often than me, it was Hunter. Taking the most distant desk would only serve to force them closer together.

In an effort not to be a jerk to one of my few friends, I took the spot next to Alex.

The minutes ticked by, and my discomfort grew as he stared out the window. For some reason, despite how much he disliked me, I was drawn to him, wanted to know him. If someone else told me they felt this way about a guy, I'd want to slap them, but I just couldn't help myself.

Finally, the silence became unbearable. "Hi, Alex. That assignment from yesterday was killer, huh?"

Alex snorted and the pit in my gut deepened, even as my jaw began to clench tight.

Should I confront him? What does he have against me, anyway? I don't get it . . .

I still hadn't decided on how to proceed, when Hunter and Eva burst into the classroom. They spotted me and made their way to the back as the owl hooted, announcing the start of class.

I arched an eyebrow, taking in the disheveled state of Eva in the desk next to mine. "Dude. What's up with your hair?" I whispered, as Eva dug into her bag for her book.

Eva froze. "What do you mean?"

"It's all messed up." I pursed my lips to keep from laughing, but Eva glued her eyes to the floor and didn't notice.

"Must've gotten all windswept when I ran here." She began patting her hair down self-consciously.

Hunter, on the other side of her, chuckled.

Alex snorted again and, unable to help myself this time, I glared at him. Why did he always do that? If he didn't like me, or what I had to say, he didn't have to listen to my conversation. I opened my mouth to tell him that, just as the professor spoke.

"Good afternoon, class. Today we will be doing something rather unusual." Ms. Seeley, a unique witch with piercing purple eyes and long, blonde hair that broadcasted her mixed fae and witch heritage, stood at the front of the class. She was the only mixed magical on staff, and one of my favorite instructors.

"Does anyone remember the species of fae we discussed last time? The one that creates rings to make their way in and out of our realm to Faerie?" the professor asked.

A few hands shot up, and Ms. Seeley scanned the class. "Yes, Amethyst?"

"Faerie rings are traditionally made by the Pixie Court. But sometimes other courts use them too."

Ms. Seeley's violet eyes sparkled. "Very good, Amethyst. Now, does anyone remember how I described these rings? Specifically, how they would look should one have been closed by magic?"

This time, no hands shot up. I wracked my brain but came up empty on the specifics of what faerie rings looked like.

Amethyst raised her hand again.

"Amethyst?"

"Didn't you say they would look a bit like small crop circles, with the innermost circle being in the shape of an oval and then expanding from there?"

Ms. Seeley clapped her hands, and I couldn't help it, I released a frustrated sigh.

Alex whipped around and glared. The motion startled me, but I met his gaze, still miffed about his earlier exasperation. Then he *dared* to roll his eyes.

What the hell!

"I hope everyone heard what Amethyst said, because today we are going into the forest and looking for dormant faerie circles." Ms. Seeley began doing a headcount. When she finished, she smiled. "Wonderful. Our numbers are even. Everyone pair up with the person to their left, and we'll get a move on."

My stomach dropped, and I turned my head to the left to find Alex Wardwell's jaw clenched tightly.

"I'm sure we can find other partners," I snapped, unable to keep tension out of my tone.

"I was about to suggest the same." Diana appeared out of nowhere and sidled up next to Alex, batting her eyelashes. "I'll be your partner, Alex. We should probably work with people at *our* skill level, anyway. Efraim doesn't mind working with the Legacy." She gestured to the front of the room, where Efraim, a short and impressionable guy, stood waiting.

My lips parted at Diana's insult, and anger began bubbling inside me. But contrary to my instincts, I kept quiet. I'd *just* said we could switch partners, and here Diana was, offering a solution to what was sure to be an uncomfortable class, albeit condescendingly.

To my great surprise, however, Alex shook his head. "No. There's no need to make a fuss. We need to learn to work with those we don't see eye-to-eye with." He bolted out of the room.

Don't see eye-to-eye with? My eyebrows arched. We hadn't spoken to each other since the day he'd healed me after my fight with Tabitha, and only a handful of times before that. How would he know what we did or didn't agree on?

"Hey. You should partner with Hunter. I'll convince Alex to work with me," Eva offered.

"And let jerkface know he affected me? Oh hell no." I followed my partner. Perhaps if we worked together, I'd finally get some damn answers.

Ms. Seeley led us out toward the lake and stopped close to the spot where I'd heard Tabitha screams. I joined the rest of the class, keeping a good distance between Alex and me, and scanned the grass and trees with unease.

"Flashbacks making you nervous, Legacy?" Alex whispered.

"Excuse me? What's that supposed to—"

"As you all know, Spellcasters has been on these grounds for less than a century. Before that, it was a school for troubled human teenagers. During that time, these woods used to be rife with fae. Since Spellcasters hired me, I've deactivated a dozen rings. Your assignment today is to locate one of those rings."

"But what if we come across an active one? How do you tell the difference?" Mina asked.

"To determine the status of a faerie ring, all you must do is wave your hand over it, and say the word 'reveala'. It's a basic indicator charm that I placed on the circles in case I forgot where the previously discovered ones were located. If someone has discovered the ring already, it will glow a soft lilac hue. If it's an undiscovered ring, which would surprise me, the charm will do nothing. Active faerie rings do not glow unless a fae has recently passed through it."

I wondered how Ms. Seeley had come up with her own

charm, and if this was really as basic as she thought. After two-and-a-half months of school, we'd only covered a few incantations, most of them in Conjuring class. In our practical classes, we'd largely stuck with learning how to manipulate our innate, raw magics. It was magic that all witches were capable of—the basics. They considered charms more advanced, since they could intensify our natural powers, similar to how totems and familiars worked. Of course, many people already knew over a dozen spells because their parents had taught them before they arrived at Spellcasters.

I was not among those people, and hoped we'd learn more charms soon. Knowing a few more magical words might give me a boost during my first trial.

"Oh, and one more thing." Our professor smiled, and two sweet dimples appeared in her cheeks. "The teams that find a faerie circle will receive a reward green-lighted by the headmistress herself. Best of luck to you all." Ms. Seeley swept her arms wide, and we trudged into the forest.

CHAPTER FIFTEEN

Alex led the way into the woods. The evidence of Fall became more obvious and enchanting the deeper we trudged into the forest. Whereas the academy lawn was still pure green, thanks to concentrated magic floating in the air around the main building, inside the forest looked very different. Many of the leaves on the trees were now various shades of flaming reds, vibrant oranges, and golden yellows, which made my heart quicken. In L.A., we didn't have four distinct seasons, so experiencing a traditional East Coast autumn was amazing.

All of a sudden, Alex whirled around with a pointed stare, ripping me from taking in the pleasant scenery, and making my heart skip a beat.

Whoa, calm yourself, ovaries. You may be stupidly attracted to him, but he hates me, remember?

"Did you hear that?" Alex asked.

I turned away to enhance my concentration. After a moment of standing in silence, nothing obvious hit my ear.

"What was it?"

"I thought I heard . . . faint humming."

My eyebrows furrowed, and Alex rolled his eyes.

"Don't you remember what Ms. Seeley said about looking for faerie rings?"

My mind raced, but nothing I recalled seemed to fit this scenario. "I only remember her saying it would glow lilac with that charm."

He shook his head. "Not earlier *today*. When she first introduced the concept. All the discovered faerie circles around Spellcasters have been charmed closed. People have been searching for decades, and they've only found twenty. Twelve were discovered by Ms. Seeley because—well, she has a special connection. But I *swear* there was humming, and that's a sign of an *open* faerie circle." Alex spoke slowly, like he thought I wouldn't get it, but I brushed it off in light of the interesting information.

"But we're not very deep into the woods. Wouldn't they have found something this close to the academy a long time ago? Especially with Ms. Seeley's connection?"

Alex chewed his plump bottom lip. A vision of me reaching out and stroking his jaw to relieve his worries arose in my mind before I pushed the dream away.

Dammit, why do all the hot ones have to be so frustrating?

"You make a decent point, Legacy," he gritted out.

My hands landed on my hips. "I don't appreciate—"

A sound hit my ear, and my mouth snapped shut as I whirled about.

Alex rushed to my side. "You heard it, didn't you?"

I nodded. "Do you think it's one of our classmates screwing around? Or maybe Ms. Seeley is trying to throw some people off? Make the hunt harder?"

"I don't think so. Can't you sense the magic in it?" For the first time since I'd known him, Alex's tone didn't sound short or hold the slightest bit of disdain for me.

I closed my eyes and listened. It came in fits and spurts, but every time a low note reached my ears, I realized he was right. There was a power to the music, a resonance and energy my bones recognized, like when I used my magic—but alien.

"Yes. Holy hell, Alex! This could be amazing! What would the professors do if we found an active faerie circle?"

Alex almost looked like he wanted to smile, but instead he took a step toward the sound. "Let's find out."

We followed the hum deeper and deeper into the woods.

"Alex? Where does Spellcasters' property line end?"

"All the way to Wandstown and fifty miles on the other sides."

I cocked my head. If the property was so vast, could there really be fencing on all sides that connected? And if there was, how would they know if it had been breached? Why did Headmistress Wake think it so preposterous that someone had gotten onto Spellcasters grounds when I'd found Tabitha? Most of all, why would she question my parents' concerns about the perimeters not being fully secure? There had to be a weakness somewhere.

My mind drifted back to the howling that had pierced the air that night, and I gulped. We were hearing humming now, and I'd heard howling the night of Tabitha's death. What if it wasn't just one creature that had found their way onto Spellcasters property, but many?

"We're getting close," Alex said.

"Isn't it odd that we latched onto it and not Ms. Seeley?" I asked, shocked that I hadn't considered it before.

Alex tilted his head. "No," he said unconvincingly.

Yeah right. I rolled my eyes, recognizing the signs of a guy trying to be all strong and proud. My dad pulled that move all the time.

"Nice try, Al—oooh!" I leapt backward, my hands flailing, as a figure stepped out from behind a tree.

"It's just me!" Amethyst shrieked, ducking away from my frantic swatting.

I paused in my assault. "Amethyst? What are you doing?! You scared me!"

"The same thing as you guys, obviously." She looked around. "You heard the humming, didn't you?"

I nodded. "But where's your partner?"

Amethyst's chin wobbled, and only then did I realize how messy her hair looked.

"I don't know. I was leading the way, and when I turned around, Mina was just *gone*!"

My blood froze. Humans often thought of the fae as sweet, dainty little creatures. And while there were *some* like that, a lot of the fae were actually mischievous, or worse, violent and bloodthirsty.

"I just realized I lost her when I heard you guys talking. And I thought it would be best—"

"We should stick together," Alex said before Amethyst finished. "But we should still try to find the circle. What if the music mesmerized Mina, and she got shifted through?"

The idea sent a shiver up my spine. Fae could lure people into Faerie, or shift them through, with music, if they were able to match the individual's energy resonance. Those who were shifted through were often used as slaves in various Faerie courts, unless someone—usually a magical—bargained for the person's freedom. They succeeded with humans more often than witches. Still, it wasn't unheard of for a fae to latch onto a witch and pull them into the faerie realm.

Amethyst nodded. "I considered that. But I didn't want to find it by myself and risk being shifted through, too."

"Should we—" My mouth snapped shut as the humming vibrated through the air again, loud and from the right. "It's coming from right over there!" I pointed to a small clearing a short distance away.

Alex's eyebrows furrowed. "You heard it?"

I nodded, confused. "Yeah. Didn't you?"

Amethyst shook her head, and Alex's eyes narrowed. "No . . . how did you, if we didn't?"

"We don't have time. Grab hands," Amethyst instructed.

I tilted my head in question.

"Ms. Seeley hasn't talked about it yet, but the fae can't take numerous people through faerie circles at the same time. Just one. If we link up, we're safe."

Immediately, I grabbed Amethyst's hand with my right hand, but my left hesitated. Alex was standing on the other side of me, looking very conflicted about having to link up with me.

I bit my lip. *Is he going to walk around me and take Amethyst's hand? Oh my God, how mortifying would that be?*

A half dozen other embarrassing scenarios raced through my mind before the hum sounded again, ripping me back to the moment. My eyes landed on Alex, who had tensed. Slowly, his gaze lifted to meet mine, and even though the look of frustration had not vanished from his face, he extended his hand.

Amethyst shuffled in my periphery, and cognizant of how odd our trepidation must seem, I took Alex's hand quickly, gripping his palm tight with mine.

The next thing I knew, a shock of electricity zinged up my arm. Heat pooled in my pelvis, and every hair on my body stood on end. My head jerked up to see Alex's reaction.

All the annoyance of having to touch me had vanished. His eyes were wide, and his lips parted, then slowly, he looked up and met my gaze.

Warmth pulsed through us, and my breath hitched.

"Let's advance," Amethyst said, breaking our connection.

What the hell was that? My hormones? Had he felt it too? I gulped down my many questions, knowing that it wasn't the time.

Later, though. I would ask later.

The leaves crunching beneath my feet, the scurrying of a squirrel, and the breathing of my classmates all echoed in my ears as we walked, amplifying with the tension running through us. Still, my eyes never left the clearing.

We were only a few feet away when I spotted it.

"Look." I took the hand attached to Alex's and gestured to a point fifteen feet up, nearly hidden in a mess of branches on a robust tree.

An oval pattern glowed white on the tree's trunk.

"It's active," Alex whispered, and on my other side, Amethyst nodded, her eyes growing impossibly wide.

An active faerie ring. Holy shitballs!

We approached the tree one careful step at a time, our hands still clenched. The electrical hum that had shocked me when Alex and I first linked was still there, but less noticeable in the face of danger. On the other side of me, Amethyst's arm trembled violently. Even though I didn't feel strong, I realized that I had to be. Alex couldn't be the only one carrying our group.

And we had to find Mina.

With every step, twigs cracked beneath our feet, until

finally, we were standing at the base of the tree, looking up at the glowing swirl.

"I'm confused. I thought they were closer to the ground," I said, just to break the overwhelming silence.

"They are," Amethyst replied, her voice stuttering. "Which means whoever created this one, did so purposefully. It's high up so that most people wouldn't see it, especially not Ms. Seeley."

My breath hitched as her words sank in. She was right. Ms. Seeley was only five feet tall. She might not notice a circle that far above her head if she was looking closer to the ground.

"What do we do?" I asked.

"Nothing, witch," a sharp voice rang behind us, and we turned, breaking our chain in the process.

Twenty feet away, a fae stood, his black wings shining behind him, a dirty cap on his head, and a dagger pressed to Mina's throat. Tears rolled down my classmate's cheeks, and whimpers escaped her lips.

"It's okay, Mina," I said. "It's all gonna be okay."

The fae chuckled, and my attention shifted.

"*Is* it going to be *okay*, witchling? Or am I about to enter Faerie with four new slaves for my court? That would please my queen oh so much."

"You can't bring all of us through." Alex crossed his arms over his chest, and even though I was freaking terrified, my heart rate still kicked up at the sight of him being all assertive and hot.

"Unless," the fae allowed the "s" sound to trill out in a

hiss, "I'm not the only one here."

My eyes darted around. I didn't see anyone else, but fae could glamour themselves and hide. For all I knew, there could be dozens of others surrounding us.

Amethyst shook her head, and despite the chin wobble, she looked rather brave. "Impossible. Only one fae can come through faerie rings during the sun cycle. One per day. You're alone."

"Well, pooey. I see they're teaching the baby first-years more than usual," the fae scowled as he pressed the blade deeper into Mina's skin. "Fine. We'll do this the old way. If you want your classmate back, what will you give me?"

"What do you want?" Alex asked.

The fae made a show of considering what he might request, but as his eyes trailed up to the faerie circle above us, I knew what he would ask for.

"For your classmate's life, I demand your silence about my faerie ring. Should you break this promise, one of you will join me in Faerie as my personal slave at court." The creature arched a bushy eyebrow and extended his hand. "Do we have a deal?"

This was the worst possible scenario. We could get Mina back, but the threat was real that the fae would return later and simply take someone else. If we told, however, we *knew* he would take someone else, and it would be one of *us*.

Amethyst turned slightly to face us. "Guys, I—"

"No deal!" Alex leapt forward, and crimson magic burst from his hands.

It shot toward the fae and engulfed the creature's arm

before blooming into fire. A second branch of magic split from the main one and formed a tiny shield between the blade and Mina's throat. Alex moved fast, which was good, because as soon as the fae screamed, I saw him apply pressure to the blade and heard it *crack* on Alex's shield.

"Mina! Move!" I screamed.

But instead of fleeing to safety, Mina fell to the ground, coughing and sputtering and grabbing her arm which was smoking. The fae had incapacitated her.

Alex shot another beam of power at the fae before his attention shifted to Amethyst. "Can you conjure iron?"

Amethyst gaped, and I understood why. So far in Conjuring, we'd only conjured representations of items—illusions with little to no actual mass behind them. But an *illusion* of iron would not defeat this fae. Only the real thing.

"I can try," Amethyst said as her brown eyes filled with anxious tears.

"Do it," Alex growled, and then he turned his startling eyes on me. "Send up sparks."

I did as he said, sending up a shower of pink sparks and holding my breath until they reached just above the tree line. I hoped that Ms. Seeley was looking our way, and would see the signal of distress agreed upon by Spellcasters students and faculty.

When I turned my attention back to the ground, I saw that Alex was already in motion, tossing crimson magic at the fae every chance he got and muttering who-knew-what kind of spells under his breath. Amethyst's eyes were narrow, and her face scrunched up as she worked to conjure a solid weapon.

I'd never felt so helpless in all my life. But even if I was the weakest witch among us, I just knew there had to be *something* I could contribute.

What, I wasn't sure. But I figured I'd discover it in the moment, as I rushed forward to fight the fae.

CHAPTER SIXTEEN

"Did you alert Ms. Seeley?" Alex gasped as I joined him, and he threw up a shield to protect us both.

"Yeah," I grunted as the fae slammed a large tree branch into Alex's shield. "Do you have any tips on how to defeat this guy?"

I'd gotten better at magic, but fae and witch magics were different. Witch magic was a manipulation of energy, whereas the magic of the fae races was largely elemental. They had control over earth, water, wind, fire, and sometimes aether. The fae who could control all five elements were the most powerful.

"This one is a redcap." Alex repositioned his glasses, which had gone askew, as he shot off a spray of power that missed our opponent and singed the bark straight off a tree. "Warrior fae that dip their hat in their enemies' blood. Some make deadly potions out of them. I think that's what's causing Mina's skin to burn." Another spray of magic, another singed tree.

The fae cackled, and for the first time, I noticed that the hat on his head was indeed discolored at the tip.

As if he knew exactly what I stared at, the fae lifted his arm and pointed gleefully at the point of his cap. "Looks like I'll be adding witch blood to the mix soon!"

My lips flattened, and just to shut him up, I sent my power, a beam of pink, intending to burn him.

The fae cackled even more maniacally when I missed. "I always wanted a weak and pretty little slave."

I wanted to scream for him to get away, to leave us alone, to disappear back to his faerie hole and no one would get hurt, but an intense gale of air flew over me before I could even open my mouth. I fell to the ground with a yelp, and a second later, Alex grunted and landed beside me. A large rock flew out of nowhere to hit his head with a *crack* and Alex's eyes fluttered closed as blood began to pour from his temple.

I scrambled to my feet and stood over Alex, my breath catching in my throat. The fae had taken advantage of our moment of weakness and had crossed the clearing. He now held his long dagger against Amethyst's jugular. My gaze strayed to the iron weapon Amethyst had been conjuring until the fae took her hostage. It lay on the ground a fair distance from the pair, as if the fae had batted it away. The weapon was almost solid, although the blurred lines made it clear that it was not *quite* there. If I got my hands on it, would I be able to complete conjuring?

"You can try, weakling," the fae spat. "By the time you reach it, Faerie will have a new slave."

My stomach churned. He was right, the blade and the portal were in different directions. But I wasn't powerful enough to call items to me, especially not an item that someone else had conjured. I could either fight him with my magic, which I was positive was not strong enough to best him, or I could take a chance and use Amethyst's weapon.

There was only one option.

I lunged right, and the fae moved left. My hands were on the cold, almost-solid blade a second later. I pushed all the magic I had into it, and nearly fell over from shock when a burst of strong, fuchsia magic that I'd never seen before flew from my hands, and the iron solidified.

Hell yes!

I scrambled to head-off the fae and Amethyst, who was screaming and dragging her feet, trying to slow her captor from abducting her. My feet moved faster than they ever had before. If I just got close enough, the iron would end him. Amethyst would be safe.

"Odette! Stop!" A woman's voice shot through me.

But I couldn't just *stop*. Amethyst was mere feet from being shifted through, and I was her best chance.

Or so I'd thought.

Suddenly, a cloud of lilac whooshed by me, the intensity of it sending a shockwave of energy through my body and throwing my balance off. My scream rang through my ears as lilac magic swirled all around me, nearly blinding me with its brilliance as I fell.

~

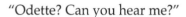

"Odette? Can you hear me?"

I groaned as my hand found my pounding temple, and my eyelids fluttered open to find Ms. Seeley leaning over me. Hunter and Eva knelt right behind her, their mouths gaping. Alex stood at our professor's side, and whereas the others looked concerned, his lips were flat, his expression calculating.

"What happened?" I asked, taking in the smoky woods, and Mina on the ground crying, and Amethyst lying nearby, cradling her arm.

"Thank goodness everyone's fine." Ms. Seeley leaned back on her heels. "I'm so sorry. When I assigned this challenge, I didn't expect an event like this to occur. I see now that I should do more thorough searches for faerie circles."

Faerie circles. My eyes snapped open, and I twisted my neck to take in the tree behind me. The faerie circle we'd spotted was glowing lilac. "Did it get away?"

Ms. Seeley nodded. "I tried to capture the redcap, but couldn't get a clear shot. So instead, I went a different route. It caused him to drop Amethyst, but also gave him time to escape." Her lips pressed together until they turned white. "I still need to close up the circle."

"But don't you think you'd be smart to send someone through and see if we can't find him? To question him?" I pressed on, needing answers. Deep in my gut, I knew that this had to do with the curse on our year; it was too big of a coincidence.

"Why would she do that? The longer we keep it open, the higher the chance that more get through," Alex snapped.

"But wouldn't it be worth the risk to understand what was going on?"

Ms. Seeley shook her head. "Alex is right. We can't take that chance with students on the grounds. In fact . . . " She clapped her hands together, and a cloud of lilac magic burst from them, then pulled out into a long thin cord, and slithered through the forest.

I watched in awe as she held one end of the cord, and not a minute later, a voice came out of it.

"Professor Seeley? What's the meaning of this magical intrusion into my chambers?"

"I apologize, Headmistress Wake, but we have spotted a fae on the grounds of Spellcasters. And not the peaceful kind that live among humans." Ms. Seeley's tone dropped. "It injured students. Please send infirmary witches to collect them. I'm remaining in the forest to double-check that the faerie circle is sealed, and to patrol the area . . . just in case."

The line fell silent for a moment. "Very good, Professor Seeley," Headmistress Wake croaked. "I'll send reinforcements right away."

The lilac wire evaporated, and Ms. Seeley let out a long sigh. "Someone will be here to escort you back to Spellcasters soon. For the moment, we're safe."

Even though I wanted to believe her, I knew that after today, that was impossible. I'd only been at the academy for four months, and already one student had died, and another had almost been shifted through to Faerie. If there was one place on Earth where I was unsafe, it was at Spell-casters.

CHAPTER SEVENTEEN

Since the fae fiasco, things had gotten a little better. Word had circulated that I'd tried to fight the fae, and as a result, fewer of my classmates ignored or sneered at me. My change in circumstances was fortunate. October was slipping through my fingers, and the Samhain Trial was approaching way too quickly. A few more friendly faces helped reduce my stress about the momentous event—especially seeing as one of my peers would be my partner.

Of course, not everyone changed their minds about me. Diana still sneered at me every chance she got, and although we'd worked together that night, Alex kept his distance.

I so did not understand that guy.

A small part of me had thought we'd bonded while saving Mina, but apparently, I was way off base. In fact, Alex seemed content to act like *nothing* of note had happened between us that day, whether it be saving classmates, or experiencing the electricity that had passed through us when we touched.

Thankfully, I didn't have time to dwell or distract myself with Alex's odd mannerisms. I was too busy studying, practicing, and hoping that my powers would strengthen in time for my trial.

Which was how I found myself awake in the common area at the ungodly hour of five in the morning on a Saturday, flipping through our Demonology text.

The Samhain Trial had to include an adversary of some type. Demons, fae, or malicious vampires seemed the most natural choice. Since we hadn't been taught a single class on vampires yet, I was hedging my bets between demons and fae.

Goosebumps crawled up my arm as I took in an illustration of a daeva. While I'd seen many images and conjurings of demons since school started, they still elicited a visceral reaction. They were just plain ugly, and to imagine them inside people, possessing them, always made me want to take a shower.

De Spina introduced us to daevas only days before. While their diminutive size and relatively human characteristics made them *slightly* more palatable than other types of demons I'd seen, these little guys were real assholes who thrived on chaos and destruction. They could produce noxious gas from their hands and mouth to force their victim to pass out before possessing them. And after that, things only got worse for the human, as the gases the daeva continually created caused the person to rot from the inside out.

After I finished reading the page on the daeva, I held my breath, knowing that evidence of how a daeva possession affected humans was coming next. I flipped the paper over and sure as hell, a photograph of a decomposing human corpse stared up at me.

My stomach heaved. "Ugh!"

"Some of our books should come with a trigger warning, huh?"

My head shot up to find Amethyst standing before me.

"Hey," I said with a smile. "You're up early."

Amethyst nodded to my books, and a chunk of her purple hair fell out of her topknot. "You're not the only one feeling the Samhain crunch."

My lips parted, and I leaned back. Amethyst was tops in Conjuring, and fairly strong in our other classes. Only Alex, Diana, and Hunter consistently beat her outside of Conjuring.

"Don't take this the wrong way, but that's kinda nice to hear."

Amethyst smiled and sat down in the gray armchair opposite mine. In her hand she held our Battle Magic book, which was as surprising as her admission. Since we'd arrived in July, we'd only cracked that text once.

Unlike the act of conjuring, which often required an incantation and hence, more studying, the discipline of battle magic ran on emotions. How well the caster manipulated and used their feelings generally determined their strength. Some theorized that this was an advantage, as emotions were always with us, whereas a forgotten incantation could lead to death in battle. Or course, if witches could use both, they had a major advantage.

I wasn't so sure I believed the emotions theory. I was at the bottom in our Battle Magic class, and it pissed me off, but my frustration didn't seem to help one bit.

"Have you been reading that?" I gestured to the text.

Amethyst nodded. "On and off. I know Thrax doesn't believe in teaching by the book, but there's some interesting stuff in there. Things about harnessing your ancestors' experiences and using them in battle."

"That sounds . . . advanced." Not that what Amethyst said surprised me. She wasn't the best in our class, but that was partly because her primary interests were in fields of magic that we wouldn't be taught until later years—like divination, tarot, and scrying. "And cool. If I could access my ancestors' power, that'd be major." I thought back to the night Eva had barreled into my room and told me all the amazing things Deliverance Dane had done.

"Yeah, ancestral magic is *super* advanced," Amethyst admitted. "Most of us need to learn to master our own magic first. We—"

The door to the common area burst open, cutting Amethyst off and making us jump.

Headmistress Wake bustled in. "Ladies! Good to see you up and studying." The headmistress' voice boomed, and I winced. After the quiet of the morning, her tone was a little much. "I'm about to announce an impromptu field trip."

The headmistress took in my robe and Amethyst's flannel pajamas. "What do you say you get changed, and meet me back down here in half an hour?"

An impromptu field trip. My heart thrummed with excitement even as my brain told me this was the worst timing. We hadn't been outside of Spellcasters since our parents left in July. Four months of consistent study and work had begun to make me batty, but still—our first challenge was less than a week away. If I ever needed to study, now was the time.

"But, Headmistress Wake, we need today to prepare. Samhain is so soon." Amethyst stood and voiced my exact concerns.

The headmistress, who had been making her way to the staircase, stiffened and turned to face us. Her laser-like gaze bore through Amethyst before she replied, "I'm well aware of Samhain's date on the calendar, Miss Rhines. However, a spy's schedule is dictated by their missions, *not* the calendar. Do you expect to never be interrupted when performing operations for your country?"

"I guess not," Amethyst's voice wavered.

"Good. Because that would be foolish. And if there's one thing my students cannot be, it's foolish." Headmistress Wake turned around and snapped her fingers. "Hurry along and get changed. I'll rouse the rest of the class."

Thirty minutes later, the entire first-year had congregated in Kyteler Hall, a smaller version of Agnes Sampson Hall that I had yet to see firsthand. After a quick assessment, I deduced that I hadn't missed much. The room was bare.

"If we're going on a field trip, why'd they bring us here?" I asked Hunter and Eva. "Won't we need a bus?"

A few feet away, Diana snorted. I rolled my eyes. If she wanted to answer my question, then great, but I wouldn't ask her for help. I'd long since learned that Diana Wake was a witch best ignored.

Hunter rubbed his eyes and yawned. "I think they're gonna warp us there."

"Of course that's what they're going to do!" Eva rubbed her hands together, chipper as she always was in the morning. "Why else would we be in such an empty room?"

My eyes widened. I'd never seen warping done or known anyone with the skill to create a warphole. Like necromancy, spirit walking and talking, or telepathy, warping was a rare and dangerous magical skill.

"Wow," I breathed. "That's awesome."

"What, Legacy? Your parents don't have any fancy friends in Beverly Hills who warp? And I thought it was all about who you know." Diana had shuffled closer without my noticing, and I released an irritated sigh.

"I've never met anyone who could do it."

She snorted. "And once again, it's revealed to me that money can't buy everything. Even if it can get a lackluster witch into an elite school."

I whipped around, ready to retaliate, but Diana had slipped through the crowd of peers at my back.

Suddenly, the doors to Kyteler Hall slammed open, and

Headmistress Wake strode into the room with Professor Tittelbaum behind her. My mouth fell open. The thin, severely academic looking professor of Magical Languages was a warper? Talk about unexpected.

"Initiates, gather 'round!" Headmistress Wake clapped once. Her appraising gaze ran over the crowd. "Who here has never warped before?"

My hand shot up, but no one else had raised their hand. I pressed my lips together firmly, trying to hide my embarrassment. How was it that out of a class of thirty people, I was the only one who had never warped before?

Someone way in the back of the group sniggered, and I knew without looking that it was Diana. But instead of getting all riled up, which was what she wanted, I kept my hand proudly in the air and stared the headmistress straight in the eye.

Unlike her daughter, Headmistress Wake didn't seem bothered. "Fewer than normal, but I suppose that's to be expected in a class this small. This way, Dane." The headmistress waved me forward, and I moved to join her. "Professor Tittelbaum is highly skilled at warping and it is something you will be expected to have undergone before the Samhain Trial. I always like to give students lacking in this experience first choice. So, Miss Dane, would you like to go first or last?"

"First," I blurted out. No way in hell did I want to wait around and watch everyone go while my nerves mounted.

"Excellent," Professor Tittelbaum stepped forward to stand in front of me. "Now, there's no need to worry.

Creating warpholes is just a manipulation of energy, like any other magic we work. It simply dives deeper into our being."

"Then why is it so rare?"

The professor studied me for a moment before answering. "Warping costs more than most can bear."

I pressed my lips together. "Does it hurt you to warp us?"

He shook his head. "Not anymore. Many new warpers have died from overextending themselves, but I was always careful. In my opinion, the pain of learning was worth it. Warpers are the only witches who can transcend two levels with their magic—space *and* time. Alas, I'm not a time traveler, but I can move you from one place to another."

My eyes widened at his mention of time travel.

Professor Tittelbaum's face softened. "Now, as it's your first time, I suggest that you take ten long breaths in and out. Double the length of your exhale compared to your inhale. This relaxes the nervous system, and reduces the chance that your magic will fire and interfere with my manipulation of energy."

I nodded, knowing what he meant. Breath-work was a relaxation technique my mother had learned in yoga. She'd taught it to me when I started theater. I closed my eyes and focused on inhaling and exhaling. My pounding heart slowed and the tingling sensation of my skin lessened within seconds. After a dozen long exhales, I opened my eyes to find Professor Tittelbaum smiling.

And a freaking swirling vortex of light right next to him.

I jerked back. *How did I not feel him create the warphole?*

"Shh," Professor Tittelbaum cooed. "We wouldn't want to spike that lovely, calm heart rate you've achieved, now would we?"

My eyebrows knitted together. The professor of Magical Languages was *much* more powerful than he let on if he could create warpholes and suss out how fast my heart was beating. *What kind of wizard is he?*

But I didn't get to ask, for the next second, the professor gestured toward the vortex. "Keep calm and walk through. People are waiting on the other side for your class to arrive."

This is so weird, I thought, but instead of asking all the questions swirling around in my head, I figured I might as well get it over with. People were waiting, and I was curious to learn who.

Taking one more long inhale and exhale, I squared my shoulders and walked toward the light.

CHAPTER EIGHTEEN

When I emerged on the other side of the warphole, the first thing I heard was the clicking of keyboards, high-pitched beeps, and phones ringing somewhere in the distance. I blinked, trying to force my eyes to refocus after being in an intense vortex of light. Slowly, the dots disappeared.

I stopped blinking and opened my eyes. I was in a typical, bland office filled with gray-blue cubicles and computers. The only intriguing aspect was that the room seemed to be mostly empty except for a group standing before me. My eyes swept the mass of people, and a smile spread across my face as I recognized one of them.

David Chena stepped forward, his lips quirking up in a smile. "Odette Dane! It's a pleasure to see you again. Welcome to Paranormal Intelligence Agency. Why am I not surprised that you're the first through the warphole? The old-timers tell me that your parents were brave. Must be an inherited trait."

I grinned. This was our field trip? A tour so we could network and check out our future place of employment? It was right up my alley.

"Honestly, I was the only one who'd never stepped through a warphole, and I just wanted to get it over with," I said, already feeling comfortable in David's presence.

"And modest." He waved me forward. "Step over here. Your classmates will come through soon, and not everyone pops out of a magical force field as gracefully as you managed. We cleared most of the office, just in case someone shot out like a bullet, magic blazing."

Warmth rose in my cheeks, and I did as he said just in time for Eva to appear. She stumbled her way out of the warphole, and David arched an eyebrow at me.

I shook my head. "Doesn't count. She's kinda clumsy all the time."

"I'll take your word for it." He chuckled and then turned to say something to a colleague as Eva approached me.

"I swear, I've done that before, but it never goes smoothly. Something about not knowing where I'm gonna step is so freaking awkward! How did you do?"

I shrugged. "Okay."

She nodded and looked around. "Interesting choice of field trip. My parents always told me about how they went to Wandstown and other historical witching sites around the world. This seems much more third-year stuff—more business oriented."

Now that she mentioned it, I realized that she was right. Why were we at paranormal headquarters? It's not like any of us were skilled enough in magic or diplomacy to get a job yet. Even Diana, who knew the most about theoretical diplomacy and governments, didn't ace our exams. And Alex, the all-around best at magic, wasn't even close to as good as the third-years who I'd seen practicing.

"Yeah, you're right." I turned to watch our peers as they popped out of the vortex faster and faster. A few minutes later, all of us were present, with Headmistress Wake and Professor Tittelbaum as chaperones.

"Welcome to the PIA," David said once we'd all gathered around. "We thought you may want to see what your future office looks like. Maybe even meet a couple of skilled colleagues who are in the office today and begin building connections. Who's up for a tour?"

Hands shot up, and David chuckled. "Follow me."

While I liked David, I didn't want to look like a suck-up again, so Eva and I took up the rear of the group. I was surprised that Hunter didn't join us. That was, until I spotted him near the front, chatting up David.

David led us through the halls of the PIA, pointing out areas of interest along the way. Occasionally, he'd introduce the group to a member of the staff. It seemed to me that they were all human, but I could have been wrong. Discerning power in another magical still wasn't easy for me. Eva could do it from yards away, but I needed to be close enough to touch them and suss out their energies.

We stopped in front of the cafeteria, and the aroma of fresh brewed coffee tantalized my nostrils. A chorus of sighs flew up from our group, and David quirked an amused eyebrow.

"I take it no one has had their coffee yet?"

Everyone shook their heads.

"Perfect! You can all try our state-of-the-art espresso machine. It just came in from Italy, and I have to say, it makes a stellar latte."

Headmistress Wake pursed her lips at the sudden detour, but said nothing as David led us into the cafeteria.

Five minutes later, I scooted away from the espresso machine, sipping a delightful americano. That was, until Mina bumped into me and almost made me spill the precious nectar.

"Oh, crap!" Mina's face scrunched up. "I'm so sorry, Odette! Did it get all over you?"

I shook my head as I wiped a couple splotches off my hand. "You're all good. It's a little crowded in here, though. I think I'll step out into the hallway while everyone else gets their drink."

Mina gave me another apologetic smile, but I didn't mind. No harm, no foul, and I did actually need some air. Crowded spaces were not my thing. I exited into the hallway, shut the door to the cafeteria, and immediately, my shoulders loosened a touch. Getting away from the crowd was akin to entering a church after being on a busy road. Kinda blissful.

I heaved a sigh of happiness, only to have my zen shattered a second later by a loud shriek piercing the quiet.

What the—?

I started, spilling coffee on my hand again, as two massive men burst into the hallway and rushed toward me with an old woman between them. She was kicking and screaming like her life depended on it, while the men fought her every step of the way. Clearly she was a handful, because neither man saw me standing there with my mouth hanging open.

Finally, the man wearing a newsboy cap noticed me. He swore and glanced at his partner.

"Students shouldn't be back here," the other man said.

I gestured to the coffee. "Sorry. What's going on?"

"It's classified." Newsboy-cap-guy shot his partner a warning look.

The woman's hand grabbed me. Hot coffee sloshed everywhere as our skin met, but that wasn't what made me gasp. My skin tingled at her touch. She was a witch.

"Don't trust anyone! *Anyone,* I tell you, girl!" the woman shrieked. "They'll—"

But I never got the chance to figure out what anyone would do, because at that very moment, Newsboy Cap clocked the witch over her head, and she passed out.

"Hey! What the heck? Why did you do that?"

"Like I said, classified," Newsboy Cap snapped, and the

men kept moving toward the door at the other end of the hall.

Oh hell, no. You will not just dismiss me.

I barged forward after them, only to have a pair of hands reach out and stop me. My head whirled about, and I saw David Chena, his brows furrowed with worry.

"Are you okay, Odette? Did she hurt you?"

I shook my head, perplexed by the question, and all the air left David's chest.

"I'm so sorry. First-years should never have to see something like that," he said, concern in his eyes.

"I'm fine," I insisted and pointed to the woman. "But what's wrong with her? Why are they forcing her to go somewhere? They're being super rough."

"She's ill. Very ill. And she's been threatening to unveil the government and witches' relationship."

My blood froze, and I shot a nervous glance at the door that the witch had disappeared through. Why would someone want to do that? Why would they endanger us all?

"Do you want to sit down?" David asked.

I shook my head and suddenly became aware that my classmates had trickled into the hallway. "No, let's just get on with the tour. I'm fine."

"All right. But if you feel even the slightest bit off, you'd tell me, right?"

My lips formed a thin smile. "I promise," I said. My word seemed to be enough for David, who released me and began wrangling my peers into a group again.

A few moments later, our informational tour started back up. Once again, I stayed to the back of the class, shooting glances at the door that the witch had disappeared through until it was no longer in sight.

CHAPTER NINETEEN

The scene from the PIA played in my head for the hundredth time during Demonology the following Monday. By now, Eva and Hunter had heard my story and agreed that it sounded odd, but not unprecedented. Eva's mother had known a spy who'd rebelled and disappeared from the agency overnight.

But the question of why a witch would rebel remained. Magicals had a good thing going for them. We could use our gifts for the greater good, and governments kept our secrets from the wider populaces—a demographic too varied to ensure the peaceful acceptance of magicals.

"Answer the question, Miss Dane." Professor de Spina rapped his pointer stick against my desk with a loud *thwack,* and I nearly fell out of my seat.

"Sorry, Professor de Spina. What was that?" I asked, trying to play it cool while a few people tittered, and de Spina glared at me.

"I'll accept your apology if you can tell me what this is." De Spina swung his arm to the right and twirled his fingers in a move I'd now seen many times. A ghost-like creature appeared and began to glow as if it were on fire. The demon's narrow eyes were glowing red, and his lips curved up grotesquely, like an exaggerated clown smile.

I shivered as I always did when our professor introduced new demons. The illustrations in our textbook were not as sharp as his conjurings.

"Ummm." I studied the monster, taking the most interest in the way his hands and feet glowed like flames. "A fire demon?"

"And whatever gave you that impression, Miss Dane?" Professor de Spina arched a brow.

I blushed as a few peers, Diana among them, chuckled. I supposed I deserved that. It had been obvious.

The professor twirled back around to face the whiteboard, and the marker began moving of its own accord across the board.

"This is an ifrit. A demon from the Middle East that, as Miss Dane has so intuitively stated, is a fire demon. They're like a genie in that they can grant wishes if tamed, which is difficult. Most importantly for our purposes, an ifrit is one of the top three demons skilled in possession. They're often sent from the underworld to inhabit diplomats, presidents, or religious leaders. Ifrits adore those in power, particularly those who do not know how to free themselves and gain access to wishes."

I leaned forward. Demons never gave humans anything.

They sucked the life out of you, and often, fed off the energies of those around you too. If a person remained alive long enough to undo the possession and collect wishes, that was very intriguing.

"Unfortunately, the human normally does not realize the possession in time, so they rarely get the chance to take advantage of their wishes. And what's worse, an ifrit can only live in the human's body for so long before the person suffers . . . irreparable damage."

De Spina twisted his hand again, and a new conjuring materialized of a woman in a pantsuit. I cringed, taking in her appearance. The suit was burned in places, and raw, oozing skin showed underneath. What looked like cigarette burns riddled her face, and her lips were so dry, they looked like dead worms.

"This is what a human looks like after a long ifrit possession. Often, people believe these humans consume illicit drugs. Really they're being burned from the inside out." The professor glanced at the illusion of a woman he'd created. "They don't last long past this stage. The internal organs can only take so much scorching."

I squirmed in my seat, imagining being burnt from the inside out for days. *What a terrible way to die.*

"Professor? How do you extract an ifrit? And if you do, are you able to take advantage of the wishes, or is that only if it possessed you?" Mina leaned forward in her chair and twirled a lock of her long black hair in her fingers as she spoke to de Spina. I held back a chuckle. She was always trying to flirt with the young and handsome professor.

"Excellent question." de Spina turned back toward the board. "Anyone can take advantage of an ifrit's wishes, as long as they bind the demon. As for how to do so, there is an incantation."

Pages turned and pens clicked as everyone awaited the incantation. Most magic was linked to the caster's will or emotions, but sometimes, witches needed a little extra *oomph*. Often when other supernaturals were involved. Before coming to Spellcasters, I hadn't known a single incantation, nor had I ever needed one.

But now a dozen were drilled into my mind. I had yet to get them to work for me, but I still memorized the magical words, and dreamed of the day when my magic would cooperate.

"The incantation to bind all demons—except for greater demons and the royals of Hell—is '*relligo*'." The word appeared on the board and Professor de Spina turned back to the class. "It works best when you're touching the item you'd like to bind the demon to, but merely laying your eyes upon the binding item would suffice in a pinch. I would recommend not to choose anything too large. Remember, portability is key if you're to attempt this feat. You'll want to keep the demon close to make sure it doesn't escape. And *never* bind an ifrit to your own body, unless you want to be possessed."

Efraim Eastey raised his hand, and de Spina nodded.

"So, once we've pulled the demon from the person with the incantation and they're bound, how many wishes do we get? Three?"

The professor's lips turned up in a crafty smile. "That depends on your skill level. If you can bind an ifrit, they will remain for as long as you can hold them captive. Witches have gotten dozens of wishes from the monsters. But if the ifrit is much stronger than the witch, they may only get a few. For comparison's sake, I'll divulge that I have pried ten wishes from a single ifrit."

Efraim frowned. I understood his sentiment. The explanation didn't sound promising. At least, not for witches at our level.

The professor waved his arm about, and the conjuring disappeared. "Time to switch to the other demon I wanted to cover today. One that is also a master at possession." The professor twirled his hand and then curled his fingers in so that his thumb and pointer finger touched. "However, unlike the ifrit, a fenrir is not as cunning or brilliant. Greater demons, the generals of Hell, often assign fenrir's more mundane possessions."

I tilted my head. *Mundane?*

A figure materialized in front of the class. It was a middle-aged man in a wife-beater and trucker hat who looked as though he drank a six-pack nightly.

"Greater demons often send fenrirs to possess normal people. They are skilled at appropriating a man's faculties and causing him to slap his wife, or provoking a child to set an outhouse on fire. Not that these things are small. In actuality, these acts of violence often fester into something sinister. Fenrirs tend to irrevocably change the people they possess."

"How?" Hunter asked, looking very troubled.

"Because fenrirs are shapeshifters, they can insert a little of themselves into the heart and mind of each person they possess. This ensures that the cycle of evil perpetuates for years to come. For the human to be clean again, a witch must perform a full exorcism. And we all know how likely humans are to seek a witch or an exorcism."

"Are we ever sent to perform those?" I asked, barely repressing my shudder.

De Spina shook his head. "Generally, spies would not deal with mundane possessions. But that doesn't mean that they aren't important, or that you shouldn't know about them. My motto is if you spot one, always help. Does everyone remember the exorcism incantation for lesser demons?"

"Evellam," we all chanted, and de Spina nodded, pleased.

I leaned back in my chair, wondering how many normal people were suffering possession.

The professor continued to blather on, but I allowed my mind to drift. Eva would take excellent notes. If I needed to, I could just look at those.

I was just running through a list of not-so-nice parents I'd known in school, wondering if maybe a fenrir had gotten to them, when something outside caught my eye. A van had pulled up to the school. From its doors poured a dozen people around my age.

My eyebrows knitted together. *Who are they?*

A piece of paper landed on my desk. I looked up to see

Hunter grinning at me. I wasn't much of a note writer, but Hunter couldn't go a full class without talking to someone. He was always passing notes to Eva and me.

I unfurled the paper and read it.

Students, third years, returning to watch the Samhain Trial.

My stomach dropped. A dozen students had come out of the van, but considering the trials were still days away, there would probably be more. Apparently, we would have quite an audience present for our first major test.

As much as I enjoyed performing, this was one show I was definitely dreading.

CHAPTER TWENTY

As the final days leading up to Samhain flew by, Spellcasters filled up with students who I'd never seen before. Third-years walked the halls like they owned the place, cocky grins on their faces. One attractive young man actually winked and blew me a kiss as we passed in the hall.

"Yeah, yeah. So you know something I don't. What else is new?" I muttered beneath my breath.

"Excuse me? Whatcha talking about, crazy?" Eva teased.

I blushed. "It's just all these upperclassmen acting superior around us. Why can't they tell us something about the trial instead of smirking all the time? It's annoying!"

Eva chuckled and shook her head. "It's also forbidden, remember?"

Ugh, why was Spellcasters so frustrating sometimes? I huffed out a breath. At least we would only have to suffer the third and second-years' smirks, winks, and condescending chuckles for one more day. After the trial, maybe they'd actually talk to us like we belonged.

If we passed.

The fact that some students didn't pass was terrifying. And even if you passed, your results might be lackluster. The Samhain and Beltane Trials ranked initiates from strongest to weakest in their year. Those who were the most capable had first dibs at choosing summer internships after our Culling and Grind-years. Not only that, but Spellcasters reserved subjects like necromancy and spirit walking or talking for only the top Crucible-year students.

I wasn't sure if I even wanted to take necromancy, or have anything to do with spirits, but I knew one thing: I sure as hell didn't want to come in last and have my choices limited.

"How do they choose the partners, anyway?" I asked, trying to ignore the pit in my stomach that kept on growing.

"No idea," Eva said. "I think it's random. Same with the Beltane Trial at the end of the year."

Well, damn. I hoped that I wasn't paired with someone like Diana or her little minion Phoebe. Or Alex, who, despite the strange connection we'd had—one I couldn't stop thinking about—hadn't acknowledged me since the day in the forest. Although I shouldn't have been upset about it, since we weren't friends before, it still hurt.

I thought there had been something between us during

the fae fiasco. Something real. But clearly, I'd just watched too many romcoms.

I shook my head, annoyed that I was obsessing over Alex again when he wanted nothing to do with me. So many things in my life mattered more than my little jerk-face crush. I couldn't let thoughts of Alex Wardwell destroy my confidence and ruin my chances in the Samhain Trial.

"What do you say we ditch the library and head back to our rooms and do facials?" Eva said out of the blue.

I arched an eyebrow. "Right before the trial? That's a terrible idea, isn't it?"

Eva's eyes twinkled. "Probably the worst. But we're both uptight and we've been studying nonstop for days already. Hell, my brain hurts! The first trial is tomorrow. I think we deserve a few hours to pamper ourselves. We can study again after the ceremonial dinner, if we need to."

I stopped in the dead center of the hallway. Masses of students flowed around me, but I barely noticed them. The flood of relief that I wouldn't have to go to the library and stare at a pile of books and feel frustrated and worried and overwhelmed was too strong.

"Yeah, good idea. And let's blast your beat-up, old stereo." I did a strange little jig, and Eva giggled.

"Only if you promise to teach me that dance." She threw her arm around my shoulder, and we pivoted to return to our rooms.

For the first time in days, the hard knot in my stomach loosened. And though I knew it wouldn't last long, I welcomed the brief relief all the same.

That night, the Agnes Sampson Hall felt very different from the night of orientation. The most pronounced of these differences was the unbridled enthusiasm that radiated from the upperclassmen as they took up spots next to friends at the long communal tables and began catching up.

Although I thought I might vomit at any second, I smiled at the scene of two more senior girls reuniting and hugging one another. Depending on our ranks and mission rotations, that might be Eva and me soon.

I shot a glance at my best friend, dressed in a long, sage green dress that set off her blazing hair, and my heart clenched.

"I think they've put the initiates in the front." Eva pointed to the long table near the stage where Headmistress Wake would announce the theme of this year's trial and our partners.

"The better to view our horror-stricken faces that way," I replied, not relishing the idea that we were being put on display. There was too much riding on this trial. Only when it was over would I breathe freely again—I hoped.

We made our way to the table, and I was pleased that Hunter had saved us a seat.

"Ladies." He stood at our approach. "You look amazing, as always." His green eyes stuck on Eva, and she turned pink beneath his smoldering gaze.

"Thanks," I replied with an easy grin, now used to Hunter's flirtatious ways, especially around my bestie.

Eva hadn't come out and told me yet, but I was positive they were hanging out and not just as friends. Hunter still flirted with any girl who breathed, but he treated Eva differently—with reverence.

As if to prove my point, Hunter pulled out a chair and gestured for Eva to take a seat. My heart melted, noting how he pushed it back in carefully and brushed her copper tresses to the side so it wouldn't catch between her back and the chair. And while Hunter pulled my chair out too, the gesture was different, less weighted and more friendly.

What I wouldn't give for a hot gentleman to treat me like a queen.

My eyes trailed down the table and settled on Diana, whose hand was on Alex's shoulder, as she laughed at something he'd just said. Jealousy roiled within me at the sight of them touching. Even though it was clear they both despised me, which meant they probably deserved each other, seeing them together annoyed me an irrational amount.

Why can't I just let him go? He isn't that hot, I lied to myself.

As if he could hear my thoughts, Alex turned and locked eyes with me. An involuntary shiver ran up my spine, and I glanced away. Dressing up for the night's occasion had been mandatory, and Alex did not disappoint. His black suit clung to his tapered waist and broad shoulders. He'd styled his hair in a way that was both a little careless and so devastatingly attractive that my fingers yearned to run through his black locks.

I fanned my cheeks and thanked the universe when Headmistress Wake took the stage and gave me a reason to focus on her.

"Welcome, students," she said, her tone warmer than usual. "It's a pleasure to see so many familiar faces. The staff at Spellcasters loves the first-year trials, for it's an occasion where we get to not only test our newest students, but see our more advanced students all in one place again."

Someone in the crowd let out a whoop, and shockingly, Headmistress Wake gave them an indulgent smile.

"Initiates, as you can see, unlike at the orientation feast, we have not served you yet. That is because for the Samhain Trial, I will pair you with another student in your class." A hush fell over the room. This was the moment many of us had been waiting for. "Once the pairings are announced, you will sit with your partner. Relationships are often best built over a warm meal. Take that advice to heart as tonight is your *only* chance to discuss strategy before the Samhain Trial begins."

I shifted in my seat. The entire room was scanning the table, sizing up our class. Since I was one of the weakest in our year, I figured I would be at an advantage pairing with pretty much anybody, and yet I still hoped to avoid Diana or Alex. No matter how skilled they were, the Samhain Trial would be hard enough without one of them as my partner.

"The pairing will take place after I announce the magical species you will oppose this year."

Murmurs rose from the tables where the second and third-years sat. Many of them were leaning in, pushing money to the center of their tables. A smirk lifted my lips. I wondered what else they were betting on tonight. Perhaps which team would return soonest or most unscathed?

"So, because we are all famished and curious, allow me to get on with business." Headmistress Wake's arms flung wide, and blue smoke unfurled from her hands, shimmering and undulating like a wave on the beach.

I gasped. Every witch and wizard's magic was a different color, or sometimes colorless, depending on their aim. Producing colorless magic took more energy, but for some instances, it was necessary. Like when you wanted to do magic in front of a human, or during a secret spy mission. However, when we were at full strength, proud and strong, our magic always looked the most beautiful.

Headmistress Wake's power was probably some of the most radiant I had ever seen. I sat there mesmerized as the blue waves began forming a body. Eyes and lips and hands carved their way out of smoke, and just when it was clear that whatever we would face had a humanoid form, the headmistress snapped, and the image crystallized into perfection.

I fell back in my chair, taking in the wrinkled gray skin, rows of razor-sharp teeth, and glowing red eyes that stared back at me.

Upperclassmen either cheered or groaned, depending on the bet they'd made.

"Wraiths," Eva muttered.

"As you can see here, I've conjured a replica of a wraith." Headmistress Wake echoed Eva's proclamation as her fingers moved up and down the body of the conjuring. "However, do not assume that the creature you will meet tomorrow will be a wraith. It can be *any* sort of lesser demon. After all, you will not always be spoon-fed every bit of information in the real world. You must learn to think fast, adapt your knowledge, and pivot easily. And once you discover who your partner is, I recommend that you discuss strategies for conquering the larger classes of the Hell-born."

I shuddered, completely positive that I couldn't beat *any* race of demon. Not unless I had my can of magical mace, which I doubted they'd allow me to use in the trials. So far, none of the techniques I'd used in our Battle Magic class had worked. I simply couldn't reach deep enough to trounce anyone. And incantations? Well, I knew them by heart, but that was about it.

"Now for the pairings." She began to list my classmates' names.

Eva's name was read off with Alex's, and a few names later, Headmistress Wake paired mine with Hunter's. I straightened my spine and smiled at my friend. This was lucky. Hunter was not only one of my best friends, he was near the top of our class. Only Diana and Alex consistently outperformed him.

"Now that you know your partner, please sit with them. You have until the end of the feast to discuss how to prepare for the big day. When you leave here tonight, you are to go straight to your rooms and spend the evening and next day alone, until we call you. Be warned, the professors will charm the doors to your rooms. Should anyone try to lift these enchantments, there will be severe repercussions."

I shook my head as everyone in my class got up and rearranged themselves. As Hunter already sat next to me, he just scooted over, and we gave each other a high-five.

"Lucky we're partners, huh?" Hunter grinned.

"Yeah, lucky us. We're gonna kill the Samhain Trial." I beamed back at him and hoped with all my heart that what I said was true.

CHAPTER TWENTY-ONE

I trudged down the hallway silently with the rest of my class. Hunter walked at my side, and though he'd been all bravado and pep while we brainstormed for the trials the day before, today, the dark circles beneath his eyes betrayed him.

Just like the bags under my eyes spoke of the hours I'd spent studying. I'd read my Demonology text for so long that I'd fallen asleep with my arm wrapped around the tome.

Unfortunately, there were *hundreds* of types of lesser demons, and mine was only a beginner's edition. Compared to the door-stopper books in the library—which I probably should have looked at more often—our texts were basic. So basic that it barely mentioned greater demons—largely incubi, succubi, and cambion. All it said was that greater demons were considered middle tier and smaller in number, but were vastly more powerful than lesser demons. They served as the officers of Hell under the six royal demons Lucifer, Ishtar, Xaphan, and Erinyes, also known as the three furies.

Not that Spellcasters would send us to fight a greater demon, anyway. The academy might be intense, but the Trial wasn't *that* crazy. Very few witches tangled with greater demons and lived to tell the tale.

I twitched at the mere thought of coming across one. The jerky motion caught Hunter's attention.

"How ya doing, Dane?" He mumbled his first words to me since we'd met at our dorm's entrance.

"Okay." I smoothed the wrinkles on my black T-shirt, a fidget that whispered of the truth. "Tired. I studied for hours after dinner. I wish they'd allowed us to research and practice more together—or even talk."

Hunter nodded as our group began to descend the stairs that led to the entrance of the academy. "Me too, but you know Spellcasters, they're sticklers for tradition."

I'd never believed those words more. A staff member had delivered breakfast and lunch to each initiate earlier that day, negating any reason we might have to leave our rooms. We'd had access only to the bathrooms—one student at a time—so no one could confer with someone else about the trial.

"So," I said, realizing we'd fallen into silence. "Did you learn anything new that you want to share?" Even as I asked, I hoped he'd say no. What good would new fighting tactics or incantations be if I couldn't practice them? Once we stepped foot in Merlin Amphitheater, the rules of the Samhain Trial forbade magic until our challenge began.

He sighed. "Nothing new. Just what we already learned in Demonology. Which, despite the fact that my brain always felt like mush after that class, doesn't seem like enough now."

I let out a huff of air as we stepped outside and the cold whipped across my face. Wasn't that the truth?

The uproar that assaulted my ears upon entering Merlin Amphitheater shook me to my core.

"Holy shit," I whispered, taking in all the people. "I didn't realize we would have such a massive audience. Or that the amphitheater was so huge."

Merlin Amphitheater was reserved for special events, such as the Samhain Trial, the Yule Ball, the Beltane Trial, and Convocation—the graduation ceremony that occurred after our Crucible-year. Unless you were partaking in those events, the amphitheater was off limits.

"My older brother has been through the trials," Hunter said, his mouth open wide as he took in the room. "He couldn't tell me anything specific. The enchantments that they put on students who have been through them to keep their mouths shut are intense. But he did tell me that an audience would be present." He gestured to the stands opposite where we entered. "The middle sections are for the second and third-years. It's a rite of passage that they get to watch us do what they recently accomplished."

He then pointed to the ends of the oblong arena.

My eyebrows narrowed together. I didn't recognize a single person over there.

"Those are humans."

"No freaking way!" As a general rule, humans did not know about witches and warlocks.

"They work for the PIA," Hunter added. "It's practically the entire office."

It would have to be. Each end held at least one hundred people. With that many humans knowing of our existence, it was a wonder that witches could keep themselves hidden. Not to mention the fae, shifters, and vampires at other academies who did similar types of work for the humans.

"My brother says that when a human signs onto the agency, they take a binding oath." Hunter's voice was low. "They know about us, but outside of work, they can't tell anybody. And when they retire," he arched his eyebrows, "well, one of our memory witches has quite a job of rearranging a life's work."

I shuddered. The prospect of losing a lifetime of memories was terrifying. But I had to admit, those rules ensured my safety. The fewer people who knew about magicals, the less chance there was that human hate groups would target us. We already had enough fighting between various magicals; we didn't need to add humans to the mix.

My eyes swooped to the final side of the arena, and I saw that adults lined that part of the stadium. "I recognize our professors, but who are the rest of those people?" I asked.

"Spies—probably spymasters from around the world, too. They like to take stock of those coming up the ranks."

My eyes bulged. Spymasters were top-level spies and rare. That spymasters were here, to watch *our* Trial, drove home the importance of this task.

Sucking in a breath, my gaze swept the amphitheater, taking in everything from the star-spangled ceiling, to the crushed crimson of the seats, and the scent of brimstone—an aroma that served as a universal warning in the witching world that dangerous magic was afoot.

I closed my eyes and my mantras ran through my mind.

You will be amazing.

Everything will work out.

You will be amazing.

Everything will work out.

"First-years, this way!" Headmistress Wake waved us toward the dais in the center of the room. We got closer, and she gestured to the chairs, designated for our class.

"When it is your turn, I will call you up. Two groups will go at a time, as that is the maximum number of warpholes any magical feels comfortable being around at once. Because of the small class size this year, I expect this Trial will not last as long as normal."

"Thank God," Hunter whispered.

I had to agree. They kept much about the Trial secret, but that some had lasted for days was common knowledge.

"You will be under the constant watch of no less than two spymasters and three academy professors. Should the challenge become too much at any moment and you wish to withdraw, you need only to touch this bracelet," she held up a handful of what appeared to be plain gold chains, "and speak the universal surrender incantation that you learned in Battle Magic. Help will only be given if you *call* for it—expect no one to rush in and save you otherwise. That is not how things happen in the real world, and it is against Samhain Trial rules. Does everyone recall the spell?"

"*Cessio,*" we all chanted.

"Excellent." Headmistress Wake jerked her head in a tight nod. "Withdrawing your candidacy via surrender is grounds for academic probation. If you surrender and also fail the Imbolc challenge, you will be expelled from Spell-casters."

My heartbeat kicked up. Failure would be devastating.

"Though you may not have studied the race of demon you are about to encounter, each case has been monitored and deemed appropriate for your level. The warphole will only reopen once you defeat your adversary or surrender. Do not lose the bracelets. They are not only your lifeline if you cannot save yourself, but they allow the warpers to follow you through your trial, and for those present to view your performance. We have given you all the tools for success, now let's see what you do with them."

The headmistress clapped her hands together, and two warpholes popped into existence and expanded until they were about the size of small cars.

"Let's begin, shall we?" Headmistress Wake cast a circle around all the initiates, binding us to our seats. "This year's

Samhain Trials have officially begun. I call Diana Wake, Efraim Eastey, Amethyst Rhines, and Mina Köhler first."

Five hours later, I was still sitting in the same chair. My legs had fallen asleep at least a dozen times, and my butt had long since gone numb. As I watched my classmates stride through the warpholes to face their trials, the dread I'd felt since that morning only deepened. To make matters worse, while we could see everyone enter the vortex, and even hear their voices from time to time, what happened on the other side was a mystery. This limitation was placed only on the initiates, as made obvious by the occasional gasps or cheers that rose from the crowd.

It did not surprise me that Diana Wake had entered her trial bravely and emerged first. Sure, her head was bloodied, and I'd never seen her eyes so wild, but she composed herself quickly. Her partner, Efraim, on the other hand, did not instill as much confidence. Blood covered him from head to toe, and infirmary witches rushed him out right away.

A few others stumbled out of the warpholes, terror in their eyes. And yet, no one had needed to use the surrender incantation, which was comforting.

Finally, only two teams remained.

"Odette Dane, Hunter Wardwell, Evanora Proctor, and Alexander Wardwell, to the dais, please," Headmistress Wake called.

"Woooo! Go Alex!" Diana cheered, her gaze locking with mine as she smirked.

I tried to ignore the roar of possession that cut through my intense nerves, and rolled my eyes so obviously that she'd have to be blind not to notice. She was such an Alex groupie, it was ridiculous.

"Ready, partner?" Hunter asked, ripping me back to the moment.

I nodded, and we stood together, clasping hands and squeezing before letting go.

You'll be great.

You'll be great.

You'll be great.

I repeated my mantras over and over as I approached the headmistress, spymasters, and professors who would assess our performance.

"We got this," Hunter said, as if trying to convince himself.

I gulped, shot Eva a nod of encouragement, and took the gold bracelet Headmistress Wake handed me.

"Yep. We've got this." I turned toward the warphole.

Heat caressed my skin as we stepped through the vortex. I shivered, delighting in the warmth after the cold walk across the academy grounds. Then, an even more familiar sensation hit my nostrils.

Salt. Seawater. The sound of the ocean coming through an open window.

My eyes took in the room that we'd landed in. I realized

that not only did I recognize the smell and texture of the air, I knew where we were.

"Senator Smith's mansion," I whispered.

"What was that?" Hunter asked, his eyebrows furrowed.

"We're in San Fransisco. My parents are friends with a state senator. I've come to his San Fran house a few times for galas and charity functions. This is the bathroom near the kitchen." I pointed to a one-of-a-kind black marble statue of a woman holding three cats and a parakeet perched on her head. "I know that statue. Senator Smith told his wife she could have it, but it couldn't be in the main living areas because . . . well, it's weird."

Hunter nodded. "This definitely looks like a wealthy person's bathroom," he gestured to the gold gilding along the ceiling and the top-of-the-line marble vanity. One might even call the toilet classy with its gleaming gold lid and handle.

"So, the next question is why are we here?" Hunter asked.

I shook my head. Senator Smith and his wife, Amelia, were kind people. They donated to many charities, and were always willing to lend a helping hand.

"Maybe they're hosting a function tonight, and someone dangerous is attending," I guessed. "I'll try to sneak down the hall and see what's up. Then we can conjure appropriate clothes."

"I'll wait here."

I slipped out the door and had made it halfway down

the hall when a woman I recognized rushed by at the end. She was a well-known socialite, clad in a blue, silk gown and dripping with diamonds. There was classical music trickling in from what I recalled was the ballroom area.

The senator and his wife were definitely throwing some sort of fancy social function.

A party with a demon in attendance.

I pressed my lips together. To have to deal with a possession at a high-profile event was tricky. It was something we'd have to do all the time when we became real spies, which made it an ideal challenge, but I wished I didn't have a personal connection.

But Spellcasters hadn't given me a choice.

I scurried back to the bathroom, and after giving Hunter the scoop, we began conjuring clothing appropriate for the scenario.

Five minutes later, I wore a striking, red, silk number that left one shoulder bare, and had a slit up to my thigh. The dress ensured I would garner attention, which was part of the plan. Since Hunter was more skilled in every type of magic, we'd decided that I would distract and charm others, while he took care of the actual possession.

"Damn, Dane," Hunter wolf-whistled. "If I didn't already have my eye on someone else, I would be all over you."

"Thanks." I tried not to roll my eyes.

Hunter and Eva still thought no one suspected their relationship. I wasn't sure why they hadn't told me yet, but seeing as I was weird about relationships too, I didn't pry.

They would tell me they were gonna get married and have beautiful, bright-eyed babies when the time was right, and I would be happy for them.

For now, I had bigger concerns.

I held my arm out to Hunter. "Let's find a demon, shall we?"

CHAPTER TWENTY-TWO

I scanned the packed ballroom, searching for familiar faces. Would Mom and Dad be here tonight? Our family wasn't a regular fixture at the Smiths' parties, but we weren't complete strangers either.

While I missed my parents and yearned to see them, I also hoped they were still in L.A.—I didn't want anyone claiming that I'd ridden their coattails through this challenge.

"Should we split up?" Hunter asked.

"Let's stick together until we get the lay of the land. People don't go it alone at these functions unless they arrive single. They cling to their dates."

Hunter arched an eyebrow. "I would've thought the opposite, seeing as these people are the rich and famous, but I'll take your word for it."

"The rich and famous are just as insecure as everyone else. A lot of them are just better at hiding it."

We wound through tables filled with guests drinking champagne and talking animatedly to seem like they were having the time of their lives. I cringed. This was too familiar. While parts of Hollywood had attracted me—producing movies, storytelling, and working with creative individuals—I'd gladly left all the fakery behind.

"Dude, that woman laughed so loud she burst my eardrum." Hunter wiggled his finger in his ear.

"I'm betting she's a new actress. She's talking to an up-and-coming L.A. film producer," I answered while scanning the room for our target.

What kind of demon were we looking for? A wraith? A fenrir? An ifrit? Not a daeva. Their smell would be too obvious, and this crowd would take offense.

"Odette Dane!" A high-pitched, almost shrill voice came from behind me, and I turned to find Amelia Smith, the senator's wife approaching.

My eyebrows knitted together. She looked different from the last time that I saw her. *How long ago was that?* I thought it had only been a year, but Amelia's face reflected almost a decade of aging. She was still a beautiful woman, but the bags beneath her eyes and the deep wrinkles on the sides of her lips were undeniable.

My spine stiffened. Was Amelia the person they had sent us for? Could a demon be inside her, destroying her body from the inside out until she actually rotted?

"Hello, Mrs. Smith. It's a pleasure to see you again." We shook hands, and I allowed my power to rise to the surface of my fingertips and do an initial probe for any sensation of magical penetration. There was none that I could discern.

"Yes, it is a pleasure . . . and a surprise. Your parents declined the invitation to come tonight, but made no mention that you would take their place." Immediately, Amelia's cheeks pinked as she heard her own tone of voice. "Not that I mind. I'm sorry if I sound a little off-kilter. I've been so incredibly tired lately, and Stephen decided to have this gala just two weeks ago, which didn't help at all." Her blue eyes traveled across the room.

I followed her gaze and caught sight of the senator, looking as young and jovial as ever, shaking hands and making connections.

"I'm Hunter Wardwell." Hunter extended his hand.

Amelia let out a startled gasp. "Oh my goodness! I am so sorry! I didn't mean to ignore you. Like I said, I've been so tired, I don't know what's come over me."

"Why don't you rest over there?" I pointed to a bench at the edge of the room near the water station. "I can do the rounds and make sure people are entertained for a bit. If you need anything, just wave."

The excuse was as good as any to do a bit of snooping. This way I could play at host and get a better read on the people in the room.

"Oh . . . thank you, dear. That would actually be a great help. I wouldn't mind a sit-down, and I trust you to do a good job. Your mother is an excellent hostess, and you know how tedious entertaining can be."

I nodded. "I insist. Hunter, see to it she gets a bit of food, too, will you?" I locked eyes with him, and his eyebrows furrowed. *"Change of plans,"* I mouthed the minute Amelia turned her back.

Hunter's eyes widened, but he nodded, fine to go with the flow, and escorted Amelia to the edge of the room.

My toes tapped beneath the folds of my red, silk dress. Thirty minutes had already passed, and I'd found nothing. I was trying to figure out how to best exit yet another mind-numbing conversation about Hollywood politics, when *finally* I felt something worth paying attention to.

Magic caressing my back.

I stiffened, determined to pinpoint which direction it had come from.

"Uh oh, Odette are you okay?" the starlet who had been fawning over me placed her hand on my shoulder in mock concern.

I'd met her many times before, and she always acted as if we are best friends. Which we obviously weren't, as she was going on thirty and I was only eighteen, but she had ulterior motives. Being the lead in one of my parents' films would make befriending an eighteen-year-old seem worth it.

"I'm fine," I lied.

"Are you sure? You look a little green." The starlet's doe-like eyes ran over my face. "Did you overdo it on the champagne?"

I glanced down at my glass of sparkling water served in a champagne flute. "No, this is actually—"

"Because I know sometimes that stuff can turn my stomach," the starlet added.

A few women around me nodded, and belatedly, I spotted my chance for a smooth exit.

I placed my hand on my stomach. "Actually, you may be right. I think I should go to the restroom, just in case." I extradited myself and plowed through the crowds.

With every step I took, I searched. Someone had been trying to perform magic on me, and I had to find them.

Unfortunately, everywhere I looked, the attendees appeared normal, if eccentric—which was basically normal for this kind of crowd. I'd done one slow lap around the entire room when I spotted Hunter flapping his arms to get my attention.

I pursed my lips. Two things were odd about this scenario; the first was that Hunter was still sitting beside Amelia. It would've been natural for him to remain with her for a short period, and then part to find our target. The second was how ludicrously he was trying to get my attention.

Why doesn't he just come over and talk to me?

I made my way through the crowd, and as soon as I approached Hunter, he whispered something under his breath. A faint green shimmer floated from his hands and caressed Amelia's face. Her eyes glazed over, and I stiffened.

"Why are you using magic on her?" I looked around. "That was risky!"

Hunter snorted. "You've got to be kidding, right? These people are so into themselves that no one's even looked our way since we sat down. Well, almost no one." He patted the spot next to him.

I arched an eyebrow.

"We need to talk," Hunter said, and I obliged. As soon as I sat, my partner leaned close and pointed to the far side of the room. "It's him."

I followed his finger and shook my head. His target was unmistakable.

"The senator?" I asked incredulously. "Are you—?"

My mouth snapped shut, for at that very moment, the senator turned, and his eyes flashed red for a millisecond. It was such a short time that a human unfamiliar with magicals, would have thought their imagination was running amok.

A demon probably wouldn't even cross their mind.

I sucked in a breath. Hunter was right. I'd steered clear of the senator so as not to get pulled into one of his long-winded stories, and of course that was the one person they had sent us to find. What a dumb mistake. Especially after seeing the state of Amelia.

"What are we going to do?"

Hunter didn't answer, and silence hung between us for a full minute before I loosed a frustrated sigh.

"Well, one thing is for sure. We have to lure him away to exorcise the demon."

Hunter took a massive inhale. "We could use her."

"'Her' who?" I asked, checking out the room for someone who would be an obvious choice.

"Amelia."

I bit my bottom lip. Senator Smith's wife. If anyone could lure him away from the crowd, it would be her. But still . . . after realizing that the demon was the source of her pain, it felt very wrong to involve her.

"I don't like it, either," Hunter admitted. "When we got over here, she didn't want me to leave her. I think she felt like he might come over and force her to do something, or—"

"Feed on her energy," I muttered. "I bet that's why she looks so terrible. Last time I saw her, she looked much younger and very vibrant."

My eyes ran over the once-statuesque blonde with the reputation of lighting up rooms. The fact that others weren't even approaching her to socialize said a lot. Either they were those rare humans who were sensitive to demonic energies, or they'd already dismissed Amelia as washed up.

I heaved a heavy breath. "You're right. Amelia's our best chance. We can have her say there's a problem with their son. The senator wouldn't dare brush that off in public. Not even a demon would be so stupid as to make the human they were possessing look bad like that. Lift her enchantment. We need to have a talk."

Hunter did so, and Amelia came to, blinking hard. She looked at me, then Hunter, then back to me. "Odette? I feel weird. And you're looking at me funny. Is something the matter?"

"Let me explain," I said, and figuring there was no reason to delay, dove right in.

Shockingly, Amelia was not at all astonished to learn that demons existed, or that one had possessed her husband. Her reaction hinted at the horrors she'd probably been hiding.

"You'll be waiting in the nursery, right?" Amelia checked for the third time. She didn't want to be alone with her husband for even a second.

"I promise. We'll rush up there as soon as you leave," I assured her.

Amelia gave a jerky nod and took a deep inhale. Immediately, the shaking of her shoulders quelled a tad. I wondered how many times she'd had to forcibly calm her nerves to keep up appearances.

I placed a hand on her arm. "After tonight, you won't have to live in fear. Everything will be back to normal."

"Back to normal," Amelia whispered hopefully.

"Mr. Smith will once again be the amazing man you married," I added. "I promise."

A small sob escaped her, but she cut the emotion off. "Okay. I'm ready."

As soon as the senator's wife disappeared through the crowds, I grabbed Hunter's hand and led him out of the ballroom to the nursery. I knew where it was. On one of the nanny's nights off, my parents had recruited me to babysit the Smiths' son while the four adults indulged in too much wine. I'd been so annoyed that night, but not anymore. Their desire to party then had given me the insider knowledge I needed to pass my trial now.

Or so I hoped.

We climbed the stairs two at a time and dashed into the nursery a few minutes later.

"This is a nursery?!" Hunter exclaimed, spinning on the spot. "It's as big as a freaking tennis court! How much room does one kid need to play? And why does he need toys the size of small cars?"

"Who cares? Hurry up, we have to hide." I pointed to the window with thick, navy curtains. "Get behind those. When they come in, wait until you hear Amelia say the code word."

Hunter nodded, and I gestured for him to go first. If his body was invisible behind the heavy curtains, I would have no problem hiding. Once he was situated, only the gleaming tips of his shoes stuck out. He had massive feet, so that was no surprise. After a few seconds of analyzing just how visible his black shoes were in the dark, I decided it was fine. We wouldn't be hiding behind the curtain for long anyhow.

I took my spot.

While we waited, I wondered what the audience in Merlin Amphitheater was making of our performance. So far, there hadn't been as much spectacle as I'd heard from other trials, but that was okay, right? I couldn't imagine all real-life spy missions being epic battles. We practiced stealth and charm for a reason.

The door to the nursery *snicked* open, halting all my doubts and sending ice through my veins. It was time.

"He's just in here, honey," Amelia said, her tone cheery.

"Shouldn't he have gone to bed hours ago? What kind of nanny are you hiring for our son?" The senator's voice was clipped, almost a growl.

"He woke up and wanted to join the party, but Raven persuaded him to play with his toys. It was a smart move. You know how distracting Ethan can be. You'd get no work done if he appeared downstairs."

Senator Smith grunted. "Well, where is he? Ethan? Are you hiding from Daddy?" A few more steps resonated through the room and then stopped. "Dammit, I have work to do! Where is he, Amelia?"

Whatever demon was inside the senator, it had a mega short fuse.

Amelia cleared her throat. "He must be playing hide and seek again. Ethan, honey where are you?"

Her heels clacked on the wood floor as she pretended to walk around. I hoped she was making her way back to the door like we discussed.

Thirty excruciating seconds later, the tapping of heels on the floor ceased, and Mrs. Smith took a shaky breath. "Or maybe he's playing pineapple pin drop?"

My heart lunged in my throat. There it was. The nonsense code word Hunter had come up with.

"Pineapple pin drop? What in the hell is that—"

The door slammed shut.

"Amelia!" Footsteps sounded, moving away from us. "What's going on?"

We stepped out from behind the curtain just in time to see the senator reach for the doorknob. A burst of Hunter's green magic flew past the senator, freezing him in his tracks and locking us in with the demon.

"Hello, Senator Smith," I said.

The senator turned, and a look of recognition swept over his face. Whatever demon possessed him had been there long enough to read some old memories.

"Odette Dane? Why are you here?"

"I'll tell you why, but only after the demon inside you comes out to play."

Senator Smith's spine straightened, and a bone-chilling smile that I'd never seen on his face stretched impossibly far over his chiseled cheekbones. "You want me to come out and play, little witchling?" he growled.

I took a nervous step back, and Senator Smith began to laugh, a low, rumbling, non-human sound.

"Oh . . . did I scare you?" The senator stuck his bottom lip out. "Pretty little things like yourself should be careful what you ask for."

"Well, maybe you should be careful who you possess," I shot back. "You were careless, if we're the ones here to stop you."

"Careless? Or brilliant?" The senator cocked his head, but before I could puzzle out what he meant, he charged.

CHAPTER TWENTY-THREE

"*Evellam*!" Hunter thrust his hands out, and his magic surged, slamming into the demon-possessed senator.

Under the tide of magic, Mr. Smith began convulsing and whimpering. I winced, but kept alert. When the demon emerged from its victim, I wanted to be ready.

"*Evellam*!" Hunter yelled again. This time when his green power hit the senator, the man's jaw cracked open wide, and the demon flew toward the door.

Spotting my opening, I shot a burst of pink magic across the room and swept the unconscious senator behind us, depositing him against the wall. If the demon wanted to possess Mr. Smith again, he'd have to go through Hunter and me first.

"Damnable witches!" The demon's shriek lifted all the hairs on my body.

I whipped around to face the vile creature, and recoiled. *These things are even more hideous in person.*

The wraith's skin was dark gray, the color of a rotting corpse, and slimy. His three rows of teeth glinted, sharp and jagged. His hand moved, and my eyes locked on his claws —half the length of my fingers, and dripping with slime. To top it all off, the wraith's eyes shone an eerie garnet red.

Hunter moved, and I followed. We advanced just as we'd planned, Hunter at the forefront, green power flying from his palms. I flanked him, my magic primed to shield us from any demonic energies the wraith might spew.

Professor de Spina's lessons ran through my head as we prowled forward. Wraiths were cunning. They had magic, but weren't the most brutal fighters—just the smartest. We needed to expect sneaky attacks.

The thought had barely registered when the wraith leapt into the shadows of the massive nursery.

Right . . . And wraiths are difficult to see in the dark.

My eyes scanned the room, and I shook my head. Ethan Smith had way too many damn toys, most of them oversized. Hiding spots *abounded* in the vast, dark nursery.

"Turn on the light," Hunter whispered.

"And separate?! But—"

"We need it, and I should stay central," he cut me off.

I huffed an annoyed breath, but didn't argue. Hunter was right.

"Okay, be ready." I took one step, and then two, my gaze never leaving Hunter.

"Go," he insisted. "I'll be fine."

Though my intuition screamed not to, I listened to Hunter. He wasn't the third best wizard in our year for nothing. And the sooner I got the switch flipped, the quicker we could do away with the demon and get the hell out of here. I was across the room seconds later, my hand reaching out, touching the switch and then flipping it.

"Argh!" I wrenched my eyes shut as light flooded the room.

Hunter grunted. Neither of us had been considering that, which was pretty freaking dumb. We may be fighting a demon, but even a human knew . . .

I tensed as a cold, wet finger trailed across my collarbone. My eyes snapped open, and a scream ripped up my throat. The wraith stood right in front of me, three rows of sharp teeth bared, and crimson eyes gleaming.

My heel slammed down upon the beast's instep. The demon screeched, and I bolted.

Before I'd even reached what I deemed a safe distance, I heard Hunter grunt, and then the sound of something falling to the ground.

I whirled around and a gasp flew from me. The wraith had reached Hunter, who'd probably been distracted by my dumb ass running away, and ripped open my partner's thigh. Blood had already pooled on the floor around Hunter, who was clutching the gaping wound.

A low rumbling sound cut through my terror. The demon was laughing.

"Stupid witchlings," he chuckled, and black tendrils of

magic began dripping from his fingertips to wrap around Hunter's neck.

Oh hell no!

The guttural sounds of Hunter choking pushed me past my terror, and I rushed forward.

This had so not been the plan. My weak power and a few punches wouldn't do shit against a demon. Hunter was supposed to be the hero of our squad.

But now Hunter depended on me.

I was halfway across the nursery when the demon wrenched his attention from choking out my partner and turned his glowing eyes my direction. He sneered and pulled the sinister tendrils tighter.

My heart stopped as Hunter wheezed.

"Music to my ears." The demon hurled a bolt of black magic at my feet. "A perfect tune to dance to, wouldn't you say, beautiful?"

A second ebony ball of energy soared past my shoulder, followed by another, and then another. I yelped and performed some fancy footwork that had me thankful for my dexterous feet. Yet even as I leapt and darted lithely out of the way, the demon was yanking the life from Hunter. Desperate to help, but unable to get closer, I directed a beam of pink power at the wraith. It floated across the room, its pace languid compared to the demon's bullet-like magic.

The wraith's eyes widened, and he swept my power to the side. "This is what Spellcasters sends to best me? Thank Hell!" He barked out a laugh. "My lords and ladies of darkness will see their time on Earth sooner than we hoped!"

My jaw tightened, and I shot another assault at him. Though this one was brighter and faster, the demon flicked it away and continued to roar.

"If that's all you got, you'd do well to jump out that window and save yourself, witchling. Because this boy is *mine*." The demon whipped around and gripped Hunter by his neck. "Open wide." Black tendrils of magic rose from the floor, pooling around Hunter's mouth and opening his jaw wider and wider.

I forgot how to breathe. *He'll possess Hunter. The demon will have access to Hunter's powers on top of his own.*

Throwing up a prayer to the universe, I sprinted across the room, watching in horror as the demon's lips curled back, exposing razor-sharp teeth. Once they latched onto Hunter, only an incantation could force the demon out of him. As I hadn't gotten any other incantations to work, I didn't have hopes for this one.

God dammit! Why does my magic suck?!

"Say goodbye to your pretty boy." The demon chuckled, and the sound of his mirth, juxtaposed with Hunter's terror, sent rage bubbling over my fear.

"Over my dead body!" I roared and thrust out my hands. "*Nex*!"

As soon as the spell left my mouth, the unexpected happened.

Bright fuchsia magic burst from my palms, stopping me in my tracks and wrenching a gasp from my throat. It was power like I'd never seen, a million times faster and more potent than the watery pink power I'd grown used to seeing.

And it hit the demon square in the back.

He roared as the energy I'd produced seared a hole through his fiendish flesh. Black pus dripped to the floor, as smoke twisted and twirled upward. The wraith dropped Hunter, who scooted backward.

We both watched wide-eyed as a plume of blackness filled the room and the stench of sulfur from the demon's rotting body threatened to overwhelm us. A second later, the demon's body fell apart, like a stone turning to sand—albeit with a lot more goop.

I stared at the spot in disbelief.

"What happened?" Hunter rasped after a prolonged silence.

I shook myself back to the moment. "Not sure. Are you okay?" I knelt at his side, and Hunter's blood and acrid demon pus soaked the silk of my dress.

"Will be. Once we get back."

As if his words had conjured it, the warphole expanded before us, and I blinked. Everything had happened so fast that I barely believed it. But it *had* happened. We'd done it. Hunter and I had passed the Samhain Trial.

I stared astonished into the inky depths of the warphole, now large enough for us to step through.

"Yo, Dane. A little help?" Hunter pushed up from where he lay on the ground covered in demon goop, and even though it was disgusting, I grabbed his slime-covered hand and pulled him up.

"I can't walk on this leg," Hunter admitted once he was up.

"I was afraid of that." Shimmying my shoulder beneath his, I took most of his weight, and got covered in slime in the process. "So you know, Wardwell, I don't touch demon goop for just anyone. I must really love you."

Hunter grinned, and together, we took a step forward through the blackness, toward home.

Cheers filled my ears as we stepped out of the swirling vortex into Merlin Amphitheater.

I scanned the seats before me, taking in my classmates. Amethyst gave me a thumbs-up, and Mina was clapping her hands together high above her head. Even though they couldn't see what had happened, they were proud. We'd all gotten through the Samhain Trial. No one had surrendered. Our entire class passed, and only Efraim had been sent to the infirmary.

"Eva isn't here," Hunter said, and although we'd just returned victorious, his tone dripped with worry.

I tensed, understanding his reasoning. In the Samhain Trial, Eva and Alex were the strongest duo. Alex was the top of our class, and Eva was nearly as good as Hunter. If Spellcasters had deemed the individual challenges equal, and we were back, they should have returned forever ago.

"I wonder—"

The words died in my mouth as I caught sight of people in the crowd leaping to their feet and pointing. Around the warphole that Eva and Alex had walked through to begin their trial, professors burst into arguments, and Headmistress Wake wrung her hands as she peered into the darkness.

What the hell is going on in there?

"Someone needs to go through! Who cares if it's against Samhain Trial regulations? Initiates can't handle *that* on their own!" Professor Umbra screeched, her mop of graying hair flying everywhere as she whipped her head around frantically.

A group of spymasters from the crowd joined the professors and added their support to Umbra's opinion. Thrax, with his red plait flying behind him, barreled into the group and voiced his opinion. De Spina appeared at the warphole a moment later, tension lining his normally cool facade. The arguments continued, and all the while, most of the professors couldn't take their eyes off the warphole.

I took in the stadium again. Most people were standing and trying their best to peer around those in front of them. All wore a look of shocked fascination mixed with horror.

Wrenching my shoulder out from under Hunter, I stepped forward. Hunter faltered and whimpered, but I didn't care. He was here and safe, but something was happening to Eva, my best friend, and if anyone had a right to know what the hell was happening, it was me.

Screw protocol.

I pushed past the spymasters and professors who were still squabbling so much they didn't even notice, and stood directly in front of the warphole. I sucked in a shocked breath as my hand flew to my mouth.

Fire ravaged what looked to be the interior of a decrepit house. It looked like I was peering into hell itself.

"Where are they?!" I screamed.

A dozen pairs of hands grasped me, and I swore. Why had I been so dramatic? I should have just jumped through and seen for myself.

"Portland, they're—" Headmistress Wake's clipped tone filled my ears, but fell silent just as a vision of Alex, glasses-less, covered in ash, and carrying a lifeless Eva, filled the warphole.

CHAPTER TWENTY-FOUR

"Odette? Are you awake?"

A smooth baritone cut through my dreams, and my eyes snapped open. I shot up from where my head had been resting on the book I was supposed to be reading. The page ripped a little in the process, and I swore.

"Sorry, I didn't mean to startle you," the voice—Alex's—said, sending shivers up my spine.

I brushed the sleep from my eyes. "It's okay. I need to wake up anyway and get some studying done." I tried to gaze out the window of the infirmary, but it was all the way on the other side of the room, and someone had drawn the curtains. How long had I been out?

"It's after dinner," Alex replied. "As a matter of fact, I brought you some food. I noticed you haven't been eating in the cafeteria."

"Err . . ." I blinked, unable to form words.

Alex Wardwell was bringing me dinner? The fact that he was *talking* to me was a shock.

He winced. "I guess I kind of deserve that reaction." Alex gestured to the chair on the opposite side of Eva, who remained passed out in her bed. "Can I join you?"

Still unsure of what to say, I nodded, and took the bag he handed me. Inside, I found a turkey sandwich and a cup of soup. I wished that it was a slice of Hawaiian pizza, my choice comfort food, but my stomach didn't care. It rumbled all the same, and I realized that I was ravenous. When was the last time I'd eaten? Since the Samhain Trial, everything had been a blur.

"You've missed three days of classes. Have you been here the entire time?"

I nodded and stuffed an oversized bite of sandwich into my mouth.

Alex's lips tightened, and he shifted his gaze to Eva, taking in the many lacerations on her face, and shaking his head.

The tension in the air mounted as I studied him, unable to work out why he was in the infirmary. He hadn't been friends with Eva before the Samhain Trial. They'd barely talked, except for . . . *Oh!*

I wanted to facepalm myself. Alex probably felt major guilt over what had happened to Eva.

I swallowed and took a drink of the water that the healers always kept on Eva's bedside. "I can leave you alone with her," I offered.

Alex bit his lip and a conflicted look crossed his face

before he spoke. "Actually, I came to see both of you. Since you're the only one awake, it looks like you get my full attention." He inhaled sharply, and the following sentence gushed from him as if he needed to get it out as fast as possible. "I owe you an apology, Odette."

I dropped my sandwich. "What?" I cleared my throat. "I mean—I don't understand what changed."

Alex let out a long exhale. "No, you wouldn't. You, unlike most people here, aren't as up on witching drama. I'll try to explain my faulty thinking as best I can. You're aware that Hunter's family and mine don't get along, right?"

I nodded.

"It's a feud that goes back generations. His great-great-grandfather screwed mine over. Ever since, the branches of the family have hated each other. When Spellcasters cropped up before World War II, the families met for the first time in years. For a while there, it looked like they would make up and attend the same school." His lips flattened.

I leaned forward, intrigued by the supernatural drama. "What happened?"

"Hunter's side of the family brokered a deal with the headmaster. They excluded my family from attending Spellcasters and the feud lived on, hotter than ever. Hunter and I have known of each other's existence our whole lives—family members still like to send birth announcements to spite the other half. That being said, we've only met once, and it was on accident."

"How?" The question popped out, and while it should have embarrassed me that I was prying into someone else's family business, I couldn't help it. The history of the Wardwells was like watching an addicting soap opera.

"I was going to a concert in New York. Hunter and I may have never met, but social media ensured that I knew what he looked like. I noticed Hunter at the concert. He acted so entitled, so manipulative, using his magic in public when humans weren't looking." Alex shook his head. "He was probably just being an idiot sixteen-year-old guy, trying to impress girls, but I got unreasonably pissed and tried to leave. Hunter saw me, and we ended up getting into a massive fight."

"So how did you get into the academy?"

"My parents are both physicians. A few months ago, Headmistress Wake's husband arrived at our family practice after an expedition that went wrong. My family saved him and bargained my admittance." He shrugged. "They'd been training me as if I was already enrolled at Spellcasters for years. The plan was to petition for it anyway, but the leverage was too good to pass up."

I leaned back in my chair, taking it all in. "Okay, so I get why you don't like Hunter. But why were you such a dick to me when we first met?"

Alex's cheeks reddened, and a tingle of desire trickled through me. "I'm ashamed to admit it," he began slowly. "When you arrived, Hunter and I had just argued over being placed on the same floor. My fuse was already short.

Then I saw you, and . . . let's just say you reminded me a lot of him."

"Entitled?"

"Well . . . not exactly. But definitely a legacy—from a good family, wealthy, attractive. That you hadn't bothered to read the paperwork frustrated me. It reminded me of something that I believed Hunter would do. So I took all my anger out on you. With every class, it became more clear that you were unprepared to be here. And I'll admit I thought you were glory-seeking when the fae was trying to shift Amethyst through the circle. That only added fuel to my fire."

I let out an exasperated huff. "This apology is going south fast."

"It was dumb—all of it," Alex amended, "but I took my first perception and ran with it. Some say the Wardwells have a temper—although I'm pretty sure that's only my side of the family. Hunter seems to charm everyone."

I let out a chuckle. That much was true.

I ate a few more spoonfuls of soup, mulling over what he'd told me and watching Eva's chest rise and fall.

"What made you change your mind?" I asked finally.

Alex nodded to Eva. "After we returned from our trial and I saw your face, I knew that I'd misjudged you. You may not be prepared to be here, and you might have gone a little overboard with the saving Amethyst thing, but it's just because you *really* care about others. You're not some entitled legacy."

He sucked in a breath. "And honestly, I think seeing a

greater demon helped put a lot of things into perspective. You know . . . what's important, and what I'd been trying to deny. I'll admit that since the moment I saw you, I've been drawn to you. It only made me more annoyed that you could charm me so easily. All my prejudices combined and festered inside me, and I acted like an ass."

"Yeah, you did," I agreed.

My gaze settled on Eva, and I took in what he'd said. I had every right to be mad at him, but Alex seemed to be laying it all on the table, and there was no denying that I'd been drawn to him too all these months. Maybe there was a reason for that? Were we supposed to be friends? If that was the case there was one big issue.

I took a few long breaths before speaking again. "You know that Eva and Hunter are a thing, right?"

Alex's eyes widened.

"Not officially," I amended. "They're being all secretive about it. Of course, just because you're apologizing doesn't mean we have to be friends, but I have to say . . ."

My eyes lifted to meet his stunning blue ones, and my breath hitched. The same tingles I'd felt the night we'd held hands while a crazy fae attacked us pushed through me. Perhaps it was hopeful or naïve, but after Alex's admission, I didn't believe that this chemistry was one-sided.

"I wouldn't mind it. And if we're hanging out, Eva will be there, which means Hunter will be too," I finished.

Alex chewed his lip for a few seconds before finally speaking. "I understand. And for the record, I'd like to hang out, too. As for Hunter, well . . . it will undoubtedly take some time, but I'll try my best."

I nodded. That was good enough—for now.

"Let me get this straight, you and hunk-of-the-year Alex Wardwell bonded over my unconscious body, and you've hung out every day since? I've been awake a full day! Why didn't you tell me?" A grin spread on Eva's scarred face.

Spellcasters' healers had tried all the regular remedies to cure the greater demon scars. Nothing had worked, and many believed the creature who had scarred Eva was more powerful than most. They hinted that the marks would never fade. Thankfully, Headmistress Wake had sent out inquiries, and well-respected healers from around the globe would arrive in the next few weeks to offer their opinions.

Eva had returned to our suite after a week in the infirmary, and I couldn't have been happier. A part of me was conflicted that I was leaving her alone tonight, but I'd made plans with Alex to have dinner in Wandstown, and my hopes were great that the dinner would benefit Eva as well as myself.

"I hardly wanted to talk about my crush with all those healers and professors around, and they were *always* there. Plus, as of now, we're still just . . . friends . . . learning about each other. We haven't even held hands." My eyes shifted to Eva, and my lips curled up in a smirk. "You know about being 'just friends,' don't you?"

Eva's cheeks colored, and she dropped her gaze to her hands. "You figured out that Hunter and I are . . . doing whatever we're doing, huh?"

"You guys were obvious. I legit walked in on him kissing your hand in the infirmary. Sorry, but no guy *friend* does that."

Eva rolled her eyes. "I swear, he is such a hopeless romantic."

"You should have seen the way he leapt up."

We shared a good laugh that petered out into an uncomfortable silence.

Aw hell, let's get this over with.

"I don't understand why you guys wanted to keep it hidden. It's not like I would've cared. I mean, Hunter's hot, but I always thought of him like a brother."

"I didn't think you'd be jealous," Eva explained hurriedly. "You never had eyes for anyone except Alex."

I gaped, and Eva laughed.

"Odie, you stare at him all the time! Hunter and I knew you liked Alex. We didn't want to make you feel like the third wheel and change the dynamic of our trio. Especially when everyone else—Alex included—was being such an ass to you." Eva pressed her lips together, clearly still annoyed by the rudeness of our peers.

My heart clenched. Her explanation made perfect sense and rang true to my friend's character. "Well, thanks. But for the record, you don't have to hide a part of your life for my comfort. I can handle going it alone. I'm a tough cookie."

"So Hunter tells anyone who will listen." Eva arched an eyebrow, and I smiled.

A door slammed outside, and Eva glanced at her clock. "Don't you have a hot date, like now?"

"Ha. Friends, remember?"

She pursed her lips. "We'll see how long that lasts."

I sighed. "How do I look?"

Eva's blue eyes ran up and down my body. "Hot. Have I ever told you how much I love that piece?" She gestured to my long, leather jacket.

"Well, you can't have it," I teased. "It was my mom's. She got it on one of her first missions in Venice. It gives off an espionage vibe, doesn't it?" I twirled.

"Or dominatrix, whatever." Eva grinned, and I swatted her shoulder."Hey now!" she cried out. "Remember, succubus scars!"

My face fell. "I'm so sorry. Are you okay if I go out? You won't feel alone?"

She'd given me the rundown of what she could remember from her trial, and it had been horrific. Apparently, she'd just killed the lesser demon that Spellcasters had sent them to fight when a greater demon appeared: a super strong succubus. The bitch had thrown acid at Eva's face, barely missing her eye. Eva had passed out shortly after that.

"I'm kidding. Apparently, no regular cure can heal them, but they don't actually hurt. I'll be fine," Eva assured me.

"Are you sure? I can cancel dinner."

"No. It's okay. Hunter's busy tonight, too, so I was gonna use the time to catch up on some classwork. I'm behind. Basically, I need this time to study, so *puh-lease* leave!" Eva gave me a playful shove.

I inched toward the door. "Okay. Get lots done, and don't stay up too late," I said like a total mom.

"Okay," Eva said. "Get lots done and don't forget to jump Alex's bones."

I shook my head and, cheeks flaming, rushed out of my room.

CHAPTER TWENTY-FIVE

"It's so cute!" I exclaimed as we stopped in front of a bistro in Wandstown.

No one had been more surprised than me when Alex asked if I wanted to get off campus for an evening out. Of course I'd said yes. Not only was it dinner with Alex Wardwell, but after staying in the infirmary with Eva for a week, I needed to get away. Then I'd come up with a brilliant plan to make my life easier, and everything fell into place.

Well, almost. That last bit remained to be seen, but I was hopeful that it would work.

A few people turned to look at us as we entered the bistro. Three older couples smiled and waved. Alex waved back, which I thought was a little odd, but didn't question. I was too busy wondering what the people in the bistro thought we were. An established couple, casual daters, or friends?

"Reservation for Wardwell," Alex said to the hostess,

and as she searched her sheet, I hoped that Ms. Seeley had honored his request to book a reservation. Simple things like that were a lot harder without cell phones.

"Right this way, please."

Thankfully, the hostess led us to the table for four. Alex helped me out of my jacket, which sent butterflies fluttering in my stomach. I took the seat facing the dining room. I didn't want him to know about my plan until the very last minute.

"So, how does it feel to be out of Spellcasters?" Alex asked as he sat down.

I heaved a breath. "Amazing. When I got to the academy, I thought I would never want to leave, but after this last week . . ." I shook my head, taking in everything that had happened. "It was intense. Eva finally told me what happened at your trial—or at least, what she could remember. I can't believe you guys faced all that."

Alex's blue eyes darkened. "You and me both."

"How did you get out of there without it following you?"

"I killed it."

My eyebrows furrowed. "You *killed* it? But we haven't learned any incantations *that* advanced in Battle Magic or Demonology. Only those that can deal with lesser demons."

"My parents taught me," Alex said as if he was admitting something he shouldn't. "Remember how I told you that they were determined that I enroll in Spellcasters?"

I nodded.

"Well, they taught me a few things that we won't learn until third year to cinch my admittance."

I gaped. Alex knew Crucible-year stuff? *Holy universe, that is so hot.*

Alex shrugged as if trying to brush it off. "They didn't teach me that much advanced stuff. They're only two people and I had normal school, which took up a lot of time. But what they really wanted me to know, they drilled into me. The curse terrified them. They wanted to make sure I could defend myself."

The curse. Of course. The curse that had made *my* parents lie to me all my life. The curse I still had yet to bring up to them. The curse that had affected the lives of everyone in my year.

"What else did they teach you?" I couldn't help but be curious about this boy whose upbringing had differed greatly from mine.

"Healing. That's my favorite branch of magic. A little about conjuring, although not too much." Alex smirked. "I guess they thought no child should be able to conjure whatever they wanted. Definitely not a teenage boy." He chuckled and gave me a sheepish look that sent shivers up my spine. "Healing, Battle Magic, and Magical History were our main subjects."

"So healing is your favorite magical art to study?" I leaned forward, interested by his unexpected answer. "What do you like best about it?"

To my surprise, he leaned forward too, and placed his hands inches from mine.

We both seemed to notice their proximity at the same time, and stared down at them, our conversation stagnating. I gulped as the scent of his cologne washed over me, and Alex squirmed in his chair. The air between us began to sizzle, and despite my assurances to Eva that Alex and I were just friends, the whole thing felt *very* much like a date.

"Healing is a puzzle," Alex said finally, his voice raspy. "I find that the most gratifying things in life are often puzzles." He licked his lips, and his brilliant blue eyes strayed to my mouth.

Oh my God what is happening? Are we flirting? Play it cool, Odie.

Blood thrummed in my veins, and I floundered for something to say to elongate this magical moment.

"Oh?" I choked out. "Like what else?"

Alex arched an eyebrow. "Well, to be honest, like y—"

"Thank you." A very familiar voice cut through me, and I let out a quiet groan as Alex jerked back and the hot tension between us shattered.

Why in the hell had I invited Hunter? He'd screwed up a moment that I'd been dreaming about for months!

"Hey, partner, hey, Cuz, what's happening?" Without waiting for an invitation, Hunter pulled out a chair and sat down next to Alex, who tensed.

My emotions swerved from aroused to nervous in the space of a heartbeat. While it hadn't been easy getting Hunter to agree that the cousins needed intervention, I'd managed to convince him. Mostly by using my trump card.

Eva.

I'd sworn to Hunter that if he didn't meet up with Alex and do his best to make amends, I'd monopolize as much of her time as possible.

But I held no such power over Alex. Hell, he'd gone months hating me. What would stop him from walking out right now?

After a full minute, which felt like a year, Alex inhaled sharply. "Hello, Cousin. Fancy seeing you here." He turned to me and arched an eyebrow. "I imagined this moment arriving on my terms, but clearly, by courting you, I must get used to working outside my comfort zone."

Hunter clapped his hands. "Ha! You and me both. Eva isn't a play-by-the-rules kinda person, either. Then again," he smirked, "neither am I. Not on the level of your side of the family, anyway."

"Oh? Is that so? And what do you know about my side of the family?" Alex turned his full attention to Hunter, and the pair began to banter.

I barely heard them.

Courting me? Had Alex insinuated that we were dating—or almost dating?

A smile spread across my face.

Apparently, I'm dating Alex Wardwell. Oh hell yes!

I beamed and then, realizing that I'd left two feuding cousins to their own devices, snapped back to attention.

"And at that concert! Cuz, you were all strait-laced, standing in line and scowling at me while I rode the mosh pit." Hunter burst out laughing at the memory, and Alex's lips flattened.

Shitballs, time for a redirect.

"Alex?" My voice cracked a little. "We have to deal with the issues between you two if we all want to be friends." My eyes darted back and forth between him and Hunter, and I inhaled a long, calming breath before laying it out on the table. "I guess what I'm saying is that you two better make up tonight, because with Eva and me, it's sisters before misters."

The right corner of Alex's lips twitched in amusement. "Obviously. And yes, I'm okay with this. A little warning would have been nice . . . but I understand why you sprang it on me. However," he locked eyes with Hunter, "let's do this right. We're here. We need to confront each other's issues and hurts. We talk it out like adults, no hiding from the past. No joking around and pretending everything is fine. I want a *real* discussion."

The jovial smile disappeared from Hunter's face, and for a second, he looked like he might refuse. Then he nodded. "All right. I'm in. We'll do it your way, Cuz."

The coil of tension in my gut loosened, and I leaned back. I'd remain for moral support, or if things got out of hand, but they needed to work out their differences on their own.

CHAPTER TWENTY-SIX

A month later, things between Alex and Hunter were going so well that I couldn't help but feel pleased with myself. Of course, there had been a few tense moments—no relationship was perfect, and certainly not one that had been so fraught with dislike for years—but the guys always worked them out.

Now, if only my magic would freaking cooperate with me, I thought, running my hands over Alex's torso. He grinned up at me from where he lay on the cold, metal examination table, and my heart skipped a beat.

"Has someone's mind slipped from trying to diagnose me?" Alex teased.

I swatted him playfully. "Oh hush. Close your eyes."

He obliged, and my heartbeat slowed. Those darn blue eyes distracted me, and Alex was right, I needed to concentrate.

After Eva's encounter with a greater demon, world-renowned healers had flocked to Spellcasters to see her baffling wounds firsthand, and help Eva if they could. Spotting an opportunity, Headmistress Wake propositioned the most skilled healers to put on a weekend of workshops.

As Tiberius Thorn's time was valuable, he consented to do the workshop as long as it was an option to teach the Culling, Grind, and Crucible-years all together in half-day sessions.

Attending sessions with the upperclassmen made it clear how much a year of study changed things. While many had already called out the "ailment" that Tiberius had enchanted their partner with, and received a new one to puzzle out, the initiates' success rate was lower. I, for one, had yet to sense any amiss energies within Alex's body. All I'd been doing for the last thirty minutes was roving my hands inch-by-inch over his torso, hoping to feel something other than desire.

I supposed it shouldn't come as a surprise. While I'd been killing it in the academic classes, the ones in which we used magic were not going as well. It was frustrating, since I'd seen that accessing powerful magic was possible. During the Samhain Trial, my magic had been astounding. But since then . . . nothing.

Is Diana right, and I shouldn't be here? Tears began to prick in my eyes.

"Hey. What's wrong?" Alex asked, sitting up and grabbing my hand.

A spark of pleasure ignited in my belly, pushing away the darkness. If it weren't for Alex, Hunter, and Eva, I might have already gone home. Spellcasters had always been my dream, but my failures were crushing my spirit.

"I'm *so* tired of sucking," I admitted. "The only time I've done anything impressive magic-wise was in the Samhain Trial. And that was all adrenaline or something."

Alex shook his head. "No way. You're strong. Hunter told me about your trial. That wasn't just a fluke. You just haven't figured out how to harness it yet. You'll get there soon."

I closed my eyes and exhaled. Easy for him to say. Alex was at the top of our class and never seemed to struggle.

"Want to switch?" he asked. "Be my patient?"

I nodded and took Alex's spot on the table. Closing my eyes, I tried to focus on my breathing so my brain would turn off. I would probably only have a minute before Alex detected the false illness Tiberius had planted inside me. Healing came so naturally to him that Alex had started attending the second-years' healing seminars whenever possible.

Although my eyes were closed, I still sensed his hand floating over me. I wasn't sure how, but I was always aware of a certain energy coming off Alex. I'd never experienced it with any other boyfriend, but then again, I'd never dated a wizard before. Maybe that's how it was with witches and wizards? If so, I liked it . . . a lot.

"Hmm."

My lips curled upward at the familiar, thoughtful sound.

"Joining the ranks of stumped first-years?" I teased, keeping my eyes closed.

"You might say that."

"Welcome. I'm Queen Odette of the Confused." I mimed placing a crown on my head.

"You're my queen, but not in that way," he growled sexily, and my eyes popped open to find Alex's face inches away.

A small gasp escaped me, and our lips crashed together.

My bad mood disappeared as his velvet-soft lips pressed against mine. I doubted anyone could feel bad for themselves when receiving a grade-A kiss like this. Hell, if anything other than ecstasy gushed through their veins, I didn't know what was wrong with them. Must be faulty nerve endings or something.

"Um, hello, this is a *healing* workshop, not an intro to baby-making," a comically nasal-toned voice teased, and I giggled right in Alex's mouth.

We broke apart to find Eva and Hunter off to the side, their hands entwined.

"Tiberius excused us for lunch." Eva's eyes twinkled. "We have an hour before the next workshop."

"Thanks for the heads up," I said.

"No problem, you just have to get your enchantment taken off, or else you'll actually start succumbing to its effects," Eva said. "We've already had ours removed, and want to get out of here. It's mac and cheese day in the cafeteria. I'm not missing that again. Want us to get you guys some?"

We declined, and Eva and Hunter scurried off to indulge in one of Spellcasters' most popular entrées.

Alex placed his hands on my waist and helped me off the table. Together, we strode up to Tiberius Thorn, who waved his hands over our abdomens and arched his eyebrows.

"Any guesses?" he asked.

I shook my head. "No idea," I admitted easily. Much of my frustration had vanished after our makeout session.

"And you, Wardwell?" Tiberius asked.

"She has congested arteries. They're reducing her blood flow and might cause a heart attack or stroke," Alex said, surprising me.

When had he figured that out? He'd seemed so confused right before we started kissing.

Tiberius beamed. "Correct. You're the only one in your class to hit the nail on the head."

"Thank you, sir." Alex nodded and grasped my hand.

We left Agnes Sampson Hall together, and though my feelings of defeat still lingered, the hand I held made things a lot easier.

CHAPTER TWENTY-SEVEN

I have the best friends.

Even if they had just kicked my ass one-by-one, I could say that with confidence. After all, they were giving up a sacred day off to help me train and hopefully pull my magic out of me.

Most of our class had headed down to Wandstown, intent on chugging ale and letting off some steam in the witching town that turned a blind eye to underage drinking, and the shenanigans of Spellcasters students. Our parents would arrive the following week for Yule, and while I was looking forward to seeing Mom and Dad—and questioning them about the curse—many of my classmates were dreading their reunions.

Poor Efraim had actually burst out into hives at the idea of seeing his parents.

"How did that time feel, babe?" Alex asked, his blue eyes narrowed as he wiped his glasses clean.

"About the same. Like I can push my magic only so far before I hit a wall." I heaved out a big sigh and threw up my hands. "Maybe magic is one area where I'll never be as good as I want to be. If I get through Spellcasters, I'll be that spy who relies on her charm and smarts. Or have to partner with somebody who's superb at magic."

Eva placed a hand on her hip. "No way, girl. You can do this! Everyone's magic is different. Professors try to fit us into boxes, but it's possible that you don't fit into a box."

Every time this topic came up, I felt that Mom and Dad had failed me in teaching me how to be a witch. Even if they wanted me to be self-sufficient without magic, it made little sense. Especially considering the curse.

"Okay." I shook the negative thoughts from my mind. "What do you say we do one more round and then break for lunch? This time, Hunter and I will be on the same team, and you guys attack him. We'll try to recreate Samhain."

Hunter gaped. "Gee, thanks, friend. Thank goodness Eva isn't annoyed with me today, or I'd think you had it out for me."

Eva wagged her eyebrows. "After this *morning,* there's no way I'm mad at you, honey bunch. You—"

"Okay, okay," I cut her off. "No one needs details, here."

Eva was a *major* over-sharer when it came to her relationship with Hunter.

"All right." Alex waved his hand, and crimson magic

burst from his fingers to form a tiny, brass cup in the center of the room. "We'll battle for this cup."

He pointed to both ends of the Battle Magic classroom, which was long and rectangular. "We'll start on opposite sides and work toward the middle. Nothing is off limits. Since it worked once, we'll do what Odie said—go for Hunter and try to pull her protective instinct out."

It would kind of suck if I could only perform strong magic in life-and-death situations, but at least if this worked, I would know for certain what my capabilities were.

We faced off at the opposite ends of the long room, and when Alex gave the signal, we charged at each other. I shot off an array of magic. But no matter how strong the intentions or emotions I channeled were, my magic was always weaker in appearance than the vivid sunshine yellow beams, crimson tendrils, and green waves of smoke that my friends produced. It was like my power was less vibrant; watercolors versus acrylics.

Hunter was doing most of the work of advancing our team toward the cup, which meant we were moving slower than our opponents.

Why am I always freaking behind?

Annoyance bubbled in me, and my teeth ground together. Harnessing that emotion, I shot a beam of power straight at Alex.

It hit, but instead of searing his skin like I'd intended, it absorbed, and he kept moving.

I pressed my lips together and threw off another bloom

of magic, this one directed at Eva. She deflected it with an easy wave of her hand, yellow energy washing away pink.

Ugh! What the freaking hell is wrong with—crap! I fumbled and caught myself before I hit the ground. When I looked back up, I cringed, as a stream of crimson magic slammed Hunter square in the chest.

"No!" I yelped as he fell to the ground about fifteen feet from the cup, and full-on convulsions began to wrack his body.

He released a long moan, and I rushed over to him.

Surprisingly, Eva and Alex stopped advancing toward the cup. I furrowed my eyebrows. Why wouldn't they just go for it? Nothing was off limits, and we had an infirmary down the hall skilled in healing injuries that students inflicted on each other. Then again, Hunter's screams sounded pretty terrible. Or were Alex and Eva waiting until I exposed myself, to incapacitate me too?

Whatever their diabolical plan, I couldn't help but drop to my knees at Hunter's side.

"Are you okay?"

Still convulsing, Hunter's lips quirked up, and he winked. "We're so close. Get the prize while they still think I'm dying."

I snorted. *Oh my God.* He was freaking brilliant—and a good actor too.

"You got it," I whispered.

I leapt up, twirling as I moved, a victorious grin on my face.

And then I ran straight into a demon.

A shriek ripped up my throat, and I leapt backward, over Hunter. But before I'd gone more than a few feet, Hunter began screaming.

Twirling around, I saw the demon leaning over Hunter, his teeth exposed. My hands thrust outward. "Nex!" I screamed.

Pink magic trickled from me, but as the demon's mouth lowered closer to my partner, it transformed as if someone had turned a hose on full blast.

And it shot straight at the monster.

The creature exploded on the spot, and I heaved a massive breath. My heart rate began to slow, and I refocused on Hunter.

It took me only a few seconds to deduce that something was off. Where was the inky blood or the goopy guts that had covered him the last time we'd faced a demon? And how the hell had one gotten inside Spellcasters?

A slow clap began, and realization dawned over me. I whipped around to find Alex and Eva beaming.

"Which one of you assholes conjured that?" I pointed to the spot where the demon had been.

"We did it together," Eva said, pride in her voice, although her expression of joy had dimmed. "We thought, if we reproduced your Samhain Trial—"

"That you could give me a freaking heart attack!" I threw my arms in the air. "Mission accomplished."

I stalked to the other side of the room, slid down the wall, and flung my head into my arms. *What the actual hell?*

Did this exercise just prove that I need to face off with an evil demon for my magic to work?

Soft footsteps followed me, and I knew without looking who they belonged to. A few irregular heartbeats later, Alex slid down the wall to sit beside me. Still I didn't lift my head.

"Sorry. We shouldn't have scared you like that."

My head snapped up. "Oh, really?! It's one thing when de Spina does it in a class, but when it comes out of nowhere like that—"

"I agree," Alex said, before making his signature thoughtful sound. I usually found it charming, but right now it made me want to slap him.

"Oh, don't be going all *Mr. Pensive* on me. All you should be doing is getting me apology chocolate."

He chuckled. "I'll get right on that." He paused, and his tone dipped. "*Although,* say theoretically I had an idea about why your magic is acting odd . . . would you like to hear it?"

My breath hitched and my eyes grew wide. *What? Is he serious?*

"I thought so," Alex said, reading my expression. "I've been considering this since we started hanging out. After the healing workshop last weekend, I was *almost* certain, but didn't want to bring it up in case I was wrong. Seeing your magic today, how you reacted to the demon . . . well, now I'm sure."

"Oh my God! Spit it out, Alex!"

"I think you have lots of magic," he began, his tone careful.

"Why the hell can't I use it?" I pressed.

His gaze locked with mine, and a strange pressure built in the air between us.

"Because, Odie, you're spellbound."

"I don't get it," I said. "What do you mean by spellbound? And how do you know? How has no one else known?"

Alex had made the three of us leave the Battle Magic classroom for privacy before he explained his line of thought. Now that we were secure in my room, I couldn't get my many questions out fast enough.

"I mean that your magic is tied up inside you. I think it's in a tight ball. You're able to access it through a hole, kind of like a pinprick in a water balloon, except you don't explode. The hole lets a little power out, but not enough to be considered strong or dangerous."

I pressed a finger to my lips. "What makes you believe that?"

"I know how energy should flow in a body. It should be free, running through you in a cyclical fashion. I've noticed that yours was different before when we . . ." His cheeks pinked as he trailed off, and Hunter wolf-whistled. Alex cleared his throat. "My mind wasn't fully there during those times. I'm only a man, after all. But during Tiberius' workshop, I could concentrate. I finally realized that your energy felt . . . stagnant, which isn't like you at all. It was confusing, but I didn't say anything. I did, however, begin to wonder."

"And spend a crapload of time in the library," Hunter added.

He was right. Out of the four of us, Alex naturally spent the most time in the library, but for the last week, he'd been spending an excessive amount of time in there—even for him.

"Yup, and that's where I found information on binding. Usually it's reserved for black witches and warlocks who have committed heinous crimes, but sometimes . . . parents bind children who have too much power. In that case, the binding is less severe and is often loosened over time." His blue eyes leveled with mine. "I think that's what your parents did to you, Odie. Kind of. The difference is I don't think they ever loosened it, *and* I'm pretty sure they added a safety mechanism. They allowed you to access your magic if you were in a life-threatening situation."

"Like Samhain." I fell back on my bed, dazed.

Although what he said sounded kind of crazy, it also felt right. My parents had always been safety freaks. And this explained why they didn't put much emphasis on magic in the home. They didn't want me to question my lack of power.

It also explained why they didn't want me going to Spellcasters.

Anger flared within me. All my life, they'd advocated for me to make my own choices about my body, and then they went behind my back and did *this*? They'd restricted my magic? A part of my very nature?

Or was it because I was dangerous—a natural-born black witch?

I had to know.

"How can I get rid of it?"

"I'm pretty sure I can help." Alex gulped and took a long, steady breath. "But it will hurt. A lot."

CHAPTER TWENTY-EIGHT

"Are you ready?" Alex asked, cracking my bedroom window.

I nodded. "If I say stop—even if I beg—*don't*. I want this done. No . . . I *need* it done. Do you promise?"

A flicker of discomfort rushed across Alex's perfect features, but he nodded as he sat in a chair next to my bed. "I promise."

Sure he wouldn't let me down, I leaned back and laid my head on my pillow

"Eva and Hunter, stand at my sides. Be prepared to block any wayward power." He gulped. "When Odette's magic is finally free . . . well, results vary, but most say that it's like a small explosion."

I shot back up. "An explosion?! You're just mentioning this now? Why are we doing this in my bedroom?"

"Not like a bomb," Alex amended. "An explosion of

light and vibrational energy is most common. It will be intense, almost blinding, and it'll shake up every cell in our bodies. Thankfully, all the bedrooms in Spellcasters are warded against destructive magic, so the room should be fine. I just wanted everyone to know what to expect, and maybe Hunter and Eva can save your stuff from getting damaged if the vibrations are too much."

The pair nodded, although the tightness of Eva's lips told me that worry still clung to her.

"You two don't have to stay," I said. "I understand if you want to wait it out in your room."

Eva shook her head. "No way in hell am I leaving my best friend to do this by herself." She stepped forward and grasped my hand. "I'm right here with you, Dane. And don't you forget it."

Tears pricked in my eyes. "Thanks, girl."

I lay back once more and closed my eyes. "Let's do the damn thing."

A soft chuckle floated from Alex, and the tightness in my chest loosened at the sound, only to cinch up again a mere second later.

Magic filled the surrounding air—Alex's—but different from his usual energy. He was tapping into something more powerful than normal. For what felt like the billionth time, my boyfriend impressed me. Hopefully, after the unbinding was complete, my power could rival his.

"Breathe, Odie," he whispered, and I realized I'd been holding my breath.

Literally and figuratively.

A long-fingered hand decorated with rings rested on my shoulder, grounding me. Eva's. My lips lifted in a small smile, and I began reciting a mantra.

Everything will work out as it should. Everything will work out as it should. Everything will work out as it should.

Soft murmurings filled my bedroom. Alex had started the incantation. I braced myself for pain, but a dozen heartbeats later, I felt normal.

He stilled, but I could not discern anything different going on inside me. Maybe, like everything else in this damn school, I was an exception.

Does this mean I'll never be unbound?

Frustration spiked at the thought, then vanished just as suddenly as my ribcage constricted, pushing out the little air that remained in my lungs. I gasped, and my eyes flew open as my hands flew to my chest.

"Hold tight, babe," Alex said, his palms hovering over my heart as crimson magic poured from them. "We're almost there. The bind's weave is loose. I just have to pull it out of you."

I squeaked, fighting for air.

"Hurry, Alex!" Eva whisper-shouted as she grasped my hand and squeezed it. "She can't breathe!"

"Calm her down. Her heart rate is too high, she's burning through oxygen," Alex countered.

He was right. My heart was pounding so hard that it wouldn't surprise me if it actually shot out of my chest.

Every beat pushed blood through me faster and faster, until the desperate thrum of it filled my ears. Someone grabbed my hand and began rubbing the webbing between my thumb and pointer finger.

"Shh, Odie, it's okay. Try to breathe," Hunter said, his normally exuberant tone calm as he leaned close.

Easy for him to say. It didn't feel like an elephant was sitting on his chest.

I tried to retort, but a sensation so powerful came over me that all thoughts disintegrated.

Instinctively, I gazed down toward my navel and loosed a scream. My ribcage was opening like a set of double doors. It hurt like hell, but what was worse was seeing my bones in the unnatural position, bending as though they were noodles and not hard flesh.

Hunter rubbed harder, and Eva squeezed my other hand tight.

"One more push," Alex growled, and a surge of red magic flew from his palms straight into me.

My body began to convulse. His magic was inside me, ripping my skin from the muscles and muscles from their bones. Everything was stretching apart, and if he didn't stop soon, I'd break.

"St—st—stop!" I screamed, but as he'd promised, Alex didn't listen.

Instead, his power surged out faster and harder. Spots began to cloud my vision. I closed my eyes, determined not to see what I was sure would be the end. My heart pushed against the confines of its sternum, and I groaned.

Eva whimpered. "Maybe we should—"

"She's almost there!" Alex snapped.

Another surge of power, riddling my inside with holes, ripping me apart. My muscles gave up fighting, and I fell limp against the bed, numb from overstimulation. This was it. This was the end. At least it was light—painless.

A grunt, followed by a squeal, hit my ear, but I remained turned inward, unable to take on anyone else's hardships at the moment.

And then my heart dropped right back into place, and breath—blessed air—filled me, giving me life once more.

I lunged upward, but Alex's strong hand pressed me back down.

"Wait." His tone was raspy.

Was he injured?

I opened my eyes, and a gasp flew from me. Fuchsia magic, more vibrant and intense than anything I'd ever produced, swirled and spun above me. My friends looked shell-shocked, the energies messing with their bodies. Only I had been spared, because this power was mine—a part of me.

And *damn* did it look like it could kick some butt.

It took a few minutes, but thankfully, Alex had had the foresight to crack the window, and my magic leaked outside. When the air in my bedroom was barely tinged pink, my friends shook their heads as if coming out of a daze.

"Holy hell," Hunter murmured.

"Yeah, what have you been hiding, Odie?" Eva asked, blinking.

I had no answer, so I locked eyes with Alex, who regarded me with awe.

No one knew what powers had been hiding inside me, but I was ready to find out.

CHAPTER TWENTY-NINE

A long exhale left my lips.

"It'll be all right," Eva said, pinning her red curls up for the Yule Feast. "You have every right to be frustrated with your parents. And no matter what they say, unbinding your magic should be your choice, anyway."

I didn't disagree with her. What I *was* worried about was what they would say.

Since my binding had been released two weeks ago, my entire world had changed. I'd gone from the absolute bottom of our class to somewhere in the middle. Alex thought I could shoot to the top, but I had my doubts. Having raw power—which I apparently had a ton of—was one thing; control was another. Since I'd never had to temper my magic, I lacked in that aspect.

It was terrifying.

Maybe Mom and Dad knew I wouldn't be able to control this

much energy, so they'd taken precautionary measures? Am I a menace to society? What if the smart thing to do is bind myself again?

I shook myself. No. That was impossible. Even if I could barely handle the tremors that wracked my body when I performed the most basic of spells, I doubted that I could go back to being half a witch.

"Oh my God, girl. I can feel the tension rolling off you. You're shaking, and it's not from the heater being wonky. Here," Eva handed me a glass of wine from a bottle that Hunter had somehow snatched from the kitchens. "To calm your nerves."

I took a sip, and even though my anxiety did not diminish, the warmth that slipped through my veins was welcome in the cold bathroom.

Setting the glass down, I finished curling my hair. The Yule Feast would begin in thirty minutes. At that time, I would see and speak with my parents for the first time in months.

And I'd finally hear what they had to say.

Merlin Amphitheater—the only space large enough for all three years of Spellcasters students, their parents, and the staff—looked totally different from the night of the Samhain Trial. But even with the festive streamers, mistletoe, floating candles, and massive pine wreaths scenting the air, the hair on the back of my neck lifted as Eva and I entered.

I wasn't alone in my trepidation. Eva actually stopped on the threshold, her eyes wide and staring at the spot where the warphole had been during her trial.

"It's okay." I grasped her hand. "Nothing like that will happen tonight."

She nodded. "I know, it's just . . ."

"Hard."

"Yeah."

"Eva! Odie!" a voice called, and I scanned the room to find Hunter waving us over. Not far away, I spotted my parents. They had claimed the end of an empty table and were speaking so intently they hadn't even noticed our arrival.

Unlike Orientation, which separated families, Yule was a time for community. Each table sat at least twenty people. Hunter's family had claimed the north side of the amphitheater, while Alex's family resided in the south. The boys had made it a point to arrive right when the amphitheater opened to find their parents.

And they'd arrived together.

I wonder how that went over?

Judging by the diamond-hard set of Hunter's dad's jaw, and the narrowing of Alex's mom's eyes, I guessed not very well. The guys had expected that. Their parents might not forgive and forget in one night like they had, but seeing their children together was a start.

"I don't see my parents yet," Eva said. "Bet they're still socializing in alumni housing. They plan on spending the whole freaking weekend here." She stared at Hunter and his family, longing in her eyes.

"Go meet them." I nudged her. "I should talk to my parents alone."

"Are you sure? You don't want emotional support?"

Truthfully, I wanted to pull my parents into a private room and interrogate them. But the feast would start soon, so there wasn't time for that.

"I'm sure. I just want to get this over with."

Eva gave my hand a comforting squeeze, and we parted. I crossed the room, wishing a happy Yule to Olivia García and what looked to be three generations of her family, complete with five other chihuahua familiars. The ruckus the other families made was so intense that I made it halfway before my parents saw me coming.

"Odette!" Mom leapt up, ran over, and embraced me. "I missed you so much, honey!"

"I missed you too, Mom," I said.

Dad took his turn next, enveloping me in a giant bear hug.

Then he stiffened.

I frowned. "What's wrong, Dad?" I asked, my voice falsely innocent.

Dad gulped and pulled away. Our eyes met, his hazel ones wide.

"Pea . . . We—"

"Wanted to restrict my power? Wanted to hide an integral part of me from myself? Thought I was a menace to society and needed managing? Pick one and tell your tale, because I'm all ears." I pointed to their table.

We returned to their spot. Dad could barely look at me, while Mom had gone sheet white. I sat down, tented my fingers beneath my chin, and waited.

After a strained minute of silence, Mom spoke. "We didn't want to do any of those things, honey. The truth is, we bound you—for your own safety."

I arched an eyebrow. "It seems to me that sending a spy-in-training out into the world without access to her full power is *awfully* dangerous. The exact opposite of protecting me. Unless another reason existed? The curse of my year, perhaps?"

Dad winced.

Bingo.

"In fact, honey. You're right. It has everything to do with the curse." Mom inhaled a shaky breath. "We wanted to hide you from whoever is attacking children. *Powerful* children. By making you appear weak, we were protecting you."

"And humiliating me," I muttered. "Do you know how many classes I spent frustrated? How many insults I listened to?"

Mom pressed her lips together. "I hate to admit this, but that was part of the plan too. When you expressed interest in enrolling at Spellcasters, Dad tightened the bond. We thought if you weren't good at magic, that you'd—"

My eyes widened. "Give up on my dream!" I shot up

from my chair. "Why would you want me to fail? And what about putting me in danger during the trials?"

"Pea, we made sure that if you truly needed your power, you could access it. Now, please, sit down," Dad pleaded, but I refused.

"You always said I could be whatever I wanted to be, but then you manipulated my power behind my back to ensure that I wasn't prepared. Why?"

"We didn't want anyone to come after you," Dad said. "If you appeared powerless, why would they?"

"Is that why you quit espionage? So you'd draw less attention to the family?" They shot nervous glances at each other. My eyes narrowed, and I sat, intent on getting answers. "What else aren't you telling me?"

Dad's jaw worked from side to side, and then he lifted his hand and waved it in the air. Although I couldn't see his power because he'd made it colorless, I felt it swirl around me like a protective cocoon.

"What don't you want others to hear?" I asked

My parents leaned closer to me, and after a tense moment, Mom spoke. "We knew the black witch who cast the curse. She acted as my midwife."

I gasped. "You hired a black witch to deliver me?!"

Mom shook her head. "No. Not really. I've gotten used to calling her a black witch because in witching circles that's expected, but Desdemona was anything but dark. She was an old woman who kept to herself. She used to deliver babies long ago and had stopped about a decade prior. Desdemona delivered your father and acted as the family healer for years, so when he approached her to deliver you, she agreed. Her favor to our family might have been her downfall." Tears pricked in Mom's eyes, and she wiped them away. "Desdemona wouldn't hurt a fly, and certainly not children. She actually came to our house the morning before the curse became public knowledge. We weren't around."

"Why would she stop by the house?"

"She'd been feeling off for days, but was a tough cookie and went about her business. In retrospect, we think she felt the vision building," Dad replied. I narrowed my eyes, and he expounded. "As your mother said, Desdemona was our midwife, and I'd known her all my life. I don't believe she cast a curse that day, but experienced a vision. Her first and only. First visions often take hours, if not days, to come to the surface. Once the vision was closer to being revealed, she probably figured out what was happening, but didn't understand why. She was quite old to be experiencing visions, after all. So she came to us. When we weren't there, she went to our office at the PIA to look for us, but the vision spewed out before she was even completely in the building."

"And then she just died?" I asked, my tone disbelieving.

"Yes, honey," Mom said softly. "Contrary to what you see in the movies, being a seer takes a great deal of training. If you simply have a vision—or a prophecy, like Desdemona did—it's detrimental to the body. Too much energy flowing through you wreaks havoc on your cells—just like it would if you cast a powerful curse without preparation. She was old and didn't survive."

I pressed my lips together. There was action all around us, people laughing, hugging, and talking. I experienced none of their glee, only confusion.

"So you think it isn't a curse, but a *prophecy*? Aren't those inaccurate and kinda laughed at in our society? A curse sounds more likely. Clearly, a lot of other people think so too, and have raised their kids accordingly."

"You should know, pea," Dad whispered, "that when Desdemona came by our house, she also left a note. Well, more of a scribble really. It was difficult to read, which only lends credence to our idea of a vision building—they can scramble the brain."

My heart rate accelerated. "What did it say?"

Mom and Dad shared a long, pointed look before turning their full attention on me once again.

Dad gulped. "It said something dark was searching for you."

Even though my frustration at Mom and Dad lingered, I broke bread with them at the Yule Feast. We didn't talk about the curse, or prophecy, with others around, but that didn't stop my mind from whirring with questions.

Was there more to the prophecy? How did we know it was reputable? Prophecies were notoriously flimsy, but there *had* been a few oracles throughout history who'd been spot-on with everything they'd predicted. Because of this, prophecies could never be entirely discounted.

Alex and Eva joined the table after dessert. I introduced them to my parents, and Dad and Eva launched into a rousing discussion of the latest anthropological thriller that had just hit the big screen. Mom and Alex, on the other hand, struck up a dialogue about healing. Both conversations gave me time to continue mulling over what I'd learned.

It was only when Hunter arrived, greeting my parents and swooping up Eva to dance, that I snapped out of it and noticed Mom was watching me carefully.

"We can't let them have all the fun, now can we?" Alex asked, holding out his hand.

For the first time that night, something other than anxiety and confusion ran through me. But of course, I played it cool around my parents. The last thing I wanted was Mom asking for intimate details about Alex and me. How embarrassing.

Despite my nonchalance, I felt my parents' eyes following me as Alex and I twirled around the dance floor. Once a slow song came on, my parents joined us. At one point, I caught Mom's eye, and she winked.

I sighed. She would definitely be asking too many questions later.

"Are you having a good time? Alex asked, his hand shifting lower on my back, compelling me to press closer to him.

"I am," I said. While I intended to fill my friends in on

what my parents had told me, now wasn't the time. I wanted them to enjoy the night. "I always do with you."

A smile bloomed on Alex's face, and he dipped his lips to meet mine. And even though my parents were right there, even though just months before, I would have *died* if they saw me kissing a boy, I didn't even balk.

Instead, I let the night dissolve in his kiss.

CHAPTER THIRTY

"We had so much fun with you, honey." Mom pulled me into a tight hug.

"I had fun with you guys too," I said, meaning every word.

After the Yule Festival, I spent the next three days with my parents. We'd split the holiday break between Portland, Maine and Wandstown. As my only prior experience in Wandstown had been devoted to staging an intervention, my second trip was much more relaxed.

Plus, since Mom and Dad felt bad about keeping the prophecy a secret, they'd spoiled me rotten. I scored a cute pair of winter boots that would look amazing with my leather jacket. They also bought all the snacks I liked, and a sound system for my room. While I didn't really miss having a phone, I definitely longed for streaming music services. This system used satellites, and once I programmed it, I'd have beautiful, crisp audio. Eva would be so stoked.

"We loved meeting all your friends, pea," Dad said. "I'm glad you're fitting in here."

"Even if you didn't want me coming here?"

Dad pulled me into an embrace. "We don't want you to be miserable. Just safe."

"Actually, after meeting your friends, I feel a bit better about everything," Mom added. "They all seem capable . . . especially Alex." She winked, and I was glad that Dad didn't see it.

Although I'd done everything to avoid relationship talk, Mom had cornered me in a shop and made me spill about Alex. I'd begged her not to tell Dad; I could only take so much mortification.

"They're all great," I admitted as Dad and I broke apart. "They monopolize the top of our class rankings."

My parents shared a look that I couldn't decipher, and Mom cleared her throat. "That may not last for long, honey. Now that you're unbound, you may find your power advancing quickly."

I nodded. I had been getting better, but I was still nowhere near Hunter and Alex, or even Eva. "Well, I can't say that I wouldn't mind kicking their butts in a few magical subjects."

Dad roared with laughter. "That's my little pea!"

Mom smiled. "I'd expect nothing less from a Dane. We'd better get going, but promise me one thing?"

Oh my God, please don't say anything about using protection. I can't take that talk again.

"What's that?" I asked innocently.

"Don't go looking for trouble."

"Duh, why would I do that?"

"No reason," Mom said. "I just wanted to make sure I said it. Mom duties, you know? Stay safe, my love. See you after your summer internship—we'll plan a late birthday celebration."

With that, my parents slipped into the rental car, and I waved goodbye until they were out of sight.

"Oh my God! This sound system is legit!" Eva exclaimed as I turned the volume up one more click. "We're gonna have the party suite!"

I laughed. While I hoped what she said wasn't true because I loved my space, it made me happy that she enjoyed my present. I'd received it at the perfect time, as tonight we'd be celebrating Alex's birthday, which was the next day, and New Year's Eve.

Actually, where are the guys?

I glanced at the clock. It was 9:00 p.m., and Alex had said he'd be at our rooms by fifteen till. It wasn't like him to be late.

As if the universe had heard me, someone pounded on my door.

"Come in!" I yelled, and the guys appeared, both holding bottles of champagne.

"What!? How do you always get booze?" Eva laughed as she rushed up to Hunter, leapt, and wrapped her legs around his hips.

"I have my ways."

Eva pulled back. "Is it worth the risk, though? What would happen if you got caught?"

For the first time, I considered the scenario. Witches were way more lax about alcohol than humans. In Wandstown, academy students never got carded, but Spellcasters was strict, so her concern was valid.

Hunter shrugged. "It would be worth it. It's my first year celebrating my cousin's birthday! Plus, it's New Year's Eve!" he said, prying a smile out of Eva and taking her mouth in his.

I beamed, reveling in the ease that surrounded my friend group. The last week had been weird and tense while the Wardwell parents were around. The guys tried to make the most of it, and while neither branch of the family was talking to the other, they had gotten within a few feet of each other without screaming.

It was progress. I was glad they'd made some, but I was also happy that things were back to normal—just the four of us.

"Hey, sweets," Alex said, coming up to me and brushing a wayward chocolate brown tress behind my ear. I shivered. "Hope you don't mind. Hunter thought a celebration was in order. You know, a birthday, Yule, New

Year's, and most of all, no one in our families killed each other."

I laughed. "We all deserve to let loose."

"Hell yeah, we do," Eva said, jumping off Hunter and ripping the foil off the bottle of bubbly. "Honestly, if my parents had to stay one more day, I'd have tramped into the forest and searched for a faerie hole to jump through."

Everyone laughed, and in no time at all, bubbly filled our glasses, and we were kicking up our feet.

"Man, I could get used to this." Hunter leaned back in my desk chair, his hands behind his head. "A whole week without classes does the body good."

It was true. Even if time with my parents had been stressful at first, I'd needed the rest. I was still acclimating to the intensity of my changing magic, which seemed like it flowed through my body differently day by day. In fact, it only acted normal when Alex was around. I put it down to him being so damn hot that I couldn't focus on anything else.

"It was an excellent reprieve," Alex agreed, his voice rumbling through me so pleasurably that even though I sat on his lap, I couldn't help but lean into him. "But I'm ready for classes to start." He kissed my neck. "I want to see how your powers have changed."

"Me too," I admitted.

The room fell into a hushed silence, and I sucked in a breath. The time had come.

I cleared my throat. "I want to tell you guys something else. About why my parents spellbound me."

"Didn't they do it so you'd leave Spellcasters and not be affected by the curse?" Eva sat up straighter. She'd asked about my parent's reasons for spellbinding me right after Yule. While I planned on telling her everything eventually, that night I'd held back the bit about the prophecy. I needed time to mull it over for myself before sharing it with friends.

"Yes," I pressed my lips together. "But they said something else too. They believe the curse of our class is really a prophecy."

"A prophecy!" Hunter leaned forward, and champagne sloshed out of his glass. "Spill, Odie."

The story of Desdemona flowed from me, and after I finished, my friends stared at me, eyebrows furrowed and mouths gaping.

Eva snapped out of it first. "But if the prophecy is about you, which the note would indicate, why did so many others die? I don't know guys, it seems more like a curse placed on a group to me."

"Actually," Alex drew the word out. "A prophecy makes a good deal of sense. A curse can affect many, yes, but it can also be broken by the right witch. Odette's parents were strong enough, and yet they didn't break it. Neither have countless others who have tried. No one has, as indicated by the fact that kids our age keep dying mysteriously. Doesn't anyone find that strange?"

When we didn't comment, he continued. "Lauren and Joseph were at the top of their game when Lauren retired. Everyone thought she just went on maternity leave, but she never came back. Not even for temporary jobs, which the PIA would have provided for her because of her status. Joseph kept at it for about a year more before he quit. If it was a curse, and they just had a kid, wouldn't one of them at least *try* to break it? Instead, they shed their witching community identities, and took on normal human jobs."

"What my parents do for a living is *hardly* normal."

"More normal than paranormal espionage," Alex countered. "Or demon bounty hunting, diplomatic liaisons for magicals, or even working for the government in a safer position, all of which they were qualified to do."

"It was a deliberate choice," I agreed. "They wanted to distance themselves from the witching community so people would forget about them—and me. They weren't just protecting me by binding my magic, they were hiding me from *everything* having to do with the magical community."

"I agree." Alex's lips pressed together. "I think that whoever is murdering our peers doesn't know exactly who or what they're looking for—just like we don't. But once they make themselves known to their targets, they can't just walk away, so they eliminate those who have seen them. They kill. So the smart thing to do would be to figure out what the prophecy has to do with you."

CHAPTER THIRTY-ONE

Blood thrummed through my veins, and I rubbed my arms, trying to fend off the February chill, as my class wound its way through the corridors of Spellcasters to where the Imbolc challenge would take place.

Unlike the Samhain Trial, which had garnered much pomp, and necessitated preparation beforehand, Spell-casters had told us nothing about Imbolc. I'd overheard Diana telling Phoebe that even if she wanted to inform others about the challenge, she couldn't. Her mother had erased her memory of the day every single year. Now *that* was a rule-following mother.

"What do you think it's gonna be?" I asked, grasping Alex's hand and squeezing it tight.

"No idea. We've already battled demons. If I had to guess, I would say that the Beltane Trial will probably be similar to Samhain's because it's the final trial. Plus, on the wheel of the year, it makes sense to have mirroring tests. Following that logic, the Imbolc Challenge will be different." His lips pushed to the side. "Would they send us to another realm?"

Another realm? Ice flew through my veins. The only other realms that witches could enter were Hell and Faerie. Neither of which I wanted to visit.

"No way," I said. "That's way too advanced. There aren't many known cases of witches journeying to either Hell or Faerie and surviving. Unless they go to reproduce, those trips don't usually end well for witches."

Alex looked impressed. "Where did you learn that?"

"I did some research before school started."

"What? Then why didn't you know how to get into your room?"

"I only said I didn't read the orientation paperwork." I gave him a playful shove. "You're the one who decided that meant I didn't do any research at all."

His lips turned down. "I was a fool. If only I'd pushed past my prejudices sooner, I wouldn't have wasted so much time not knowing you—or how amazing you are."

My cheeks warmed as I beamed at him. Our relationship had changed so much from the day we met. Alex really believed in me, and it warmed my heart.

At the head of the column, Professor Umbra stopped before a set of brass double doors that I had never seen. We were close to the wing where the professors lived, an area I avoided.

"Behind these doors lies your next challenge," Professor Umbra flung her arms wide and beamed. "Be advised that some of you will fail."

A few murmurings arose from the crowd, and defiant glares flashed up at our professor. I, too, felt annoyed. We'd all completed the Samhain Trial. What made her so sure that we'd fail this?

"It's not that you're unworthy." The professor smiled as if to soften the blow. "It's the facts. This challenge is very . . . specific. Some people succeed right away, while others will take a lifetime."

I gaped. A lifetime? *What the hell could we be doing?*

But instead of answering the questions plastered over all our faces, Professor Umbra stuck the key in the lock and opened the door.

A whoosh of air left me as I entered the room. Everywhere I looked, there were weapons, jewelry, and even a wall of wands that had gone out of fashion centuries ago.

"These," Professor Umbra gestured to the surrounding items, "are totems. Items imbued with magic. Many consider them to be magical amplifiers. Some say totems are analogous to familiars, and to an extent, I have to agree. Professionals have tested each totem in this room, and every single one revealed sentience to some degree. The primary difference between totems and familiars is that familiars bond to only one witch or wizard, whereas totems can have many partners."

"Partners?" Efraim spoke up, his eyebrows knitted together in confusion. "But they're things."

"Did I stutter when I said they were sentient?"

A couple students snickered, and Efraim's face pinked.

"Yes, they are items, but totems have acted on their own —they've even saved the life of the witch they bonded with when the witch wasn't strong enough. It's because of this that when you pick up a totem, you must be very honest with yourself. Claiming a totem that does not belong to you could end in disaster for the person who was meant to have it—and the witch or wizard who took the totem against its will.

"That being said, go forth and see if you bond with a totem. If you do not, have no fear. Yours will still be out in the world, waiting. Spellcasters graduates are constantly returning to campus to see if their totem has cropped up. You will fail this trial only if you take a totem against its will." The professor arched her eyebrows. "And believe me, we will know if you choose an improper totem."

"But how do *we* figure it out?" Alex asked.

"It is different for everyone," Professor Umbra said. "However, those who have discovered their true totem have all agreed that a profound sense of . . . rightness . . . overcame them when they found it." She shrugged.

"Duhhhh, bae," I teased, and Alex rolled his eyes.

"Proceed as you wish."

Professor Umbra ushered us forward, and the group surged toward the items.

Alex and I broke apart. He gravitated toward the swords, whereas I went straight for the wands. Even if they were considered old-fashioned, I couldn't help myself. I *really* wanted a wand as a totem. My fingers found a light wood one first and trailed the length of its twisted grain embedded with emeralds, my birthstone. It was so beautiful that it made me want to cry, but there was absolutely no spark or a sensation of "rightness" as Umbra had said.

Dejectedly, I set it down and moved on.

The next one was carved from dark wood and was almost as pretty as the first, with its elaborate, curved handle. But again there was no epiphany, so I set it down.

I moved on to a wand with an identifying card beneath it, and when I read the card, my jaw slackened.

I'm looking at freaking Merlin's wand? Oh, please, please, please, let this be my totem.

Equal parts nervous and excited, I grazed the wood with my fingertips, but once again, nothing sparked inside me.

I let out a huff.

I supposed it wasn't surprising that Merlin's wand wasn't mine. Something of that caliber should go to a witch like Alex or Diana, but still, what a bummer.

Continuing on, I picked up each wand one by one, held it for a second, and set it back down when no sense of "rightness" overcame me. After I'd held every wand on the table and felt nothing, profound dejection settled in. I needed to pause and collect myself, so I scanned the room to see if anyone else had lucked out.

It didn't seem like that was the case. Eva had also gone

straight for a table of wands, and was frowning down at them and muttering beneath her breath. Alex and Hunter were still at the wall of weapons, along with every other guy in our class.

I rolled my eyes. How typical that all the dudes would want a weapon. Unfortunately, none of them had bonded with a totem yet.

As if to emphasize that fact, Efraim threw up his hands, whirled away from the weapons, and strode up to my table, his lips pursed with annoyance.

"No luck?" I asked.

"Zero," he said, shaking his head. "One actually burned me." Efraim raised his hand, which was blistering and red.

I cringed. "That sucks. I didn't have any luck either, but maybe this table will be better for you. I need to move onto something else." I turned and began making my way to the next table of wands.

"No way!" Efraim cried.

I froze before whipping back around. There Efraim stood, in the same place that I'd just been, with Merlin's wand held aloft.

And the damn thing was singing.

"Excellent, Efraim!" Professor Umbra cheered. "Efraim is the first initiate to bond with his totem. And quite a sensational one it is, too."

"Heck yeah! It cured my hand!" Efraim said excitedly, looking from his wand to his once-blistered hand in amazement.

"Very good, indeed! I've been waiting years to see who claimed that piece of magical history." Professor Umbra gave Efraim a pleased nod and turned her attention to the rest of the room. "As for the rest of you, let that be a lesson that your totem will probably not be an item you are initially drawn to. They will more likely be something that you need."

Something I need? I tilted my head. Honestly, I knew I didn't need any of the stuff in this room. I'd grown up with plenty, and if I requested it, my parents would buy me whatever I wanted. It was a charmed life that made claiming that I "needed" any material item difficult. Still, Professor Umbra knew better than me, where totems were concerned, so I pivoted away from the second table of wands that I was about to peruse and scanned the room.

My next inclination would be weapons. We were spies-in-training, so weapons seemed useful, and I was attracted to two daggers with pearl inlaid handles.

Which meant I should probably look elsewhere.

Keeping that in mind, I ambled over to the least crowded jewelry table.

"If only that one would have chosen me," Amethyst said when I stopped at her side. "Then life would have made sense."

I barked out a laugh as I took in the piece she pointed to. It was a necklace with a massive, silver-dollar-sized hunk of amethyst as the centerpiece.

"Be glad it didn't," I said. "A show-stopper like that

wouldn't go unnoticed in many settings. You'd have to be super creative with your outfits."

Amethyst let out a sigh filled with longing. "It would have been worth it. I guess I'll go try the wands next." She wandered off.

Someone came up behind me and wrapped their arms around my waist.

"Any luck?" Alex asked, his touch sending a shiver up my spine.

"Not with the wands," I admitted, kissing his cheek. "I haven't picked any of these up yet. I'm trying to be more discerning. I don't need a necklace slicing my finger off, or something crazy like that."

Alex snorted as he let me go to stand at my side. "The sword only attacked Efraim because he was begging it to choose him. You're not that dim."

I beamed at him. "What do you say we try choosing totems for each other? Clearly our first opinions weren't very trustworthy anyway. And we seem to know what the other likes and needs in some aspects," I suggested, eyebrows wagging.

Alex stepped closer and dipped his lips to meet mine. Our bodies pressed together as our kiss deepened. Tingles rushed through me, as they did every time we kissed. How in the world had we been able to deny this chemistry for months?

"Ugh, get a room," someone mumbled, and we broke apart laughing.

"I'm game," Alex said. "I had no luck with weapons.

Maybe I'm more in the market for a beautiful necklace?" He pointed to the amethyst honker.

"Talk about an awkward totem-and-wizard combo."

Alex chuckled, and together, we gave the display our full attention.

My gaze traveled over the trinkets and baubles. There was quite an array, ranging from elaborate, costume-style pieces, to rings that appeared to have been crafted by a very amateur smith. I didn't relish the thought of walking around with a poorly made ring. It would limit my fashion choices drastically.

Shaking my head, I focused on what to choose for Alex. While he was always well dressed, he was also generally very classic. He preferred jeans or tailored trousers and a button-down shirt. Depending on the shirt, cufflinks would do nicely, whereas something like the necklace with ruby red salamanders would not compliment his tastes.

Of course, the salamander necklace might *actually* be his totem, but if it was, I wouldn't be the one springing it on him.

I gravitated toward a simple, sterling silver band. The label said it belonged to a wizard from Basque country who'd been renowned for his fairness and skill in healing. Alex would like that.

"Try this one," I said, and then rattled off what the label specified.

Alex's grin grew with each word, but when he placed the ring on his pointer finger, I could tell that it wasn't a match. When Efraim had found his wand, he'd been ecstatic.

"That's not it. But perhaps I found one for you." He picked up a bracelet dotted with emeralds and diamonds.

"Beautiful," I murmured and extended my wrist. As soon as the metal touched my skin, I knew it wouldn't do.

"But not for me." I admired the bracelet once more before setting it down.

I chose one of the pounded metal rings, and Alex slipped it on. He once again shook his head.

His next choice for me was also a ring. This one made of yellow gold and bearing an amethyst and sapphire. As beautiful as it was, I couldn't claim it was mine.

"I can't help but think we're doing this all wrong," I said with a frustrated sigh.

While we'd been choosing for each other, three of our other classmates, Olivia, Kira, and Joseph, had discovered their totems.

"I agree." Alex frowned down at the table. "Although, I get a more positive vibe about this table. At the wall of swords, I felt nothing. What about you?"

I focused inward and found that he was right. I hadn't noticed the welcoming sensation before, probably because being around Alex always made my insides fuzzy.

"You're right. I think I'm meant to be here, too."

I cocked my head and took in the table once more, trying to see all the pieces at once, rather than studying them one at a time. Then I had an idea.

"I think I need to choose more with my heart, rather

than my eyes. I'm gonna close them and wave my hand over the table."

Alex shrugged. "Hell, it can't hurt. Not like we were having any luck before."

I grinned and took his hand.

"Even better," he murmured.

"On three?"

"On three."

I counted down and extended my hand over the table, swiping from right, inward. I moved deliberately, not wanting to miss any telling sensations. At one point, I thought I felt something was off, and stopped. Dropping my hands, I fingered the piece that I recognized as the salamander necklace. Thankfully, no sense of rightness overcame me, and I released the jewelry.

Soon we'd both reached the middle, and our hands collided.

"I think closing my eyes helped," Alex said. "It was more intuitive. Want to switch sides?"

I nodded before remembering that he couldn't see me. "Yes. I'm keeping my eyes closed to stay in the zone."

We shuffled around each other, and somewhere in the room, I heard a few more shouts of glee. I was almost positive that one of the exclamations had been from Hunter.

Once we were in position again, Alex and I began swiping the opposite way.

My palm had covered about half of the table when I sensed it. Heat radiated from the center of my palm out to every fingertip. I released a loud gasp and trying to remain calm, lowering my hand toward the warmth.

As soon as I cupped the full weight of the jewelry in my palm, my heartbeat kicked up, and a warm cocoon smothered me, making me feel nearly euphoric.

"Odie, open your eyes," Alex whispered.

Savoring the sensation, my eyelids fluttered open. The necklace in my hand was stunning beyond belief. It had a moonstone as its centerpiece, and I watched, amazed as the gem changed colors right before my eyes. It went from pink to purple to gold.

"Oh my God, it's beautiful," I whispered. Then, realizing that Alex still hadn't found his totem, I turned to him. "Keep going. You were drawn to this table too. I bet yours is here."

Alex gave me a smile, as if he no longer believed what he'd said earlier.

"Close your eyes again. It's like Professor Umbra said, you'll know it when you feel it."

He started where he left off, his hands trembling. I grasped the other one and sent him mantras for encouragement. He was in the middle, where our hands had collided the first time, when he stopped and sucked in a breath.

"Grab it," I encouraged.

Alex complied, his hand dropping languidly to the table and curling around a simple gold ring, decorated with two garnets surrounding a moonstone.

The moment his hand was wrapped around the ring, my necklace began to tremble, and a beam of light shot from the pendant to the moonstone on Alex's ring. And then, just as quickly as the connection had ignited, it vanished.

I blinked. "Did you see that?"

Alex nodded, his eyes as wide as saucers. "Yeah. But what does it mean?"

CHAPTER THIRTY-TWO

"You will not freaking believe what just happened!" Eva burst into my room, out of breath and her hair all over the place.

"Umm, you lost your hairbrush? Girl, you are a hot mess," I teased.

Eva jumped on the bed, where I was writing a paper on magical heroes and feminism, and swatted my shoulder. "No! I ran all the way here to tell you the most exciting news of the year, and this is the thanks I get?"

I laughed. "Okay, I'm sorry! *Please,* most kind and amazing friend ever, tell me your exciting news."

Eva sucked in a breath and slammed her hands against her thighs. "We've been invited to a party!"

I cocked my head. "Okay . . ."

The initiates' dorm had put on a couple parties, but considering our small class size and that half of my peers were a bunch of sticks-in-the-mud, the parties were never that great. Except for that one time when Olivia García and Kira Johnston had initiated a dance-off. I'd lost, but seeing Olivia and José perform a traditional Jarabe Tapatío, and Kira jam her way to the top in a jaw-dropping hip-hop dance had been memorable.

Still, I had more fun just hanging out with Alex, Hunter, and Eva in our rooms.

"In the third-years' dorm!" Eva squealed and threw up her hands.

My eyes bulged. "What? Are you serious?!"

This was as unbelievable as seeing a dragon in the wild . . . which I'd learned was possible, but extremely difficult. The third-years were *super* cliquey. Sometimes they let a couple second-years hang with them, but they'd ignored our entire class since we arrived.

"Yup! The second-years are coming too! I guess it's some stupid tradition for the upperclassmen to spurn the newbies until after the Imbolc Challenge. They don't want to waste their time with anyone who's cast out after the first two tests. It kinda makes sense, if you think about it. They have so little time at Spellcasters, there's not much to spare on people who they may not see again."

In the framework of a spy's life, she was right. Operatives almost never got to reveal their true selves to those in their daily lives. Because of this, real, honest relationships were coveted. If the upperclassmen were going to hang with us, they wanted to make sure we could pass a couple tests and stick around first. Time and relationships were precious.

"When is it?"

"Now! Come on girl, let's get ready! I already told the guys, and they're gonna pick us up in thirty." She rushed to the bathroom before stopping in her tracks. "Oh, and we're supposed to bring our totems if we bonded with one. The upperclassmen want to see what we got."

I chewed my lip. I didn't want to do that. Even though my totem was gorgeous, I didn't like carrying it around. Two weeks had passed since Imbolc, and I still didn't understand why my totem had reacted to Alex's the way it did. Our ignorance bugged me—and him—and because of it, we often left the magical amplifiers in our rooms.

"Do we have to?"

"Yup. It's the entrance fee," Eva yelled, already rifling through her makeup. "And don't you dare say it's not worth it. They'll have theirs too. It's kinda like a show-and-tell. Think about it, Odie. We can see if our totems are related to a second or third-years'. That could be beneficial."

That was true. One of these older kids could be our mentor in the field during our first year of real espionage. Creating a tight bond in advance could help.

"Okay," I agreed. "Are you wearing a cocktail dress?"

Eva's head popped back into my room, a look of incredulity on her face. "Are you from Mars? They're throwing a college party, not a ball! Put on some tight jeans and a cute top, and you're done!"

"You got it, chica!" I heaved myself off my bed, already forgetting about my homework.

Once we were ready, Eva led the way, plowing down the hallway from the first-years' tower all the way to the opposite end of the academy, and then down a stairwell that I hadn't even known existed.

"How the hell do you know where you're going?" I asked.

"When my parents dropped me off, they made sure I took the most thorough tour *ever* to really sell me on Spellcasters. They even insisted that I see where the staff and professors live, like I'd be waltzing through there for tea or something." She rolled her eyes.

We reached the bottom of the stairwell, and I tilted my head as Eva pressed open a door that led to the outside. "The third-years don't have a tower like us?"

"No, silly," Eva said. "There are four towers. We have one, the second-years have another, the professors that live in the academy have another, and the rest of the staff has the final tower. Third-years get the privilege of having their dormitories off-site from the main building."

In the middle of winter, I didn't see how having a dorm outside the main building was a privilege. It was flipping freezing.

I rubbed my hands against my arms and Alex pulled me close.

"They probably cast an enchantment over themselves to keep warm," he said, as if he could read my mind.

Alex, Hunter, and I followed as Eva wound us down a well-trod path, through woodland. We'd seen nothing but dense trees for about five minutes, and I was just beginning to wonder if she'd accidentally veered too deep into the forest, when the trees cleared.

The third-year dormitory was not as spectacular as the main building of Spellcasters, but it was close.

Made of glass, with the windows on the upper floors tinted for privacy, it looked modern and ritzy. Lanterns illuminated the walk up to the building, their light reflecting off the glass. There was a massive porch where a few students lounged on outdoor furniture. A keg sat off to the side, and I grinned. We might be at an elite spy school, but some things about Spellcasters were just like how I envisioned they'd be at a normal American college.

"Hey, Firsties! What are you waiting for? Get your green asses up here!" A boy who I'd seen once or twice waved us toward the building, and we jogged up the path.

"Where are your totems?" The boy arched an eyebrow.

I let go of Alex's hand and unzipped my jacket. The chilly winter air grazed the skin of my chest, exposed by the plunging neckline of my snug, cashmere sweater. My necklace glittered there, the moonstone a ruby color that matched my sweater.

I didn't know how the center changed color or why, but every time I put it on, it tended to morph into whatever color I needed to complement my outfit. Or at least, it did when Alex wasn't around. Had I been touching Alex when I showed my totem to the third-year, the moonstone would have shifted through a kaleidoscope of colors. Both Alex and I weren't comfortable letting others know that our totems reacted to each other's quite yet—

we hadn't even told Eva or Hunter. It just felt too . . . private.

The boy nodded and allowed me to pass.

Eva pulled her hand out of her pocket and revealed a bracelet, and Hunter unsheathed the dagger he wore on his hip. Alex went last, and I made sure to keep a safe distance when he showed his ring. Nothing happened, and I breathed a sigh of relief.

"Here's a beer." The guy gestured back to a girl holding out two red cups, while another student filled two more. "Welcome to the King's Castle."

I barely held back my snigger. *'The King's Castle'? Damn, these third-years are cocky.*

We entered the fancy dormitory, and I blinked, taking in the chaos in front of us. I was sure that on any normal day, the King's Castle was neat and sophisticated, with its high-end finishes, sleek furniture, and modern design palette. Tonight, however, it looked like a well-to-do frat house.

Beer cans were everywhere, and a few bottles of alcohol sat open on the table in the center of the living space. From the entry foyer, we could see the main living area, an open kitchen, and even a gaming area with pool and foosball tables.

"Pool!" Hunter's eyes lit up. "I'm about to show these upperclassmen what's up. Anyone wanna join? Sugar?"

Eva shook her head and kissed Hunter on the cheek. "You have fun. I want to look around first."

Alex and I also declined, which didn't seem to bother

Hunter at all. He rushed off like a kid running after the ice cream truck.

"Odette! Eva!" A shrill voice pierced through the general chatter and raucous laughter.

I followed it to find that Mina had already arrived and was clearly drunk.

"This is a great party, isn't it?" She stumbled as she took a step toward us, and saved herself by grabbing onto someone's shoulder.

"It looks super fun, Mina," Eva said when our classmate had gotten close enough to speak at a normal volume. "How long have you been here?"

Mina shrugged, the gesture exaggerated. "One hour. Maybe two. I don't know, I got here when the sun was still up."

Considering that we were in the middle of winter, I guessed that Mina had already been here for four hours. No wonder she was so drunk.

"Did you come with anyone?" I asked, curious if I should keep an eye out for her.

"Oh yeah, Efraim, Kira, Thor, and I rolled up together. We were kinda nervous about the party, but everything has been great, and we split up. I don't know where they are."

She squinted and shielded her eyes with her hand, as if she were outside in the sun rather than in a dimly lit room. "Ah! There's Efraim! The ladies have loved him all night." Mina gestured to the left, and I followed her finger to find that what she said was, surprisingly, true.

The short, blond boy who had bonded with Merlin's

wand swung his totem around wildly, as a circle of older girls watched in wonder. I'd never pictured Efraim as a ladies' man, but clearly I'd been wrong.

"They're really impressed with his wand." Mina's eyes opened wide, and she arched her eyebrows high. "*If* you know what I mean."

"I have no idea what you mean," Eva deadpanned, and Mina's face fell.

"Don't be a jerk," I admonished, trying not to laugh. "She's too drunk for sarcasm." I turned to Alex. "Would you mind making sure Mina gets some water? I need to run to the bathroom real quick."

Alex nodded and gave me a peck on the cheek.

"I'll come with you," Eva said. "I want to make sure I still look hot."

"What does that matter?" I asked, an eyebrow arched. "You're with Hunter, and he's already head over heels for you."

"That doesn't mean I don't want to look fabulous for everyone else. Odie, you're Lauren and Joseph Dane's daughter. You have higher status than a lot of us in the espionage world. You don't have to try as hard. But some of us, like myself, have to be on point all the time."

I blinked. At the beginning of the year, it had seemed rather obvious that being a Dane meant something at Spellcasters. But since then, I'd felt like it didn't matter as much. Particularly when my magic had sucked, I'd felt like I needed to try just as hard as everyone else.

But then again, if I hadn't been a Dane, would I still be here?

We followed signs to the restroom down a long hall, past the library, what looked to be a study room, and through a secondary living area with a built-in theater.

"The third-years live in the lap of luxury," I muttered.

Eva nodded. "I think it's to prepare them for the real world. They expect spies to get into high-profile places and situations and act like they belong. After living in dorms for two years, you need time to acclimate to nicer surroundings."

I could sort of relate. It had been an adjustment to move from my Beverly Hills home into a small dorm, but I'd ended up loving it. A lot.

We did our business and split off, Eva to join Hunter, while I searched for Alex. I found him again, rubbing Mina's back while she sat with her head between her knees.

It was a sweet scene, except for one thing.

Diana Wake sat on the opposite side of Mina, holding our classmate's hair back and chatting animatedly with Alex.

I huffed. While Diana either avoided or sneered at me, she sought out my boyfriend whenever she got the chance. Of course, I couldn't really blame her, Alex was a stud. But that didn't mean I had to like her talking to him.

Pushing away my negative thoughts, I went to join him.

"Hey. Thanks for getting her water, Alex."

"No problem." Alex stood to kiss me and offered me his seat. "I was just about to go get more. She guzzled two cups down like a camel in an oasis. I think she really needed it. Do you want something?"

As much as I did not want him leaving me alone with Diana, it would be smart to get Mina more water. "I'm good. I'll wait with her."

Once he left, an uncomfortable silence descended over our trio, punctuated only by Mina mumbling the lyrics to the song that was playing.

"Sooo, Diana, how have . . . things been?" I took a stab at being civil.

The smile that had spread across Diana's face when Alex had been around vanished, and her blue eyes hardened as she assessed me. "Still at the top spot for our class. I'll take that as a win."

"Yes, it's very impressive," I admitted. "You always perform well."

"I do," Diana sneered. "In all aspects of my life."

This girl just can't help but get sassy with me. What the heck do I say to that?

I decided on nothing. It wasn't worth my energy.

Seconds ticked by in silence, and I suspected that Mina had fallen asleep, when suddenly, Diana spoke once again.

"He's too good for you, you know that right?"

"Excuse me?" I asked, my tone super high-pitched.

"You may be a Dane, but Alex is a *Wardwell.* Their family lineage has been the strongest in our community for centuries. And even if he's from a different branch than that playboy, Hunter—"

"Hey! Hunter is not a playboy, he—"

"Maybe not anymore. Your little friend got her hooks in him good, but that doesn't matter. Their family is renowned for serious espionage and magic. Alex needs someone who can match him. Not just waltz in and bank on having a pretty face."

"Diana," my tone dripped with exasperation. "I'm sorry that my relationship with Alex offends you, but it's none of your business. And when are you going to get over me not taking the entrance exam? I've been progressing a ton. Are you telling me that counts for nothing?"

Diana's blue eyes pierced through me. "Yes, that's exactly what I'm saying." She pursed her lips, and I could sense something else coming. "You know we kissed, right?"

I blinked, and a wide smile spread across Diana's face, making my gut sink like a rock tossed into a lake. *She'd kissed Alex? When? And why hadn't he told me?*

"Ahhh, I see he kept our tryst a secret. I wonder why?"

I scowled. Diana was loving that I was in the dark, which pissed me off. A nasty retort was on the tip of my tongue, when a blonde girl burst through the front door and threw a massive beam of magic across the room to get everyone's attention.

"Someone's dead in the forest!" the girl screamed. "Come quick!"

I shot up and ran out the door.

CHAPTER THIRTY-THREE

I exited the King's Castle to arrive in pure chaos. Everyone was running around, trying to find the corpse. Someone called out for the person who had spotted the body. It soon became clear that while others had run outside, she had stayed *inside*. Two third-year girls went back in the dorm to find her, and emerged minutes later with the trembling blonde between them, her skin pale and eyes wild.

"You said you found a body." A third-year male with a barrel chest and a shaved head stepped forward from the crowd. "Where?"

The girl pointed into the woods that separated the King's Castle from the rest of Spellcasters. "That way, just off the path, about thirty feet in. I spotted a shining light, and followed it and found—" She gulped, and one girl supporting her patted her on the back.

"Two initiates, go get Headmistress Wake," the guy with the shaved head ordered. "Everyone else, let's go find the victim."

My stomach sank. Did I want to see who had died? I already suspected they were in my year.

Unfortunately for me, Amethyst and Mina, who seemed to have sobered up extraordinarily fast, darted toward the academy before I could volunteer. I could either search or bow out, a coward's move.

Just call me Corpse-Finder Odie. I sighed and joined those tramping into the woods.

"Did you check for a pulse?" someone asked the blonde who had found the body.

"Yeah, just like Professor Medella taught us. I couldn't feel it, but his wand was glowing when I first saw him." She gulped. "I turned to get help, but then, the light went out . . ." Her rambling explanation trailed off.

My ears perked up. What did that mean?

"So he was still alive when you first saw him," a second-year guy supplied.

"He's right here!" someone called, deeper in the woods. "It's a firstie!"

I sucked in a breath and followed the voice. When I arrived at the site, I was totally on edge and as soon as I saw the body a choked sob wrenched itself up my throat.

Efraim lay on the ground, sprawled out as if he were making a snow angel. His face looked younger in death, and there was no blood, revealing that whoever had killed him had done so by magic.

"What's up with his clothes?" A girl with long, brown hair pointed at Efraim. "They're torn."

I looked closer. There were three two-inch-long rips on his shirt.

"Probably just happened during the fight for his life," someone else said.

Diana approached Efraim's body, and I scowled, recalling her proclamation that she'd kissed Alex. *Where is he anyway?* I wondered glancing into the crowd.

A few upperclassman began to murmur, pulling me back into the moment.

Diana had straightened Efraim's shirt and then pulled the cut portions aside, exposing his chest. There was a mark carved into him—a square with lines through it, and blood smeared all around his skin. I was just about to ask what it was when a second-year girl pushed her way through the crowd and gasped.

"Do you . . . recognize that, Sam?" a guy asked, his eyebrows furrowed.

The girl nodded. "I'm in a mentorship study with Professor Adyto. That's a demonic rune made by a lesser demon, as indicated by the liberal slathering of blood well past the normal confines of the cut. The demon must not have run away very fast. He took the time to brand the initiate so he could find him again. I think the demon planned on coming back and getting information from this boy."

Once they arrived, Headmistress Wake, Professor de Spina, and Professor Thrax broke up the party and herded everyone back to their dorms. The headmistress led the initiates to our tower and forbade us from leaving until classes started the next day.

Who the hell would want to go into the woods with a demon on the loose? I sat down on Eva's bed and tried to gather my thoughts, which seemed to be everywhere and nowhere all at once.

Eva shut the door to her room, and turned to face Hunter, Alex, and me. "We have to go back and check out the murder site," she announced.

I flinched. "Ummm, excuse me? The professors will be patrolling the woods. What if they catch us?"

Plus, what if the murderous demon still hadn't made its way to Hell? The third-year girl had explained that the brand on Efraim was used to locate a person. The demon must have gotten interrupted while fighting Efraim and fled, but not before branding him. Which meant the demon had expected Efraim to survive.

For the first time in my life, I wished that a demon was right.

"True, but that means they won't be near the body," Eva retorted. "No killer would just hang around the scene of the crime. The professors will have to search all the acreage around the academy."

"But why do you want to go back?" Alex asked. We'd been separated since he went to get Mina water, but in that moment I was reminded of Diana's proclamation that she'd kissed my boyfriend. A million emotions swirled inside me. I knew now wasn't the ideal time, but still the question of what the heck Diana had been talking about had nearly bubbled up my throat when Eva spoke.

"Didn't you hear that girl who found Efraim say that his wand was lit when she first spotted him?" She raised an eyebrow.

Pushing aside my personal issues I thought back to the events of the night. After a few seconds of recollections, we all nodded.

"I didn't see a wand when we found the body. Did you guys?"

I can't believe I let Eva talk me into traipsing through the woods with a killer on the loose. Goosebumps rose on my arms as I considered all the terrible things that might happen.

It was even darker outside than it had been an hour before, and to make matters worse, using magic as a light source was out of the question. The professors would spot us too easily.

Eva led the way once again, although this time, she moved more cautiously. The rest of us followed, keeping an eye out for danger.

We'd gotten about halfway to the King's Castle, when Eva shot into a crouch behind a tree. My heart leapt into my throat as I mimicked her, dropping low.

Thirty seconds later, Professor Thrax emerged a fair distance away to the right.

"Bloody demons. I catch one, I'll . . ." His mumblings quieted as he disappeared toward the school.

Right behind me, Alex placed a gentle hand on my elbow. "Let's move," he whispered.

His touch reminded me once more of what Diana had claimed and I whirled around, no longer able to hold my curiosity back. What if a demon attacked us and I died not knowing the truth? "Did you kiss Diana?" I blurted out.

"E—excuse me?" Alex stuttered, his eyes widening. "What are you talking about, Odie?"

"Diana told me that she kissed you. Is it true?" I placed my hand on my hip and vaguely heard Eva and Hunter stop trekking through the woods to wait for us.

Slowly, Alex released a breath, and then, he nodded.

My heart tore in half, and when he grabbed my hand I pulled it away. "Don't touch—"

"Wait! Stop! It's not what you're thinking!" he hissed softly. "It happened before classes started. During the testing period last May."

I tilted my head. "Okay . . . then why didn't you tell me?"

"We weren't together then. It only happened once and was so long ago. Plus, I know how you two feel about each other," Alex said, his tone measured. "Do you think I'd lie to you?"

"No," I whispered quickly because if there was one thing I was sure of, it was that Alex had always been honest with me. "I don't think you would, but I do wish you'd have told me. Clearly Diana was waiting for the right time to . . . cause trouble in paradise." I stopped and chewed at my lip for a second. "Did you like her then—at the testing?"

Alex chuckled darkly. "Not like that. I mean, I can't deny that she's attractive but honestly, it was a whim. You see, Hunter and I attended the same testing session." Alex shot a glance at our friends who were still waiting for us. "He was . . . popular with the ladies, and because we were feuding at that time, I wanted to show him up. Diana and I already knew each other and I got the sense that she liked me so . . ." he shrugged. "I let it happen."

"That's unlike you," I said.

Alex's cheeks reddened. "Yeah, but like I told you, my side of the Wardwell clan can have a temper. It was a dumb way to feel like I was showing Hunter up, but it happened."

I thought that over for a moment and then exhaled. *Thank goodness these guys made up. I can't handle stupidity like that.* "Anything else I should know regarding you two that Diana might spring on me?"

"We helped solve a crime."

What? Cryptic much?!

"I meant romantically, Alex." I tried to keep the exasperation from my tone.

He shook his head. "I swear, we only kissed once, and right after I told her I wanted to be just friends. I'm not sure if she believed me, but I really meant it."

His tone was genuine and he looked me straight in the

eye when he spoke. I believed him. Thank goodness, because now was so not the time to be getting into my boyfriend's past with Diana Wake. "In that case, let's keep moving." I gestured to where Hunter and Eva stood waiting, their eyes wide with question.

I caught Eva's gaze and gave her a look that said I'd tell her everything later. I had no doubt that Diana had known what she was doing, and while I wasn't going to give her the satisfaction of knowing she'd caused even a blip of strife in my relationship, that didn't mean Eva wouldn't help me get out my frustrations. After that, I'd forget all about it. Diana would never know that she'd ruffled my feathers, which would probably kill her.

We made it the rest of the way to the murder site without issue. I couldn't hear the other professors, which meant that they were likely deep in the woods, searching for the killer. The only evidence that something had happened at the scene of the crime were a few magical lights set up by Headmistress Wake. The tension in my shoulders loosened a bit. Those would make searching for the wand without our own light a little easier.

"Spread out," Eva, who had transitioned to an amateur sleuth in the last hour, commanded.

We did as she instructed, each of us taking a quadrant and working outward. After fifteen minutes of fruitless searching, I concluded that whoever killed Efraim had taken his wand. There was only so far the thing could fly in a skirmish, and Efraim would have to be an idiot to intentionally toss aside something that would be helpful in an attack.

"No wand," Eva said as we converged on the murder site. The greater demon scars that no healer had the skill to remove from her beautiful face glinted in the pale moonlight, making me shudder. "I wonder what that means? Do you guys think it's related to the prophecy?"

"I'm not sure about the prophecy. No one has gone after Odie, but I might have another theory," Alex whispered, stealing everyone's attention. "It's very tenuous, but during testing to get into Spellcasters, I overheard Tabitha bragging about her family line."

I arched an eyebrow, not seeing where this was going.

"It seemed that the Goodes believe they're descendants of Merlin."

My mouth fell open. "Are they serious?"

Alex shrugged. "Who knows?" He turned to Eva. "Does your family claim descent from Merlin?"

Eva snorted. "My parents might be proud as hell sometimes, but they'd never say something like that. It's too grandiose, even for them."

Alex nodded, and even though Eva had been dismissive, I understood why he'd asked her. Eva had been attacked by a greater demon, which had not been the planned portion of her Samhain Trial. That meant someone was gunning for her too. If Alex tied the events together, it might help unearth more information.

"Well, even if you weren't, Efraim bonded with Merlin's

wand. And if Tabitha's family thought they were related . . ." I shrugged. "There might be a thread there."

A twig snapped in the woods, and the hairs on my arms sprang up.

"We should get back inside," Alex said, his eyes wary.

He grabbed me by the hand, and the four of us rushed back to the academy.

CHAPTER THIRTY-FOUR

A month passed, and still no one could pinpoint Efraim's murderer or their motive. Just like Tabitha's murder, his remained unsolved.

I couldn't get either case out of my mind. Efraim's attack was the third demonic attack outside of our trials. If you added in the fae fiasco, five initiates had been attacked in less than a year.

"What's the connection? Is it me? But how?" I murmured out loud, and set my pen down.

I was supposed to be working on an essay for Faeology, but nothing stuck. No matter how many times I read the material and synthesized my hypothesis to answer the question Ms. Seeley had posed, I just couldn't put it into words. My mind was elsewhere—trying to piece together the attacks on my classmates with the prophecy, and now the new information about Merlin.

Was there a connection? Were my parents just wrong,

and it was a curse? Were all Spellcaster initiates actually the targets?

None of the pieces seemed to fit.

I wasn't the only one stumped. Alex had been in the library every free minute since Efraim's death, researching everything he could about Merlin. He was convinced that the attacks must have something to do with the enigmatic and mysterious wizard. Even after Mina, Amethyst, and Eva had all insisted that they didn't have a single personal tie to Merlin.

A knock came at my door.

"Come in," I said, already knowing who to expect, from the tempo of the knock.

Eva appeared a second later, with Hunter right behind her.

"Hey. We're heading to dinner. Want to join?"

I shook my head. "I need to finish this essay, and it's taking forever. Bring me back something, will you? Lasagna, if they have it?"

Eva nodded, and they left. I resumed trying to focus on my essay, but after a few minutes, the sound of yelling from outside caught my ear. I peeked out the window.

Diana and Thor ran about the academy lawn, practicing battle magic. As I watched, my eyes widened. Thor, as his name would suggest, was a massive guy with the makings of a true warrior.

And Diana was kicking his ass.

She's become even more aggressive. I cringed at the thought.

As the calendar on my wall reminded me every single day, we were less than two months from the Beltane Trial. The trial that would determine our rank and missions during the Grind-year, as well as prospects for summer internships. I knew I should be practicing battle magic more, but our homework load had become so great that I often found myself having to work super hard to balance the practical side of magic with the academic side of spycraft, governmental machinations, and history.

I'd set my pen to paper and began to write once more, when another knock came on my door. Throwing the pen down on the desk, I pushed my chair back and gripped the sides of my head with my hands.

"Come in," I said, annoyance clear in my voice.

Alex burst through the door. His blue eyes glinted with a wildness that I'd never seen before, and his glasses had gone crooked, probably from the sweat dripping down his forehead.

I shot out of my seat. "Alex! Are you okay?"

"What? I'm fine. I just have something to show you." He looked at the mess on my desk, which I normally kept neat. "Am I interrupting something important?"

"Don't even worry about it." I eyed the book in his hands and swept the papers aside. "Here."

I gestured for him to set the book down, which he did with the reverence that he showed every tome. Then he flipped the book open and turned straight to a marked page.

"I found something in the library. Something about Merlin."

It took everything I had to not roll my eyes. "I told you, Alex, I—"

"I know all I had was guesswork before, but this is different."

My mouth snapped shut. Alex never interrupted me; he always treated me with the utmost respect and consideration. It was that more than his tone or the frantic look in his eyes that shut me up.

"I'm all ears." I perched on the edge of my bed and folded my hands in my lap.

Alex gave me a grateful look, before continuing. "I've been reading this book for a while. There's a lot of Arthurian legend in it, and tall tales about Merlin. But today, I stumbled across something intriguing that I think might actually be true. Let me read it to you."

When I didn't respond, he continued. "'Merlin, the famed wizard of King Arthur's court, lived a long and varied life, of which there are many tales. He's said to have transformed lives and performed miracles, but like most celebrated men, he did not do so alone. Merlin had disciples, pupils—many of them nearly as powerful as he. But one, Morgan Le Fay, King Arthur's half-sister and a famed witch, was the pupil Merlin revered above all others. Morgan was young and beautiful and skilled in the magical arts. She was Merlin's protégé, and as rumor has it, his lover.'"

I listened with interest. Of course I'd heard about both

Merlin and Morgan Le Fay, although I knew little of either. I'd often stopped to gaze at their portraits in the halls of Spellcasters, especially Morgan's because she was so striking. But most of my knowledge on the pair came from a Disney cartoon that my mom loved.

Alex went on reading for at least two pages, speaking of the trials and tribulations that Morgan and Merlin had undergone together. How they had shaped the world and made it a better place. The more he read, the more enchanted I was by the tale.

Then he stopped. "Odie, can you come here?"

"Is that it?" I was filled with sadness that the story was over.

"There's a lot more," Alex said. "You can read it later, but I want you to see something important first."

I hopped off the bed and stood by my boyfriend. "Okay, show me."

Alex turned the page, and an image illuminated with colored ink was revealed. It was of a man and a woman, working magic together, the vortexes of energy swirling between them. The caption identified those people as Merlin and Morgan.

"Do you see anything spectacular about this image?" Alex asked.

My eyebrows knit together. Anything spectacular? To me, the image *defined* spectacular. Though the artist rendered it in common paper and ink, it was almost like looking at a photograph.

"What do you mean?"

Alex's finger trailed over the page to land on Morgan Le Fay. He tapped her neckline, and I inhaled sharply.

"Is that my necklace?"

Alex nodded. "And look at Merlin."

My eyes snapped left, and I felt faint. While Morgan wore my totem, Merlin, with his hand outstretched and magic pouring from it, wore an item of jewelry too. A ring with a multicolored gem in the middle surrounded by two red stones, the same ring that Alex had bonded with at Imbolc.

Our totems were from Merlin and Morgan Le Fay.

CHAPTER THIRTY-FIVE

"Oh my God, I *sooooo* needed this workshop," Eva declared as she filled a rocks glass with bourbon, sugar, bitters, and ice.

"You and me both," I agreed, placing a strainer over my own shaker and pouring out a pineapple juice and vodka concoction that I was experimenting with.

Since learning who my totem belonged to, Alex and I had either been studying, practicing magic to prepare for the upcoming Beltane Trial, or researching Morgan and Merlin. I was holding out hope that if we found information that related our totems to Merlin and Morgan—or M&M, as I now thought of them—it might give us a lead on the prophecy. So far, we'd had zero luck on both fronts. Just the thought made my heart race, so I took a sip of my martini.

I make a mean pineapple martini!

"You ladies know that the point of this workshop isn't to

get drunk, right?" Alex teased, joining our table after an extensive search for a grapefruit.

I shot him a look filled with mock shock. "Who on Earth would put a room full of underage college kids in a cocktail-making workshop and expect them not to drink? Live a little, Alexander Wardwell!"

Alex snorted and shook his head, but it was clear I wasn't the only one who thought this way. This was one of the more fun workshops we'd had all year, and many of the first-years were taking advantage of it. As were the upperclassmen, who walked by and mimed for my classmates to bring them a drink.

Whatever the rules of the bartending workshop were, I was damning them. I'd had a hell of a week, and while I preferred champagne, I was making sure my drinks had enough juice in them so that I'd find them palatable.

"How strong do you think Professor Medella will want drinks to be?" I asked, wondering if I might have made my cocktail too fruity. "And does anyone else think it's crazy that the academy's healing professor is in charge of this workshop? Or that this is our first experience with him, and he's probably gonna end up wasted?" The ancient professor was already walking a little oddly after only five "samples".

"Hey, yours is over half juice. That's vitamin C. A healer would appreciate that," Eva reasoned, and snuck a not-so-tiny sip of her Old Fashioned.

"I've heard he prefers his drink on the stronger side," Hunter grinned, clearly in agreement with the academy's self-proclaimed mixology master. "The better to hide potions and poison in."

"Or remedies." Professor Medella, the extremely tall and gray-haired professor of Healing, sidled up to us. "Which, mind you, all react to alcohol differently. But you'll learn more about that during your infamous Grind-year. Has anyone perfected their signature cocktail? While it's smart to have a wide range of recipes at your disposal, every intelligencer *must* have a signature drink."

I held a martini glass out for the professor. "Here's my drink."

Professor Medella took it and sipped. After he'd had about half of it, he set the glass down. "That, Miss Dane, is a well-rounded beverage. Few people can make such a versatile pineapple martini. No doubt you inherited your skills from your mother. If I recall, your father relied on 'a stiff scotch' as his signature drink."

I laughed. "Thank you. And Dad still isn't much of a mixologist, Professor Medella. As for my drink, are there any potions or poisons it wouldn't work well with?"

Since we weren't enrolled in healing yet, I knew very little about remedies, but I was skilled in our Herbalism, Potions, and Poisons class. More so with poisons, which Alex always liked to point out was creepy, but whatever.

The professor's head nodded. "I would *never* pair pineapple with belladonna, especially if you were trying to subdue other magicals. And any nettle-based potion would not leave a pleasant taste in one's mouth."

I nodded. "Okay, no nettle or belladonna with my pineapple. I'll make a note of that."

Professor Medella moved on to my friends' drinks, declaring them also good, and Hunter's spectacular. After a few more tries at variants of our signature drink, plus a few other concoctions to build our repertoire of cocktails that Professor Medella believed every good spy should know, we were all feeling damn tipsy.

"Wowza." Eva exited the class with one arm wrapped around Hunter. "I wish all our workshops were like that one! I mean, this has got to be the coolest college ever!" She stopped and tilted her head. "Do you think the Feds know? Oh my God, I'm so glad we don't have Physical Conditioning today. There's no way I could run right now."

Alex and I burst out laughing, and he wrapped his arm around my waist.

"I don't think they care, sugar." Hunter kissed a rambling Eva on the top of her head endearingly. "If us making a good drink is gonna get the bad guys, they're probably all for it."

"Touché!" Eva exclaimed.

We strolled through the halls at a leisurely pace, not having any plans except for studying—which probably would not be as productive as I'd hoped, considering my current state.

Maybe tonight is just a chill night. I can't remember the last time I had one of those.

We were halfway up the stairs, when fast footsteps sounded behind us. I turned and saw Olivia sprinting our way, her face lined with terror, and her yappy familiar following close behind.

"Help! Thor just fell over and he's puking!"

I nearly fell down the stairs. "Wait? What? From the booze?"

Olivia placed her hands on her knees and took a moment to catch her breath. "I'm not sure! I teased him about that, but he was adamant that it wasn't from the alcohol. Then he started vomiting—*super* violently."

"Why didn't you get Professor Medella?" Alex asked.

"I tried!" Olivia wailed. "He'd already locked up the classroom and left. I was just running to find him when I heard you guys. You've taken healing seminars, right?" Her eyes locked with Alex's, shining with hope.

Alex bit his lip. "Err, yeah, but I—"

"Come on, then!" Olivia grabbed his hand and took off down the stairs.

When we reached Thor, my blood went cold. He laid face-up on the floor, his mouth filled with vomit.

"Help me turn him over!" Alex yelled, and Hunter rushed forward to comply.

A moment later, I knelt at Thor's side and whacked his back hard to force the vomit out. Then I saw it. Thor's eyes were wide open, and his pupils were like massive marbles in his light blue eyes.

I sat back on my heels. "He's gone, you guys. Check out his eyes."

No one listened to me. They were all running about,

shouting instructions. Eva was already halfway down the hall, searching for Professor Medella.

"Listen to me, dammit!"

Alex, Hunter, and Olivia all froze, their eyes wide.

"Look at his pupils."

Everyone's gazes fell upon Thor.

Alex connected the dots first. "Belladonna," he whispered. "It had to have been a strong dose to work on such a big guy so fast. Olivia, do you know what Thor's signature drink was?"

"A margarita," she supplied, looking confused.

"It couldn't be that. It's not floral enough to hide belladonna," Alex said. "Were you his partner? What was your cocktail? Did he drink it?"

"Rum and lilac syrup. And yeah, he drank it all. I don't like booze, but my mom likes that cocktail, so I've seen it made plenty of times."

Lilac. A floral taste, just like belladonna.

"We need to test the syrup you used," Alex said and stood.

"Wait . . . are you saying *I* did this? I *killed* him?" Olivia's face fell.

"*You* didn't kill him, Olivia," I assured her. "But we think someone planted a poison in place of your syrup. Probably hoping one of us would drink it. It was a sloppy attempt, but effective."

My stomach sank as I spoke, and one question ran through my mind.

Had I been the target?

CHAPTER THIRTY-SIX

Ostara was upon us. Although I did not usually adhere to the normal witching holidays, this year was different. Ostara, when daylight equaled the dark, the spring equinox, was symbolic of the dance between the living and the dead. And now, more than ever, I felt the need to honor its symbolism.

The ceremony involved a candle being brought into a natural area in the middle of the night. It was representative of our kind beating back the evil trying to encroach on our world.

I walked out to the lake with Alex on one side and Eva on the other. Alex's solid, strong presence lifted me up. Although I still felt the effects of Thor's death, which had been just days earlier, it only intensified the sensation that being here, alive, was so, so special.

The entire student body of Spellcasters, along with the professors and staff, fell into line around the edges of the lake. Cold and snow clung to Maine, even in early Spring, but someone had shoveled walkways for us to make the ritual easier. So, despite the fact that the wind whipped my nose, and my toes were on the verge of freezing, I couldn't complain.

I was here, I was alive. Tabitha, Efraim, and Thor weren't. Knowing that, there was no way in hell that I could take the breath in my lungs for granted.

In front of me, Alex slowed to a stop. I scanned the lakeside and saw that we were almost all in position.

"How are you?" Alex asked, his tone soft.

"Sad. Scared. Selfishly grateful. Take your pick."

"Me too, sweets. Me too."

I squeezed his hand just as the sound of snow crunching underfoot hit my ear.

Headmistress Wake stalked up the snowy path last, her candle, which was as tall as a toddler, burned with a blue flame as it floated in front of her. She took her spot along the lakeside, about thirty feet from us, and grasped the hands of those beside her. Everyone else followed suit, reaching for their neighbor.

"Witches have celebrated this day for millennia," the headmistress' voice boomed out over the ice-covered lake. "Although as with all things in life, the meaning and name has transformed over time, one aspect of Ostara has remained true. That the balance of light and dark is in flux." She drew a heady breath. "Tonight, we honor those who have come before us, those who have passed through the veil, those who help us as we continue to balance the light and darkness of this world and the other. To those ancestors and all the deceased, I offer my light." Headmistress Wake dropped her neighbors' hands, and with her palms face-out, thrust her candle toward the center of the lake.

At her right side, Professor Tittelbaum twirled his left hand, and a smaller candle, this one with a bright purple flame, appeared. "I offer those dead before us my light."

It went on like this, down the line of professors and staff. Then the third-years and second-years had their turn, before the words ended with my class.

I inhaled a shaky breath. Conjuring had never been my strongest subject, although I was far better at it now than I had been weeks ago. Still, I didn't want to mess this up. I didn't want to disrespect the dead, especially since some of them might be dead in my place.

At my side, Eva spoke the general conjuring spell, and a sunshine yellow candle with a bright blue flame appeared. She pressed the offering out to hover in the center of the lake with the hundreds of other flames already there, lighting up the ice below. She turned to me.

"I offer those who have perished before us my light." I closed my eyes, and the faces of Tabitha, Efraim, and Thor flashed in my head. The pit in my stomach expanded, but instead of allowing the sorrow to consume me, I harnessed it. *"Pario,"* I said and envisioned a simple white candle as clearly as I could, even imagining the flame's heat on my face.

A few murmurs flew up and down the line.

"Odie, look," Alex whispered.

I opened my eyes, and jerked back.

Before me was not *one* candle, as I'd intended, but a sea of them, all on the small side with white bottoms and a bright fuchsia flame.

All mine. My penance. My prayer. My hope that I could somehow change the future.

A tear slid down my cheek, and without hesitation, I swept the candles toward the center of the lake, giving my offering to anyone who would have it.

CHAPTER THIRTY-SEVEN

"The largest vampire clan in the United States is Clan Nightblood." Professor Artibus pointed to a spot on the map outside of New York City. "Nightblood's headquarters are here. And like many of the clans, Nightblood has historically been wary of aligning themselves with humans."

Vampires. Always looking out for number one. I shook my head.

"Clan Nightblood has been behind some of the most horrific terrorist acts in the modern century."

Words began to appear on the whiteboard in Artibus' tiny, scrawling script. I leaned forward to read the writing, and my mouth fell open.

Nightblood was behind all those attacks? Why didn't we learn about them sooner?

"I'm sure many of you are wondering why I didn't open

with Nightblood, back when term started in July. Why would I save such a dangerous clan until mid-April?"

Everyone in the room nodded, and relief that I was not the only one questioning Professor Artibus' teachings flooded me.

"The answer is simple." Professor Artibus pointed to the whiteboard again. "While Nightblood might have been behind all of these attacks, recently—as of December, in fact—they have been in talks with the United States government. Last week, the U.S. government took them off the paranormal terrorist watch list. You, my students, are witnessing history in the making."

Professor Artibus continued to drone on, and while just moments ago, I'd found the lecture riveting, I lost interest. I often preferred learning about our enemies rather than our allies. In this class, Artibus focused a lot on allies.

I thought that was a mistake.

Four attacks on my classmates meant we should focus on our enemies at all times. One might think me a little paranoid, and they would be right.

Since Alex had discovered the illuminated illustration of M&M, I'd been on edge. Whenever we had free time, Alex and I were in the library, reading everything we could find about the famed Arthurian wizard, trying to learn how we fit into the events unfolding around us. Unfortunately there wasn't much, and there was even less about Morgan Le Fay.

Alex believed this was because Spellcasters kept much of the material regarding Merlin in the Rare Book Room, where only Crucible-year students and professors could venture. I'd asked the head librarian once for access. I even pulled the "my parents are donors" card; a privilege I'd never used before, but in this instance, it felt warranted.

She'd flat out denied me.

"Miss Dane." Professor Artibus stopped before my desk, ripping me from my musings.

I blinked. "Yes?" My spine straightened, and while my classmates stared, I did my best to look as if I had been listening the entire time.

"I understand that your workload has been getting to you. It's often that way among first-years as Beltane draws near. But please refrain from exhibiting your inattention so bluntly."

I tilted my head, not understanding, and the professor gestured to my desk.

I glanced down, and my cheeks warmed. Apparently, I'd been doodling while my thoughts wandered. A depiction of Alex and me showed on the page, almost lifelike. We were locked in an embrace beneath a crescent moon in the middle of the forest. And even more embarrassingly, we were kissing.

While it was no secret that we were together, I didn't think everyone wanted to blatantly view the details of my private relationship, and *I* definitely didn't want them to know.

I set a book over the sheet. "I'm sorry, Professor Artibus. It won't happen again."

"See that it doesn't." He resumed lecturing.

Everyone else turned around, their attention back on the professor. Everyone, that is, except for Diana, who was scowling at the paper.

A knock sounded on my door, and I released a frustrated sigh. "Come in!"

The door opened with a whine, and Alex shuffled in. "Hey, babe. I just wanted to come see you before bed."

Though annoyance had filled me only a moment before, all my frustrations vanished. How could I be mad at the guy who was working as hard as I was to figure out the connection between our totems, the prophecy, and M&M?

"You could never bug me," I said, pushing my chair back.

Alex arched an eyebrow, and a chunk of black hair fell over the rim of his glasses. "Even if I wore plaid with stripes?"

I winced. "Okay, there's absolutely no reason to test me on that."

He chuckled and sat down on the bed. "So, I spent the last two hours in the library, looking up Merlin and Morgan again."

"And . . .?"

"Still nothing." Alex threw up his arms, and I noticed the glint of his totem on his finger.

That was odd. Like me, he never wore his totem, or carried it around. Since we didn't want to answer questions about how they interacted, we opted to leave them in our rooms.

"You're wearing your ring," I said and pulled my chain out from under my shirt. "That's kinda weird, that we chose to do it on the same day."

"I needed inspiration."

I nodded, knowing what he meant, because I too had put the necklace on for inspiration. For two people who were *very* different, sometimes we thought so alike that it was scary.

"Well, how's your poisons essay going?" I asked.

"All right. I started it yesterday, but ended up having to do a million other things. It's waiting for me in my room. Is that what you're working on?" He nodded to the desk where my essay sat.

"More like I was staring at a blank page. The professors are throwing so much at us lately, my brain feels like mush. I need, like, a million massages."

"A million massages, huh?" Alex's voice deepened, and the exhaustion that lined his face moments before disappeared. "I may not be a great masseuse, but I can think of a few other stress relieving activities." He patted my bed.

My heart rate spiked at the thought of Alex's arms wrapped around me, his muscular body pressed against mine. *Yassss, this is exactly what I need.*

I straddled him, and our mouths crashed together. His hands roamed my back before landing on my butt. I smiled self-satisfactorily. Alex was definitely a butt man.

I moved to the side, nibbling at his ear and teasing my

fingers down his neck, just the way he liked. I was rewarded when he released a long moan. I giggled as he tried to muffle the sound in my cleavage.

"Eva heard that one," I whispered.

In response, Alex pressed his face deeper into my chest, and my boobs began to vibrate.

"Oh my God!" I began to laugh uncontrollably when I realized he was motorboating my cleavage. "Stop! It tickles! Stop! Oh my G—*what the shit*!"

Suddenly, my totem shook, lit up, and began flashing through every color of the rainbow. Pressed against my backside, Alex's ring vibrated too. Then a beam of light shot out of my necklace.

"Alex, what's going—"

"Descendants, hear us!" two voices, one male and one female, boomed from behind, cutting me off.

Despite their odd wordage and accents, something deep inside me recognized the voices, and although they should have freaked me out, they didn't. Instead, I turned around and found two balls of light floating in the air. One held the visage of a white-bearded man, the other a beautiful, red-haired woman who I knew on sight.

"Merlin and Morgan," Alex whispered, echoing my thoughts.

"Children of our ancestral lines, we bring a warning." Morgan spoke, and though the light made her eyes appear misty, there was an undeniable hint of caution in them.

"The dark ones will soon seek you out. They will want to use you for their own vile reasons, and to keep you apart." As Merlin spoke, his eyes shifted to Morgan. "As they did us."

"Do not make the same mistake we did." Morgan spoke next. "Do not succumb to their delights for temporary bliss and power easily given. It will not last, and the world will be worse off."

Merlin's hazy lips quirked up in a smile. "As always, my lost love is right. Heed her, and know this: should you stay true to your destiny, together, you will change the world."

My lips parted, and questions bubbled to my lips, but before I could ask a single one, the lights from our totems flickered out.

CHAPTER THIRTY-EIGHT

The next day, all my classes blurred together. It was very obvious that Alex felt similarly confused after our strange experience the night before. Professor Thrax even commented on Alex's poor performance in Battle Magic, which was a first.

"Okay, what is wrong with you two?" Hunter asked as the four of us sat down for lunch. "I know that classes have sucked lately, but you're like zombies. Did you not sleep last night or something?"

"Nah, they slept. Believe me, Odie's room was dead quiet," Eva said. When I didn't respond, she dropped the fry she'd been eating. "Whoa, something is seriously up. Odie should've blushed over me hinting about her *intimate* life. You guys . . . what happened?"

I caught Alex's eye. "Should we tell them?"

He shrugged. "Sure. Maybe they'll have some freaking idea of what it all means."

Omitting the private bits, our story spilled from me, starting with how our totems were from Merlin and Morgan and ending with the night before. A few minutes later, Hunter and Eva sat there with their mouths hanging open.

"So, you two are connected to Merlin and Morgan Le Fay. And they spoke to you in a . . . what would you even call that?" Hunter asked, his eyebrows knitted together.

"No idea, but yeah, they spoke to us. Apparently, Odie and I are related to them. If our totems are any indication, she's of Morgan's blood, and I'm of Merlin's. Oh, and they mentioned that dark creatures are after us and we're meant to change the world." Alex threw up his hands. "You'd think that after however many hundreds of years those balls of light spent in that ring and necklace, they could have come up with a more enlightening way to relay information."

"For reals," I huffed. "We don't have time for *more* research. And I totally did not need this stress right before Beltane."

The final trial was a few days away, and my attention had been so divided lately with all the totem stuff and the murders that I felt fried. Adding a direct message from M&M only made me even more terrified for the final trial that would determine my future.

"Well, that's . . . I don't even know what to say about it." Eva picked up her fork and began to play with her side salad. "A lot of weird stuff happens to us, you know?

Between my scars, which by all accounts should be healed by now, and this Merlin and Morgan thing we're probably the strangest bunch at Spellcasters."

Our table fell into silence and we began to eat again. Before we knew it, the owl hooted, signaling the end of lunch. Wordlessly, we stood, deposited our trays, and rushed off to Conjuring.

I flung a beam of intense power at Alex, who barely got his shield up in time to block his face.

"Damn, babe! What did I do to you?"

I shot another stream of magic at him, this time aiming for his knee and delivering.

His jeans began to smoke, and before Alex could put out the budding fire, Eva whipped her power around like a lasso to cinch it tight around Alex's torso and pull him to the floor.

"Bam!" I shouted, punching my hand in the air.

"Girl power!" Eva added, and we broke out into a victory dance.

"Whenever the pair of you are finished reveling in your victory, feel free to let us loose," Hunter called from where he lay on the ground, a victim of one of my prior attacks.

Eva beamed. "I'm not sure how long that will be. I'm kinda liking the sight of this right now."

In truth, so was I. While Eva and I were not as magically

skilled as Alex and Hunter individually, we worked better as a team. The boys were always trying to impress one another with showy displays, whereas Eva and I had long since learned to work *with* each other. The sight of them on the ground, and us standing over them, victorious, was almost enough to make me forget my exhaustion.

Almost.

Despite having just been sparring, a yawn climbed its way up my throat and let loose. "What do you guys say, one more round and then we hit the hay?" I asked, glancing around at the Physical Training Facility.

An hour ago, the entire first-year class had been present and working their asses off. Everyone wanted to be prepared for the Beltane Trial. But in the last few minutes, a couple people had left. I assumed they were off to get ready for bed, and I desperately wanted to be in their squad.

"That sounds perfect," Alex said. "But you still have to let us up."

"Oh, right," I said. Eva and I smirked as we waved our hands, and the magical binds around the guys dissolved. "Before we start, though, I need a water and bathroom break."

"Ditto!" Eva proclaimed.

The guys rolled their eyes. They thought Eva and I had the bladders of children, but really, everyone knew that staying hydrated was important. Good for the body meant good for the magic.

We were crossing the magical training room, about to

pass over into the gym section, when Headmistress Wake's voice shot through the din of treadmills running, and weights hitting the floor.

"Phoebe Pudeator? Phoebe Pudeator, are you here?"

Everyone in the gym looked around, and a second later, Phoebe's head popped up from the bench press. "Right here, Headmistress Wake."

"Miss Pudeator, your parents are here. They—"

A rotund man of significant height, and a thin woman no taller than five feet burst into the gymnasium.

"Phoebe! Grab your things! We're going home," the man yelled.

"Dad! What are you talking about? What did I—"

"I can't believe that Spellcasters has fallen so far. They don't even inform the parents when students are being killed off like mice! What are you still doing standing there, Phoebe? I said get your things."

Phoebe placed her hands on her hips. "I don't want to leave. The Beltane Trial is in just a few days. I've trained my ass off for this. I'm participating."

"Oh no you're not. You're my daughter, and you *are* coming home with me."

The father and daughter volleyed threats back and forth for a few more minutes, until Headmistress Wake suggested that they move their family business to a more private area.

Although Mr. Pudeator seemed far past caring if anyone heard what he had to say, he nodded and marched out of the facility with his wife trailing behind him, and Phoebe following reluctantly a second later.

"Whoa," I breathed. "What are the chances we'll see Phoebe tomorrow?"

Eva bit her lip. "Who knows? With the way things are going around here, that question applies to everyone."

CHAPTER THIRTY-NINE

We didn't see Phoebe the next day. Or Olivia, who apparently had *requested* that her parents come get her. That left our class at an even twenty-six taking part in the Beltane Trial. One year at Spellcasters, and we were down five students.

And rumor has it the Grind will be even worse. I shuddered at the thought and nearly poked my eye out with my mascara wand.

"Don't think about it," Eva said, her voice terse as she applied blush to her cheeks.

I didn't answer, and a second later, Eva sighed. "You're right. Who am I kidding? What do you think they'll throw at us?" A blood vessel twitched at her temple.

I bit my lip, taking in the lines of stress on my friend's face. We all had a right to be worried about the trial, but after what Eva had gone through I would understand her extreme anxiety.

I hoped that they paired her with someone strong and calm.

"Probably not demons," I offered, and Eva's shoulders loosened.

"So that leaves black witches, vamps, shifters, or fae." She counted them off on her fingers, and her lips smooshed to the side.

"Humans?" I asked.

Eva snorted. "Too easy."

A knock sounded on Eva's door.

"That must be the guys." She spritzed herself with perfume before answering the door.

Hunter and Alex appeared a moment later, both dressed in jeans and sports jackets.

"Hey, babe." I stood on tiptoe to kiss Alex, who dipped to meet my lips.

"Hey, gorgeous," he replied as we broke away. "You look stunning. Are you ready?"

I shrugged. "As ever." I tried to keep the anxiety out of my voice.

For hours, I'd been obsessing over what the ball of light had said—that we should stick together. Soon we would discover our Beltane Trial partner. While I knew that it would be a little too perfect if we were partners, I still held onto a shred of hope.

"We only have five minutes before they close the doors," Eva said, glancing at the clock on her wall.

Hunter grabbed her hand, and a bit of the anguish on her face vanished. Although I wasn't sure if it was wise for

Hunter to be Eva's partner—he was too likely to put himself in danger to save her—I sort of hoped he was anyway. After what happened on Samhain, Eva deserved an easy Beltane.

Unfortunately, nothing ever came easy at Spellcasters.

The pre-Beltane Trial feast took place in Kyteler Hall, the little sister to the Agnes Sampson Hall. It was far less grand, but had the distinct advantage of windows that looked out into the woods, which I found calming.

"No upperclassmen?" I asked, glancing around.

There were only six large tables laid simply for dinner, with three tapered candles at various lengths, and plain white serveware.

"Looks like it," Alex said, squeezing my hand.

"Initiates! Please take your seats," Professor Umbra called from the table farthest from the door.

A few of our regular professors and Headmistress Wake sat beside her. Each instructor wore strange, black robes very unlike their normal garb.

What is this? Hogwarts? I thought as we claimed a table.

At the next table over, more professors congregated. Professor Tittelbaum did a headcount and nodded to the headmistress, who stood and clapped her hands.

"Let the pre-Beltane rituals begin," she proclaimed.

Rituals? I thought we were just having dinner and learning about the upcoming trial.

I shot a glance at Alex, who shrugged, and I didn't even have time to check if Hunter or Eva knew what the hell was going on, before Professor Thrax's dulcet Scottish tones rang through Kyteler Hall.

"Bring in the chalice!"

A set of doors at the far end of the room slammed open, and three figures dressed in hooded cloaks glided forward. One of them held a silver goblet in their hands.

My mouth fell open. *What the hell sort of secret society crap is this!*

"Initiates, step forward," de Spina's voice boomed.

My attention swiveled to the front of the room to find that our professors had donned their hoods, formed two lines facing one another, and conjured an illuminated pathway for us to walk between them. The headmistress was positioned at the end, her hands lifted in supplication.

I shivered. Spellcasters was always a little creepy—a building as old and darkly beautiful as this one couldn't help it—but this was a new level of creeptastic. Still, I did as they told me, and rose to fall into line right behind Alex.

We entered the tunnel of lit magic, and my lips parted in awe as a dozen colors swirled and spun all around us. The figures of our professors were visible through the kaleidoscope of magic, their hands working to keep the energies flowing.

Right behind me, Eva nudged my back. "This is awesome," she breathed, and unable to form words, I merely nodded.

Alex was the third person in line, so when we stopped, we were near the front, facing Headmistress Wake, whose dark eyes did not stray from the ground.

"Who joins me in the sacred ritual of the Beltane Trial?" she asked, her eyes still on the floor when the three hooded figures accompanying the chalice halted to stand behind her.

The tallest figure clutched the cup, which up close I noticed was encrusted in emeralds. He stepped forward first. "It is I, Headmaster Ezra of Nightdwellers Academy."

I gaped. The headmaster of Nightdwellers was here? Why would they invite a vampire?

"I join the witches of Spellcasters Spy Academy in the Beltane Trial," Headmaster Ezra continued in what was clearly a preplanned speech, "so that I may give testimony to the events of the rite, and act as an impartial judge. In doing so, I bind myself to the ritual."

A flash of metal shot out from the voluminous sleeve of his cloak, and the vampire lifted his arm. Blood poured into the chalice until, almost as quickly as he'd cut himself, the wound healed.

I stiffened. *They expect us to drink that blood? Please be wrong.*

Despite the churning of my stomach, I watched in grotesque fascination as Headmistress Cristala of the Fae Academy of Elemental and Arcane Arts, and Alpha Conon of the Shifter Academy of Spies approached the goblet. They recited a similar speech and added their blood to the chalice.

Finally, Headmistress Wake took the chalice, stuck out her palm, and made a one-inch cut. Red blood welled up, and a few drops of her lifeblood flowed into the cup.

"The power of all the schools representing the newest generation of the United States Supernatural Society of Spies has been united. Contingent on your performance in the Beltane Trial, partaking in this ritual binds each initiate into the Supernatural Society of Spies. First initiate, please step forward and drink."

My gut flipped, and saliva began to pool in my mouth. *What the what? A little heads-up about all this blood-drinking would have been nice.*

I briefly considered bringing it up, when the first person in line, Mina, stepped forward, took the chalice, and took a sip without hesitation.

What the hell, Mina! Now I'll just look like a wimp if I say something.

"Excellent, initiate Köhler," Headmistress Wake said, her tone flat. "Now that you've completed the first portion of the ritual, seek Professor de Spina to claim the packet bearing your Beltane Trial partner's name. Refrain from opening it until I command you to do so."

Amethyst went next, followed by Alex. Both took the blood like a pro, claimed their envelope, and sat down like all of this was no big deal.

But when I got to the front of the line and stood before Headmistress Wake, I didn't feel that way. Despite the many mantras running through my head, telling me that everything would be fine, the room was spinning.

When Headmistress Wake passed the chalice to me, it took all I had not to throw it back at her.

My shoulders shook as I lifted the emerald-encrusted

goblet. Desperate to look anywhere but at the liquid in the cup, my eyes shifted to the side and caught the gaze of the vampire headmaster. His lips turned up in a self-satisfied smile, and I shuddered. He was probably getting a lot of joy out of this, the sicko.

Just do it, I told myself as the chalice came closer to my mouth.

The scent of metal flooded my nostrils, and saliva filled my mouth once more as my stomach threatened to heave its contents into the cup.

But then, I noticed something else. The blood in the cup didn't just smell like metal. There was another aroma there too, something I couldn't quite put my finger on, but had smelled before. I pressed my lips together in thought.

The vampire headmaster shifted, and I caught him glance up and tilt his head toward the tunnel of magic churning above us.

Magic. There isn't only blood in the cup, but the power of the predominant magical species of Earth.

My eyes popped open. While I wasn't sure that drinking in magic would do a damn thing for me, it made the blood more palatable.

Riding the wave of realization, I brought the cup to my lips and sipped.

It tasted like blood, but there were pleasant undertones too. Tastes that evoked images of green woods and moon-filled nights and ancient rites and blood-filled wars.

It was four cultures of magicals in one glass.

"Are you quite done, Miss Dane?"

Headmistress Wake's stern tone snapped me out of my revelation.

"Perhaps this one should be at my school?" the vampire whispered, and the shifter chuckled from beneath his hood.

"Yes." I returned the glass to my headmistress, and went to claim the envelope that held my partner's name.

I returned to the table and sat. Alex was on my one side, Eva on the other. The wax-sealed envelope burned beneath my fingers. I hoped that when I opened it, I'd see Alex's name.

The line moving through the magic tunnel dwindled, and soon, the final first-year had completed the ritual. As soon as they claimed their envelope, the tunnel vanished, and the professors, along with the heads of the other schools, sat. Only Headmistress Wake remained standing.

Her heels clacked against the wood floor, and I couldn't help but think that while we were all sweating bullets, the headmistress probably lived for these moments. She paced through the tables twice before stopping in the center of the room.

"Who here is interested in knowing what species of magical will be your opponent this Beltane?"

No one spoke, but we all leaned forward, telling of our interest.

Headmistress Wake smirked, and her attention turned to the table at which the other heads sat, still hooded. "Will the representative for the oppositional species please reveal themselves?"

The tallest figure stood, and my blood froze, knowing who it was before he took off his hood.

Vampires.

Eva's hands shot out to clutch both Hunter's and my forearms, while murmurs rose from the rest of the tables.

Of course it would be vampires, the magical race we'd only recently begun studying, and never encountered. Why would we even consider anything else?

Headmistress Wake was still smirking at the front of the room, but Headmaster Ezra had retaken his seat. The only tell that he was enjoying himself at all was the faint upward curl of his lips.

The headmistress strode toward the middle of the room. "There is one more thing that you should be aware of, before you discover your partner's identity. During the Beltane Trial, we allow you use of your totem."

I gasped, and Alex gripped my hand. This was huge. Other people had been practicing with their totems for months, and some were getting pretty good at using them. While Alex and I were not among those people, ours were connected to Merlin and Morgan Le Fay. In proximity, they reacted to one another.

My hope that we'd be paired multiplied by a thousand.

Headmistress Wake lifted her arms, and a hush descended on the room. "Now that you know what you shall face, and the advantages you will have, I give you permission to open your parcels and learn the name of your partner."

Papers rustled all around me. Eva practically tore hers

in half to get it open. Concern about her pairing overwhelmed me, and my envelope remained on the table.

My best friend unfolded her paper and her blue eyes widened.

"Who is it?" I asked, unable to take the suspense any longer.

"Amethyst," Eva breathed and leaned back in her chair.

I mimicked her reaction. That was good. Amethyst tested consistently near the top of the class and had progressed to conjuring solid objects with ease. If they needed a stake or cross, Amethyst could provide one.

Hunter and Alex had torn their envelopes open too, and both were staring at them in wide-eyed wonder.

"What about you guys?" I asked.

They lifted their heads and pointed to the other Wardwell.

No freaking way.

I heaved a sigh of relief, even as regret that Alex wasn't my partner seared through me. Thank goodness they'd made up earlier this year. Now they'd have each other. The guys would be fine.

Which left me.

My hands found my envelope and brushed the creamy paper. If it couldn't be Alex, Hunter, or Eva, who did I want beside me? I hitched a breath, unsure of the answer, but ready to discover the hand fate had dealt me.

My finger slipped beneath the wax seal, and I applied the slightest amount of pressure to crack it open.

"You've got to be kidding me!" a voice screeched. "I'm

partnered with *her*? Two of my friends are *gone* because of her! This is foul!"

I dropped my paper on my lap and whirled about to see Diana stomping toward the entrance to Kyteler Hall.

My stomach clenched, and I bit my lip. *No, she can't mean—*

I ripped open my envelope and unfolded the paper quickly to find the name "Diana Wake" scrolled in emerald green ink.

CHAPTER FORTY

The pit in my stomach deepened with every step I took toward Merlin Amphitheater.

"You haven't talked to Diana yet?" Eva asked.

"Nope. No one spotted her in the dorm after they allowed us out of our rooms. She wants nothing to do with me."

"To be fair," Alex started, "it's against the Beltane Trial rules to confer with your partners."

Frustratingly, he was right. Headmistress Wake had insisted that if the partners had been sitting together at last night's dinner, they separate. And just like before the Samhain Trial, we'd been locked in our rooms after dinner, ensuring no one could talk to anyone else. The professors had released the spell only a half hour ago so we could make our way down to the amphitheater.

"To be *fair*," I stuck my tongue out as I mimicked Alex playfully. "Diana wouldn't have conferred with me, anyway. She hates me. I only wanted to hash out a temporary peace before the trial to give us both the best chance."

I ran my hands down my cheeks. The Samhain Trial had been hard enough, and Hunter and I were friends. Working with someone who despised me, and actually succeeding without a temporary understanding was difficult to imagine.

As soon as I crossed the threshold into the stadium, I sensed the excitement in the air.

"There are more people present this time," I said, noting that the tension was far greater than before our last trial.

"How can there be?" Hunter asked as we strode deeper into the building. "During Samhain, every Spellcasters student, all our professors, and people from the PIA were present. Who else would they allow to—"

"Our parents!" Eva yelped, her eyes sweeping the stands to the right as we entered the open space of the amphitheater.

My heart clenched as my eyes scanned the crowd. It took me only seconds to find my parents in the sea of silver, black, white, and green—Spellcasters colors. Mom particularly stood out in the long, yellow dress she always wore for special occasions. Just seeing it made me smile.

"They said nothing about inviting our parents," I commented.

"Big surprise there," Eva said.

She looked even more tense than before, and I had an inkling why. Eva's parents, more than anyone else's, would want her to succeed during the Beltane Trial. Them being here put immense pressure on her.

We made our way into the wide open space, toward the same dais we'd waited upon before. A handful of our classmates already sat in chairs. I found Diana wedged between Kira Johnston and José Valdez. I shook my head, I'd never seen her talk to either of them. Clearly, she'd only sat there to keep *me* from sitting next to her. Unfortunately for her, I was not so easily swayed.

Plopping down in the seat behind Diana, I wasted no time tapping her on the shoulder.

"Diana. We should talk."

"Isn't it enough that I will be the one who ensures you progress to the Grind-year, Legacy?" Diana said, her back resolutely to me.

My lips parted in surprise. "You're not even going to try to talk to me before the biggest test of our lives? What if I have something to offer that's helpful?"

Diana snorted. "Admittedly, you are getting better. However, you know nothing that I don't." She whipped around, and her blue eyes bore through me. "Let's just take this for what it is—an annoying twist of fate that brought us together. There's no need to bond." She turned back around.

I slammed my back against my chair and crossed my arms over my chest. Fine. If she didn't want to talk to me now, I could handle that. But once we went through that warphole, she couldn't ignore me so easily.

She might even need me.

Of course, I was not the first to face my trial, as I would've liked to have been. I was dead last.

Again. What does the universe have against me?

At least I'd been able to witness Eva and Amethyst return from their trials unscathed. That, and because my peers had gotten through their trials in just under three hours, when Headmistress Wake called Diana and I up alongside Alex and Hunter, I still felt fresh.

While my partner sneered at me, my boyfriend squeezed my hand reassuringly as we approached the warphole. The headmistress handed out the same gold bracelets that we'd worn for the Samhain Trials as a way of calling aid should we need it.

"And now, Diana Wake, Odette Dane, Alexander Wardwell, and Hunter Wardwell shall begin their trial. Your test starts now."

Without further instruction, Diana stepped through the vortex, and I followed. For the first time, the heat of the warphole caressing my skin and the energy tingling over me didn't startle me, and I landed on the other side with grace.

I scanned our surroundings. We'd landed in an alleyway.

My gaze shifted to Diana, who was pointedly looking away. "Do you know where to go?" I asked.

Diana snorted and pointed toward the mouth of the

alley. "Already you need my help? *Obviously,* we need to get onto the street, Legacy."

She stomped away, toward the bright lights of the street. I refrained from rolling my eyes and followed. If I had to, I would try to keep my attitude positive for both of us.

When we emerged onto the street a smile cracked the tension riddling my face. "We're in Brooklyn."

"How do you know that?" Diana asked, her tone sharp.

"Before my parents dropped me off at Spellcasters, we spent a few days in the city before heading to Portland, Maine. I wanted to explore Brooklyn and remember this spot. There's a popular goth hangout just down there called 'Fangs and Fetishes,' which could be a perfect place for—"

"Vampires," Diana finished, and took off in the direction that I pointed.

We spotted the bar from a couple blocks away. "Fangs and Fetishes" wasn't a subtle name for a vampire establishment, but sometimes hiding in plain sight was best.

We ducked into an alley, and Diana conjured us both appropriate clothing. I'd asked for tight, faux leather leggings, a skimpy top, and glittery Converse sneakers. Diana looked similar, except for the severe stilettos she wore on her feet. I had concerns about whether she could fight in those, but thought it best not to bring it up. Either way, our new outfits would fit right in with the scene we were about to enter.

We pulled out the fake IDs that Spellcasters had supplied their students for instances such as these. Thankfully, there was no line, and after the bouncer examined our fraudulent cards, he let us in.

As soon as we stepped foot into the bar, pounding music filled my ears, and the scent of bodies, sweaty and lustful, teased my nostrils. Fangs and Fetishes wasn't just a bar, it was a strip club.

"So, do you think—"

I didn't get to finish my question, because Diana walked toward the bar.

I released a sigh and went to join her. "I understand that you don't want to talk. To be honest, I'm not super big on it either, but the faster we get through this trial, the faster we can go back."

Diana didn't answer, but I wasn't about to let up. "And that means working together. I—"

"Just stop." Diana cut me off in her usual brusque manner. "As much as I hate to admit it, you have a point, Legacy. I, too, would like to get this over with. If you want to work together so badly, give me your theory on who they have sent us here for."

As much as her rudeness grated on my nerves, now was not the time for confrontation. Real spies didn't let personal shit get in the way of their missions, so I wouldn't either.

I scanned the room. All manner of people were in the bar, but if my experiences with Spellcasters had taught me anything, it was that we should look for someone—*a vampire*—who could get some shady shit done. Someone who exuded power.

Keeping that in mind, my gaze paused on a group of

men all wearing sleek business suits, in the far back corner of the room. One in particular caught my eye. His skin was gleaming white beneath the bright neon lights, his cunning eyes scanned the bar even as he joked with those around him, and at nearly seven feet tall, he looked *exactly* like a mob boss.

I continued to watch as at least three people darted up to him, and the guy spoke and pointed as though he were giving instructions. He was definitely a top dog in this bar.

"My money is on the back right corner."

"I agree," she said. "Now the only question is *why* are we here?"

My mouth snapped shut. I'd been wondering the same thing since they had announced that vampires were our adversary. Working against demons was self-explanatory, mostly they wanted to gain access to our realm to feed off the life here and cause havoc, but vampires could have *many* motives.

Diana shook her head. "Yeah. I'm not sure either, but I have a hypothesis. I bet you anything it has something to do with blood."

I nodded. That made sense. Many vampire clans were notorious for operating illegal blood rings. Professor Artibus had mentioned a dozen just last week. Considering the name of the establishment that we were in, it wasn't hard to believe that something of that nature operated out of here.

"That's a good guess," I said after a few seconds of mulling it over. "Should we go talk to the head honchos?

See if they have any speciality blood in stock for wicked potions?"

"I think that's our best first step," Diana agreed. "In fact, I even know of a potion that will work for a cover. Let's do it."

I let her take the lead, and as we approached the circular booth filled with powerful vamps, every bloodsucker looked our way.

"Good evening, witches," the vampire I suspected was the leader said as we stopped before their table, striking a sexy pose. "To what do we owe the honor of having other magicals in our establishment this evening?"

"We hear this is the place to come for procuring materials of a darker nature." Diana set her hands on the table, and leaned forward so that her thick, blonde hair poured over her shoulder.

Damn. Who knew Diana could play the seductress?

The tall vampire met her gaze like a hawk preparing to go in for the kill. "No matter how tight your pants are and how much skin you reveal, I have to say I don't believe you. You two don't look like a pair of black witches."

A few of the men in the circular booth nodded, and I cocked my head.

"Is that so? And what, might I ask, do you believe black witches look like, *vampire*?" My tone was sassy as hell, not at all telling of my nerves. Thank the universe that acting had taught me how to keep my cool under pressure.

The laughing stopped, and the vampire leader turned his attention from Diana to me. "I might not be a witch, but

I've been around long enough to know when I'm seeing a witch who's turned the dark corner, and when I'm not." His gaze leveled with mine, and I noticed for the first time that the outermost rim of his irises were a startling red. This vampire had fed, and recently.

I shook my head as if he were an idiot. "Perhaps that's true," I shrugged.

"And perhaps it's not," Diana played off me, and we shared what I thought might be our first smile—although admittedly, it was more like a smirk.

"Fine." The lead vampire crossed his arms over his chest. "Maybe I'm wrong, and you're black witches. Maybe I've lost my touch. But I don't think so. There is one easy way to find out . . . What are you here for?"

Diana mirrored the vampire, crossing her arms over her chest. "What else would someone come to a vampire bar for? Blood. We're concocting a necromancy potion, and were hoping you'd have fae on hand—pixie, specifically, although elven will do in a pinch. I'll want to smell it first, though, before I buy."

What the what? How the hell does she know about necromancy potions!

The lead vampire nodded to a guy with a scarred lip at the edge of the table. "Go ask our girl to fact-check what this witchling just said. Pixie or elven blood in a necromancy potion."

The guy with the scarred lip strode off.

We waited, trying to keep up our confident appearances while the vampires in the booth studied us. My heart rate began to climb, but instead of letting it show, I pursed my lips and placed a hand on my hip, as if waiting was the most annoying thing in the world.

Finally, after five minutes that felt like five months, Scarred Lip returned.

His eyes latched onto the lead vampire's and he nodded. "She had to look it up, but she says that what these two asked for is legit."

The hawkish vampire turned to us. "In that case, it would be a pleasure to do business with you, ladies. Steve, take 'em to the supply room and show 'em our stock."

Another vampire—Steve, apparently—grunted for us to follow, and we did.

"The price goes up if you decide you want aged blood," Steve said as we broke through the crowds of bodies, and he unlocked a door at the back of the bar.

"Naturally," Diana said. "Whoever heard of paying the same amount for fresh fae blood and aged fae blood? I only want the best, which means the magic needs time to cure."

Steve nodded, obviously impressed.

Damn she's good.

We walked down the hall, and I caught sight of an exit sign, indicating that we were near the rear of the building. I was just wondering if we were about to head outside, when we took a sharp right through a false wall and entered what looked like apartment buildings. I took note of another exit sign as we walked to the end of a very long corridor. Two minutes later, we were descending a flight of stairs. A damp chill washed over me at the bottom, and a musty odor filled my nostrils. Then the vampire opened an ancient-looking side door and entered.

"Where are we?" Diana demanded.

"These are old interconnected basements where we store supplies."

We nodded, and Steve moved on.

Almost immediately, we began taking twists and turns through hallways that I feared Diana and I wouldn't remember. What if we had to kill this guy? The rest of the way had been easy to memorize, but there would be no easy way out of this underground labyrinth. I had to make one.

I called my magic to my fingers, and began brushing the side of the wall. Fuchsia flashed against the cement and then disappeared, ready to reveal itself again when I needed it. It was the magical equivalent of leaving bread-crumbs for us to follow.

I was feeling satisfied with my contribution, when a scream up ahead cut through my core.

"What was that?" I asked, stopping in my tracks.

Steve turned around, and one corner of his mouth lifted in a devious smile. "Let's just say they're occupants. We don't call the bar 'Fangs and Fetishes' for nothing."

A louder moan and a cry for help shot through me, and suddenly I realized why we were there.

This bar was involved in human trafficking. We were here to set the captives free.

The vampire was still staring at me, so I nodded as if I'd

suspected what he told me all along. "Smart to have them so close so you can use them whenever."

"It's a treat, and I do *so* like to indulge," Steve said and then turned back around.

He made it three more steps before I sensed the shift, the manipulation of energy.

Then Diana lunged forward and stabbed him in the back.

The vampire disintegrated before my eyes, and Diana transferred the wooden stake that she'd just conjured from one hand to the other.

"It seems as though we've discovered our trial. What do you say we get to saving some humans?"

CHAPTER FORTY-ONE

"We need to figure out where the humans are being kept, and fast." I gestured down both directions of the dark hallway. "We've passed ten doors, and there are probably a lot more. Split up, or stay together?"

Diana's aquiline nose wrinkled. "I'm not—"

A shriek ripped down the hall, sending my heart racing.

That was close. Very close.

"Follow me," my tone dipped, suddenly aware that vampires might be behind many of these doors, taking their fill of human blood or pleasure.

Diana didn't even argue. As silently as possible, we walked ahead, past four more doors.

When we reached the fifth on our right, I spotted light coming out from the crack at the bottom of the door. I dropped to my knees and put my ear to it. Immediately, I caught the sounds of creaking metal and soft whimpers, as if someone's cries were being muffled by a cloth.

I stood. "There's one in there. You still have that stake handy?"

Diana held it up.

"Good. I'll bust down the door, and you rush in and stab. Sound good?"

Diana's eyes narrowed. "So I'm the one that has to get close to the fangs? Are you trying to get me killed, Legacy?"

I refrained from rolling my eyes. "No. It's just that you're faster. If you want to trade, give me the stake. Or conjure me one, too."

I hated to ask, but despite my growing powers, I was still behind in Conjuring, which required a great deal of control. It would take me too long to make a stake of the same quality as the one that Diana had in her hand, and time was not on our side. If we didn't reappear in the bar after a reasonable amount of time, someone would come looking for us.

A smirk bloomed on Diana's face. "No, you're right. I am faster. Plus, like they say, if you want something done right, you have to do it yourself."

I inhaled and pushed thoughts of slugging her from my mind. "Fine. As soon as the door opens, rush in, and I'll distract the vamp."

She nodded, and I moved off to the side and held my hands out, right over the lock.

The old me wouldn't have been able to break the lock,

but now I had the utmost confidence in myself. Despite the fact that my hands began to shake only seconds after my power attacked the metal, I kept my cool. My magic was strong, and while I might not have the best control over it, in this situation, destruction was what I wanted.

A little more.

I pushed harder, and an intense burst of fuchsia exploded from my palms.

There was a *crack,* and I kicked my leg out, shattering the mechanism and throwing open the door.

Diana rushed inside, and I was hot on her heels. Magic continued to flow from me, coloring the entire room fuchsia. I shot a beam straight at the vampire, a big, ugly brute who had already turned around, but he couldn't move properly because his pants were caught down near his ankles.

Fuchsia beams slammed into him, hard, and he wobbled, disoriented.

"Now, Diana!" I said as loud as I dared, and my partner hurtled through the air, stake extended, and slammed it into the vampire's heart.

Gray ash mixed with shimmering fuchsia energy as the vampire exploded. A muffled sob from the woman he'd been enjoying met my ear, and I rushed forward. She lay stomach-down on the mattress, her face buried in the pillow. Surprisingly, she was still clothed, although three fresh bite marks decorated her neck. The bed beneath her was filthy, black from dirt and red from blood, and the general state of the room wasn't any better. Apparently, the clientele of Fangs and Fetishes didn't expect cleanliness.

I was almost at her side when the woman seemed to snap out of her stupor. Her head shot up, and at the sight of me, she opened her mouth to scream.

I held up my hand. "Shh! It's okay. We're here to help you. Don't yell. If there are more, they'll hear you."

The woman's mouth snapped shut.

Diana joined me. "Can you walk?" she asked the captive, her tone terse.

"Dude, Diana! A little empathy?" I said.

"We don't have time, Legacy. This woman needs to get up and take us to the others. I'm assuming there are many people being kept down here, right? Do you know where they're located?"

Diana's eyes bored through the woman, who still looked too terrified to speak, but she nodded.

"Good." Diana held her hand out to the captive. "We'll get you all out of here."

The woman didn't say a word, but she managed to lead us to another door. Diana and I worked together, burning off the lock in record time, and swinging the door open.

I scanned the room, and a mixture of emotion welled up, threatening to overwhelm me, before I pushed it down. I would deal with emotions later, but right now, the scene before me needed all my attention.

Three men and at least twenty women were being held captive in a small, dank room, with only four buckets to relieve themselves in, and no visible source of water. It was hot and smelly in the small space. Most of the captives wore few items of clothing, while others had on period costumes. They were kept in chains. About half of them appeared drugged, while the other half simply sat there, trembling in fear, or scampered to the corners of the room.

"Tell them we're here to help," I said to the woman we saved.

Her lips parted, and slowly, she spoke. "They saved me from . . . Gair."

At least half the women in the room winced.

Gair must have been a real asshole. I was glad we'd eliminated him.

"They'll save us," the woman finished, as if she couldn't believe what she was saying.

"Yes. We're witches, the good kind, and we'll get you out of here." Diana stepped forward. The command in her tone was severe after the woman's meek voice. "But you must cooperate. And don't just run off. That puts everyone in danger. Can you do that?"

I wasn't sure if they knew witches existed before, but no one looked surprised. Maybe already knowing vampires were real, made anything seem possible. Or perhaps they were just so desperate to be freed, we could have said anything. Whatever the case, most people merely nodded at Diana's proclamation. Those who didn't appeared so drugged that I wasn't sure they even knew we were there.

"Okay, good." Diana moved to the closest woman. "Now, hold out your hands, I'll sear off everyone's chains.

Legacy, watch the door. No one comes in or out." She tossed me her stake. "We're all leaving at the same time."

I did as she said and watched as Diana moved from one person to the next, breaking their chains. Only one woman tried to escape right away, but a captive with filthy blonde hair and scratches all over her face stopped her.

"Didn't you hear them," the blonde hissed. She shook the runner. "Don't go running off and getting us all caught again, you idiot."

The runner calmed after that, and we had no more trouble. Once Diana had seared through the last chain, she turned back to me. Sweat shone on her forehead, and I winced. I should have insisted on helping.

"Are you okay?" I whispered as Diana joined me.

She grunted and smirked. "Okay? That was nothing, Legacy. Wait until the real fighting starts, because ten to one, it's coming." She turned to the crowd. "Do they keep captives in other rooms?"

A man shook his head. "Not that I'm aware of. They keep the other rooms open for . . . their pleasures. I heard a vamp once refer to this room as the 'human corral'. I think we're the only ones, and everyone is present."

Two other women echoed his belief.

"Good. We can make a run for it right away," Diana said.

My eyes took in the captives. Most of them were too skinny, and some were so drugged they needed help to stand. I gulped, sure that Diana was right about a fight coming, and knowing that not everyone in this room would make it out alive.

Thank the universe I'd left breadcrumbs of magic to guide my way back to the surface. We found our way without having to backtrack, and wound up on the ground floor of the apartment building next to the bar. The exit sign twenty feet away shone like a beacon, and my heart leapt.

We made it!

Of course, that was the moment a trio of beefy vampires entered the corridor from the bar side.

The women and men who had been following us screamed, and my jaw clenched. There was no way Diana and I could fight off the vampires *and* keep these people alive. This was the best chance that they had to run.

I blasted magic at the vampires, hoping to slow them, as I sprinted toward the bloodsuckers. Steps sounded behind me, and a wave of purple power flowed over my head to slam into a vamp. Diana was right behind me, and I maneuvered to one side so she could sidle up next to me.

"Run!" I directed the captives, and pointed as we passed the exit. "Get the hell out of here!"

I tossed another bolt of power at the vamps, trying to keep them back long enough for everyone to escape.

The sound of footsteps followed, and I knew the humans were doing as I instructed. A few seconds later, a door slammed against a wall. I took ten more steps before I dared to glance back. My stomach clenched. The tail end of the group was just disappearing through the door, but one of the heavily drugged women lay motionless on the ground not far from where we'd entered the hallway.

I stopped in my tracks, spun around, and created a shield around the unconscious person. Diana swore loudly, and then something knocked me to the ground.

"Thought you could pull a fast one on us, little witchling?" the vampire who'd rushed me growled as he ripped my stake from my hand and threw it to the side. "Well, it seems you just earned yourself a new position down in our basement. We've never had a witch before. I'm sure some of our clients will pay handsomely."

"Over my dead body!" I bucked and kicked, desperate to escape. The vampire had pinned my hands so I couldn't fight back or use magic. For the first time in my life, I was totally at another creature's mercy.

The vampire watched me, amused, and began to chuckle. "How about an undead body? Some humans have a definite predilection for female vamps, but we don't have any as pretty as you. Until now." He began lowering his mouth to my neck.

In a futile attempt, I tried to wrench my wrist—the one wearing the gold bracelet that would call for backup—out of his grasp, but the vampire was too strong.

His breath was hot against my neck when I realized it was too late. He was going to change me.

"See you in three days, sweetheart," the vampire breathed.

I closed my eyes and released a scream as his lips brushed my skin.

Then, suddenly, ash filled my mouth, and I began to cough.

"Get up! There's one more left!" Diana commanded.

My eyes flew open to find Diana standing over me, her stake gripped in her hand.

She'd saved me.

"Th-th-thank you," I stammered.

"Whatever. Get up. I—*Agh!*"

She loosed a horrendous wail as the third vampire flew at her from behind and latched onto her neck.

CHAPTER FORTY-TWO

I moved on autopilot, rolling toward my stake. As soon as it was in my hand, I turned to face the last vampire.

My stomach fell to my knees. Only seconds had passed, but all the blood from Diana's face seemed to have already drained out, and she hung lifeless in the vampire's grasp.

His vibrant, blood-red eyes bore into me, narrowed and appraising. Then he broke his latch on Diana's neck, and smiled. "Ahh, it's been ages since I had a witch. This one's as good as I remembered. A pity she's thin and there's little blood. I'm already nearly finished."

Diana moaned, and I took a step forward.

The vampire held out his palm. "I wouldn't come any closer. Not if you want your friend's body to be presentable at her funeral." He tilted his head. "Which is rapidly approaching. You'd be smart to save yourself, witchling."

Do I risk it and stake him? Or . . .

My heart skipped a beat as the truth came crashing down. There was no other choice. The vamp would injure or kill her either way.

I flew into motion, sprinting toward the vampire. If I hadn't been watching him so closely, I would not have caught the infinitesimal widening of his eyes. He hadn't expected me to fight. He'd expected me to leave Diana and run the other way.

My mind worked wildly, hoping that meant he would run if he was attacked.

I flung my hands forward and loosed a hailstorm of magic. As I'd hoped, the vampire dropped Diana to the ground, turned tail, and sprinted away.

But I was one step ahead of him. Another shot of fuchsia power soared over Diana, past the vampire, and formed a wall in front of him. He collided straight into it and staggered backward, disoriented for the moment.

A moment was all I needed. I willed my magic back to me, and it formed a net, scooping the vampire up and hurtling him toward me.

Straight into my stake.

I'd barely wiped the ash from my eyes when Diana moaned.

I have to get us out of here.

I placed a shield around Diana, and turned to the passed out human. I couldn't just leave her here. Our mission wasn't over. We had to save her.

"Home . . ."

Another of Diana's moans cut through me, and I realized she was right. There was only one place we could safely go, and *all* of us would go there, whether it was against the rules or not.

I released my shield over the human, and dragged her dead weight closer to Diana.

As soon as they were close enough for me to grip each with one hand, I called the warphole using the bracelet. A speck of blackness to my right popped into existence and ballooned. When it was large enough to walk through, I pulled both women forward.

The blackness encompassed us, but it was only temporary, and soon enough, the sound of a screaming audience met my ears.

Headmistress Wake joined us in an instant, her arms folding around her daughter's body as she tried to revive the unconscious Diana. Others joined her and called for stretchers for the human.

But a larger crowd surrounded the other warphole—Alex and Hunter's—and it looked like they were confused and arguing about something.

Unease coiled in my gut as the night of Samhain came rushing back. This was familiar, but more intense. Something felt very off.

Then a blood-curdling scream ripped through the amphitheater.

The switch flipped, and unlike the night of Samhain when everyone had simply gaped and stared, the crowds in the stands stood simultaneously and charged toward the exits. A handful, probably seasoned spies and a couple of professors, rushed forward.

I searched the crowd and saw that my parents were among those surging toward me, terror in their eyes.

My heart clenched, and everything in my body grew cold. I rushed to the other warphole and shoved myself past the professors and spymasters on duty. Was it another greater demon? But chances of that happening twice was ridiculously low, right?

"Bow before me, witchlings," a voice boomed out of the warphole, and the hairs on the back of my neck stood on edge. "Forsaken by my subjects, I have returned! I am your new ruler, the Queen of Darkness, Ishtar."

A spymaster shrieked and bolted the other way, and my body felt like it would collapse. A queen of darkness? An actual lord of Hell was in there with Alex and Hunter?

"Why isn't anyone helping them?" Tears pricked in my eyes as those in charge scurried about, their fear and indecision plain.

"No witch in living memory has survived an altercation against the the royal demons of Hell. I'm closing the warphole," Professor Tittelbaum said, his thin face lined with effort and his glasses nearly falling off his nose. Without waiting for an okay from anyone, the black vortex began to shrink.

"You can't!" I screamed, but Tittelbaum didn't listen, he didn't even look my way.

So instead of arguing, I dove through the blackness to help my friends.

CHAPTER FORTY-THREE

My shoulder hit marble, and I rolled to minimize the impact. When I leapt up, I found an actual beast before me.

Ishtar, Queen of Hell and wife to Lucifer, was at least five times the size of a normal man. Her blue horns curled toward her forehead, and her tasseled tail flicked as she caught sight of me.

"Ah!" Her red eyes glowed with delight. "Are you the one we've been searching for?"

Alex's head whipped around, and terror filled his eyes. "Odie! Get out of here!"

Laughter boomed from Ishtar. "The idiot girl can't. The warphole is gone. Whether you're who I seek or not, you three are *mine*." She lunged toward Hunter, hands the size of sheet pans grasping for him.

Hunter leapt out of the way just in time and shot a beam

of green magic at her. The power hit Ishtar's right horn and reflected off without even causing a scratch.

What the hell were we going to do? I'd never heard of anyone battling any of the six royals of Hell. In fact, I wasn't sure that anyone knew how to beat them. They'd been banished for far too long.

"How many magicals and demons did you have to kill to come here?" Alex screamed, as a stream of magic left his hands and seared Ishtar from her thigh all the way to her breast.

A gaping hole opened, revealing black muscles for a second before healing.

Ishtar grinned, not at all bothered by Alex's display of power. "Smarter than the average witchling, I see. Someone's taught you the ways of Hell. Could it be that you are the one I seek? The blood of Merlin?"

Ishtar opened her palm, and tendrils of onyx flooded forth and whirled around Alex, lifting him high into the air.

The indecision that had gripped me only moments before vanished, and I dashed forward, releasing every iota of power I possessed to break the chain of Ishtar's magic so Alex could squirm out of her grasp. It worked, and Ishtar's gaze shot to me.

"Or is it you whom I seek?" Her massive hand moved to grasp me, but I was ready, an incantation on the tip of my tongue.

My magic surged out of me and slapped her across the face.

A dazed expression came over the Queen of Hell, but the show of power had not drawn blood.

"Nothing we do will stop her. We have to get out of here now!" Fear dripped in every syllable Hunter spoke.

We whipped around and sprinted toward the door. Seconds before we got there, it slammed shut, and Ishtar roared with laughter.

"The only way you're leaving here is with me. Now, come to your master."

I watched as her eyes began to glow red, and suddenly, a compulsion to obey her overcame me.

She only has to make eye contact to possess us. The realization struck like a lightning bolt to my heart, and my eyes snapped shut as I tried to pry the door open.

"Yes, handsome boy, come to me."

What?!

I whirled around and squinted one eye open. What I saw stole all the breath from my lungs. Alex was walking toward Ishtar. He was submitting to the demoness, possessed by her.

I had to save him.

An intense wave of energy flew from my hands, and I staggered backward. It slammed against Ishtar, bowling her over. Her eye contact with Alex was severed, and he broke from her hold and darted backward, closer to Hunter and me.

The next second, however, Ishtar was back, her mouth set in a determined line, and her eyes narrowed as she took me in. "So, it is you." Her hand shot toward me again, and our trio scattered.

I dove right, but Ishtar must have been expecting it, because her fingers brushed my ankle. I loosed a scream as the skin there burned with the fire of a thousand suns. I crab-walked back, but was unable to rise.

The queen laughed. "Did my little mark sting, witchling? Perhaps you don't possess much of Merlin or Morgan after all. Now, come to me."

Again the sensation of losing myself came over me, and I rose from the ground to go to her, only to have Hunter slam into me.

"No, Odie, don't submit."

I wrenched him off me and socked him in the jaw.

Ishtar laughed. "Yes! Show him what you're made of! Come to me and leave the weakling boys behind."

"No! Odie—"

I pulled my arm back to punch Hunter again, but he twirled out of the way. A heartbeat later, Alex took his place, his hand stopping mine, cupping it, and weaving his fingers through mine. As soon as our skin touched, our totems began to glow, and I came back to myself.

Ishtar's eyes widened. "It's both! The blood of Merlin and Morgan has reunited!"

Alex and I locked eyes. Our grips tightened and, suddenly, beams of light more intense than any I'd seen before burst from our totems. Without our instruction, the light flooded around our trio, forming a protective orb of power.

The demoness roared, and her eyes narrowed. "You can't keep me out. I'll take all three back with me!" Her screams shook our shield.

She was right. We might be safe for now, but the orb wouldn't last forever. Ishtar was too powerful.

"How the hell do we get out of here?" Hunter asked.

"We can't kill her. We have to send her back to Hell—somehow," Alex said, his tone tight from the energy it took to keep the orb over us.

I gaped. We hadn't learned the sacred incantation to send a queen of darkness back to hell—shit, we didn't even know how to do that with greater demons, which were far less powerful. But Alex's words had sparked a memory from my first time walking through a warphole.

"Guys! A warphole is just a lot of magical energy, right? Enough to bend space and time?"

Both boys nodded.

I looked up at the shield. The magic was fuchsia, tinged with rivers of red. Although months ago I wouldn't have believed it possible, most of the power coming from the totems was mine—sort of. I wasn't sure how to describe it, but the power above us resembled my own energies, but it was different too. Like it was actually coming from another source. Someone a part of me, but stronger than I was on my own.

Morgan Le Fay.

The shield pulsed above us, even more vibrant fuchsia than before. I was on to something.

"Alex is right. We need to send her back." I gestured up

to the shield. "I think we can send her to Hell using this. *It* came from . . . somewhere else." My words teetered off. I didn't know where the magic in my totem came from, but surely it wasn't only my power. "Maybe it can send her somewhere else too."

Alex's eyes widened. "You mean using the totem energy?

I nodded, seeing that he understood what I was getting at. Probably because he felt the difference between his magic and the magic of his totem too.

"Smart, but you should do the shield," Alex said. "It's more yours than mine."

"I agree. Let's slam her together, then you guys hold her off while I manipulate the shield. We'll be unprotected while I'm figuring it out."

"You got it," Hunter said.

I inhaled a massive breath. "Okay. I'm letting the shield down . . . *now*!" I screamed.

A hole appeared in front of us, and we thrust our hands forward, shooting beams of energy toward Ishtar.

The howls the queen emitted when our magic pummeled her were otherworldly. Even if she had the ability to regenerate, even if she was practically *invincible,* we were doing *something* right.

"I'm letting go! Cover for me," I screamed.

A surge of power came from both guys, and I turned my attention to the magic our totems had generated. It churned above, crimson and fuchsia, in wild and powerful waves.

Please let this work, I thought, as I gathered as much

magic as I could muster, combined it with the power from our totems, and hurled it straight at Ishtar.

The combined force of my magic and that of the totems slammed Ishtar straight in the chest. She groaned, and for a second, I thought it wouldn't work, that we'd given up our best protection for a stupid idea.

But then a black hole appeared and began sucking Ishtar through.

"Noooooo!" the queen roared as her legs disappeared, and the vortex continued to pull her through, inch by inch.

The last we saw of Ishtar before she vanished through the swirling hole of black and fuchsia were the tips of her horns, and one hand grasping for us.

As soon as her body disappeared, I willed the hole to close, and it responded rapidly. It was nearly all the way shut when a chorus of screams cried out from another dimension. The sound of demons welcoming back their queen.

The next second, the hole sealed itself shut, and silence vibrated through the room. I gasped, relishing a moment of unexpected victory, before my entire body went slack. I fell to the floor and gripped my leg where Ishtar had branded me.

"Babe! Are you okay?" Alex fell beside me.

"I'm . . . alive. It looks like she burned a mark into me." I tried to lift my pant leg, but had no energy to do so.

"We need to get out of here." Hunter began pacing the room. "I take it that no one knows we're still alive?"

I shook my head, and a searing pain shot up my leg

again as Alex helped me sit up. "I jumped through the hole right before Professor Tittelbaum closed the warphole. They—"

"You don't have to explain," Alex said, his jaw clenched. "They couldn't justify endangering everyone else."

"Still." Hunter's fists clenched, and tears pricked in my eyes for the boys.

"Yeah," I agreed. "It still sucks. But we can deal with that later. How are we going to get out of here?" I looked around the room that I hadn't fully been able to take in yet. It resembled a capitol building or some other official structure.

"Where are we?" I croaked, the searing sensation from my leg not letting up one bit.

"A courthouse. I think in New York," Hunter said. "There was a vampire here, but after we beat it, a lesser demon showed up and . . . sacrificed herself. We think many others must have done the same in Hell, because Ishtar arrived right after."

New York. The guys had been only miles away from me during my trial. Just miles, and yet our circumstances had been vastly different.

"I suppose we could always drive back to Spellcasters," Hunter continued. "It would take all night, but I have enough energy left."

"No," I said. There was no way that I was risking being out in the open after what had just happened. Spellcasters wasn't totally safe either, but the wards and gates around it were more secure than the flimsy metal of a car. "I'll try to open a warphole to Spellcasters."

Hunter gaped, and Alex placed a careful hand on my shoulder.

"What?" I demanded. "I just made one to Hell. Do you doubt me?"

The boys cringed, but recovered quickly and shook their heads.

"It's not that we doubt you," Alex said. "You just look so spent—rightfully so, if you finished your challenge and came to save our asses afterward."

Well, that *was* true. I was exhausted, but something told me I could do this.

"Help me up and then stand back," I commanded, and the guys acquiesced.

I unclasped my necklace. Holding it in both hands, I extended it as far as possible from my body, not wanting to be struck by its erratic magical energy, should it come rushing out. Sure, it had helped me a second ago, but who knew what else my totem was capable of? It seemed to act on emotional whims and needs.

My spine straightened. *Needs. Do I need to tell it what I require?*

Take us home. Take us home. Take us home. I repeated my desire like a mantra, willing every drop of power to pour from me.

Fuchsia energy flooded out of my hands and formed small wind funnels, whirling and spinning in different directions. I tried to push the funnels out so they'd encompass both guys too, but they stayed close, hovering over my skin. It was like they didn't want to do my bidding—or couldn't, with what I'd given.

'Creating warpholes is just a manipulation of our energy, like any other magic we do. It simply dives deeper into our being.'

Professor Tittelbaum's words from the first time I'd experienced a warphole rang through my head, and suddenly, I realized that doing this alone was impossible.

"I need help," I said.

"What can we do?" Hunter asked when they'd joined me.

"You can hold me up." I gave him a weak smile. "And, Alex, I need you to place your totem in my hands."

Without hesitation, Alex pulled his ring off his finger and placed it in my palm.

Instantly, the skin of my hands warmed. Judging by the widening of Alex's eyes, he felt it too. Another stroke of intuition hit, and before he could remove his hand, I grasped it tight.

"We'll stick together." My gaze locked on his. "Can you pour energy into me? I think I know how to do the rest."

He nodded, and not a second later, crimson magic swirled in the air to complement mine. The energies resonated around me, some the same, some dissonant, but all constructive.

You can do this.

I gave it all I had left. A flash of fuchsia and red shot through the air, stopping and hovering like a ball of light a few feet in front of us.

Help, I begged the totems. *Please take us home.*

Both the necklace and the ring began to glow and vibrate. I asked once more for help, and tendrils of smoke emanated from the totems, red and fuchsia, and floated toward the ball of light.

The second the tendrils joined the ball of light, the colors disappeared, and a black hole expanded before us.

I sucked in a breath, but doubt still creeped in. How had it worked? Had it actually worked, or was this something else? There was only one way to know.

With Hunter's assistance, I took a step forward and listened.

Squabbling voices met my ear, and the stern tone of Headmistress Wake was among them.

It had worked. I'd made a warphole home.

I released a breath I hadn't realized that I'd been holding. "This will take us to Spellcasters."

The guys slid their shoulders beneath mine, lending me their support, and we stepped through together.

CHAPTER FORTY-FOUR

Eva studied me as we entered Agnes Sampson Hall. On my other side, Alex helped me walk. He had clung to me like glue since the Beltane Trial, which I didn't mind. When we'd walked through the warphole into Spellcasters after the trial, members of the faculty, spymasters from the PIA, and our parents had descended upon us and hadn't let up since. Having his support made the many questions and scrutiny much more bearable.

Right after returning to the academy, the headmistress had whisked us away to her office with our parents. Hunter recounted our story there—including the fact that Ishtar had marked me.

No one knew what being marked by one of the six royals of Hell meant, and they'd charged Professor de Spina with figuring it out. After a day of researching, he'd come up with something.

Unsurprisingly, being marked by demonic royalty—or

demon-touched, as some texts called it—was rare. So rare that there were only two other recorded cases. In both those cases, the markings were made right before the Hellgate had been sealed shut, leaving demons only one way to travel to our realm—blood sacrifice. The more power a demon possessed, the bigger and more elaborate the sacrifice needed to be, which was why royal demons had not been sighted in centuries. But even though the royal demons had been banished, the marks stayed with the demon-touched people for the rest of their lives.

The markings would allow the monarch who'd marked the person to find them, anytime, anywhere, as long as they were in the same realm. It was like the demon rune we'd seen on Efraim, except Ishtar hadn't needed to draw a precise rune into my skin, nor smear me with her blood. She'd only needed to *touch* me.

What was worse, the mark might even allow the royal to possess a weak-willed person without eye contact. Thank the universe I was stubborn and had sent Ishtar back to Hell. I had a feeling the royal demons wouldn't be performing another mass execution to get her into our realm again any time soon. The numbers they must have sacrificed had to have been astronomical.

Of course, some didn't believe that I'd sent Ishtar back to Hell, but they hadn't been there. They hadn't seen what we'd experienced.

They were wrong.

"Our parents are sitting together." Eva pointed through

the crowds of families in Agnes Sampson Hall, and a smile bloomed on my face.

"That's amazing, they—" My words fell away as two other families approached mine. The Wardwell clans—together.

My eyes shot to Alex and then Hunter. "Did you guys know?" I nodded at their parents, who were a little stiff, but attempting to be civil.

Alex's eyes widened. "No."

Hunter's lips turned up in a small smile. "You were both in the infirmary. Mom mentioned something about interacting with my uncle, but I didn't know that *everyone* was talking. She said that after they saw us coming through the warphole together and nearly dead, they realized something had to change. They must've made up last night in alumni housing." His eyes were misty, and a lump formed in my throat.

"Well," Eva said, her voice thick with emotion. "Why don't we join them?"

The four of us made our way to the table, and the families scooted over so we could sit in the middle, next to each other. Alex gripped my hand, and our totems, which we both decided we were never taking off again, flared brightly.

"What does that mean?" Mom asked, catching the light.

"We're not sure," I admitted. "But after Beltane, you can bet that we'll find out."

Alex leaned over and kissed my cheek. "We're gonna find out exactly what the prophecy is and how we're related to it. Even if we have to travel back in time to visit Merlin and Morgan themselves."

My eyes bulged. Was he talking about using a warphole to travel through *time*?

A sly smile played on Alex's lips at my reaction. "That last bit was a joke, babe."

Everyone chuckled, and before anyone could broach another subject, the sound of a small bell rang through the hall, capturing our attention.

Headmistress Wake stood on the stage, along with the headmasters and headmistresses of the three other spy schools of the United States. It was the first time that I'd seen Headmistress Wake looking flustered and exhausted. I was sure that the last two days had been nearly as hard on her as it had been on me. Between worrying about her daughter healing from the vampire attack, and dealing with the drama around the school, she had been the busiest person on campus.

"Thank you all for being here tonight," Headmistress Wake said, her tone heavy. "After the Beltane Trial, I'll admit that I expected some of our students would not return for their final ceremony. Let alone for the Grind next year. It seems, however, that I have underestimated you. Just as I have done in small ways all year." Her gaze met mine, and my breath hitched. "I will not be making that mistake again, for today, you become more than hopeful initiates of the Supernatural Spy Society of the United States. You all become full-fledged members."

A flare of blue magic rose behind her, and three emblems appeared in midair. "Five of you— students decided by your professors and the heads of the other spy academies—will earn something more. As you all know, the PIA ranks spies of the witching race in three ways, depending on their skill, courage, and dedication to the cause. The level you will begin at when you join the PIA is the lowest rank, the rank of emissary spy." The symbol on the far right lit up bright white. "The second level, which many of you will achieve after some years of the agency, is sorcerer spy." The center emblem began to glow an otherworldly shade of silver.

"And the third level is spymaster. This is reserved for only those spies who show the utmost dedication to their cause, their country, and their peers. At Spellcasters, we rank the top five initiates approaching their Grind-year as junior spymasters. They will be the leaders among their peers in their next academic year. The top two of the five will be awarded the supreme honor of head spymaster."

Murmurs flew up from the crowd as everyone in my class began to fidget and squirm in their seats.

Headmistress Wake smiled and released a heavy sigh. "As you all know, these last few days have been . . . full . . . and I'm aware you want to spend time with family and friends before your internships begin. So without further ado, I shall begin by announcing the three junior spymasters for next year's Grind class."

Her eyes swung across the room, taking us all in, and sending chills up my spine. I'd heard of this ranking, but had barely given it a thought. At the beginning of the year, it had seemed so out of reach, but now . . .

Could I make the junior spymaster cut? Could the second half of my year make up for my poor performance in the first term? It was a long shot, but not impossible.

Headmistress Wake cleared her throat. "The first junior spymaster I'd like to congratulate is Hunter Wardwell."

Hunter's family shot up from their seats and began to cheer. Even Alex's parents smiled and clapped. My heart clenched for my friend, whose green eyes were wide as Eva's lips crashed against his.

"The second junior spymaster will be Diana Wake."

Everyone cheered, and Headmistress Wake actually hugged her daughter before taking the stage again.

"And the final junior spymaster for this year's initiate class is . . . Evanora Proctor."

My stomach dipped with regret for my loss.

Guess my first term was too awful to overlook. Maybe next year I'll have a chance. Then pushing aside my disappointment, I beamed and gripped my best friend's hand. "You made top-five! I'm *so* proud of you."

"The judges must be drunk." The grin on Eva's face belied the sarcasm in her voice.

The cheering died down, and Headmistress Wake gave everyone a pleased nod. "And now, it is my great pleasure to introduce you to the head spymasters for the upcoming Grind-year." Her voice shook with emotion. "For the gentlemen, the head spymaster is . . . Alexander Wardwell."

All the Wardwells shot up from their seats, and

everyone hugged and cried. A lump formed in my throat. I turned to Eva, who was bawling at the sight of the two families rejoicing together.

"Silver lining?" I asked.

"If I *had* to get attacked by a succubus, then this made it all worth it," Eva sniffed.

"And the female head spymaster of Spellcasters' upcoming Grind-year is . . . " Headmistress Wake's amplified voice cut through the excitement, hushing the crowd. She paused dramatically, her eyes sweeping the room.

"Odette Dane," Headmistress Wake finished.

My lips parted, and everyone toppled on top of me. Mom's scent of vanilla and myrrh overwhelmed me.

"Odie! Odie, you're number one!" She was crying.

And the truth was, so was I.

Adrenaline was still zinging through my veins when Eva and I said goodnight to my parents that evening. They traipsed off through the woods to alumni housing, swinging their hands and laughing. The news of our rankings had kept the Wardwells, Proctors, and Danes up for hours. It was a fun celebration, but the truth was that I was exhausted and my leg hurt. I was ready for bed.

Eva, as if knowing exactly what I was thinking, nudged her shoulder beneath mine.

"Off to bed?" she asked.

I nodded. "Yes, please."

We made our way back toward the first-years' tower. Alex and Hunter had left with their families two hours ago so the Wardwells could reunite in private. They might not see each other again until after the guys' summer internships, which would start in a week.

We were approaching the initiates' tower door, when a figure stepped out from the doorway and threw an awkward wave.

Diana?

Eva halted, and we shared a confused glance.

"Hi. . ." Diana stepped forward and wobbled a little.

My eyes shot to the puncture marks on her neck. Shouldn't she be sleeping to heal from the attack?

"I was wondering if we could talk, Odette?"

Diana Wake wanted to talk to me? Almost immediately, my heart rate kicked up. Was she mad that I'd gotten head spymaster?

"Diana, I—"

"It's not what you think," Diana said, hurriedly. "Eva can even stay, I don't care. I just wanted to . . . thank you."

My jaw dropped.

"Thank me?"

Theoretically, I understood why. I had saved her from the vampire, and pulled her back to safety. But the shock that she acknowledged that was great.

"Well . . . you're welcome. The trial was a hard one, and we both performed well. I probably wouldn't have even gotten into the bowels of that bar without you."

Diana shifted from side to side. "It's not only that." Her

voice broke as she came a few steps closer. "I wanted to thank you . . . *and* congratulate you on becoming head spymaster."

"No way," Eva breathed, and Diana glared at her before resuming a more humble expression.

"Yes way," Diana said, and Eva blushed. "I have to say, Legacy, I didn't think you had it in you. But . . . what you did the night of Beltane was remarkable. It was something a true leader and spy would do, and I respect that." She gulped loudly, and I realized how much this was costing her pride.

"Thank you, Diana. I never thought I'd say this, but I'm happy we'll be working together to lead our class next year. We'll do an excellent job."

I caught the slightest upward tick of Diana's lips before she nodded, wiping the movement away. "See you next year, Dane." She walked past me and was nearly out of sight when she turned and cleared her throat.

"Oh . . . and one more thing."

I tilted my head.

"That thing I said about Alex and I kissing . . . it was nothing. Just a stupid crush really. I wanted to make someone else jealous, and then it seemed opportune to do the same to you during the party. Sorry I was such a jerk all year." And with that she spun and disappeared down the dark hallway.

Damn, when Diana decides to make amends she doesn't mess around. Then again, when does she ever?

I watched her go, and the immensity of how much had

changed washed over me. My first year at Spellcasters was over. The next day, we'd choose our summer internships, and as head female spymaster, I'd get first pick.

I already had an idea what I'd choose, too.

A grin bloomed on my lips. I'd survived the Culling and found my tribe. If I could survive this year, I was sure I could survive anything.

Even the Grind.

A MARKED WITCH, SPELLCASTERS SPY ACADEMY SUMMER INTERNSHIP

SPECIAL NOTE

A Marked Witch, Spellcasters Spy Academy 1.5, Summer Internship is told from Eva's point of view, rather than from Odette.

CHAPTER 1

The rotting floorboards creaked beneath my feet. Behind me, my trial partner swore softly. I bit back a smirk. *Silly Alex. It's not like the demon doesn't know we're coming.*

We'd been tracking the woman possessed by a monster through Portland, Oregon, for an hour. Eventually, she'd led us to a run-down area in the southeast quadrant. It was unclear why the academy had set this as our Samhain Trial. Usually, spies in training took on more diplomatic tasks for trial. But this was what we'd been dealt, so we were rolling with it.

A rat scurried out of a hole in the wall, and a shiver tore up my spine. I held my breath as we tiptoed down the long hallway, peeking into each room. What sort of dumbass demon would choose *this* place over the cute, historical craftsmans or the newly built homes we'd passed on the way here? This questionable choice made me assume we were chasing a fenrir or an angul, since neither race was particularly bright.

"Are you *positive* that she entered this house?" I asked Alex after I passed yet another empty room.

As if in answer, the whine of rusted hinges came from somewhere further down the hall.

"It came from the right," Alex whispered.

I pressed my body up against the wall. As we approached the next doorway, a glow, soft and flickering like a flame, became noticeable. My breath hitched, and I waved Alex forward.

We reached the door. I motioned for Alex to ready himself and inched my head around the corner.

A fireball zoomed past my ear, and I jumped back.

"An ifrit!" I screamed, and we sprang into action, barreling into the room with shields of yellow and crimson magic blooming in front of us.

The fire demon was still encased in its human shell. The poor possessed woman's eyes glowed red, and flames licked at her fingers, surely causing irreparable damage to the skin of her fingertips.

"We need to exorcise it," Alex grunted as a stream of flames tore past us, nearly catching his sleeve.

"*Evellam*!" I screamed the exorcism incantation, and my power poured from my hands to hit the woman in the chest.

She convulsed, and a groan rang from her. Right away, I knew my magic had overpowered the demon's will to remain in the woman's body.

Sure enough, the fiend surged up the woman's torso and squeezed through her neck, so it looked like she was about to vomit out a tennis ball. I pressed my lips together, knowing what was coming. A grotesque moment later, a creature resembling fire flying on the wind zoomed out of the woman's mouth, unfurling its blazing ghostlike body as it soared straight for us.

Frantically, I searched for an object with which to trap the ifrit. But nothing looked strong enough to bind the demon so that we might take advantage of the wishes ifrits were known for granting.

Fine. Screw the wishes.

"*Nex*!" I cast the spell we'd learned to kill lesser demons.

It missed, but forced the ifrit backward. That was good; I didn't want the hellfire creature getting too close. No burning insides for me, thanks.

Alex mimicked me, and for a few glorious minutes, we worked like a well-oiled machine, one of us attacking while the other maneuvered themselves into a better position. I was poised to strike, but instead of defending itself, the demon did something I wasn't expecting and rammed straight into Alex.

My partner fell to the ground, and his head smacked against the wood with an awful *crack*.

Shit!

I scrambled toward the door as the demon rushed me next. I couldn't leave Alex here, but I also couldn't expose myself to the fire monster by going to help him either. Once it latched on, which was all too easy for something that did not take a corporeal form, it would possess me.

"Or I can take him," the ifrit said, as if reading my mind.

I didn't respond, only shot a blaze of yellow magic between the ifrit and Alex.

It darted away, and I ran to position myself between the demon and my partner, hoping Alex would wake up soon. We parried back and forth, me hurling magic, the ifrit throwing fire that was slowly but surely lighting up the place. After one close call that singed off a chunk of my hair, I was done messing around. I let out a war cry and charged the damn thing.

I was ten feet away when he blasted three lines of flame. One came straight on, while the other two caged me in, flying past my sides. I dropped to the ground and curled into a ball. After one perfectly executed forward roll, I leapt into a crouch.

"*Nex*!" I screamed the death incantation and shot a beam of magic at the beast.

His eyeholes widened, but there was no way he was escaping my assault. It hit him dead-on, and my power seared through the demon. A high-pitched wail ripped from his mouth as he disintegrated on the spot, leaving only the scent of brimstone behind.

I rushed to Alex and shook him. "Alex! Are you okay? We did it! We can call the warphole! The Samhain Trial is over!" I glanced around, taking in the pockets of flames that were eating up more ground by the second. "We *really* should get the heck out of here. This place will be a tinderbox soon."

Alex coughed as his eyes fluttered open. "What happened?"

"The ifrit knocked you out. But don't worry, I kicked its fiery ass. Are you okay? Can you stand?"

Alex shook his head. "I'm fi—"

"Don't even say 'fine,' witchling," a voice growled.

I froze. *Who the hell is that? I already got rid of our demon. The trial should be over.*

Alex was staring straight behind me, his blue eyes wide. In their reflection, I saw a figure move in the doorway, coming closer. I spun and let out a gasp. With creamy, pale skin, long black hair, ruby-red lips, and curves that didn't quit, the creature was one of the most lovely beings I'd ever set eyes upon.

Except for her garnet flashing eyes, which screamed of her demonic nature and freaked me the hell out.

"Eva, call the warphole," Alex whispered. "It's a greater demon."

"*Succubus,*" she hissed and twirled a lock of raven hair. "And to clarify, the higher-up demons like myself, actually prefer the term 'generals of Hell'."

"But, how did you . . . ?"

My words trailed off as the succubus lifted both her arms. Manicured nails grew into claws and began dripping a poisonous green substance.

"No time for questions, little witchling. Now let's see,

which one of you was I sent here for?" she mused as a stream of chartreuse shot toward me.

I lunged up, and a strangled scream left my lips as I gripped the burning scars on my face.

"Sugar! Eva! Are you okay?"

I sucked in a breath and twisted to find my boyfriend, Hunter Wardwell, in bed next to me. His green eyes were full of concern, and his hands raised in a gesture of surrender. He knew better than to touch me right away after a night terror. My power had reacted instinctively and poorly to his kindness twice before.

"Eva? Was it the dream again?"

My heartbeat slowed as Hunter's voice pulled me back to myself—to the place where I was no longer being attacked by the succubus who'd disfigured me months ago. I was in Portland again, but this time, I was safe.

I flung myself onto the mattress and wrenched my eyes shut. "Fine. Yes, it was the same dream."

Hunter's soft hand found my shoulder, and I turned to press my face into his chest, needing comfort.

"I'm sorry, sugar." He stroked my red tresses. "So sorry this happened to you. I promise I'm searching my mentor's potion books for any remedy that will help you sleep."

My heart clenched. My boyfriend was one of the sweetest men I'd ever met. Not only had he chosen to complete his academy-mandated, post-first-year internship here, because I had come to Portland, but he'd also chosen an internship that could benefit me—potions.

"I know you're trying your best," I whispered.

The burning sensation from my scars, a feeling I experienced as a result of PTSD whenever I thought of last Samhain, began to dissipate and my breathing calmed.

We stayed like that for a few moments, until the scent of bacon wafted into our bedroom.

"Odette's up." I gestured toward the door.

"She has a hard time sleeping if Alex isn't here," Hunter said. "I heard her walking around a few times last night. The night before too. Thank goodness he's coming back Thursday. He calms her. The Beltane Trial screwed them both up."

I could relate. My best friend and I were strong women, but I had to admit that having Hunter by my side made me feel stronger. I knew Odette felt the same about Alex—perhaps even more so, considering the strange circumstances involving their magical totems.

"I feel bad that I never hear her wake up at night," I said. "She might want to talk."

"You need all the sleep you can get, especially with how these dreams have been affecting you." Hunter kissed my shoulder.

"What time is it, anyway?"

Hunter glanced at the phone on the nightstand. "Almost eight."

My heart rate spiked, and I leapt out of bed. "Oh my God! I have to go!"

"But your internship doesn't start until nine, and it's right down the road." Hunter watched me pull on leggings and a tank top.

"Master Exeter asked me to come early today. He wants to do an excursion through Mount Tabor and thinks that if we go earlier, there will be fewer humans around."

"Oh, okay. See you at dinner?" Hunter asked, sitting up in bed. With his blond hair tousled sexily from sleep and his washboard abs on display, it was almost impossible to leave.

But I had to.

I settled for pressing my lips to his, savoring his masculine scent as we kissed. "Of course, honey bunch. It's my night to cook. I'm making my famous lasagna, so show up hungry. See you later."

"You know I'm *always* hungry." He swatted my butt playfully, and with a grin I rushed out the door.

CHAPTER 2

I dashed inside the bungalow my mentor called home, right outside Mount Tabor, a city park in Southeast Portland. "Sorry I'm late, Master Exeter! I slept in!"

"Well, isn't that a surprise, Evanora Proctor," my mentor's jovial voice called from the kitchen.

I winced. He was right. I'd been late nearly every day of my internship. It was unlike me, but since I'd returned to the city of my attack, my sleep pattern had been awful.

"Sorry," I replied, unwilling to give details.

Of course, he knew about the attack. It felt like half the witching world did. But I kept the night terrors to myself. This was a professional internship and one that, unlike my enrollment at Spellcasters Spy Academy, I actually wanted.

While my parents had the power to keep me at Spellcasters by holding the promise of fully paid tuition to my choice of a college and a grad program over my head *after* I graduated spy school, my internship was different. I'd chosen this course of study for myself. Master Exeter was on the forefront of studying other magical cultures, like the fae and the demons of Hell. It was anthropology for magicals, and that was so my jam.

"No matter." The gray-haired master poked his head out of the kitchen. "The coffee's finished. It's the good beans from down the street. What do you say I make you a thermos, and we'll get on our way?"

I shot him a thankful smile and set the to-go cup Odie had made for me on his console table. Odette was a great friend, but the girl couldn't make a good cup of coffee to save her ass. When I joined Master Exeter in the kitchen, he was already pouring the liquid gold into thermoses, so I sat at his table and took a second to take in my mentor's kitchen for the millionth time.

Swords hung on the wall from fae who had come over from the Faerie realm and needed favors to fit in. Claws from a shifter friend who had passed away were displayed lovingly by the knife block. Stakes with vampire blood discoloring the wood hung in the shape of an *X* over the doorway. The cloak from a powerful black witch who'd tried to spellbind an entire town in Romania was one of my mentor's favorite items and was showcased by the table.

"So, what exactly are we doing today?" I asked, realizing that my mentor was watching me.

His face lit up. "I've sensed unprecedented energies building for the last couple of days, but yesterday, they became *very* noticeable. They seem to be coming from Mt.

Tabor, and I want to examine them. You're staying in the area—have you noticed anything strange?"

I bit my lip. Master Exeter had been at this for decades. For a wizard of his capabilities, it was easy to discern whether a fae or demon had opened a portal and entered our realm. He could even determine if a vampire had taken his fill of blood within the neighborhood. Every instance of magic left a precise energy footprint behind and Master Exeter knew how to tell them apart.

Unlike my mentor, I rarely noticed irregular or unique energies. My first week in Portland, he'd sensed an open faerie hole from half a mile away, whereas I'd only felt the magic from the faerie hole when I stood in front of it.

"I can't say I've noticed anything off," I admitted, heat rising in my cheeks.

"No worries, Miss Proctor. You're still a babe in the woods. That talent will come with time." Master Exeter winked at me, reminding me of my boyfriend—if Hunter needed a cane, and his golden-blond hair had faded to silver.

I quickly decided that wasn't a bad thing. If we were still together in sixty years, and Hunter was like Master Exeter, I'd probably be having a blast.

"Here you are." My mentor handed me a thermos that smelled like heaven. "A two-second pour of cream and two sugars in yours, just how you like it. Now, what do you say we go find what's causing the magical disruption?"

From Master Exeter's house, we walked to Mt. Tabor and climbed the hill. All around us people jogged by—

tennis players enjoyed the courts, slack-liners walked from tree to tree, yogis meditated, and Portlanders enjoyed nature. After a ten-minute trek, we reached the public restroom next to a playground, and Master Exeter stopped.

"The energy is coming from that direction." He pointed right, far away from the main trails that led to the top of the hill, which boasted a spectacular view of downtown Portland. Then, arching a bushy gray eyebrow, he pointed the other way. "And that direction."

"Together or separate?" I asked.

Master Exeter winked conspiratorially. "How would I test your skill if we proceeded together? Send up a stream of sparks if you come across something suspicious. People are always setting off fireworks around here in the summer. No one will bat an eye, and I'll be able to find you."

"I'll go this way." I started walking.

I turned onto a random trail about one hundred yards away and was immediately surrounded by lush greenery. Moving a few more yards in, I closed my eyes and attempted to focus on the energy my mentor had felt.

The vibrations of nature, human activity, and magic buzzed all around me. Those were normal, pleasant. My lips quirked up as I walked deeper into the woods, moving aside for a runner, before resuming my hunt for a unique resonance.

Blocking out the sounds of children yelling and screaming as best I could, I kept inching down the trail. Two minutes of ridiculously slow walking later, I latched on to something odd.

Humming—almost ethereal in nature.

Memories of the day my first-year Faeology class had gone searching for faerie holes in the woods outside Spellcasters Spy Academy instantly came flooding back. My bestie, Odette, and her boyfriend had heard humming that day too, right before they ran into a fae.

Had it sounded so creepy, though? I shivered as the sound hit me again—harder this time.

Pulling myself together, I walked toward the humming. Master Exeter would be so excited if I found a faerie hole here, practically in his backyard. Maybe he'd write me a great letter of recommendation. Getting a leg up before our second year at Spellcasters was appealing. After all, the academy didn't call it "the Grind" for nothing.

The sound intensified, and I followed it. Turning down a smaller path, I found myself in a dark patch of woods. The sunlight did not seem to penetrate the canopy as strongly in this area, and an unnatural cold permeated the air.

I shivered. Was the cold what Master Exeter meant by "strange energies"? If so, I was close.

Closing my eyes once more, I zoned in, and for the first time, I felt something . . . off. Whether from the cold or my fear, the demon scars I'd earned last Samhain began to tingle.

I gasped and my eyes flew open.

Right in front of me, something glinted against the rough bark of a tree. I squinted. Whatever I was looking at was magical—and probably sinister—but it didn't resemble a faerie hole.

"It looks like a rune," I said to myself, as I inched forward and the symbol clarified.

Two lines horizontally crossed an *M* shape, and wavy embellishments flowed off the horizontal lines.

There were thousands of runes, and I'd only been studying them for two weeks. Before that, the only rune I'd ever seen had been carved into a dead classmate's torso—not something I liked to remember. Still, even with my limited experience, the rune looked familiar.

I walked right up next to the symbol and practically pressed my nose against the tree. A tangy, metallic scent filled my nose, and I furrowed my eyebrows.

"What are you?"

As soon as I voiced the question, the rune glowed.

I leapt back with a squeal. The symbol had taken on a red tinge, and I realized what the metallic smell was.

Blood.

"Do not touch it, Evanora," a voice boomed, startling me. "That's a fae symbol. It might shift you through to Faerie if you lay a finger on it." Master Exeter came up behind me, his walking stick clamoring over stray rocks and roots.

I hadn't even heard him approach, which told me the rune had called to me by locking onto my personal resonance. I'd almost let it shift me through to Faerie.

Ice flew through my veins. "Thanks for warning me," I said, working to commit the rune to memory.

"As soon as we parted, I knew something was amiss. I

did not mean to interfere with your learning experience, but first and foremost it's my duty to protect my pupil."

"I'm not offended. I'm glad," I assured him, although that wasn't the whole truth.

I was also flabbergasted and full of questions. The most pressing of which being, why did darkness seem to follow me?

CHAPTER 3

Hot air rushed at my face as I pulled the lasagna out of the oven. I beamed, taking in my creation. It was *perfect,* the cheese bubbly and browned, and the sauce oozing over the side of the casserole dish, promising piping-hot goodness inside. My stomach rumbled, and I obligingly set the dish on the stovetop and fanned the pan to cool it faster.

The door to the condo we were renting flung open.

"Oh my God! That smells amazing!" Odette flew inside.

My eyes bulged. Her long brown hair looked like a rat had been dancing in it, and dirt caked her clothes. There was even a faint smudge of mud between her soft brown eyes. She must have gotten a lot of strange looks on her walk home. "What the heck happened to you?"

Odette set her bag on the floor and rolled her eyes. "I created a warphole—one of my first since Beltane—and I misjudged my exit location and landed in a mud pit outside my mentor's house." She glanced down at her filthy jeans and off-the-shoulder top. "I hope I can get all the stains out."

"There's stain remover in the laundry area. Do you want me to do it?" I offered, as I cut tomatoes and threw them on our salads.

Odette had grown up with maids, and Spellcasters did our washing while we were at the academy. Because of this, I'd never seen her do a single load of laundry, and suspected that she didn't know how.

"That'd be great, but can you show me how to work the machine? It's about time I learn," Odette said, confirming my belief. She peeked into the living room. "Where's Hunter? He's usually home before me."

The second she finished her sentence, the doorknob twisted, and Hunter rushed inside. "Sorry I'm late! Oh! Hey, ladies." He ground to a halt, and his green eyes narrowed as he took Odie in with interest. "Looks like someone else had a hectic day."

"How about we talk about it over dinner?" I kissed him and gestured to the pan of lasagna. "I'm freaking starving."

My friends ran to wash up, and I set the table. The moment they returned, we filled our plates and dug in without saying a word.

Silence at the start of our meals had become our routine. Much like Spellcasters, our summer internships were a massive drain of energy. But unlike academy courses, we weren't acclimated to them yet. It was only after Odie and I had inhaled almost our entire meal, and Hunter had gone back for seconds, that I felt energized enough to chat.

"So, Hunter, you had a *day* too? What happened?"

"What *didn't* happen? A potion exploded in my face. Luckily it was meant for your scars, so the worst that will happen is I might peel and it will make my skin even *more* radiant." He winked flamboyantly, causing Odette to roll her eyes and me to chuckle. After receiving the reaction he desired, Hunter continued with a grin. "The other mishaps weren't so fortunate. Right before lunch another concoction burned through the bottom of my cauldron. My mentor insisted I scrub the *entire* floor, which took over an hour because his warehouse is massive. *Then,* to top it all off, Mom called. It seems that Alex's dad said something dumb that she didn't like. Trite shit, really."

Odie and I leaned forward simultaneously.

"Please don't tell me the Wardwell clans are fighting again?" I shook my head. After all their sons had been through during our Culling-year at Spellcasters, to resume a family feud seemed idiotic. The Wardwells should be cherishing each other, not fighting over trivialities.

"Yup." Hunter popped a tomato into his mouth. "She didn't seem *too* indignant though, so maybe it will blow over fast. Either way, I told her to get over it." He rolled his emerald-green eyes. "What about you two?"

Odette launched into the escapades of her day, and I laughed about her warping mishap and her mentor, who, unlike Master Exeter, was uptight but comical in her own way. Then Odie mentioned that her parents had called, and my spine straightened in anticipation of what was coming.

"Mom says they're still investigating how demons were linked to our Spellcaster trials by talking to old spy friends. But guess what they found out already?"

"What?" Hunter asked.

"This last year, a record number of spies went missing. Or at least, their friends think they've disappeared." Odette arched her eyebrows. "No one has heard from the missing people. Like, *no one*. My parents say that's odd. I guess it's common for spies to tell at least one other person about their missions—you know, just in case."

In case something goes wrong.

"How many?" I asked.

"A dozen that Mom and Dad know about. Two kids who would have enrolled in our Culling-year at Spell-casters—had their families not declined the Legacy invite—died too." Odette set her fork down and pressed her lips together tightly.

My hand landed on hers. "You can't blame yourself for any killings that happened. Obviously you and Alex are part of this prophecy thingy, but *you're* not the ones murdering people for . . ." I trailed off because we really didn't understand why kids our age were being killed yet. "This is the work of evil. All we can do is try to figure out their motivations and defeat the darkness."

Odette gave me a thankful smile, and I squeezed her hand before delivering my news. "And speaking of evil, I saw something *totally* creepy today."

I told my friends about the rune on the tree, and how after we found the first one, Master Exeter had done a thorough search of the woods and discovered three more. He'd closed them up using a powerful incantation which had exhausted him so much that I had to help him walk home.

"So he closed them, but what do they *mean*?" Odette asked after I finished my story.

I shrugged. "He wasn't sure, except that they were fae in origin but done in a unique style. Their runes are usually enhanced by magical flairs. Using blood is darker."

"Demonic," Hunter agreed. "Now that I think about it, potions specific to demons always require a blood sacrifice. Demons *love* blood. They lap that shit up."

"Didn't Professor de Spina say a blood sacrifice was necessary for demons to cross from Hell to our world?" Odette asked, her face tightening with worry. "The bigger and badder the demon, the more blood they require, right? Like a royal demon would need way more juice than lesser or greater demons?"

Hunter leaned forward. "That's why the Beltane Trial was so astounding. I don't even want to think about how much blood it took to get that royal demon into this world." He shuddered.

"But why are the *runes* appearing here?" I asked, trying to steer the conversation away from the events of the last academic year and back to the present. "Master Exeter said that Faerie holes were common enough in Portland, but he'd only ever read of fae runes in books. And he'd *never* heard of a fae rune that required a blood sacrifice."

Hunter and Odette remained silent.

I stood to take their plates. "Guess that's one more thing for us to figure out."

"Whoopee," Hunter and Odette said at the same time, before rising to help me clean.

CHAPTER 4

I slumped against a tree. A short distance away, Master Exeter was tramping through the graveyard, trying to discern where the strange energies he'd felt again just earlier that day had originated from.

Normally, I wouldn't still be at my internship at ten o'clock at night, but my mentor had requested my presence during this outing and promised me the next day off for going the extra mile. It was too good a deal to pass up.

"Evanora! Would you come over here, please?" Master Exeter called, and I pushed myself off the tree trunk to go to him.

"Look at this mark here," he said as I approached. "What does it remind you of?"

I bit my lip. He didn't need help. This was a test. For the past couple days, he had been making sure that runes and symbols and even a few Egyptian hieroglyphics—which he had never mentioned before—were on my radar.

I squinted at the scratchings in the tree's bark. "It looks kinda similar to what we saw the other day—but *very* sloppy. And obviously there's no blood."

Master Exeter nodded. "Very good. Now, can you sense its odd energies? They're slightly different from the other day, but similar enough."

In answer, I closed my eyes. Searching for errant energies was always easier without visual stimuli. Master Exeter made a soft noise of approval at my use of the tactic he'd taught me.

Once again, human vibrations were prevalent. No surprise there. The graveyard was off a busy street close to Mount Tabor. Homes dominated the area, and people walked about at all hours. As always, magic was in the air, and nature's resonance clung to this area too. None of this was strange or of note, so I searched harder.

After a minute of searching, a cold chill washed over me, and I shivered.

"It feels cold again." I shook my head. "That's all I can sense, to be honest."

Master Exeter shifted so his back was to me. For the first time, I noticed that one of his hands clenched his walking stick tightly, while the other grasped his totem, a wand I'd never seen him bring on our expeditions.

Wands, like all totems, were amplifiers of magic. They enhanced the powers a witch already possessed. If a witch had the good fortune to bond with a totem, it became one of their most precious items. That my mentor had brought his with him tonight spoke volumes.

All my senses heightened, and the darkness seemed more black, more menacing. I shuddered as the chill in the air ran across my skin again, raising goosebumps in its wake.

"Well, feeling chilled is a start. And Evanora, why would this rune exist in conjunction with the cold sensation you've been experiencing *and* a lack of blood?" My mentor's eyes darted from side to side. Something was about to happen.

My gaze went back to the tree. A lump formed in my throat as I recalled my conversation with Hunter and Odette about demons loving blood. "Either no one has applied it yet, or more likely, it's been used up to bring a demon over from Hell."

Master Exeter's head jerked in a nod, and reluctantly, I turned my attention from the tree to the large graveyard.

That was when I saw it, a hand reaching out from the ground not twenty feet away. I moaned as horrible, traumatic memories flooded my mind and the cold transformed to a blistering heat that seared across my scars.

Master Exeter gripped my wrist. "Do you remember your demonic incantations?"

"Yes," I croaked.

"Good, you will need them." He whipped around and pointed his wand at the tree. *"Occludo."*

Out of the corner of my eye, I saw the rune close, but a second later a more violent movement seized my attention. I held back a scream as a corpse—newly buried it seemed, and covered in bits of grass—dragged itself out of the dirt.

Master Exeter took a shuffling step forward. The noise caught the corpse's attention, and it turned to face us.

Its eyes burned red, and my heart lunged into my throat as images from my Spellcasters' Samhain Trial flashed in my mind, one after the other.

"*Evellam*!" Master Exeter shouted the exorcism spell and pointed his wand at the possessed corpse. Magic the color of orange sherbet zoomed toward the demon.

The creature dove, and before Master Exeter could pivot to deal a second blow, the demon reciprocated with onyx tendrils. The black magic hit my mentor dead in the chest, and Master Exeter toppled over with a groan.

No!

My heartbeat hit top speed, and despite the feeling that every cell in my body wanted to run away, my training kicked in. I sprinted toward the devil.

"*Evellam*!" I screamed.

This time, the demon didn't move as fast, and my attack struck him on the shoulder. I watched aghast as the corpse split in half, and the true beast within appeared.

A fenrir, I thought, taking in the shapeshifting demon that, in its natural state, resembled a werewolf, with its long, lupine snout and fur. *Shit. I can't let it touch me.*

Fenrirs were notoriously stupid demons, which partly explained why this dummy had possessed a corpse instead of an oblivious human walking by the cemetery. Lesser brain functions aside, they definitely weren't a class of demon to dismiss. Fenrirs *always* left a portion of themselves in those they possessed. For a corpse that wasn't such a big deal, but if this demon possessed me, a bit of him would hide in my body until I submitted to a full exorcism. It was much more involved than shouting a spell, and I *really* didn't want to undergo one. The videos we'd viewed on full exorcisms in Basics of Demonology had disturbed me for days.

"The long game it is."

I threw a shield over my mentor, protecting his body from possession, then pivoted back to face the beast.

Sunshine yellow magic flew from my fingertips as we battled, the fenrir's twisting, black powers against mine. He was fast, his animal form more agile than the corpse's, and many times, I almost landed a blow, only to have him leap out of the way at the last second.

I was trying to devise a plan to trap him, but a movement a short distance away distracted me. I shot a glance to the side, and my body clenched up. Another hand poked out from a grave.

Shit! Another demon.

The fenrir roared, probably realizing he'd soon have backup.

"*Nex*," I muttered, taking advantage of his distraction and sending a kill shot his way.

This time, my magic hit its mark, and the beast exploded. And not a moment too soon, because the second demon wrenched itself out of a grave. This one didn't seem as dazed as the first and engaged me right away.

"*Evellam*!" I yelled. Once again, the possessed corpse

ripped open, and another fenrir stood before me, all snarling teeth and sharp claws.

Sweat dripped down my face, and my scars began to sear hotter than ever, as two more hands poked out of the ground, their fingers grasping for prey in the moonlight.

"Master Exeter! I need you to wake up! Now!" I shot a glance back to find that my mentor was still passed out.

This is freaking bad.

I didn't have time to think anymore, for the second fenrir was nearly upon me. I flung five bursts of magic at him at once, the final three all being the killing spell. He disintegrated as the last one struck him in the face, and I spun to face the other graves.

"Evellam! Evellam!"

The hands wriggling out of the dirt fell limp, but that didn't stop the demons from shooting from the dirt like rockets. These were gray and wrinkled with flat, short noses—wraiths.

A groan escaped me. Fenrirs were stupid, but wraiths were cunning and good fighters. Briefly, I wondered why they'd chosen to possess corpses, but that question was quickly supplanted by a more important one.

Can I hold off two by myself?

"Evanora! Lower your shield!"

I gasped at the sound of Master Exeter's voice, and turned to find him pounding on the shield I'd put in place to protect him.

Without hesitation, I released him. My mentor raised his wand.

"*Nex*!" he screamed, and a bloom of orange magic shot from the wand, rushing over me and making my head spin.

The power flew across the graveyard, split, and hit both wraiths simultaneously. I released the longest exhale of my life as the demons dissolved where they stood.

CHAPTER 5

When I arrived home later that night, Hunter was waiting for me in the living area. I threw my book-laden bag on the couch and hugged him.

"What's up, sugar?" Hunter asked, smoothing down my wild red hair.

"Just another weird occurrence." I leaned into his chest, feeding off his strength as he wrapped his arms around me. "Master Exeter took us to a graveyard because he felt the same energies that had been present in Tabor. But this time . . . something actually happened." I shuddered, remembering the hands popping up out of the ground, and the torn-apart corpses.

Hunter's arms tensed as he took in my involuntary reaction. "Like what?"

"Demons were there," I whispered.

Hunter pulled away slightly, his sandy-blond eyebrows pulled together. "And fae runes? Like last time?"

"We actually found the *exact* same fae rune, minus the blood."

Hunter sucked in a breath. "Does your mentor think the demons consumed it?"

"Yup. He's baffled too. I mean, who's leaving fae runes with blood tributes to bring demons over from Hell? The two species don't mix, just like we don't mix with either of them. They're not even in the same world! It makes no sense."

"No . . . you're right, it doesn't."

A shrill squeal came from Odette's room, and I cocked my head. "What's she doing?"

Hunter rolled his eyes. "Alex came back early. His mentor had business in B.C. He graciously told Alex that as long as he did all fifteen items of homework he'd assigned, Alex could consider the free day a personal gift."

I snorted. "How kind."

I'd only met Alex's healing mentor, Tiberius Thorn, twice before, but that definitely sounded like something he would say. Many celebrated Thorn as an unrivaled healer, and the guy knew it. Although even Thorn hadn't been able to erase my stubborn-as-hell demon scars.

"When did Alex get here?"

"He arrived on the train at seven," Hunter said. "The three of us went out to dinner because it was Odie's night to cook. I got you something. It's in the fridge."

I chuckled. My best friend loved the idea of cooking and playing with recipes, but she was still new to it and not a whiz in the kitchen. "So Alex will be hanging here tomorrow?"

Hunter nodded.

"Cool. I have the day off too, but Master Exeter still gave me a crapload of books to study. I need to look for the fae rune we've been seeing all over the place. I wonder if Alex would know where to start. He's good at research."

Hunter barked out a laugh. "Yeah, my cuz is that kind of nerd." His eyes lit up. "Sugar! I forgot I have something to give you."

He dashed into our room and came back a second later with something resembling a laundry detergent packet clenched in each of his hands.

"Umm. Are you telling me to wash my clothes? Because you try staying clean when demons burst out of graves and come after you." I stared down at the packets, wondering if I should be offended or not.

"No!" Hunter kissed my cheek. "This is a clever, neutral package my mentor has devised for potions. That way they travel easier. These little babies are remedies. The blue one is for your scarring, and the other is to help you sleep. Just poke a hole in the packet and you can squeeze some out."

My heart swelled. Hunter was the most thoughtful guy I'd ever met.

"Thanks, honey bunch." I stood on tiptoe and kissed him. "After tonight's events, I definitely want to try it."

CHAPTER 6

The next morning, I woke up feeling like myself. For the first time since I'd been in Portland, I'd slept through the entire night and hadn't had a nightmare. I smiled, thankful for the much-needed rest. Hunter was already hard at work at his mentor's potions shop, but I couldn't wait to tell him that his potions had worked.

At least, one of them had.

As I stared in the mirror, examining my succubus scars, I couldn't say they looked any lighter or smaller. I rubbed more of the concoction on them. *Maybe they need more time.*

I skipped down to the kitchen and made a pot of coffee, a couple of eggs, and some toast before sitting down with the books Master Exeter had instructed me to go over that day. Sipping my coffee, I cracked open a tome, and flipped through the pages. Searching for runes was an easy, if time-consuming, job. Luckily, easy was what I needed that morning.

The activities of the previous week, and the restless nights, had worn me thin, but because Alex was in town, Odette and Hunter would want to go out later. Even though we were only nineteen, the fake IDs that Spellcasters Spy Academy provided to grant us more access on our missions had always worked to get us into any club or bar. And Odette's family money ensured that no one ever wanted to kick us out.

I snort-laughed, remembering how, last weekend, Odette had ordered four bottles of champagne for the table, and invited everyone and their mom to hang out with us. She claimed Hunter and I were a wild couple, but if Odette wanted to show people a good time, she pulled out all the stops.

"What's so funny?" a deep voice said.

I turned to find Alex in all his tousled hair and wrinkled clothes glory. At first glance, one might write him off as a hot mess college student . . . until they caught sight of his eyes. Then they would know Alex was on alert, just like everyone else in this house.

What group of friends is constantly on the lookout for demons coming to attack them? Oh, that's right, ours. Jesus, that's sad.

"Nothing really. Just trying to get some work done before we go out again."

Alex chuckled. "I told Odie that I'm here to see you guys, not the city—although it's great. I'm happy hanging out in the living room too."

"I'm sure she realizes that." I gave him an understanding smile. "But I think Odette kinda misses her flashy

LA life. Since Spellcasters is so strict, she probably feels like she has to live it up now. We can't take that away from her. We're only here a month after all." I paused, remembering something Odie said a couple of days ago. "Plus I think she really wants to try this new pizza place. She's been craving Hawaiian."

"Pineapple on pizza." Alex murmured and shook his head. "Sometimes she has such questionable taste."

I laughed. "It's not my favorite either, but Hunter would disagree. Between the two of them they can put down a whole large pie by themselves. It's crazy."

A siren outside blared, shattering the morning calm and interrupting us for a moment. I wondered what was going on out there.

"So," I said when it passed. "I heard you have homework to do today too. Are you off to a coffee shop? Or do you want me to make room for you?" I gestured to the table on which my books, pens, and journals were sprawled, leaving little room for anything else.

"I'll work here, if you don't mind. Tiberius gave me so much stuff to do, I'm regretting sleeping in."

"Don't. We deserve all the rest we can get."

He ran to get his books, and I made space for him. Minutes later, Alex and I were sharing the table and engrossed in our own work. The hours passed as we studied. Although I'd been through the fae chapters in half my books, I still hadn't found any rune that resembled the one on the tree. After reaching the end of yet another chapter, I slammed the book shut with a huff.

"Research not going well?" Alex asked.

"You could say that. Did Hunter tell you what happened at my internship?"

"I saw Odette off this morning before crashing for a couple more hours. Hunter was up, too, and he filled me in. Is that what you're looking for? The rune that drinks the blood?"

"Yeah. Have you ever researched runes?"

Alex shrugged, but I wasn't buying his nonchalance. Before our Culling year at the academy, Alex's mom and dad had drilled him like no other initiate's parents had. He entered our first year at Spellcasters as one of the top students, and over the course of the year even sat in on a few second-year seminars in his limited spare time.

"Really? Not even medical ones?"

As Alex's parents were witches and physicians, I didn't buy that he'd never seen a medical rune.

"I've seen a few, but I warn you, I'm not very good at rune identification. Why don't you draw the one you're talking about? It's easier than describing it," he suggested.

I pulled a sheet of paper near me and drew an *M* and the two slashes across it. I added the embellishments to the slashes, set my pen down, and leaned back to make sure it was right. It was.

"This is it. Or as close as I can get from memory. Imagine it dripping with blood and glowing, if you need a better—or more disturbing—visual," I teased, but Alex had clearly not heard my joke.

All the blood had drained from his cheeks, and his blue eyes were wide.

"Alex?" I leaned halfway across the table. "Do you recognize this?"

Slowly, he nodded. "Yes . . ."

My eyes bulged. How did my mentor, the man who knew everything about every random magical culture on this planet, not know what the rune was, but my best friend's boyfriend did?

"Well, are you going to tell me what it is?" I asked after Alex fell into silence.

"The thing is," Alex's voice was hesitant, "I know what it means. But it makes little sense, paired with your story." He picked up the page, squinted at it, and flipped it upside down, examining it at every angle. After another second, he set the paper back down. "This rune, or at least the way I've seen it, isn't necessarily fae. Actually, it's old, and no one knows where it came from. But the meaning whenever it's used is always clear."

"You're the most dramatic man I have ever met, Alexander Wardwell! Will you please just spit it out?"

"It's an arcane rune for healing," Alex said. "Some say it means to make whole. Like mending something broken."

My back fell against my chair. *Healing?!* There were about a million other words he could've said that would've made more sense than healing. A rune for healing that, combined with blood, brought over demons . . . it was so messed up, unfathomable.

"Yeah, I agree," Alex said, reading my expression. "It doesn't add up. Are you going to tell your mentor?"

I shook my head. "No. Hopefully he finds something more logical. It's possible that another culture picked it up later and decided it meant something else."

That had to be it.

A sigh gusted out of me as I opened another book and began researching.

CHAPTER 7

Even after my friends arrived home from their internships, I still had not found a solution or any clue as to what the rune meant. Relieved that I had a distraction, I pushed all the research and confusion from my mind and we hit the town. Once again, Odette insisted on taking us out for dinner before drinks. She'd even made reservations at a swanky spot atop one of the tallest buildings in downtown Portland. The food was delicious, and the view of the eastern half of the city was unrivaled.

After dessert, Hunter proposed we go down to Second Avenue to check out new bars. We usually hung out in the Pearl or inner Southeast, so I was game to try something different.

We were walking down the sidewalk, happily taking in the night, when someone hobbled out of an alley up ahead. They looked scary—drunk and rough—so we paused, letting them get further ahead.

"So, Eva," Odette said as the man walked away, "have you put more consideration into regular college?"

I took a deep breath. My best friend wanted me to join the Paranormal Intelligence Agency after we graduated from Spellcasters, but my dream had always been to continue school and become an archaeologist. The summer internship with Master Exeter had been an interesting sweet spot between both worlds, but it had also definitely gotten Odette's hopes up that I'd chosen the spy route.

Although I hadn't admitted it to anyone, I had begun to entertain the idea of a career in espionage alongside Hunter, Alex, and Odie. But I wasn't ready to make that choice just yet.

"I think about it a lot," I said, trying to be diplomatic. "But I'm not convinced yet."

Odette's face fell, and Alex slithered his arm around her shoulders. "Well, we still have two years at the academy. A lot can change in that amount of time."

"That guy went around the corner," Hunter said. "Let's get moving."

Two blocks later, we were on Second Avenue, and we walked into the first bar we came across. It was a local watering hole rumored to have entrances to the tunnels running below Portland. I'd heard that groups toured parts of the tunnels, although the whole system was too vast and sketchy to travel unless you were a professional.

"Hey," I said, inspired by the bar's name. "What do you guys think about doing one of those tunnel tours this weekend? It would be something different. They might even have a ghost one!"

None of us knew how to spirit walk or talk yet—that was a third-year class at Spellcasters—but the idea intrigued me. I was fascinated by the notion of learning from ghosts.

The boys nodded, and Odette shrugged. "I'm game." She snuggled deeper into Alex's shoulder.

"Cool. I'll look up reservations tomorrow morning."

Time ticked by, and we shared drink after drink. A haze eventually came over me, and I realized I needed to slow down.

"Does anyone else want water?" I asked.

Everyone did, so I went to get it.

I was filling the first glass when every muscle in my body stiffened. It was faint—probably muddled by all the human vibrations in the bar—but a familiar, cold sensation was creeping over me. Setting the glass down, I ran back to the table and nearly knocked over everyone's drink glasses as I skid to a stop in front of it.

Hunter stood at my approach. "What's wrong, sugar?" His green eyes were full of apprehension.

"Did you guys sense something off? Weird energies?"

Just because *I* couldn't exactly feel what Master Exeter could discern, didn't mean my friends were inept.

"Um, we're kind of tipsy, so no," Alex said, his tone light and teasing. "Is the beer getting the better of you?"

I slammed my hands down onto the table. Both guys jumped, and Odette's eyes opened wide.

"I don't think she's kidding." Odette closed her eyes.

The guys followed suit, trying their best to tune in, despite their inebriated state.

It took a full thirty seconds, but Odette's eyes popped open first. "There's . . . something. It's dark. And different. Muddy."

My heart rate sped up. "We need to get out of here," I responded. "Outside. Maybe you can get a better read."

We paid our tab and emerged on the sidewalk. Fresh air filled my lungs and helped clear my mind.

"They're here too," Odette said, her brown eyes taking in everything, from the people walking by, to the ravens flying above, and cars driving on the road. "I can't pinpoint where they're coming from, though."

"I think you're feeling the same thing Master Exeter did, before we found the runes." The image of a fenrir coming at me flashed in my mind, and predictably, my scar tingled and grew hot, dimming the chill of the energies I sensed. "All I feel is cold, but he always insinuated they felt different—odd—to him. Still, maybe I can work with that. I'll close my eyes and try to find where it's coming from."

"Let me help." Odette extended her hand to Alex. "You guide me."

We must have looked ridiculous, Odette and I, being led around like two blind mice by our boyfriends. Luckily, it didn't last for long, because Odette stopped dead in her tracks about three blocks later.

Hunter guided me to a halt, and I opened my eyes in time to see Odette's gaze turn to me.

"My demon mark is burning," she said.

I gasped and looked down at her ankle, where a royal demon had touched her. "Did it just start?"

Briefly, I questioned if hers was acting like mine, but no . . . Our scars originated from different classes of demons, and Odette's was probably much more sensitive. Ghost sensations from being in the same city as my first attack definitely seemed a more likely explanation for the tingling and warming of my scars.

Odette shook her head. "I'm not sure. I was paying more attention to my surroundings before, but then I got a sharp stab of pain. Like being tossed in the ocean after sitting in a sauna. The energies are definitely demonic, and everywhere, but nowhere that we can see."

Hunter stiffened at my side. "Sugar, didn't you say that those tunnels run all throughout Portland?"

My mouth fell open. Hunter was right. The reason we were feeling vibrations everywhere and all at the same intensity wasn't because demons were everywhere, but because they were below us.

CHAPTER 8

"Odie! Can you make a warphole to the tunnels?"

If she couldn't, by the time we found an entrance, hours might have passed. Demons could cause *a lot* of mischief in that length of time.

Odette pressed a fingertip to her lips. "Probably. It's easier if I can see where I'm going, or have seen it in the past. But as long as I can use my totem—and Alex's—I think I can do it."

I released an exhale I hadn't realized I'd been holding and pointed to the right. "There's an alley that way. Let's do it in there so we don't draw attention."

The four of us scurried into the dirty alley. Immediately, Alex stood at Odette's side and took her hand in his.

"Do you want help?" he asked.

Odette gave him a grateful smile. "Our totems will let me access a different space, but I need a ton of raw power to make it happen."

Alex nodded.

Warpers, which Odette was training to become, were rare in witching society. My best friend had only recently discovered she had the potential to magically transport people from one place to another. She still required a lot of help from her totem to actually create a warphole.

She inhaled a massive breath and closed her eyes. "As soon as it's large enough, step through. I need to keep my eyes closed, so Alex will guide me. I'll seal it once we're on the other side."

We agreed, and Odette began to work. The shifting of energy began right away. Both totems, her moonstone necklace and Alex's ring, glowed fuchsia and crimson. Then they began flashing through every color of the rainbow, lighting up and connecting to each other in their synchronicity.

Hunter and I shared an uncertain look. We were a close couple—in fact, I could barely imagine my life without him—but Alex and Odette had something else. Something my boyfriend and I didn't have, but to be honest, I wasn't sure I'd want it. Their connection was too . . . intense for people who weren't even twenty.

A dot of fuchsia popped into existence and slowly expanded. A minute later, a warphole, inky in the middle and bright fuchsia along the perimeter, hovered in the alley.

Odette loosed a strangled breath, her eyes still closed. "Is it big enough to walk through yet?" she asked.

"Yes," I said. "Let's go."

The dank smell that enveloped me after entering the tunnel left no question that we were below ground.

"You can close it now, sweets," Alex said after everyone had passed through.

Odette released the warphole, leaving us in complete darkness.

Without speaking, the four of us called our magic, and beams of crimson, green, yellow, and fuchsia light flooded the tunnel. My gaze traveled up and down the underground shaft, but I spotted no sign of demons.

"Anyone inclined to go one way or another?" I asked.

Alex, Odette, and Hunter shook their heads, each looking totally at a loss.

Dammit. Didn't foresee that. I bit my lip. "Do you guys think it would be better if we went back up to the surface and tried to feel around for a better place to enter the tunnels?"

Odette's eyes narrowed. "Eva, I can make warpholes, but not all day long. I don't have that kind of stamina yet. If we're gonna go back up and search, we have to be *damn* sure we find the exact location we want before coming back down."

Alex shook his head. "I don't think that's smart, anyway. We know there are strange energies down here—probably demonic. What if we need Odie to create a quick exit for us?"

"I get that, but—"

A sound like a can kicked down a road came from somewhere behind, and all four of us whirled around. The noise slowly petered out to nothing, leaving only the sound of my blood thrumming in my ears behind.

Hunter inched forward, and everyone else followed. We made it only twenty feet before a figure emerged at a *T* up ahead, its gait shambling, and its eyes aimed at the ground.

I sucked in a breath. I recognized that person as the man who had popped out of the alley earlier. "You guys, that's—"

The man jerked about to face us, his hand hitting the side of the tunnel with a loud *whack*, making me jump. My eyes locked with his and my stomach lurched. They were lit up and deep crimson.

"He's possessed!" I yelped as the man charged our way.

His fingertips glowed, and a memory from the Samhain Trials came roaring back with a vengeance. My knees buckled.

"An ifrit." Alex pushed me behind him and ran forward to meet the demon.

Hunter followed his cousin, but I couldn't move if I tried. My feet were glued to the floor.

"Are you okay? Eva? Is it the demon?" Odette shook me.

Unable to speak, I nodded.

"Crap! It's the exact same kind as Samhain, isn't it?" She pressed her lips together, and a line formed between her brows. Then a look of resolve crossed her face. "It's okay. The guys will take care of it. We'll have their backs from down here."

A lump rose in my throat. I was a spy-in-training, a

soon-to-be Grind-year Spellcasters student, and one of the most elite magic users of my age. Was this going to happen every time I came across a demon? Or just ifrits? Would my fear be even worse if I saw a succubus?

But Odette was right. The guys were able to exorcise the ifrit from the possessed man, who fell to the floor, and then they made easy work of killing the creature moments later.

Odette and I ran to the man.

"He's alive," I said, "but unconscious."

Alex joined and did a healing scan. "His heart is weak. I don't think he'll wake up any time soon. We need to shield him. After we figure out what's happening, we'll return and take him to the surface."

Everyone agreed, and Hunter, the best at producing shields, placed one over the man.

Once that was done, we were back to wondering which direction to go. Now at the T-intersection of two tunnels, we stared down the three possibilities. Immediately, something caught my eye down the tunnel to my left.

"Does it seem like it's kind of glowing down there?" I asked, unsure if I was seeing things or not.

My friends squinted, and after a few moments, Odette spoke. "It's *really* faint. Like maybe there's another *T*, and the glow is actually coming from another tunnel further away."

I inhaled deeply, steeling myself for action. "Looks like we know which direction we're going."

The glow intensified, like my sense of unease, as we made our way toward it. We were a mere ten feet from where the tunnels met, when a telltale chill washed over me.

"I'll peek around the corner," I whispered.

I was grateful when Hunter fell into step behind me. A moment later, we were there and, holding my breath, I peered around the corner.

A gasp flew from me, and I shot backward into Hunter.

"What is it, sugar?" he whispered.

"Runes. The ones I've been seeing with Master Exeter. There are *so* many and they're all lit up—someone is bringing demons over."

CHAPTER 9

My heart hammered, and my scars burned with the memory of the Samhain Trial as we walked down the tunnel, passing glowing runes slathered in blood.

"There must be close to a hundred." Odette's voice shook.

And yet, here we were, walking deeper into a demon pit. Hunter had suggested turning around, but I couldn't bring myself to do it.

What if there were more like the man we'd found? What if we were all that stood between demons walking the streets of Portland and the peaceful spring night above? We might not be full-fledged spies yet, but we were *here,* and we were bound to take action for the greater good.

A rune on my right flared, brighter than any other, and I leapt back. "Did you see that?"

My friends nodded, their eyes as wide as saucers. Slowly, Alex reached his hand out.

"Don't touch that!" Odette whispered and slapped his hand away.

"Yeah," I added, "Master Exeter said that fae runes might shift people through."

Alex cocked his head. "But there aren't any strange vibrations coming off them, which makes me think it's fine —at least for now."

"You don't sense anything off? No energy vibrations at all? Even though we're right next to them?" Odette asked, her eyes darting down to her ankle, where a demon mark had been seared into her skin by the Queen of Hell herself.

Alex shook his head, and my gaze went to Hunter, who mimicked his cousin.

Odette gulped and looked at me. "What about you, Eva?"

"I feel a chill, which I relate to the odd energies you're sensing. But I saw you glance down, is your scar doing something weird again?"

Odette chewed her lip for a moment. "I feel slight vibrations in it and it's kinda warm." She paused, then added, "There's also an ache. Almost a longing that pulls me toward the demons." Color rose in her cheeks at the admission.

My hand strayed to my scars as a wave of relief flowed through me. I wasn't experiencing *anything* like that. When I felt the energies, I became cold. And my scars only grew hot when I experienced flashbacks from Samhain.

Thank goodness. Being pulled toward demons would be terrible.

Odette caught the gesture. "I know you think your scars burn or tingle from PTSD. But what if it's not from that?" Her eyes searched my face. "They said the succubus who attacked you was strong. What if your scars are acting like my mark, but less potent and powerful?"

I shook my head. "I hate to say it, Odie, but I think your mark is in a different category. Mine's all psychological. That's the only reasonable answer."

Odette's lips pressed together. "But only two people have been demon-touched by royal demons before me. And we don't have much more to go on with greater demons. Why can't the marks they leave behind act similarly?"

The rarity of demon scars was undeniable, and a major reason why my face was still disfigured. There weren't enough documented cases for the healers to go on. But as much as I loved Odette, I simply didn't believe my injury was as scary as hers. The tingles, pain, and hot flashes were all in my head; a side effect of being back in Portland and dealing with demons for the first time since the Samhain Trial.

"I get that you don't want to go through this alone, Odie, but—"

My mouth slammed shut as a rune next to Hunter's shoulder seared bright red and a hand shot out of it.

"Hunter!" I ripped my boyfriend away from the stone right before a burst of black smoke flew from the wall, its tendrils outstretched like fingers. Ten more runes lit up, and non-corporeal demons whooshed out before I could even take another breath.

"Run!" I screamed. Everyone flew into motion, stampeding down the tunnel between more glowing runes, toward the light we'd spotted.

"Prepare to fight!" Alex screamed.

The distance shortened, and the glowing light ahead intensified. Behind me, the guys shot off exorcism and killing spells. The sounds of demonic grunts and pounding feet lessened after each one, telling me they were hitting their targets.

That was a massive relief, because as we approached a blind corner, my gut told me we were about to run into even more trouble.

CHAPTER 10

We swung around the corner, and my heels dug into the ground as I flung my arms out to stop my friends.

The blind corner led into an open space, kind of like a cavern. From where we stood a rock jutted out from the side, barely hiding us. My lips trembled as I took in a number of humans lumbering around in the cavern.

Some feasted on rats, others fought with other possessed people, but the vast majority were sitting on the damp ground, twitching and moaning, no doubt uncomfortable with the demon living inside them. Many appeared homeless, although I spotted a couple who looked like soccer moms.

There were at least twenty humans in the cavernous chamber. And four of us. Those were shitty odds.

The sound of pounding feet caught my ear, and I

whipped around as a demon came hurtling around the corner.

"*Nex*!" I shot a beam of yellow magic past Alex's shoulder.

It hit the demon who disintegrated on the spot.

My eyes latched onto my friends. "What do we do? We can't hurt those people! But with so many, we have to play defense as well as offense."

Unwittingly, hysteria seeped into my voice, elevating my pitch. A demon in the open space roared. I'd given away our location. We had seconds to come up with a plan.

Alex stepped forward. "Odie and I will exorcise them. Hunter, you shield the humans after we get the demons out. Anyone who gets a kill shot, take it." He turned his intense blue eyes on me. "Eva, do you know the incantation your mentor used to seal the runes? There are still many in that tunnel that are ready to open and allow demons passage to our world."

I wracked my brain, which was still fuzzy from the alcohol. "Not exactly . . . I sort of remember how it sounded. A corpse was emerging from a grave at the time, so my attention was divided. But I'll figure it out."

Alex gave a single nod. "That will have to do. Now —duck!"

I shot into a crouch as he hurled a wave of crimson magic at an encroaching opponent. Our group leapt into action, Alex, Hunter, and Odie running forward to meet the onslaught of demons head-on. I stayed on the sidelines, throwing beams of yellow at the demons to slow them while my friends exorcised the vile creatures from their human shells. All the while, I tried to recall the incantation I'd heard Master Exeter mutter in the graveyard.

Cludo? Ocald? Dammit, what was it? Why didn't I remember to ask later?

A demon interrupted my train of thought by breaking through my friends' lines and sprinting straight for me.

"*Evellam*!" I screamed.

My magic hit and ripped the demon from the person's body. I identified it as a wraith, however, this one looked different from the ones I'd seen in the graveyard. The wraith's nose wasn't flat or short. It was more . . . human.

The creature leapt forward, and I snapped back to attention.

"*Nex*!" I screamed. The incantation slammed into the demon's chest, and the wraith dissolved into dust.

My scars burned as if someone had set a hot iron on them, and my hand flew to my face as I let out a yelp.

A voice not far away shrieked, "How dare you kill the blood of His Highness!"

I followed the voice. A demon with flashing red eyes and horns sticking out of a human head sneered at me from where he leaned against the rock. He seemed to be watching the onslaught, but not taking part.

"Witches killing Lucifer's babies will be punished—violently, gloriously so," the demon continued.

I shook my head. "What are you? And why are you standing back like a coward?"

The demon let out a chuckle. "Generals of Hell do not

fight. Cambions least of all. We are too valuable. Although when I saw you killing His Highness's child—my little brother—I could not let it stand."

I killed a child of Lucifer? What the hell is this guy smoking?

But I didn't have time to muse over what the cambion said, because the next second, he lunged at me, sending me darting back into the tunnels. Black tendrils of magic flew from his palm, chasing me.

Glowing runes flashed by while footsteps sounded at my back. *Shit! I need to close the runes before more of this asshole's friends join. What was that damn incantation?*

Hands outstretched, I tried the variations I'd already come up with. Power spewed from my palms and struck the runes, but nothing happened.

Suddenly, a grip from behind wrenched me to the ground.

"Think you can outrun me, witch?" the demon hissed as he straddled me, his spittle flying on my face.

A few drops landed on my scars, and I winced as they burned again.

The demon caught the reaction and stilled. "What's this we have here? Are you demon-touched?"

I sneered. "Hell no. A succubus bitch gave me these—and died for it."

"A succubus!" The demon's eyes widened. "Was her skin as white as snow and her hair raven black?"

My lips parted in surprise. He knew the succubus who'd attacked me. Maybe I could use this to distract him and give my friends time to notice I was gone. "Yes." My voice was full of spite. "And good riddance."

The cambion slapped me, and I let out a moan. "You're worse than I believed. Killing His Majesty's children before they're even born!"

"Royal demons don't mate with other demons, you idiot," I spat.

I might be a beginner in demonology, but even I knew that the six royal demons only reproduced with humans or magicals. If they mated with others of their kind, they risked losing their personal magic. So they left the job of populating Hell to greater and lesser demons.

The cambion roared. "We shall see who's the idiot after we break open the occluded Hellgate!"

Occluded! Holy shit, that's it!

I ripped my hands out from under the demon and flung them behind me. "*Occludo*!" More power than I'd ever mustered before burst from me, stealing my breath.

Scrambling, the demon grabbed my hands and forced them back into a position under his legs, palms down.

I couldn't see if the incantation worked, but I watched as the demon's eyes followed the pathway of my power. His gaze darkened with each passing second, giving me hope.

"No matter. We shall get our allies to open more, witchling. But first . . ."

He ripped a knife from a sheath I hadn't noticed and lifted it up high. An evil grin spread across his features, and then the blade was falling toward my heart. I wrenched my eyes shut.

This was it, the end. At the very least, more demons wouldn't show up to hurt my friends.

"*Nex*!" someone shouted.

A blast of magic hit the cambion, but since he was a greater demon, the incantation meant to kill lesser demons only made him wince. His neck twisted around, his black magic twirling in his hand, ready to strike my almost-savior.

"*Morsultimus*!" the voice—Hunter's—screamed.

The next thing I knew, the demon's weight disappeared, a cloud of smoke hovered over me, and ash fluttered down onto my face. A sob wrenched up my throat. There were footsteps, and then Hunter was there, pulling me off the ground.

"Sugar! Did he hurt you?"

Tears threatened to spill from my eyes. "I'm f-f-fine," I blubbered. "How did you know that spell?"

In our initiate-year at Spellcasters, we'd learned curses to kill lesser demons, but not the greater or royal classes. Those required *sacred* incantations, reserved for witches who had proven they could handle them. Not for initiates. Hunter certainly hadn't known that incantation a couple weeks ago.

"Alex. His parents broke the law and taught him. He didn't want to make you and Odie complicit, and risk you being kicked out of Spellcasters. But I don't give a shit about that. I only care that you're safe." Hunter's green eyes shimmered, and I could tell there was a turmoil of emotion behind them. "Are you sure you're fine?"

"You saved me just in time."

"Maybe. But *you* saved all of us. Look, sugar."

I followed his finger down the tunnel to see arms and limp hands sticking out of rock. I'd closed the runes, and not a second too soon. At least four dozen more demons had been about to emerge.

A shiver ran up my spine. "Is everyone else okay?"

Hunter nodded. "We cleaned house. Alex and Odie are making sure there aren't any other demons hiding. Also, we found another room full of runes. They don't look like they've been activated by blood, but you should still close them."

I rose to finish the job.

CHAPTER 11

Blessed fresh air filled my lungs as we emerged out of the warphole onto the street.

"We need to call our mentors." Hunter grasped my hand protectively.

Odette nodded. "Good idea. They'll have local connections, and the covens can decide what to do with the unconscious humans we left down there. We should call our parents, too, so they can tell their contacts what happened."

Everyone pulled out their phones and began making calls. I dialed Master Exeter's number first. He answered on the second ring. I filled him in, my words spilling from me in a rush.

"Evanora," my mentor said after I'd finished. "You know what you four did was extremely dangerous, right?"

"Yeah."

The line fell silent for the space of three breaths before he sighed. "I'll be there in twenty minutes. Don't leave."

Master Exeter arrived, along with twelve other local witches. We gave them the rundown, and one who knew of an entrance to a tunnel led an expedition underground.

To my surprise, my mentor stayed at my side. After the other Portland witches left, he turned to me. "How did you find them? I thought you couldn't sense the energetic vibrations that I described. Did something change?"

I pointed to the markings on my face. "Every time we were near the energies—or you told me we were—I would get cold. Then, when we came into contact with the demons, my scars would burn. I didn't think the scars were a link, only a reaction from my trials, but I met a cambion in the tunnel who changed my mind. Plus, Odie helped."

I shot a glance at my best friend. I'd already told her what the greater demon had said. She inclined her head, a go-ahead to reveal information about her.

"My friend Odette was demon-touched by a royal demon a few weeks ago. And now . . . I fear I might actually be demon-touched too."

Master Exeter's bushy eyebrows rose. "But you said a *greater* demon attacked you. The curse that the demon-touched experience has only ever been noted by those touched by *royal* demons. Well, in the limited cases we have to go on."

Two cases. That's how many there were before Odette was afflicted. If my suspicion was right, that number had doubled this year.

"I suspect that things are changing in Hell. The cambion mentioned that Lucifer was procreating, and that I'd killed a child of his blood. I think the succubus who threw acid at me was pregnant with his child, so—"

Master Exeter gripped my wrist. "When her acid seeped into your blood, so too did a bit of Lucifer." He shook his head, astounded. "That must be why your scars are resistant to any healing aid. We shall have to research more."

Someone cleared their throat, and we turned to find Alex.

"Sorry to interrupt." Alex stepped forward. "But I was wondering if I could ask you something, Master Exeter?"

My mentor nodded.

"Eva was studying that rune you two found. I'm undergoing a healing apprenticeship right now and recognized it as a healing rune, but that doesn't seem to fit. Have you come up with anything in the meantime?"

Master Exeter's face lit up for the first time since he'd arrived. "Ah! Yes! I planned to tell you on Monday, Evanora! I have discovered what that rune means."

My mouth dropped open. "What?!"

"Well, I'll admit it still doesn't make much sense, but the rune was in an obscure book on the fae. It means 'to unite'. I can see how modern scholars would interpret that as healing. Both hint at something being made whole."

The cambion's words ran through my mind.

"We shall get our allies to open more."

My blood froze. "Actually, that might make perfect sense," I whispered.

Master Exeter questioned me, and I told him what the cambion had said.

"So the demons and one of the fae courts are teaming up, are they?" He shook his head. "And to make them even stronger, Lucifer is procreating—building an army from his own flesh. I wouldn't be surprised if the other royals were doing the same." His eyes dimmed with worry. "We must tell the PIA and Spellcasters. Darkness like the world has not seen in centuries is coming."

I touched my scar—my link to Hell, to *evil*—and knew he was right. Something big was coming, and it was only a matter of time until it decided to make itself known to the world.

~

Spellcasters Spy Academy Series

A Legacy Witch

A Marked Witch

A Rebel Witch

A Crucible Witch

A prequel from Diana's point of view that can be read at any time: An Academy Witch

The Spellcasters Spy Academy Boxset

ALSO BY ASHLEY MCLEO

Coven of Shadows and Secrets

Seeker of Secrets

Hunted by Darkness

History of Witches

Marked by Fate

Spellcasters Spy Academy Series (Magic of Arcana Universe)

A Legacy Witch: Year One

A Marked Witch: Internship

A Rebel Witch: Year Two

A Crucible Witch: Year Three

The Spellcasters Spy Academy Boxset

The Wonderland Court Series (Magic of Arcana Universe)

Alice the Dagger

Alice the Torch

Standalone Novels

The Alchemist of Silver Hollow (Magic of Arcana Universe)

Fanged Fae Series - A Bonegates sister series

Blood Moon Magic

Faerie Blood

The Bonegate Series - A Fanged Fae sister series

Hawk Witch

Assassin Witch

Traitor Witch

Illuminator Witch

The Royal Quest Series

Dragon Prince

Dragon Magic

Dragon Mate

Dragon Betrayal

Dragon Crown

Dragon War

The Starseed Universe

Prophecy of Three

Souls of Three

Rising of Three

The Starseed Universe (five-book boxset)

ABOUT THE AUTHOR

Ashley lives in the lush and green Pacific Northwest with her husband, Kurt and their dog, Flicka.

When she's not writing she enjoys traveling the world, reading, practicing or teaching yoga, kicking butt at board games (she recommends Splendor and Dominion), and connecting with family and friends.

For most direct access to Ashley sign up for her reader group, The Coven.

You can also find her Facebook group, Ashley's Reader Coven.

Made in United States
Troutdale, OR
10/04/2023

13419549R00289